FORSAKEN

A Novel of Horror

ANDREW VAN WEY

Forsaken is a work of fiction. Names, characters, places, and incidents either are the product of the author's grotesque imagination, or are used fictitiously. Any resemblance to actual persons, living and dead, real or surreal, or to actual events or locales is entirely coincidental (a *coinkydink*).

Chapter Art by: Andrew Van Wey

Edited by: Everything Indie / BDedting

eBook Edition: Greywood Bay, 2011

Print Edition: Greywood Bay, 2012

v.22.5.24

Paperback: 9780984015795

Hardcover: 9781956050080

For Marissa

My ideal reader, my best friend.
Couldn't have, wouldn't have, done this all without you

PROLOGUE

MY BROTHER'S KEEPER

THE CHILDREN SCREAMED and ran.

"One, two, three..." began the girl with strawberry hair as she tucked her face into her freckled arms, which were in turn pressed into the bark of the old oak tree that stood atop the hill like a watchtower.

"Four, five, six." Her voice echoed and carried like a lingering dream, down the hillside and over the twilight fields below.

Small feet carried the children past the flicker and hum of fireflies, past the tall grass and rocks, past each other. Some ran east, away from the hill and the tree and the old orphanage beyond. Others ran west, turning to silhouettes backlit by the amaranthine glow of the Nebraska sunset. A few of the first- and second-graders took refuge in the tall grass, bending the reeds over themselves like cicadas hiding away for the season.

"Ten, eleven, twelve."

Down the hill, two shadows ran faster than all the others.

"Stop following me!" shouted David to his younger brother behind him. "You'll get us caught!"

"No I won't," Daniel whined, huffing, trying to catch up.

As brothers, they couldn't have been more different. Daniel was small, scrawny, even for a ten-year-old. He hated sports, was scared of the dark, and was prone to stuttering when nervous, which was for most of his waking hours. He was an easy target for the bullies, of which there were many at the orphanage.

At thirteen, David was larger than most of the children. Not long after he discovered hair in his armpits, he sent a boy to the town hospital with three teeth bent backward for calling him a nasty name.

Crazy Davey.

Two of the teeth had to be replaced, but the nickname was never uttered again. To David, the month in detention and the forced apology were small prices to pay for the outburst. Violence didn't solve everything, but it had solved that. It put him back atop the list of kids no one wanted to fuck with. To him, that was a good place to be.

"Come on… you always get the good hiding spots!" called Daniel, falling further behind in the tall grass.

"'Cause you'll blab and tell everyone!" David shouted.

Both of these facts were true. David did have the best hiding spots, and Daniel did blab. Part of Daniel wished he could sniff out a dark corner and stay hidden like his older brother, always the last to be found. But another part couldn't resist showing others how smart David was to find such places. Places he was too scared to search out alone, yet places he knew of due to his brother's courage.

"Twenty-six, twenty-seven, twenty-eight," cried the girl, her voice now a mere whisper over the cicadas, her body a simple shadow beneath the distant oak.

"Please? I promise I won't blab!" Daniel wheezed, stopping.

She was already to thirty, David realized. Past the point of no return. If he didn't take his younger brother with him, they'd both get caught, Daniel first. That tagalong would spend the remaining twenty count trying to hide behind a rock half his size, and in the light of the setting sun, he'd cast a long shadow. A shadow that would draw immediate attention. Inevitably, Daniel would blab and point in the direction David had run, and that would be that, same as it always was. Game over.

"Please, David? Pleeeease?"

She reached thirty-five. Fifteen more to go.

"Okay, fine!" David snapped. He grabbed Daniel's sweaty hand and pulled him through the tall grass. "Keep up."

This, to Daniel, was happiness. Or as close as he'd come to knowing it in his ten years. Whenever his big brother looked after him, no one bothered him. No one gave him wedgies or charley horses or called him names. In David's shadow, he was invincible.

"Where are we guh… guh… going?" asked Daniel, forcing the lump from his throat.

"You'll see," David answered.

Daniel glanced back at the distant shapes of the other orphans all looking for their own hiding spots. He saw Raphael, the Arapaho kid from the lower dorm, legs clattering in metal braces as he tried to follow them.

"You find your own fucking spot—don't follow us!" David shouted, yanking Daniel further down the hill as Raphael clattered to a stop.

"She's almuh-most to fifty," Daniel said.

He had counted along in his head. He kept perfect time, a talent learned at night as he conjured monsters from the shadows and counted the seconds between flashes of lightning and crashes of thunder. He could count to a minute like a clock.

Forty-eight, forty-nine, he thought.

"Ready or not, here I come!" shouted the girl with strawberry hair from that distant hilltop.

"Get down," David whispered and yanked Daniel down, hard enough to knock the wind from his lungs.

They listened. Beyond the humming cicadas, a child screamed out.

"Found you!" called the girl.

Hide-and-seek had always scared Daniel. There was something cruel and futile about it. It reminded him of a monster movie he'd seen in the common room late one night. A brother and a sister visited a cemetery. "They're coming to get you, Baa-buu-rah," the brother joked, and the sister squirmed.

Then the dead people came and got him.

The sister ran and hid in a house with others, but more monsters came, building an army of the dead, changing the world bit by bit until escape was impossible. Hiding merely delayed an impending doom, and for the final few survivors, their fate was the worst. Instead of being turned into zombies, they were *consumed.*

"Found you too!" the girl's distant voice laughed.

She was building an army, he thought. And it was getting closer.

"Stop daydreaming!" David punched Daniel in the shoulder, hard. "Over here… Be quiet, okay?"

David led the way, crawling through the grass beneath fireflies floating like tiny stars. Daniel felt as if, for a moment, he was swimming in a cosmic sea. Then they emerged at the end of the field and Daniel's mouth fell open.

"Whoa…"

He found himself staring at an old house. Red paint, long since faded and chipped, clung to slanted walls. The windows were broken and boarded up. An old swing creaked in the breeze, hanging by a single rusted chain.

"Come on in," said David, walking up the steps to the porch. "Door's open."

Daniel knew the house—or at least knew of it. He'd heard stories of a place older kids snuck off to at night to smoke cigarettes and look at pictures of naked women.

"Isn't this off-limits?" Daniel asked. "Won't we, you know, get in trouble?"

"Only if we get caught," David answered, as if it were obvious. Then he paused, realization washing over his face. "You're gonna blab about it!"

"N'uh-uh."

"Yeah you will. I know it! You're gonna tell everyone!"

"No, I won't."

Another scream, then laughter from the hill behind them. The army of the dead had grown again.

"Promise? Promise you won't tell?" David's eyes narrowed.

"I promise."

"Good." David nodded. "Now get the fuck inside."

DIM LIGHT CAST DUSTY ORANGE LINES THROUGH THE SLATS AND POROUS walls of the old house. The rooms were modest and compact, made for small families back when electricity was new and winters were long. The floorboards creaked beneath their feet, littered with cigarette butts. An explosion of movement from a dark corner made Daniel yelp: blue feathers and fluttering from a startled bird as it escaped through a broken window.

"Zip it, you idiot!"

"Sorry," Daniel mumbled, embarrassed.

"Jeez..."

David was moving fast. He'd been here before, several times. Just last month he'd brought Lily James here and she let him feel her up for a cigarette. But Lily didn't know about his secret room. Few did.

"Whoa..." Daniel gasped as David slid an old set of drawers aside.

"Storm cellar," said David, pulling on a metal ring on the door in the floor. "Cool, huh?"

Daniel stared into the dark cellar. It was an abyss, and from within it came the smell of earth and decay.

"That's your hiding puh-place?"

"Yep, come on."

David disappeared below. Daniel took a deep breath. Through a broken window, he glimpsed the distant oak tree and four figures moving through the tall grass not far away.

One shadow stopped.

"Got ya!"

The army grew as a fifth form joined it, metal bracers glinting around its leg. Soon they would descend upon the old cottage, and he knew, like in that late-night zombie movie, the only way to survive was to hide.

DAPPLED LIGHT AND DECAY SPATTERED THE OLD CEMENT WALLS. THE cellar air tasted like moss and old smoke. Daniel coughed.

"Shh..." David whispered as Daniel stifled a sneeze, eyes adjusting to the darkness. Vague shapes emerged. An old wine shelf clung to the cement wall by a few rusted bolts. A stuffed deer head lay in the corner next to a pile of cracked dolls. A sledgehammer, a workbench, and a dozen rusty railroad spikes. Years of cigarette butts and beer bottles rounded out the picture.

David turned his gaze to his brother as if working out a problem.

"What?" Daniel asked.

David nodded. "I've got an idea."

He opened an old wooden trunk, pulled out some magazines and cigarettes, and threw them on the floor. Intrigued by the half-naked woman on the cover, Daniel picked up the old magazine. An ad for whiskey. A man wearing a wristwatch and sitting atop a motorcycle. A woman with a braid of flowers around her neck, emerging from a river without clothes. His eyes descended to the mound of dark hair where her legs and hips came together in a perfect V.

"Ewww," he said out of reflex.

"Gonna ask her on a date?" David laughed.

"No way." Daniel shook his head, and David took back the magazine.

"Then stop staring and get in it. Come on!"

"It," Daniel realized, was that old trunk and the reason David had been studying him. He had been sizing him up.

"In there?" Daniel asked. "You're crazy!"

David stiffened. "In there."

The trunk space was small, confined. Cracked leather lined the outer edges held in by brass bolts that had lost their luster long ago. Even the wood was faded from years of neglect. Yet somehow that old trunk still retained its sturdy structure. It looked, Daniel thought, like it would take a dozen axe blows to break through. He did the measurements in his head, but they didn't add up.

"You'll fit. I always do and I'm bigger. C'mon, hop in." David slapped his brother's back, but Daniel felt no surge of confidence or assurance, only a vast chasm between himself and that old trunk.

"I… I don't know," Daniel gulped. "What if I get stuck?"

"You won't! Just fold your knees in. Trust me. C'mon!"

Daniel peered into the empty trunk. Even on his side, he'd have to curl up tight, tighter than he thought he could. And then there would be the darkness, and that he feared more than the lack of space. The darkness, he knew, would grow constricting the second the lid closed. Suffocating, perhaps.

David sighed. "I thought you weren't chicken."

"I'm not chicken."

"I thought you wanted to know my hiding spot."

"I did!"

"Well, here it is!"

"But what about you?"

"I'll be right over there." David pointed to the workbench. The old planks of a broken sawhorse created a perfect wall of shadow where he could lie in wait until their pursuers lost interest and moved on. Daniel preferred that spot to the trunk immensely.

"Can I hide there? Please?"

"You know what? Just forget it," David said, slamming the trunk closed, sending curls of dust up into the dim light. "Let's just go, okay?"

"We'll get caught. We'll get in trouble."

"Whatever," David said. "I've already got detention." He started back toward the stairs.

"No, wait. I'll… I'll do it. Okay?"

"You sure?" David answered with a raised eyebrow that gave him an almost comic look.

Daniel wasn't sure—he knew this much—but he would pretend he was. Every instinct in his body screamed against the decision. Still, he had to make himself strong. He had to show his brother he wasn't a chicken…

He wasn't a bitch…

A shrimp…

A pussy…

He wasn't any of the names the big kids called him.

He would show David he wasn't afraid of anything. He would show himself.

"Yeah, I'm sure," he said.

"Good. Now keep quiet," David warned, opening the old trunk a second time. "And don't spaz out, okay?"

Daniel took a deep breath. He was a diver descending into the depths of the ocean. An adventurer pressing on into an unexplored cave.

"Okay," he said and climbed, one foot before the other, into the old trunk.

"Lay on your side, legs in," David coached. "There you go. See?"

David was right. The fit was tight, but somehow it was enough. Daniel placed his free hand on the lid. It was the last safeguard, the last protection against the darkness that would come all too soon. He didn't want to let go, to take that plunge. The whole idea was wrong.

"David?" Daniel asked, eyes taking in the form of his older brother, his protector, his guardian. "Don't leave me."

"Shh..." David said. A smile, a wink, and then darkness as he closed the lid on his brother.

AT FIRST, THE SHADOW WAS SOOTHING.

Daniel knew this part. He'd felt it before, hiding beneath blankets and beds, away from imaginary monsters at night and bullies during the day.

But soon, he knew, the darkness would give way to shades and sounds leaking in through the cracks. Soon his eyes would find the narrow boundaries of the box. Soon he would hear his heart racing, faster and faster, a wretched drum that would drown out that perfect clock in his head.

"David?"

Soon the air would curdle, a mixture of sweat and cedar, and his tongue would swell and his throat would tighten.

"David...?"

Soon he would find himself struggling against the edges of the shadows, the invisible boundaries of that personal universe, the extent of his existence in that cold darkness, that tomb.

"David!"

Soon he would realize that there was nothing more frightening, nothing worse in his ten short years of fear and abandonment than being alone in that infinite, unforgiving shade.

"DAVID!?"

How long had he been screaming? He didn't know.

Had it been seconds or hours or days?

Time had stretched and distorted. He felt tears against his face and snot leaking from his nose, but he couldn't tell which direction they came from, which way was up, or which way was down. He was spinning, helpless in the darkness.

"DAVID, PLEASE!"

How long had he been clawing at the edges of the shade? He didn't know. His fingers were wet, a sharp pain buried in the tips, as if they had been torn across glass.

"LET… ME… OUT!"

How long had he been screaming, begging, pleading with the shadows? His words were little more than gravel coughed forth amid pure, utter fear. This mistake, this horrible mistake… how long had he been trapped in it?

"Please…" he cried. "Please, David, please. Let me out."

But there was no one outside to hear him, no one to release him.

In the basement of the old house, both inches and worlds away, he was alone. David was gone. In the last dappled rays of the summer light sat the old trunk, a single railroad spike pushed through the metal hoop latch.

There was no one to hear him scream into the endless void.

ONE

"Art is never finished...
only abandoned."

—Leonardo da Vinci

MR. GLASS

HE AWOKE WITH a spasm, his chest heavy, skin dotted with sweat that left a salty taste in the cool breeze of the late-summer air. The last words of his dream still hung in the darkness of the bedroom. They had been screams from a boy forgotten long ago, echoing backward through time, unanswered for decades.

He rubbed his forehead. The wounds of that day had faded, and only a few scars remained, one of which was currently dulling his thoughts and blanketing the world in a migraine fog. Behind his eyes, buried deep beneath his skull itself, sat an invisible shard, a souvenir from the shadow and those twilight times in the Midwest.

Mr. Glass, he had called it long ago. Mr. Glass, his old visitor. Some people named their body parts; some even named their periods. He named his affliction, his migraine machine. Only the pills, the Imitrex that sat behind the mirror, silenced his old visitor these days. Yet tonight it seemed Mr. Glass was drifting back to sleep, too tired to whisper to him, and that was a good thing.

Dan looked around the room. In his dream, he had called out for his brother, but there had been no answer. Only now, as the dream faded and color bled back into the world, did he remember that there had never been an answer, that there never would be. That boy he had called out for had been silent for years.

"Mmm… bad dream?"

The voice came from his right side, beneath the sheets and down comforter of the warm bed. It was kind and loving and anchored him back to reality. It filled in the corners of his surroundings, sending the sharp edges of the dream curling back to where they came from until they were harmless memory. The voice was that of his wife, Linda. Her hand found his back among the curves and shadows of the comforter. He felt the warmth move down his spine. Her skin, especially her hands, had always been soft.

"Yeah, bad dream, babe."

"Want to talk about it?" she mumbled.

He looked around the darkness and remembered: this was real. The room, the woman at his side, the late-August breeze through the open window, even the warm comforter. All of it: real. This was his life. He was thirty-nine years old, married, and safe at home.

"Huh?"

"Your dream. You were shouting."

"Was I?"

"Mm-hmm. Kept saying, 'Let me out.'"

"No, I don't…" Dan trailed off. There had been his brother, the trunk, and the throbbing glass. "I don't remember."

"Well, you're safe now. Come back to bed."

Linda could feel his smile in the darkness. Ten years of marriage, a year of dating before that, had taught her these things, the sounds his body made, even his smile in the shadows. The headboard gave a reassuring creak as he settled back into his side of the bed. He reached out for her beneath the sheets. That warm, inviting skin.

"Honey… what are you doing?" she asked.

His hands traced the curve of her hip, finding that place that gave her shivers with a single, gentle touch. He felt her soft skin, that stomach that had once been so firm, even after two births, but had somehow lost its tone in the last two years. She wasn't fat, his wife, far from it. Rather, that once-slender build that rendered her elegantly athletic had settled with age. Edges and indentations and a firm tone had given way to small curves beneath her ever-warm skin. But in the darkness, she could still have that body he remembered in the black cocktail dress years ago.

"Shh…" His lips found hers in a kiss, and he felt her smile.

"It's early…" she said.

"It's never too early." He kissed her deeper. Her body agreed and came alive.

He rolled her onto her back with a quickness that made her gasp. He pulled her leg around his thigh. Between the kisses, he felt her breath grow deep, felt the warmth coming from her. How long had it been since they'd done this? Months? A year? There had been things between them, worries, concerns, bills to pay and meetings to attend, and before he knew it, he couldn't remember the last time he'd made love to his wife.

He kissed her cheek, her ear, and that spot on her neck that made her sigh. Her fingers worked on his underwear, pulling them down in short, awkward tugs, a task she'd never been good at.

"Mommy?" called a voice from the darkness.

They paused, frozen against each other, waiting for a repeat of the voice that had stopped them.

"Dad?" it asked again.

"Yeah, buddy. That you?" Dan answered.

In an instant, the adults decoupled. The shape of their nine-year-old son, Tommy, stood in the doorframe. His finger was digging into a patch of his sideways hair. His eyes held a confused glaze, as if he, too, had just awoken and was trying to recalibrate his reality.

"Is Mom okay?"

"Yeah, honey, I'm fine. What's the matter?"

"What were you doing?" he asked.

"I was—"

"Your mom lost a contact," Dan interrupted.

Linda coughed to stifle a giggle. "That's right," she said, clearing her throat.

"I can't sleep," Tommy whined.

"Why not?" she asked.

"Ginger keeps making noises."

"Tell her to go downstairs," Dan said.

"She doesn't listen." Tommy sighed, as if the notion of being bested by a dog embarrassed him.

"You want me to put her out?" asked Linda as she slyly wriggled back into her underwear.

"No, I got it," Dan answered. He liked being asked to help, to play the hero, even if it was only hero to a nine-year-old.

"To be continued," Dan said, and he gave Linda a kiss. He climbed out of bed and ruffled that chestnut hair atop his son's head. "All right. Let's go."

"What's to be continued?" asked Tommy.

"It's grown-up speak. Come on, let's wrangle up that beast of yours."

The beast, Ginger, sat at the base of the bunk bed he had bought his children two Christmases ago. Her wet nose was buried in her crotch. Enthusiastic grunts that seemed vocally impossible for such a small dog came from her curled shape. Dan was repulsed in an instant.

"Ginger, stop that!" He gave her a nudge with his foot, but she didn't stop. Few words would correct the dog's erratic behavior once she set upon an intended course. Which in this case was cleaning her crotch with her tongue.

"Come on." He gave her a sharp nudge that caught her attention.

Dan didn't care for that dog and everything she symbolized, including the price he'd paid for her on his daughter's fifth birthday. He had wanted to buy a regular dog, a Lab or perhaps a Border Collie. Something he could wrestle with and take on hikes and walk off the leash without fearing it would run beneath the nearest speeding truck.

His kids vetoed that decision the moment they spotted Ginger at the breeder's yard. To Dan, Ginger belonged in the purse or arms of a rich socialite, flaunted about as an accessory until it was no longer in fashion. She was the very definition of uselessness; she was a beast without a purpose. Nonetheless, she made his daughter smile, and true to Jessica's promise, she had taken care of her, washed her, walked her, cleaned up after her, and pampered her with bow ties and ribbons, several of which were now dangling from her absurd topknot.

"C'mere, you," Dan said, scooping the dog up with one hand. "You keeping them up?"

Ginger replied by licking him across his face. He sighed, too tired to even be offended.

"There you go, champ. All clear."

"Dad?" Jessica asked. She was awake now, blue eyes peering out from the top bunk among a dozen different dolls all arranged like some Greek chorus. "I'm scared," she whispered.

"What? Why, sweetie?"

"What if the kids don't like me?"

"Why wouldn't they like you?"

"I dunno." She sighed. "Because."

"Because what?"

"Just because."

"That's not an answer."

"Were you scared?"

"Me? Well... my first day of school was different. But yeah, of course I was scared. And you know what?"

"What?" she asked, leaning over the rail.

"I just thought of all the other kids having talks like this with their parents, and I realized they were all scared, too. So if everyone's scared, it's not that scary, right?"

She nodded. "I guess."

"Good," he said, ruffling that golden hair of hers that looked so much like her mother's. In secret, he saw little of himself in either of his children, and he was thankful for this. Thankful that they took after the best parts of their mother and not the worst parts of him.

"Now, go to bed, okay? Both of you. Big day tomorrow. No zombie face in the morning, okay?"

Tommy groaned like a sleepy cadaver as Dan gave Jessica a kiss, tucking her back beneath the Yo Gabba Gabba comforter.

"And Mr. Bun?" she asked, holding out the stuffed rabbit Linda's parents bought her the day she was born. What was left after six years of hugs resembled little more than a sock puppet with sprouts of fur, stitching, and two loose eyes re-sewn countless times. Despite its age and decay, Jessica refused to sleep without it, and on several occasions, cars had been turned around and vacations delayed only to retrieve it.

"Kiss," she said again.

He gave Mr. Bun a kiss, tucked his children in, and walked out into the hallway. Ginger struggled and squirmed in his arms the whole way.

"C'mon, go sleep in the kitchen," he said, depositing the dog at the base of the stairs. Perhaps sensing he would have been happier with her had she been a Labrador, Ginger had never taken to him the way she'd taken to the kids. As a result, he held a paranoid suspicion that she intentionally targeted his belongings or simply disobeyed him out of spite.

Sure enough, she scampered between his legs, back up the stairs, and into his bedroom. There he found her doing what the kids called "a snail dance," a series of a half dozen circles in the same spot before she lay down. "Like a snail shell," Jessica had once said. The spot Ginger chose tonight was Dan's pillow, and when she completed her dance, she sat down and resumed licking her crotch. Linda lay asleep beside her and was, Dan presumed, quite uninterested in picking up where they'd left off.

"Great," he mumbled as he climbed back into bed.

BACK TO SCHOOL

SEPTEMBER WAS AN unremarkable time of year in Northern California. The seasons blended, the transitions were subtle, and it was only in hindsight that one could pinpoint where summer had ended and autumn began. The fog came as it usually did, rolling over the foothills in waves, crashing into San Francisco, chilling the air and earth and stone well into the morning. Yet it never strayed more than a dozen miles south down the peninsula, preferring the gray of the city to the greenery of the suburbs.

There, south of the city, the mornings were warm, the skies blue, and there was no shortage of trees lining the quiet, mostly affluent streets of Alder Glen. *Arbor Day Tree City USA, 33 Years!* declared the sign at the city line south of the freeway. Oaks and maples, willows and elms, gingkoes and liquid ambers and the occasional red alder, after which the city was named, all battled for sunlight, creating a canopy above and, in the autumn months, a mess of leaves below. Leaves that changed from green to yellow or, in the case of the maple tree covering half their front yard on Greer Park Lane, a violent crimson red. Those changing red leaves made gauging the seasonal shift somewhat easier for an old Midwest boy like Dan.

He thought it ironic that the very maple Linda had fallen in love with, which in turn drove them to sign a mortgage they shouldn't have on a house a little too large, had proven for every autumn since to be the very thing he despised the most about the property this time of year. How a single tree could shed so many leaves, he didn't understand, and that morning he really didn't care to think about it. He filed the raking and bagging away for the weekend among a dozen other chores he'd probably forget to do.

As he stepped off the porch, his foot found Ginger's starfish rubber squeak toy, and on the dewy grass, it sent him sliding forward and almost into the box hedge with an absurd squeak.

"Jesus freaking—" Dan grumbled, glancing around to see if any cars had seen him. None had, but the sound of the toy alerted Ginger, who appeared as if from thin air and seized upon his slipper with a pathetic growl.

"Ginger, no! Stop it! Stop it now!"

As usual, she paid no attention to him, continuing her crusade against his offending slipper.

"Daniel!" called a voice from next door. "A word, please."

The voice belonged to Marty, who stood at the neighboring fence with a rake. He was a man of indeterminate age somewhere between retirement and death. Dan suspected he had lived next door for decades, holding a deep grudge for anything that changed his quiet street. He was active in the Greer Park Neighborhood Home Owner's Association, had fought to ban roller hockey in the street, and harbored a litany of complaints dating back to the day Dan and Linda signed the mortgage and got the keys.

"Morning, Marty," Dan said with a nod that elicited no friendly response, only the curl of a beckoning finger. Ginger continued her attack on Dan's slipper, refusing to surrender despite being dragged with each step.

"That dog of yours, Daniel," he said with a flick of his chin in her direction. "She's been at my fence again. Diggun'."

There were a lot of things Dan didn't like about Marty, but on top of the list was the way he said his name. He didn't like being called by his full name, a name he hadn't used in years, and he didn't like the way Marty said it. It rolled off his old tongue like a bad word, elongated into three syllables. *Dan-e-ul.*

Dan eyed Ginger with a smirk. "Has she now?"

"Yup. And when she gets under, there'll be hell to pay."

Dan thought of a few of his own complaints, such as Marty's seasonal habit of raking the leaves at six in the morning, seven days a week. Or the time he saw the old bastard reach over their fence and spray both Ginger and Jessica with a hose when they'd been playing outside in the summer and laughing perhaps a little too loud.

Instead, he just gave Ginger a nudge that sent her skittering back to the house.

"I'll look into it, Marty."

"Make sure you do, Daniel."

"Yup."

And that was that, same as it always was between them. Marty returned to the leaves, and Dan returned to the driveway to finish the task he'd set out to do: fetch the newspaper. Ginger, however, had beaten him to it.

DESPITE THE CHAOS AROUND HIM AND THE SHIH TZU–SIZED BITES ON THE front page, he found a brief respite in the newspaper. Not five minutes ago Jessica had been in the throes of what looked like a panic attack, a hysteria that had taken all of Linda's attention to fix, resulting in an overcooked omelet that Dan preferred to poke at than eat.

The panic had been brewing for the last several weeks, growing like a cancer. Jessica had scored poorly on her kindergarten assessment test in June. Linda had spent the summer tutoring her, and Jessica had in turn spent the summer alternating between daydreams and Disney coloring books, retaining few of the vocabulary words they practiced. In secret, Dan and Linda both felt she wasn't ready for kindergarten. Two educational consultants had agreed. Deferred engagement, they called it, perhaps even some slight ADD. It was an idea Linda brushed off as absurd on reflex. Yet the more Linda tried to bring her daughter up to speed, the more Jessica grew anxious of the impending school year and all it seemed to represent.

It was on that morning of her first day, when Tommy laughed at Jessica's sparkle hair band and the panic erupted in a chain reaction of attempting to undo and redo her entire hairstyle, culminating in tangled hair and tears. Having dealt with the dog last night and Marty this morning, Dan decided he could sit the emergency out. Linda, after all, had proven to be better at defusing such situations. Five minutes later all was right, and Jessica was smiling as if nothing had happened.

"And remember, sweetie, there's nothing to be worried about, okay?" Linda coached. "Every kid, they're all probably just as worried as you are, you know?"

"I know," said Jessica with a broad smile. "Dad told me."

"Did he now?"

"Mm-hmm," Dan replied, folding the remains of the arts section and finishing the last of his coffee.

"You look nice today, hon," Linda said, taking his plate.

"I do?" he asked, checking his shirt for pieces of egg.

"Is that a new tie?"

The tie. An overpriced limited edition silk print made by some Italian designer. A gift one of his graduate students sent him while studying in Florence over the summer. While he had worn it before, he realized he hadn't worn it around his wife. The ties she and the kids bought him for Christmas, Father's Day, and his birthday were all variations on a theme of kitsch. There were smiley-face ties, Mona Lisa ties, even a tie shaped like a fish, and he often wore them only as far as the driveway before they were removed and tucked into his glove box.

"I've had it for a while," he said, rubbing his temple. "Now, who's ready for school?"

ON THAT FIRST DAY OF SCHOOL, THE CRESCENT PARKING LOT OUTSIDE Guinda Elementary was a congested mess, just as he had expected. Eco-friendly hybrids idled curbside next to gas-guzzling imports. NPR echoed out from half the stereos. Fourth- and fifth-graders dressed as crossing guards escorted packs of younger kids across the street with a resolute determination that bottlenecked traffic half a block back. Tommy ran off to join his friends before the car had fully stopped, but Jessica lingered by the passenger door, hesitant.

"Now remember: Mom's picking you both up at 2:30, so don't leave, okay?" Dan said.

"Okay."

"Who do you find after class?"

"Tommy."

"And what do you do if a stranger tries to talk to you?"

"Scream and run to a grown-up."

"Smart girl."

He gave his daughter a kiss on her sunlit hair. She returned it with a hug of surprising strength. The experience of that desperate hug in that crescent parking lot that morning, like so many others since he'd become a father, was both uncomfortable and foreign. He didn't remember his parents, didn't know if they had planned or even wanted to be held by him the same way his daughter now clung to him like the last bit of sunlight before a dark night. No matter what memory he tried to draw upon for instructions, a way to act, a word to say, a behavior or emotion he was supposed to display, he came up empty. All he could say was, "And remember: don't be scared, okay?"

She nodded.

"Now go make some friends."

He watched her walk off, slow at first until her kindergarten teacher, a homely but not altogether unattractive woman in a floral-print dress, greeted her by squatting down, shaking her hand, and waving back at Dan.

His phone vibrated in his pocket. He checked it, surprised as a number he hadn't seen in months flashed across the caller ID. His stomach dropped as that piece of glass behind his eye began to swell. Mr. Glass was waking up.

Bad day for a headache.

NECROMANCY

LECTURE ROOM 42-14, known to the graduate students as the Archive, sat on the west end of the university on the fourth floor of the Fine Arts Building. There, the sunlight poured through the wide windows, flooding the room with a lazy glow that made the paintings come alive in the late afternoon. It was what Dan loved so much about the room. It had moods, emotions, feelings, all depending on the time of day and year. And if one knew the room the way he did, it could breathe life into the artwork within like the kiss of a god.

"Restoration, ladies and gentlemen, is the closest we will come to performing miracles." He started his introductory lecture the same way he had on the first day of each semester over the last four years: script memorized, improvised, able to be changed or discarded if needed. "It is, in a sense, the art of resurrecting an artist's original and pure vision. Taking something old, forgotten, and peeling back the layers of age and time and even death and decay itself in order to present it as new."

He paused before the sixteen graduate students seated at workbenches, all hand-selected, accepted, and even financially motivated to be in Room 42-14. He knew them all by name, first and last. He even knew some of their family stories, childhood dreams, motivations and determinations that led them to this moment.

He had to know everything about them.

At the workbench before each student sat a painting of their choosing that they would spend the next semester restoring under his supervision. Some came from the sizable collection at the university museum itself. Others from as far off as England or Beijing or points in between. Insurance policies had been taken out, backgrounds checked. Millions of dollars were now entrusted to students whose work Dan had to catechize and scrutinize and professionally sign off on before each piece would be shipped back to its owner, as close to new as an old painting could be.

"Pretty boring stuff, this artistic necromancy we perform."

The students gave a polite laugh. They always did at that part because, he knew, most were scared. In this room, their careers would be made or unmade. Of the dozen seated before him, half at least would find themselves pursuing other careers in five years. Restoration was a small field, and the jobs were few and far between.

"So let's face it: we're not Rembrandts or Rackhams. Sure, some of us may be talented with a brush or a palette, but when it comes to creating, we're not gifted. If we were, we'd be off at a gallery, wined and dined while some lawyer and an actor fought over a painting of a soup can and a ham sandwich. We're like lifeguards for the Olympic swim team. Artists create. We resuscitate."

More laughter from the students. Dan looked at each of them, smiling. There was Sergio in the second row, who'd worked his ass off to get out of some shithole in Brazil after his brother was gunned down. There was Hyuk-Jin, who'd assisted in the restoration of some of Korea's oldest palace interiors, pieces older than Dan's own country. Vicky from Vermont, the daughter of a famous vegan artist who alternated between performance art in numerous global cities and chaining herself to trees in numerous global forests.

And then the door opened and a student with hazel eyes and ink-black hair tiptoed in. A student who had spent the summer restoring frescos and oil paintings half a world away. A student who, until that very moment, Dan thought had seen the last of his lecture room. For a brief second the glass behind his eyes heralded her return like a frantic Geiger counter.

Karina smiled at the other students and took a quick seat behind an empty workstation, dropping her leather satchel on the table and meeting Dan's eyes with intensity. "Sorry," she mouthed, and a sanguine smile formed as she glanced at his tie.

He cleared his throat. "Boring stuff indeed, this line of study we've chosen to pursue. But outside the artists themselves, we're the next of kin to the masterpieces they've made. If we do our job, we're as close as the world will come to da Vinci or Van Gogh or…"

He pressed the remote on his smartphone. The projector behind him lit up with a wall-to-wall image of the ceiling of the Sistine Chapel.

"… a Michelangelo," he said and turned to the image of the Sistine Chapel's ceiling. It was old, brown, muted of color and lifeless, like a photocopy of a textbook from a few decades ago. It was an artifact.

"Take his most famous work. Over five hundred years old. Events have happened beneath it that we can't even imagine. Countless lives, come and gone. Nations born and broken. Was this his vision? Was this his ode to the glory of God and man and all of creation?"

He pressed the smartphone again. The projection was replaced by the same image from the same perspective, only it had been cleaned, restored. The colors were vibrant, the image itself three-dimensional, as if a portal to heaven had opened at the edge of that lecture room.

"Or was this?" he asked.

Karina smiled again, and for a moment, he locked eyes with her and that black hair that hung halfway to her hips, shimmering like an optical illusion. He had missed that hair, missed the touch, the smell of it, the way she put it up in a topknot or beneath a baseball cap when she worked late into the night on her paintings. She had the body of a classic movie star, back before curves and cleavage were replaced by skin and bones. Yet she hid it away behind boyish attire, hoodies and thumb holes cut into the sleeves, a secret she carried with a confidence often mistaken as indifference by her classmates.

Her expression shifted from a smile to a quick flit of the eyebrows, and Dan realized he had held his gaze a little too long. The students were trying to figure out if his speech was over. Hyuk-Jin appeared to be on the verge of clapping. Dan cleared his throat.

"Our job, your job, is to be the mouthpiece of the dead. To reach backwards, through the fog of time and decay and neglect, and to pull the artist's pure vision to the surface, to show the world what time has forgotten. Boring stuff, indeed."

The students all laughed again. All except Karina. She just smiled and pushed a lock of hair from her eyes.

THE RELUCTANT GARDENER

THE ROSE FELL into the basket with an effortless *clip*. It was a sound that Linda enjoyed almost as much as the sound of her children laughing outside. But today there was no laughter, and she had only her thoughts as company. Thoughts that haunted her in the sudden emptiness of the house and the still calm of the garden.

She once had dreams and pursuits for her future, a future that included a small boat and a few years living out of it with Dan as they chased the sun the length of the equator. She had always been a gifted cook and baker; at least that was what her friends had told her. The compliments and dinner guests had, at one time, been frequent, and she had started writing a cookbook. Now it sat unfinished, a pile of recipes next to the computer in the study, a Word document and an incomplete title. She had written poetry, too, haikus, and had even been asked to write the inscription upon her father's grave when he passed away two summers ago. She had spent weeks tweaking those words until she gave up and deferred to a simple epitaph chosen by the pastor back in Greenwich.

Those goals, those possible futures that had all lay before her as clear as a country road, had now been filed away in drawers and chests, locked deep and covered by pictures of her children as they grew up. Beneath birthday cards, written first in crayon and then in pencil. Beneath baby blankets and trinkets that she felt a compulsion to keep. Those dreams had been set aside until she no longer called them dreams but rather hobbies, and she dismissed them with ease.

Hobbies. How that word reduced a flame of passion to a simmer. Yet of those hobbies, only one, her rose garden, kept her interest season after season.

Clip went the shears as another rose fell into the basket. She noticed that some of the petals were becoming looser. It saddened her that the slow arrival of autumn, just in time for the beginning of school, would soon signal an end to those lovely reds and whites that had decorated the house since April.

Seven springs ago, when they moved into the house, she took an immediate interest in gardening. And now, after seven cycles of the seasons, she felt a small corner of the yard had attained some semblance of the dream she had in her head for all those years. She envisioned a happy little house, a cottage, tucked away like some European hamlet and bursting with greenery in a secret backyard. Flowers, she imagined, that every year would return like old friends. A garden with herbs she could use to cook for her children until her children could use them to cook for her.

Yet the house and backyard had both proven too large for her original vision, the soil too difficult, the rocks beneath it too many. Each season she revised her image of home until a small part of the yard, the rosebushes, not only matched but exceeded her dream. Dan had his job and his art. The kids had their school. What did she have? She had hobbies, she thought. Hobbies and roses and a now-empty house.

Well, not entirely empty.

"Ginger! Stop that," she said, and the dog stopped digging along the redwood fence.

Clip went the shears, and the final rose landed among the others in the basket. She took her gloves off, wiped her forehead, and glanced up at the belly of a passing airplane on the final approach to SFO. From the blue sky, a shape swooped and landed with a splash in the stone birdbath by the edge of the yard. The bird flailed about in the shallow water, squawking, pecking at its feathers, and thrashing. Its bathing was spastic, violent, as if it were attacking the water or perhaps the reflection it saw within.

There was something foreign about the bird, something askew. It was a blue jay, but not like the blue jays she'd seen in Northern California before. It was crested with a white mask around its face. Its wings and tail feathers bore white speckles between the blue and black lines. She had seen it before, she thought, but she couldn't remember where.

As she pondered that, Ginger seized the chance and jumped after the bird, missing by several feet as the bird flew to safety above. Linda smiled at the silly dog of theirs, those few instincts to hunt so useless and unthreatening. Should Ginger somehow manage to catch an animal, she would have no idea what to do with it.

"Come on," she said to Ginger, who stared up at the tree and the bird. "Let's go inside."

In the kitchen, she arranged the roses in a dappled blue and violet vase, then placed them on the counter above the sink. There they would catch the sunlight in the afternoon and, if she was lucky, last well into the week. A hobby indeed, but one her family could enjoy as well.

Outside, the blue jay squawked from a branch above and Ginger let out a frustrated howl.

"THAT SOUNDS GOOD, HONEY," DAN SAID INTO THE PHONE. "DO YOU have any preference?" He searched for a pen among the mess on his desk and scribbled Chinese or Greek food on the notepad, then crossed out Chinese.

"No problem," he answered.

His office was on the second floor of the Fine Arts Building, overlooking the quad. While it was one of the larger offices, he had managed to fill it with years' worth of stuff of indeterminate origin. It had become, as one of his students noted, what a museum gift shop in hell might look like. Some items held sentimental value, such as the century-old twin lithographs he'd brought back from his honeymoon in Peru that depicted various Spanish merchants, the hand-painted ostrich egg he'd bought at auction five years ago, or the art encyclopedias given to him by his graduate school mentor in a brief moment of clarity after the first stroke but before the second.

Other items were passing novelty at best, little more than kitsch given to him by various friends, colleagues, and students; like the ties, they were kept more for amusement than appreciation. His top shelf alone housed a Botticelli Venus coffee mug, two lamps shaped like Adam and Eve, and a set of Angkor-themed bookends mass-produced in China and probably containing trace leads.

"Okay, hon, will do. You feel better. Maybe take a bath or something?"

A knock at the door, little time to respond, and with a creak, it opened. Dan held a finger up to the visitor, recognizing the perfume. It was Clive Christenson's X. He knew this because he bought it five months ago.

"Yep, love you too, honey. Gotta go. Bye," he said and hung up.

Karina closed the door behind her, and he immediately stood up. She greeted him with a large smile, closing the distance between them in quick steps. Then she wrapped her arms around him in a tight embrace.

"Oh, Boo Bear, I've missed you!" she said.

She kissed him, twice on the cheek and a third time on the lips, holding it longer than he did. Then he broke the space between them, took her by the hand, and led her to the couch on the other side of his desk.

"You're back," he said, intending it as a question, but it had come out as a surprised statement. "How was Italy?"

"You didn't get my message?"

"I haven't checked," he said, feeling the glass behind his eye rattle at the lie.

"So Nathaniel didn't tell you?"

"Tell me what?"

"Nothing," she said, waving off the question as her eyes fell to his chest. "You got my tie? Do you like it?"

"I did. I do. Yeah, thank you."

"Oh, Dan, you should've seen it. After Florence we went to the Golfo di Taranto. A month, working on this fresco in this tiny church. Five hundred years old. Can you believe it? The fumes, oh the fumes and the heat, they actually made us sick. And what you said today, in class, I felt that, when we were there, I just... I didn't know how to say it. Not like you do."

She had said it all so fast, a burst of enthusiasm and manic energy. He was having trouble processing her return, and now her words felt accelerated.

"Sit, please," he asked. "Do you want something to drink?"

"No, no, nothing. I mean... do you really like the tie?" she asked, still smiling with intensity in her eyes, something he'd seen glimpses of before summer vacation, something he'd hoped would fade with time apart. Instead, it seemed to have grown like a cancer.

"It's just the right color." He smiled as Mr. Glass twitched with the threat of a migraine.

"Crimson. I know, your favorite. I spent all day looking for it. Come here. Let me see it on you."

She adjusted the tie, fingers tracing up his chest as she pulled it tighter. He knew those fingers, knew how tender they were when working on an old canvas that could crumble with the wrong touch, knew the blood they could draw when digging into his back.

"Why didn't you return my calls, you jerk?" She smiled, slapping him on the chest. "I missed you."

"Yeah, I missed you, too."

"Really?"

"Of course."

The glass behind his eye hummed as he flashed a smile. Not the wide, toothy kind he'd used before to dodge his wife's questions and sell her on some elaborate excuse about his late arrival or weekend seminars. It was a small, weak smile punctuated by a sigh that made his nostrils flare. The next part would be hard. She wouldn't accept it; she hadn't before.

"Karina, listen… I thought we talked about this."

"About what?"

"This. Us."

"Well." She batted her eyes as if thinking. "Talking denotes communicating, by its very nature. And you haven't returned my calls all summer."

"I didn't know I had to."

"That's because you weren't communicating, silly."

"Let me rephrase. I thought we came to an agreement."

She shrugged as if she were a toddler trying to worm her way out of a confession. "Well, maybe we did. But that was when I was going to stay in Italy."

"What happened? Why didn't you?"

"Nothing happened. It's just… The longer I was there, the more I missed you. The more I thought, *Why do this?* You know? I just… I couldn't do it, Dan. It hurt so much."

"Karina…"

"I know what you're going to say… but I can't share you. I know, I'm selfish. Call me crazy, and maybe I am. Maybe I'm just a dumb girl with a crush on her teacher…" Her hand stopped over his heart, and she took his hand, placing it on top. Dan felt repulsed that she thought the action was endearing, perhaps even romantic. "But, baby, I can't let you go. What we have is special."

He shook his head. "No, what we have is wrong."

"Shhh." She kissed him on his ear, that same spot his wife knew, and it sent the hairs on his neck upright. His eyes weakened. He thought of closing them, thought of giving in to her embrace. "Now tell me that's wrong," she whispered.

He could smell her scent, the mix of cleaning agents, designer perfume, and the hint of cola-flavored lip gloss. She was right. He missed her, missed every exquisite inch. On beauty alone, Karina was the most stunning woman he'd been intimate with. Her body took him back to a time when sex didn't lead to children and a family and responsibility but to pleasures he'd forgotten.

He could lie to them, he thought. Lie to his family. He was, after all, good at that. Just one more time and they'd never know.

"Come away with me, Dan."

"What?"

"Come away for the weekend."

"No. I can't."

"I booked us a room in Napa."

He studied her. "What? Why would you do that?"

"Why do you think, silly?"

He knew the place she'd chosen. He'd taken her there back in the spring, several times. They had lain beneath a goose feather comforter, drinking wine and staring at the ceiling beams. At first it had been fun, exciting, something that gave him confidence again, an energy to know that someone lusted after him.

Yet the more weekends he spent there, away at some fictional conference, the more he realized it wasn't her company he enjoyed. It wasn't discovering each tattoo hidden away on her firm body. It wasn't the way she whispered into his ear as they made love. It was that she made him feel younger. When he closed his eyes next to her, he felt closer to twenty than forty.

But it had been a lie, one that he no longer had the taste to tell.

"Karina," he said firmly and scooted back. "We can't do this anymore. I can't. We've been over this. I have a family."

Family. The word made her blink, as if someone had spat in her face, but she did her best to smile through it.

"So? That didn't stop you before. It's just the weekend and I haven't seen you in months. Make up an excuse. You're good at that."

"I can't."

"You can't or you won't?"

"What's the difference?"

She studied him, his posture, the expression on his face. She studied him the way she studied a painting for minutes or hours before picking her tools. There was no love or lust in her eyes, only calculation, and he knew the next words to come from her mouth would be part of a game whose moves she had already plotted.

"Do you still love me—"

A quick knock at the door interrupted her question. Dan stood up, knowing both the sound of that knock and that the door wasn't locked.

"Dan, it's Robert," said an airy voice as the door opened with a creak.

"Bob, come in," Dan answered with no other choice but to motion his boss in.

Dean Robert was his oldest friend at the university and the dean of the Fine Arts Department. He was an intelligent man, both generous and dangerous, able to weave financing for new programs from a few phone calls or reduce classes to little more than weekend electives. The old man was childless, twice divorced, and a self-proclaimed recovering alcoholic, although Dan never understood how someone who hadn't drank in two decades could still be considered recovering. Yet the man had a certain fondness for Dan, a soft spot, and Dan counted himself lucky to have an ally at a university so historically conservative.

"Bob, you've met Karina Calloway, right?" Dan asked.

"Yes, yes of course. How are you?"

"A little jet-lagged, I'm afraid." She shook his hand and brushed some hair from her face with a graceful flick.

"Karina was in Italy," Dan said, feeling a sudden desire to keep her from saying anything further. "The book you wanted? Danby, was it?"

"Yes," she answered. "I'll bring it back next week."

"Take your time."

He took the volume from the bookshelf beside his desk. In his hurry to get her out, he'd supplied her with one of his favorites, a first edition in pristine condition, worth a few thousand at least. He cursed himself as he handed it to her.

"I'll get out of your hair now. Thanks, Professor."

"Anytime."

She headed past Dean Robert, who was staring at his shoes as if he'd forgotten to lace them, and paused to give a quick glance back at Dan. She closed the door as Dan sat behind his desk.

"Have a seat, Bob."

Dean Robert sighed, still staring at his shoes with a crinkled brow. "Dan, is there anything I should know?"

"What do you mean?"

"You two, you're awfully close. You do know how it looks, I presume?"

"No, I don't." Dan laughed. "But I understand your implication and, frankly, take offense to it. She's a good girl, Bob. A good student. One of my best, actually."

The old man let out a low grunt, his wrinkled cheeks coming together in a small pucker at the edge of his lips, as if he'd bitten into something and wasn't quite sure he liked the taste.

"Of course. Forgive me," he said.

"Is that why you came here?" Dan asked.

"No, no, not at all. Rather, there's something waiting for you. A special delivery."

DEAN ROBERT PRESSED THE ELEVATOR CALL BUTTON UNTIL IT LIT UP. IT WAS an old elevator, first installed when the building was erected in the postwar boom of the early twenties. Dan thought the tacky style was more appropriate for a Hollywood villa than a fine arts department at a private university. The elevator rumbled from the basement to the second floor at a crawl, a trait that earned it the nickname the Turtle from the students who transported paintings between the four floors and the basement.

"Have a little too much coffee today?" Dean Robert asked Dan, who returned the perplexing question with an equally perplexed look.

"Come again?"

The old man gave a slight nod, pointing to Dan's right hand. His index finger and thumb were gyrating, as if tapping along to some internal song. Dan balled his hand into a fist and shook his head.

"It's Jessica's first day at school."

"Is it now? She's already that old?"

"Hard to believe."

The Turtle rumbled to the second floor, and Dan could hear the groan of tired gears. That old elevator was a tomb.

"'For if there were no schools to take our children away, the insane asylums would be filled with mothers,'" Dean Robert said with a smile.

"Or fathers," Dan added.

The Turtle opened its doors with a ding and a groan.

"Indeed," agreed the old man.

ANONYMOUS

THE PAINTING LOOMED, large and baleful, towering a few inches over him at six feet tall and almost five feet wide. His arms, when spread to their widest, could only clasp the edges. While the subject matter was not altogether unfamiliar to Dan, no particular artist's name leaped out in his mind as it often did when he was called upon to identify a work.

"Interesting," Dan said. "So who is it?"

"You don't know?" Dean Robert sounded surprised.

"Can't say I'm familiar with the artist, no."

"Funny. I thought you would be. This might help."

Dean Robert produced a card. On it, in black ink, were the words *Here in art, denial.* They were written in an almost imperceivable scrawl, as if signed by a doctor or lawyer or someone to whom legibility was of little concern.

"This? This is all that came with it?" Dan asked. "This is it?"

Dean Robert whistled. Miguel, the head of the warehouse, who had been busy eating lunch with his small crew, glanced over as the old man raised a hand.

"Miguel," the dean shouted. "Was this it? Uh… *es esto? Todo?*"

Miguel nodded. *"Si. No tiene dirección, nada. Solamente la tarjeta."*

"No return address, nothing. Just the card," Dean Robert echoed. "Courier dropped it off before dawn."

"It has... How you say?" Miguel said, pointing to Dan. "*Que tiene su nombre escrito en el.* Your name is written all over it."

Dean Robert let out a hearty laugh that seemed to confuse Miguel. "It sure is," he said. "Right up his alley."

"No frame either," Dan said, running his fingers along the edge of the canvas.

"Were you expecting one?"

"I wasn't expecting anything. Think it's a donation?"

"That's for you to figure out, isn't it?" the dean said. "Tell me, what do you make of all this?"

Dan took a few steps back, taking in the entire scope of the painting. It was a bizarre creation, both modern and macabre. The color palette consisted of earth tones that reminded Dan of driftwood and dark caves. A few dabs of color were splashed around the image: a tattered yellow dress, a golden pendulum on an aged grandfather clock, and the splotches of green leaves on a single, distant tree set in a vast field.

The composition was simple. It was set inside a nondescript room with red and gray wallpaper and a dusty bookshelf from the turn of the twentieth century. A single open window sat in the middle of the picture, similar in length and width to the canvas itself. It was the only source of light, and it cast a dim glow into the room where two figures, a boy and a girl, framed opposite ends of the composition.

The girl on the right side of the painting squatted among a pile of discarded toys, dolls mostly without limbs or heads. Her faded yellow dress hung in tatters, semi-transparent from the light through the window at the center of the image. Her head was large and distorted, egg-like and disproportionate to her otherwise normal body. The skin on her face was made from a sullied linen, like an old bag of grain stretched over something wet. Her features hung, lazy and ill-fitting, like a harlequin doll after a stroke, which obviously bore a symbolic link to the toys on the floor. Dan found that part rather trite and amateur. That artist had, in his interpretation, taken a rather simple twist on the ordinary to make it surreal. Yet there was something innocent and sad about her, as if she was, like the dolls at her feet, wounded and broken.

Unlike the girl, the boy that balanced the left side of the painting was quite lifelike. He wore patchwork rags beneath filthy overalls. He stared at the viewer through pinhole eyes that were little more than two dark holes among a scowl of disgust: a bully ready to inflict pain upon a younger victim. His stance was challenging; he was poised to fight. His right hand was balled into a tight fist while his left arm disappeared off-frame. Dan took particular note of the left arm because, like the girl's skin, the texture where it exited a filthy T-shirt beneath the overalls was not skin at all but something that resembled cracked leather.

In the center of the painting, between the two children, sat an open window looking out onto a flat field of grass with a single distant tree beneath a wide blue sky and a setting sun. The warm window and beyond were a stark contrast to the muted colors of the old room. It had an almost ethereal feel to it—even fantastical. It was as if the artist intended the viewer to be staring at two contrasting worlds, one of color and hope through the open window and one of dust and decay in that room.

Against the wall behind the boy stood an old grandfather clock, twice the height of the window. Its glass face was cracked, hands stuck at 5:55, and Dan noted it was missing the pieces at nine, ten, and eleven o'clock. The pendulum, perhaps once a reflective brass, now bore a dusty hue that impressed him with the skill that small detail required to pull off.

Still, the painting bothered him. Between the children, on opposite sides beneath the window in the center, sat an empty space of flooring and wall. It was as if something belonged there or had once sat there but had been removed or painted over by the artist. Compared to the rest of the painting, it seemed abnormally bare, naked. The empty spot beneath the window gave the painting an unbalanced feel, drawing his eyes back to that space again and again. He kept expecting to find something, yet there was nothing, only the feeling that something was missing and belonged there.

"So?" asked Dean Robert. "No idea who your anonymous artist might be?"

Dan walked around the edge of the painting. There was no decorative frame. The canvas itself was pulled taut around the stretcher bars and held to the back by dozens of small nails. The sides, the folds in the back, even the nails were all painted over.

"No visible signature," he said. "Doesn't match anything I'm familiar with. Could just be some no-name trying to get their name out. Style, take your pick. Surrealist, photorealist, elements of baroque—it's a Frankenstein mix. Hell, from ten feet away, I'd say it's no better than motel art, but up close..."

He ran his fingers over the face of the girl, traced her brown hair, and noted the dark tears coming from her distended eyes.

"What do you see?"

"Well, the detail is incredible. The brush strokes, they're hairline, nearly invisible. Yet the paint's thin, so the artist didn't make many mistakes. Still, it looks like amateur hour."

"Why do you say that?"

"The composition. What do you make of it?"

Dean Robert took it all in. He was a man of classics and had little taste for most art made in the last century. He considered most of it little more than mental masturbation and was often the butt of jokes made by other professors behind his back.

"Well." The old man puckered his lips. "I would say it's a rather well-crafted mess."

"Exactly. There's no real rhyme or reason to the composition. The whole thing's unbalanced. The kids, the window, that empty space below the frame. The viewer's eyes just bounce around, picking things up, like this broken mirror here." Dan pointed to a piece of broken mirror on the floor by the boy. It reflected something off the canvas, behind the observer's point of view. Thirteen doll heads sat on a shelf in the shadows. "If the detail weren't so incredible, I'd say the whole thing's one step up from a *Where's Waldo?*"

"Why is that?" the old man asked.

"Well, it's not just images for the sake of oddity or free association.

There is, at some level, a narrative happening, and the artist is challenging the viewer to solve it."

"The thing gives me the creeps."

"As it should. On the right, you clearly have some sort of symbol of pain and suffering represented in the young girl, the broken dolls, and the fact that their skin is similar. A loss of innocence, perhaps. A trauma. Who knows? Contrast that to the left side where you have the challenging stare and aggressive posture of the boy, hand disappearing off-frame as if holding a weapon or something."

"The skin on his right arm is different."

"Could be burnt or in the act of some metamorphosis. The point is we're really not meant to know, are we? See, the artist obscured the clues, perhaps even discarded some entirely. Imagine trying to solve a jigsaw puzzle with half the pieces."

"Between us gentlemen, I never understood the appeal of crap like this. Gerhard Richter goes for eight figures while he's still alive and Casper Friedrich dies broke and insane."

"Same stories, different endings."

"Point taken."

Dan smiled. He'd been down this road with Dean Robert a hundred times. It always ended with the older man shaking his head and shrugging his shoulders before moving on to another injustice of the art world and how it was all going to hell.

Dan turned the card over in his hand. The backside was blank. Those words—*Here in art, denial*—written in that childlike scrawl held a vague familiarity, like something seen in a dream. The black ink seemed to shimmer in the light as he rubbed it with his thumb.

He glanced back to the painting, drawing lines from object to object, searching for connections within that bizarre canvas. The two children, watchmen before a window to a world of color. Gatekeepers, perhaps, or witnesses.

For a moment Dan heard Mr. Glass whisper: *de-nye-uhl*.

The piece of glass shook as the headache slithered back into the base of his skull. He hadn't eaten since noon, and it was now almost five. At the edge of his vision, small crescents of a migraine aura began to grow.

"Daniel?" snapped Dean Robert.

Dan blinked, and with it went the auras, wiped away for the moment. "Yes, Bob?"

"This thing, it's your problem, understand? Figure out what to do with it. In the meantime, I'll have the warehouse move it up to the Archive. Who knows? Maybe it'll turn out like those Picassos they found in France, rotting away in some old basement. Wouldn't that be your lucky day?"

It would be, indeed, Dan thought. But as he stared at that anonymous painting, he felt that no such luck lay in his future.

ALL-AMERICAN SUPPER

GINGER'S PAW SCRAPED into his thigh as her warm breath wafted up from beneath the dining room table like some wretched updraft. Dan answered her incessant begging with a nudge of his foot that sent her off in search of scraps elsewhere.

Dinner that night was pizza. He had forgotten to phone in the order at their favorite Greek place, something he realized when he arrived to pick up an order that didn't exist. Pizza had been the fallback. It was fast and he could kill the time at the bookstore. He also knew the kids wouldn't complain about pizza, something they had begun doing regularly with their mother's cooking, something he silently but often agreed with.

Tommy's arm disappeared beneath the table, and Dan caught the sound of the dog's paws skittering across the hardwood floor. "Tommy, what have we said about feeding the dog at the table?"

"Sorry, Dad."

Somewhere beneath the table, Ginger crunched into a pizza crust.

"Sweetie, how was your day at school?" Dan asked Jessica, who had spent the last five minutes slurping tendrils of cheese from her plate. She stopped chewing but didn't answer him. Linda swirled her wine in the glass and gave Dan a shake of the head. *Don't ask,* her look said.

"Okay," Jessica mumbled, poking her salad with her fork.

"Just okay? Did you make any friends?"

Jessica nodded.

"Who?"

"She peed her pants at school!" Tommy exclaimed with a giant smile.

"No I didn't!" Jessica screamed back.

"Yes you did! All the third-graders heard about it!"

"Did not!" She flung a pizza crust at Tommy, but it went wide and sailed past. Ginger seized upon the crust and disappeared beneath the table, snorting.

"Thomas! You stop that. Right now!" Linda snapped.

Tommy looked down and nodded as Dan's gaze ping-ponged from Tommy to Jessica and then to his wife.

"Is that true?" he asked Linda.

A sigh. "She had an accident. It was her first day. These things happen."

Jessica sank further into her chair. Dan felt Ginger's paw back on his thigh as she awaited further fallout. "These things happen," Linda had said. Lately, it seemed they happened with all the regularity of the tides.

Tommy mouthed the words "pee-pee pants," and Dan caught it out of the corner of his eye.

"Thomas, go to your room," Dan said.

"Why?"

"Because you're being a rude little shit. Now go. No video games."

Tommy stared at his plate, let out a dramatic sigh, then tossed his napkin onto the table and stood up.

"Take your plate to the kitchen and go."

Dan hated raising his voice, hated punishing his kids, but since the summer, Tommy had become increasingly rude, not only toward his younger sister but also toward his parents. Linda blamed it on his video games and friends, most of whom were hypercompetitive in sports. His teacher blamed it on a "phase" most boys went through around the same age.

Dan didn't care about blame. Tommy was learning to press boundaries, looking for weaknesses, no different from an animal digging holes under a fence. After hearing Tommy tell his mother to shut up a month back, Dan was determined to put an end to it, even if it meant his relationship with his son would have to weather a few storms.

Tommy stomped off into the kitchen, then up the stairs, where the door slammed in a final, defiant act. He knew Tommy would probably be playing video games, but for now, his mind was on Jessica.

"Sweetie, listen… what happened, it's normal, okay? It happens."

"Dad, I'm not stupid," Jessica said, looking up at him through eyes that seemed ten years too old.

"I know you aren't, honey, of course."

"Then why did you lie to me?"

"What? I didn't lie to you."

"You said it wouldn't be scary, but it was!"

Dan gave Ginger another nudge, perhaps a bit too hard, and he heard her growl as she slid back beneath the table.

"You know, when I was your age… I did the exact same thing. But worse. See, the teachers at my school, they made us put on a big play in front of all the parents. I had to be the sixteenth president. Know who that is?"

"Abraham Lincoln," she answered.

"Wow. Smart girl. Anyways, I had this uncomfortable costume, and it was really hot, so I kept drinking water, right? So when I finally got on stage in front of all these parents, I really needed to pee, but I couldn't because the play had already started. So I tried to hold it and hold it, and when it was my turn to go out and say my speech, I couldn't hold it anymore. Then you know what happened?"

"What happened?"

Dan dipped his fingers into his glass of water—"I peed all over the audience!"—and then flicked water droplets across the table. A few spattered his daughter, who covered her face, giggling and wrinkling her nose in disgust.

"Eww, really?"

He nodded. "So if you ever get embarrassed about peeing your pants, remember, I peed on *all* the parents."

Jessica smiled, poking her pizza crust across her plate with her fork. Linda raised an eyebrow and gave Dan an approving nod.

HE PUT THE LEFTOVERS IN THE FRIDGE, FISHED A BEER FROM BETWEEN THE Lunchables and juice packs, and cracked it open with a satisfying pop. Linda ran the plates under the water in the sink and moved them to the dishwasher one by one, smiling as Dan wrapped his hand around her waist and kissed her neck.

"I didn't know they had Parents' Day at the orphanage," Linda said, closing the dishwasher and raising a mischievous eyebrow.

"You know what I was trying to do," he said.

"I do. And it was a noble lie."

She gave him a gentle kiss on the lips, smiling at that man, her husband, that big goof who had once been so uncomfortable around children he'd avoided them at her family reunions at any cost. The man who now could conjure up a lie to make his own kids feel better.

"You're a good man, Dan."

No I'm not, he thought. *I'm just a good actor.*

"I might have to go away this weekend," he said.

"What for?"

"Some stupid seminar. I'm trying to get out of it, but they've got me by the balls."

"For the whole weekend?"

"Looks like it."

She took a sip from his beer. He always loved it when she did that. It reminded him of when they sat on the hood of his car, watching the Fourth of July fireworks over the marina during grad school. Sipping microbrews and getting high as the explosions mirrored off the water. It felt like another life, and perhaps it was. He sometimes thought he didn't live one life but several, all strung together like beads on a necklace, separate but connected if only by his name.

"You're going to miss Tommy's soccer game," she said, taking another sip and handing the beer back to him.

"I know. Besides, I'm probably persona non grata right now."

"I'm sure he'll forgive you."

"He's pretty pissed."

"He'll get over it."

"You think?"

"I know."

TOMMY WAS STILL FUMING BY BEDTIME, IN PART BECAUSE HE FELT HIS DAD had been a jerk but most of all because his Nintendo had run out of batteries. Despite orders not to play video games, he did. It was only when the battery died that he realized the cable was still plugged into the wall in the kitchen. If he returned for it, his deception would be exposed. His dad, of course, would take the Nintendo for a day or a week, perhaps, just like during the summer when he teased Jessica after she fell off her trike and cried like a sissy.

If his parents weren't such jerks, he could play computer games. This idea, too, was out since he shared a room with his sister and his parents insisted on keeping the family computer downstairs in his father's study, which was off-limits.

It wasn't fair, he thought, brushing his teeth over the bathroom sink. His friends had their own computers. Sam's older brother had even stayed up with them one night, playing a game that involved stealing cars and shooting people. It was rated M and he heard words he didn't understand but knew would get him in trouble if he used them around his parents.

Not only did his friends have their own computers; they had their own rooms. This, to him, was the most unfair. To share a bedroom with someone who couldn't make it to the toilet without peeing down her legs like a baby. Even now, over the hum of his electric toothbrush, he could hear her voice through the door as she played with her dolls and sang. She never shut up.

He opened the door.

Jessica sat at the head of the play table, her dolls and stuffed toys seated around her. She counted off each toy as if taking attendance.

"This is Lamby, and this is Mrs. Pembilton, and this is Zoey Zebra, and this…" She paused, holding up that threadbare stuffed rabbit, the one that smelled like what he imagined a mummy would smell like if its bandages fell off. "This is Mr. Bun. He watches me when I sleep."

"Who are you talking to?" Tommy asked, toothpaste dripping down his chin.

"No one," she answered, as if his question was absurd.

He rolled his eyes, mumbling, "Weirdo," and closed the bathroom door.

Her gaze fell back to the table and the chair across from her, the only chair without a stuffed toy in it.

"Are you going to move in with us?" she asked the emptiness.

INCANDESCENCE

HER TATTOOED BACK glistened in the moonlight that fell across the bedsheets of their favorite hotel.

"I shouldn't have come back," she whispered, face hidden by the shadows.

"I wish you hadn't," Dan replied, his fingers running down her back. He loved watching the ink ripple, loved how the chrysanthemums and snakes, the bamboo and blossoms all shimmered and slithered with his touch.

"I'm a selfish woman. What can I say?"

"I love my wife."

"And I love you." She sighed. "It's a dilemma."

"A conundrum."

"A fustercluck."

"A fustercluck indeed," he agreed, and she shrugged as a wet line ran down her spine.

"Karina?"

Another line ran down her back, blue liquid, thick and flowing. It mixed with the red and formed a pool of violet where the sheets met the crack of her ass. As his finger slid down her back, flakes of skin came off like old paint.

"Karina!" he shouted, and her face came into the light—but it wasn't her face: it was Ginger's, and she barked at him in shrill, high-pitched yaps and the phone rang as the whole world shattered into an infinite darkness and he realized he was at home, in his bed, with his wife beside him and the dog barking at the phone in the bedside charger.

"I got it, I got it. Jesus," he groaned and flopped out of bed. The abrupt end to the dream, the confusion, the ringing phone, and most of all the barking dog fueled an instant migraine. He wound up to give the beast a kick, a real solid one. Ginger, however, read his body language and beat a hasty retreat out into the hallway as his foot caught only air.

The time on the phone read 6:47 a.m., and the caller ID displayed *STAFF*.

"Hello?" Dan answered. Linda rolled over, glancing at his slouching form, phone pressed to his ear like he was some troll in the darkness.

"What?" he gasped. "How?"

She sat up, worried. Ginger returned to the doorframe, panting and spinning, wagging her tail, ready to play.

"I'm on my way," Dan said and hung up the phone.

THE SMOKE WAS VISIBLE FROM THE QUAD. AS HE PARKED, HE SAW FIRE trucks and crowds of early-morning students already gathered outside the Fine Arts Building on the west end of campus. It took over an hour to declare the fire officially out. Dan and Dean Robert were allowed inside, but only under the escort of the fire marshal, a man who carried himself like a four-star general briefing reporters after a successful military victory. Dan found the little man annoying.

"There's no structural damage that we've found. The building is fine. The fire itself was isolated to the end room on the fourth floor."

"The Archive," Dean Robert said with lament as they made their way down the hallway, past several firefighters busy coiling up hoses and sloshing through water an inch deep. The air smelled of chemicals and paper. A mist clung to the ceiling.

"How much damage?" asked Dan.

"Considerable. I'm afraid most of the contents were incinerated. See for yourself."

They stepped into the Archive, and Dan felt his stomach drop. Considerable damage was an understatement. Industrial fans had been set up to ventilate the room. All the windows were broken, either from the fire or the attempt to control it. Rows of workstations had been reduced to featureless mounds of plastic and metal. The cement ceiling was scorched black and dripped with water, like an ashtray left out in the rain.

At the center of the ceiling, where flames and smoke had licked the belly of the cement roof, sat a single giant scorch mark, like an inkblot out of a psychiatrist's stack of crazy cards. A vague image, and when Dan gazed up at it, he thought of a bird. Water dripped from that black stain, down the scorched metal guidelines that held scraps of burnt canvas in each clamp.

Considerable damage indeed. The whole place had been reduced to some gutted meat locker, some barbecue.

Some fustercluck, Mr. Glass whispered.

Some fustercluck indeed, Dan agreed, rubbing his temple.

"It's too early to say what exactly started it. Faulty wiring, surge protectors loaded past capacity," the little man said, tapping a work lamp over one of the stations. "Hell, I've seen bulbs with half the wattage burn buildings overnight. Add chemicals to the equation, faulty sprinklers, you've got a recipe for disaster."

"I can't believe this," Dan said. A day ago, he helped his students start on their thesis projects, most of which were housed in this very room. Some of the paintings had survived wars, trips around the world, or generations tucked away in walls and forgotten boxes. They had traveled, perhaps first by horse and carriage, then by boat and car and airplane, until they arrived here, in Room 42-14. Their stories were not only in the contents of their images but in the unseen hands that had cared for them down through the centuries. Hands that had carried them, protected them, perhaps even died for them. And now they dangled, little more than ashes clamped to metal wires.

"Believe it, Dan. The administration is going to have our heads if this was negligence."

"I'm not ruling out arson either," said the fire marshal. "The door, it has a security card reader, correct?"

"Correct," Dan answered.

"How many have cards?"

Dan had to think. "Students? Maybe thirty at most. Faculty, another half dozen. Maintenance and shipping have keys as well. I don't know the exact number."

"Most security readers keep logs and time stamps of every card, in and out. It'd help to know who was here last, see if there were any irregularities we can track down."

"Of course," said Dean Robert. "I'm sure that can be arranged."

Dan found himself staring at three paintings stacked against the wall, furthest from the destruction. They were the new arrivals, and as such, they hadn't been sorted, prioritized, or assigned to a student. They were untouched by the fire—however, the sprinklers had soaked the outermost painting for hours. It was warped and torn from where the moisture had pooled around the bottom of the canvas and separated the paint. Small clumps of paint flaked off in his hands like wet scabs as he moved it aside. Another total loss.

Behind it sat that bizarre painting he received the day before. It had suffered minor water damage, a small stain along the top from where it had protruded from behind the smaller painting. However, it seemed to be minimal, and he estimated that, with a few hours, he could repair it.

"No, no no no," rose a voice that Dan recognized. Even though there were firemen outside and the area was sealed for the morning, Karina had somehow gotten access to the building, perhaps flirting her way in.

"What happened?" she gasped, staring into the remains of the Archive, her mouth agape.

"I'm so sorry, Karina," he said. He didn't have to lie. For her, he felt pity. Despite their tenuous relationship, she truly did care about her craft, and knowing that several projects she had worked on last semester were among the destroyed, he felt a sense of guilt.

Before he could say anything else, she turned and left, a single frustrated scream echoing down the hallway.

TWO FUNERALS

SHE POURED DETERGENT into the dishwasher, closed it, then wiped her wet hands on the dishtowel. She took a moment to rearrange the vase of roses, tucking a few wilting ones behind the others. She placed the vase back above the sink, next to several photos. Linda, in her commencement gown, Dan standing at her side, and they both looked so much younger that she felt like she was staring at a stranger. Had the past decade done that to her? Turned her from a girl that smoked the occasional fatty and giggled at *South Park* on the few weekends when she and Dan didn't have assignments into the woman that fought off panic attacks and arranged roses in the cold silence of a now-empty house?

Another photograph, taunting her. Her mother and father at her wedding, standing behind her and smiling those fake smiles they'd worn with such ease their whole life. That smile her father gave whenever he returned from his business trips with a present and the smell of cigarettes on his jacket. "A gift for my princess, my little fair lady," he had always said with a smile.

And he had worn that same salesman's smile when he broke the news to her family that he had, for the last decade, been raising another family with another woman in another city and that they also called him Daddy, and she knew that he brought them gifts and called them princess, too. That photo with that happy smile, that man who had shattered everything she knew about her family before she went off to college. That smile that she swore she would never return to, on vacations or holidays or ever, yet always did, hugging him a little less each time until one day, a few years before his death, she only shook his hand and gave him a kiss on his cheek. Somehow Daddy had become Father, and he no longer smiled but only nodded.

She looked at the photos of her own family: the kids at birthdays and holidays, Tommy pulling Jessica in the red wagon, Ginger curled up next to Dan when she was a puppy and no larger than a toy, and the knot in her stomach loosened. There were no false smiles on those faces, only happiness and the occasional speed bump, which was to be expected.

Her cigarettes lay hidden in the back of the drawer beside the sink, the drawer that housed old candles for birthday cakes, thumbtacks, refrigerator magnets, rubber bands, and other items that didn't belong in any single drawer. Thus, they found their way into what the kids called the "junk spot." Linda fished the cigarettes out, knowing they were safe as both the kids and Dan lacked reason or motivation to even open the drawer, let alone reach to the very back.

She lit up, stale smoke filling and relaxing her. She needed this, this one bad vice. She hadn't had a craving in weeks, but by noon she felt exhausted. Her mother had called, tipsy and talkative again before three her time in Greenwich, wanting to gossip about some celebrity meltdown and how Linda's aunt was going in for a biopsy. Earlier, at school, Jessica had clung to Linda's leg, and she had to carry her daughter all the way to the classroom, promising that she would stay in the car outside the school and wait for her until 2:30. It had been a lie, of course, and she felt a pang of guilt when she drove home to do the chores.

More valuable than the cigarettes, which she bought two months ago, was her father's lighter. It was an antique silver Zippo with inlaid mother of pearl. She had seen him use it throughout her entire childhood, a constant *click* for an after-dinner smoke, yet she had never considered asking where he had gotten it. When she found it among his items at the hospital after the cancer did its final duty, only then did she realize she never would discover its origins. Had it been a gift? Perhaps from some other daughter, some other princess in his life? Etched into one side in antique font sat his initials, yet her mother dismissed the object as meaningless with a wave of her hand. That lighter, it was a painful reminder of how little she had truly known her father yet how much she missed him in the two years since he had died.

His death had been peaceful and quiet, at least according to Dan, who was the only one present in the room when he passed away. She had been outside, smoking a cigarette while her mother slept in a diazepam haze in the waiting room and Dan kept watch over the old salesman. She had missed her father's last moments, returning to find Dan in the hall, shaking his head. She didn't cry, just listened and nodded as the doctor explained that the old salesman had expired.

Expired. How she hated that word. Hated how it reduced her father's memory to some object past its purpose and shelf life. A carton of milk, a gym membership or some batteries, all thrown away after use. He had expired, but the lies had remained. Lies that she thought about whenever she saw that silver lighter of his. Lies that had crushed her once, long ago, but could no longer hurt her.

The scent of fresh earth on her hands and roses on the windowsill cleared her memory and filled her, for a brief moment, with a sense of purpose, a sense of calm that, for all the dreams and goals she had now replaced with hobbies, there was no shame in finding happiness in roses and children and this little house of theirs, this little family, this home, free of lies.

She exhaled another satisfying cloud of smoke, staring out the window into the front yard. A few of the leaves fell from the beautiful maple. Beyond the tree, a small figure moved down the sidewalk. Yellow hair bobbed beyond the hedge, one foot shuffling one foot before the other as if injured.

It was a child.

Her daughter.

Jessica.

SHE RAN ACROSS THE FRONT YARD, CALLING HER DAUGHTER'S NAME, AND the yellow hair stopped at the gate, its form hidden behind the wrought-iron fence and box hedges. She found herself, in the few seconds before she reached the gate, scared of what she would see beyond it. A broken frame or a shambling mess—or her father, crawling across the pavement like when he collapsed in their driveway on Tommy's fifth birthday. "Feet just went out from under me, funny thing," he'd said with a chuckle between bloody lips.

"Honey, is that you?" Linda screamed.

She flung the gate open and saw Jessica standing there. Her eyes were swollen as tears leaked down her cheeks, and she wasn't sobbing so much as stuttering between words too thick to escape her throat, gagging on her own speech.

"I..."

"Honey? What happened? Oh my god, are you all right?"

"I... couldn't..."

She ran her hands over Jessica's trembling face. "What happened? Why aren't you at school?"

"I couldn't... I... could-duh-duh... unt..."

Jessica held out her shaking hands. In them sat a small object wrapped in napkins, the same napkins Linda had packed in her daughter's lunch box that morning. They had been white this morning but were now blotted red.

"Honey? What is this?"

"I couldn't make them stop poking it."

Linda unfolded the napkin. A bird, a blue jay with those same strange spots she'd seen a day ago, lay dead in the napkins. Its small talons were curled back on sticklike legs. A few wayward feathers gave it a disheveled, pathetic look. Its eyes were glazed over, staring far beyond them, beyond the magnolias that lined the street, perhaps into the sky above.

"Oh, sweetie," said Linda, and she took her daughter in her arms. Jessica's whole body shook as a sob, far too loud and pained for a child of her age, escaped from her lips.

THEY BURIED THE BIRD IN THE GARDEN, BENEATH THE ROSEBUSHES.

Jessica found a shoebox and lined it with cotton balls, and Linda placed the blue jay inside. They hadn't been able to find a lid, but Jessica didn't mind, opting to cover the bird's body in leaves gathered from beneath the maple tree out front.

Linda scooped the last of the dirt into the grave and tamped it down. Jessica put a cross made of popsicle sticks into the ground, then smiled and patted the damp soil a final time.

Then she turned to her mother. "Why did they hurt it?"

According to Jessica, the bird had struck the first-grade window during recess, and with the teacher gone, kids took turns poking it with sticks as it flopped about in the bush on broken wings. Jessica had told them to stop, and they did stop, but not until after the bird...

Had what? Linda thought.

Had expired.

"I don't know," she answered. "Sometimes kids don't know their own strength. They don't know how much is too much. And sometimes kids are just mean."

"Will it go to heaven with Grandpa?"

Linda smiled. "Yes, honey, I'm sure it will."

"Good." Jessica gave a solemn nod and repeated, "Good."

SEED

THE TEARS STOPPED five minutes ago, and now Karina's head rested on her hand, palm covering her mouth as she stared at the carpet in Dan's office. The building had been cleared by the fire department, the students and faculty allowed to return. With the exception of the morning's spectacle, the only remaining evidence of the fire lay two floors above behind a locked door or lingered in the air as an acrid chemical aftertaste. And here, in his office, in the form of a student who sat on his couch, mute, after her hysterics had subsided.

"Karina, listen, everything will be okay, all right? You'll get your grades, I promise."

She blinked. It was the first time she'd blinked in minutes. It was as if her mind had gone into some loop, like a computer, and had now finished rebooting. Her forehead wrinkled in disgust.

"My grade?" she asked, her words spilling out in rapid fire, like Morse code. "My grade? Of course I'll get my grade. I don't give a fuck about my grade, Dan!"

"Karina, please." He held up his hands. A sign of peace, anything to get her to relax and not relapse into another dramatic tangent. He knew the procedure all too well.

"Everything! Everything I worked on this year was in there. All of it!"

He nodded. "I know. I'm sorry."

"No, you don't know! The Lorenzetti, the Yate. Christ, the stupid Thomas Cole I hated. All of them. Fucking. Gone. So tell me, how am I supposed to find work when I'm done? What do I say? 'Oh, I spent the winter working on a Verduchi, but no, you can't see it because it's a pile of ash'?"

"I'm so sorry."

"Stop apologizing! Get my grade..." She laughed. "Pleeease. Of course I'll get my grade, Dan, or else everyone, including that frigid bitch you sleep with, will know about our little 'arrangement.'"

Her fingers curling into air quotes around the word "arrangement" sent the glass into spastic vibrations. "You watch your mouth," he snapped.

Her expression stiffened in an instant, as if she'd seen a ghost.

He backtracked, hands up, a white flag. "Just... don't take this out on me, Karina. Don't."

His words had come off stronger than intended, in part because he'd grown tired of playing therapist to her for the last forty-five minutes. But also because he resented that she didn't understand the immense pressure he and the department would be under as a result of the blaze. Fire investigators would be followed by insurance investigators, all of whom would pick apart every detail and moment of the program. They would analyze and scrutinize every mistake, every oversight and inconsistency that led to the moment millions of dollars of art his department was responsible for went up in smoke. It was a nightmare for everyone—and most of all for him. How could she not see this?

"I'm sorry. I really am." He softened his tone and reached out to touch her shoulder, but she put up her hands, palms out. The message was clear: *Don't touch me.*

"I just... I have to think about some things right now."

She grabbed her satchel, the one he bought her in the spring that bore her initials: *K.F.C.* Then she left, slamming the door on the way out, no different than Tommy in the throes of a tantrum. He leaned back in the chair and rubbed his temple.

SEVEN MONTHS AGO THEY HAD BEEN SITTING ON THAT VERY COUCH WHEN Dan realized that he was attracted to more than her talents, her keen eye, and the debates she often started over their differences of opinion about what constituted art.

She had brought him a book of Mark Ryden prints, *Anima Mendi,* and the two of them sat on the couch for over an hour, looking at the bizarre pictures, the fusion of the cute and the demented. Candy-colored pictures depicted strange scenes, like a boy running to a meat truck driven by a skeleton holding a puppet or children sitting in sections of a toy train driven by a somber-looking Abraham Lincoln.

Dan was familiar with the artist; in fact, there were few contemporary artists he didn't know by sight. A few days earlier he made an off-the-cuff comment to the class, a joke really, and said that time would forget Mark Ryden. It was a comment that Karina had latched onto and returned to challenge him on that rainy Tuesday.

In that hour they only looked at twelve paintings in that book, yet each time Karina defended her thesis, which provoked Dan's original dismissal of Ryden. She pointed out the similarities between other artists of the absurd, drawing a long line from Dali to Warhol to Goya, with a half dozen stops along the way. There was a determination to her opinions, a lucid and specific logic that surprised him in its maturity. He felt less like he was talking to a student and more like he was engaging his equal. And perhaps, with time, his protégé. Her enthusiasm and strong opinions sparked his interest, as well as the way her hand brushed his thigh when she turned the pages of the book and he wondered, was it an accident she sat so close?

"I'm so sorry, Professor," she had said as she closed the book. "As much as I'd love to keep proving you wrong, I haven't eaten since breakfast. I might go face-first into the rug if I don't get some chow."

She stood, slinging her ratty backpack over her shoulders. His eyes fell to where her backpack caught her shirt and lifted it, revealing a colorful tattoo that hugged her hips and disappeared behind her lower back. The shirt fell, like a curtain, hiding her inked skin, and his eyes snapped back up her body as she turned to him. He held out her book and said, "Well, you've certainly made a persuasive argument. I'll grant you that."

"It's not an argument if I'm right," she quipped. Those bright, flashing eyes of hers. That confident smile of a twenty-three-year-old girl that knew exactly how attractive she was. "Keep it," she said. "Maybe it'll change your mind about him."

"Thank you. Who knows? It just might..."

Then she walked to the door. "Bye, Professor."

"Karina," Dan called out, butterflies growing in his stomach for the first time in years. In that silence, as she turned back to him, he was aware of a great divide, a line between where he stood and where he was moving toward. Like a deep breath, a nervous step in a direction he'd never considered until he'd seen part of that tattoo and realized he wanted to see it all. Then the words left his mouth before he could stop himself. "Do you want to, I dunno, maybe get dinner together? Continue this debate?"

"HAVE YOU HEARD OF THE CARACCI INSTITUTE?" HE HAD ASKED HER.

"No," she answered, running her fingers across his bare stomach. They had slept until noon again, awoken by the lazy sunbeams that spilled through the window overlooking the vineyards.

The sex had been, as always, exquisite and exhausting. She did things to him, and let him do things to her in return, that he had joked about with Linda years ago until they were dismissed as too kinky and never discussed again. She wasn't that kind of woman, his wife. But Karina was, and it was a violent act between the two of them, an act of sheer physical domination that often lasted well into the early hours and left them both sore and short of words.

"There are women and there are wives," Linda's father had once mumbled through scotch-soaked lips as he smoked his cigarette on the porch after Tommy was born. "It's best not to confuse what we can do with each." He laughed and gave Dan an uncomfortable slap on the shoulder. Perhaps the old man, in a moment of clarity in the fog of libation, had seen a bit of his own wayward tendencies in his son-in-law.

"The Caracci Institute." Dan cleared his throat. "It's a program in Italy, government-funded. An old friend runs it. The idea is students work hands-on doing restoration all around the country. Places of historical value that, for whatever reason, can't afford to fix up their frescos and what-have-you. They get cheap labor. Students get hands-on credit. Win-win."

"Sounds nice," she said, laying her head on his chest. "I love listening to your heart. I can hear it go pitter-pat."

"The reason I ask is, well, he contacted me, just the other day, actually. He asked if I knew anyone worth sponsoring for the program. And I do."

She lifted her head, face twisting with confusion. "What are you saying?"

"Chance of a lifetime. For someone of your talent, it's a no-brainer."

"Italy, huh?" She drummed her fingers on his chest, biting her bottom lip.

"It'd be a small team, ten or so students, all hand-picked, full academic credits and, of course, full acknowledgment of the work done."

"What's the catch?"

"What do you mean?"

"Come on, Boo Bear: fully funded, a semester in Italy, credit—there has to be a catch."

"Well, I guess there is."

"So? What is it?"

"It's not a semester."

"It's not?"

"It's a full year."

"A year?"

"Summer to summer. It starts in June."

She lifted her head, those two thin eyebrows arching into small spires. "This June?"

Dan nodded. "This June."

She sat up in bed, eyes fixed on her feet, fingers tapping.

"I don't know. That only gives me a month to decide," she said, but he knew that the seed had been planted. Now all it needed was some water.

"He's already filled nine spots. He wants to know by the end of the week."

She sat there, monk-like and lost in contemplation. His finger slid down the tattoos that he found so exotic, so enticing in the first days and weeks of the affair. And now, here in this hotel room, he hoped to see them no more.

There would be doubt, of course. He knew this. She loved him, or at least she thought she did in the way that most first loves felt absolute. She also loved art, and she knew with confidence that she was better than all the other students in her class. If the seed took, he could have his life back. He could undo the mistake, cover the lie he had lived for the last few months, no different than a small blemish on a painting.

"What do you think I should do?" she asked, and he realized that for all her strong opinions, for all the times she'd been the sole voice speaking up in class, for all the fire behind her eyes, she was still a scared, confused girl.

"I think…" Dan said, choosing his words with care. "I think opportunities like this come around once, maybe twice a decade."

His fingers ran down the curve of her spine again, but she no longer purred to his touch or grew goosebumps. Instead, she stared off, eyes focused perhaps on the future, and he sensed that seed had begun to grow roots.

HOME WORK

"DO WE REALLY have to keep it here?" Linda asked, wrinkling her nose. She stood before it, the unknown painting, that enormous mismatched beast that had, until moments ago, sat beneath a cotton sheet and tarp. It was in a state of being unwrapped, like a hideous present placed at the end of the study in their house.

"Just for now," Dan answered. "We could move it off-site, but then, well, it's off-site. Personally, I don't feel like driving a few miles to sit in a cold warehouse."

Mr. Glass whistled, and when Dan considered it, he realized it had been an untruth. He had left the university intending to deposit the painting off-site at the private storage unit he kept. But as he studied the painting, he felt a strange compulsion, a familiarity with the artist or some of the clues. And that card stock note that bore those four words, a title perhaps, challenging him. Sure, he could have left it at the storage locker, in the dark and next to other half-forgotten projects he would remember once a semester when it came time to submit a report. Yet he didn't. And if pressed why, like Linda had, he simply preferred to say that he enjoyed taking his work home with him, which was as true and as good a reason, he supposed, as any other.

He snipped the last remaining tie and gathered the sheets around the base of the canvas. She took it all in. "God, it's hideous."

He took a step back and absorbed it all. The wooden room, the two children, the clock, the window, the tree, the entire unbalanced scene like some schizophrenic dream.

"It is. Unfortunately, it's all that's left. And to be honest, if the insurance doesn't cover the fire, I might be out of a job."

"I'm sure they'll cover it," she said, and he felt a spike of frustration at her simple dismissal of the problem, one that had grown more complicated when the fire marshal reported "irregularities" at the end of the day. "No, they couldn't elaborate at this time," he had said before hanging up.

Doctors spoke like that, Dan thought. Turn a head, take an X-ray, give some blood, and try not to be worried when the lab called for a follow-up. What was it the British said as the bombs dropped?

Keep calm and carry on, the glass hummed.

Yes, that's right, he thought. *That's what they said. Keep calm and carry on.*

"Well, don't stay up too late, okay?" she said and gave him a kiss before leaving him alone in the study with the painting.

WITH A POP, THE FINAL STUDIO LIGHT HUMMED ON AND BATHED THE painting in a soft white light, amplifying the colors. Odd, he thought. Yesterday the painting had appeared dim, as if intentionally rendered dark, but that had been beneath the old lights of the warehouse. Now, with the painting covered in five hundred watts of white light, he found himself impressed with how it took on a richer texture. Crimson reds, violets, indigos, some streaks no wider than a hairline, all sprang to the surface and gave the painting an unnatural depth. Whoever had painted it, he thought, might not have had an eye for composition, but their precision had become more remarkable with further study. It was as if it had been made to be viewed in the very room it now sat in.

He centered the camera on the painting, setting the resolution for max. It didn't go high, only to ten megapixels. It was little more than a point-and-shoot, but for now it would have to suffice. He stepped back until the entire painting filled the small viewfinder.

Cheese, he thought and snapped the first photo. The camera gave a chirp and a click as the viewfinder flickered and the lens captured the master shot. Another chirp, another click, and deep inside, sensors and machinery and mirrors captured the spectrum between black and white.

Satisfied with a few wide shots, he switched the camera to macro mode. Artists, he knew, left signatures, even if they didn't sign their work. A cloud, perhaps rendered with counterclockwise strokes. Spattered stars made from tiny circles that spiraled out like the Milky Way. A unique glimmer in the eyes of a portrait, a crashing wave, or even something as simple as the leaves on a tree. These flourishes, no matter how small, said more about the artist and their process than the entire painting. Van Gogh was made more tortured when one saw the depressions left in the oil that formed his sunflowers, a Monet more mesmerizing when the lilies were revealed as little more than shades dissolving each other up close. These fingerprints defined the art, and they also defined the artist. All Dan needed to do was find one.

He moved within a foot of the painting and started scanning from the little girl on the right.

Click.

A picture of her sack-like face, tears leaking from swollen eyes like overripe tomatoes.

Click.

Her hair, which had seemed brown in the dim light of the warehouse, now held hints of rust beneath it, as if it had once been dyed and the roots were growing back in.

Click.

Her left hand, clinging to a ragged sock toy held together by threads. A puff of white stuffing leaked from its disemboweled stomach where the stitching had given up, not unlike the stuffed rabbit his daughter clung to.

Click.

He panned the camera across the painted room, over the dusty window, falling upon those tiny, brooding eyes of the young boy as if the lens was pulled by magnets. They were cold, uncomfortable eyes, and Dan felt that of all the thousands he'd seen on canvas, these were the most unsettling, the most inhuman—and yet the most authentic. It was as if they were staring back at him, stripping him bare and judging him with scorn.

Click.

The leathery arm of the boy disappearing off-frame.

Click.

The grandfather clock, those three missing numbers at nine, ten, and eleven, and its hands stuck at 5:55.

Click.

The broken shards of a mirror reflecting the rows of doll heads.

Click. Click. Click.

Dan lowered his camera, his own eyes tracing a path across the canvas, from the girl to the boy and over to the window between them. That window, looking out onto that field where a distant tree stood. Again, he felt emptiness, as if it were unfinished.

Through a window, in stark contrast to the decay of the house, stood that lone green tree in the middle of the field. When he last studied the painting, he mistook the landscape for a flat field beneath a cloudless blue sky, but it wasn't. Or perhaps it wasn't any longer. Now a small hill rose from the landscape beneath the tree in full bloom. And the sun, it seemed to have dipped closer to the horizon.

Of course, it hadn't really changed, he thought. The paint had set and dried long ago, and it was only the condition and position of the light that seemed to have transformed it. That was it, nothing more.

His gaze drifted back to the canvas. Within it, there was something else he had overlooked. Behind the tree, little more than a few quick strokes of a paintbrush, stood a dark thing.

A human figure.

Sinewy hands wrapped around the tree trunk, as if it were peering out from behind the oak. No eyes, no detail, nothing other than black shadow, but there it was: an unmistakable silhouette of a figure behind the tree.

A thought occurred to him. The position of the shadowy figure, the direction of its body, even how its arm was cocked against the tree all indicated that it was staring across the field, across hundreds of yards, through the window, into the room, and at the viewer. The distance was impossible, and yet, from the few simple brush strokes that formed the shadow, he felt certain that the artist had wanted the viewer to feel viewed.

Dan felt a sudden pressure between his ankles, followed by a snort. Ginger pushed her way between his legs as if they were little more than turnstiles. She sniffed the edge of the painting, short grunts escaping her snout. Then she straightened up, backed away from the painting, back between his legs, where she let out a bark that seemed to surprise only her.

"You eat your own poop," he said, scooping up the useless dog. "You're hardly a critic."

WEDNESDAY

SPLASHED ACROSS THE front of the local paper sat a quarter-page color picture showing a plume of smoke rising from the eastern side of the Fine Arts Building under the headline *University Fire Claims Priceless Paintings*. The beginning of a headache formed like a storm behind his eyes when he read the local rag's summary of the fire. Words like "mismanagement" and "incompetence" were sprinkled throughout the article in heavy servings, opinions that a professional reporter would have been careful to back up with quotations or citations. But there were no such citations in the article, only speculation from a paper he regarded as little more than a throwaway.

Typical, Dan thought.

He hadn't expected much from the local rag, which often portrayed the liberal and affluent town as some sort of David locked in an uphill battle with the university cast as Goliath. Last year the paper claimed victory when it uncovered a photo of medical students posing with a cadaver on their Facebook page, a mistake that resulted in a dozen expulsions and ruined careers. The year before, a few hundred dollars in donations to a Republican state senator cost the dean of the business school his job as well. Carbon credits and an inadequate number of electric vehicle charging stations had been another crusade, one that uprooted his department's faculty parking spots to make room for solar-charged power outlets that sat empty year-round.

And there it was, his own story beneath a full-color picture. Insinuations in black and white that his own department had carelessly housed priceless paintings in little more than a tinder box and oily rags. If the author had her way, Dan thought, she would follow up with an article about how they, too, had lit the match.

"Honey, you're going to be late," Linda said.

He finished the last of the coffee and folded that wretched newspaper as Linda called the kids and the sounds of footsteps running down the stairs echoed out in the old house.

"All right, gang, let's go," Dan said as Tommy pushed his way past Jessica and called out, "Shotgun!"

"Tommy, you know I hate that!"

"Sorry, Mom," Tommy called, out the door in a flash.

Dan gave Linda a kiss on the cheek that made her smile. "Have a good day, hon."

"You too, love."

He closed the door, taking with him the noise and chaos of the morning ritual, leaving only silence and the half-eaten remains of breakfast. She felt a twinge of emptiness as she cleaned the now-quiet kitchen. For a moment her mind wandered to that junk drawer and those cigarettes hidden in the back, but she wiped that thought from her mind. No, not today.

She took the wet towel from the sink, turned the faucet on, and pressed the power on the flip-down TV that hung beneath the cabinets. She cycled from channel to channel, waiting for the water to warm up. Postmenopausal women sat on a couch, talking politics and cats on YouTube in the same breath. Morning news and traffic reports and some blowhard before a chalkboard calling the president a socialist. Dancing aliens, manic music, and a DJ in an orange skin suit on a kids' show. Nothing caught her eye, so she turned off the TV.

In the reflection off the TV screen, a shadow stood in the doorway behind her. It was no larger than a six-year-old girl, but Linda was certain she'd heard Dan's car pull away minutes ago.

"Sweetie, did you forget something?" she asked.

The reflection didn't move, only flickered and bent as if heat had passed before it.

"Jessica? Sweety?" Linda turned around, finding herself staring at an empty doorframe. When she glanced back at the TV, the reflection was gone. She rubbed the screen, finding a small patch of oil, perhaps spattered from the bacon she'd cooked. Whatever it was must have caught the light and, from an angle, looked like a shadow of her daughter.

At least that was what she told herself.

DAN DROPPED THE CAMERA'S MEMORY CARD OFF WITH THE DEPARTMENT'S digital printing lab technician, a graduate student named Sajid whom he sometimes had trouble understanding. Nonetheless, he was a friendly student, and the two of them often discussed Indian artwork, where Dan's fondness for Mughal painting had overcome Sajid's shyness and accent.

"I'll have them printed out in no time," he said, then added, "So sorry to hear about the fire, Professor, truly."

"Yeah, me too," Dan replied.

Two hours later, he was nose-deep in books.

The university library housed tens of thousands of volumes on art alone, and to Dan, it had always been a sanctuary, a place he could blend in and melt away among the students. It was a quiet place, not unlike a church—because a hundred years ago it had been one. Even today, Spanish saints stared down from stained glass over the stacks and stations.

It had been a good afternoon. Among the stacks, he had already found two promising books. One was titled *Modern Mysteries: Art as Enigma* by an author he'd never heard of. It displayed landscapes, most rendered photorealistically with a touch of the absurd. An Alaskan river was turned into a circulatory system where salmon swam up a river of blood. The other book, a retrospective on Appalachian art from the last hundred years, had also struck him as a good enough place to start.

The painting that now sat in his home study depicted two children, and their style of clothes, particularly the boy's, reminded him of a distant memory. He and Linda had both seen boys wearing clothes like that on paintings hanging on the walls of various cheap motels that dotted the southern half of Appalachia. They drove across the country just over a decade ago, moving from university to university, interviewing for any job he could find on a road trip that lasted all summer and resulted in Tommy's conception. A trip that had, at the time, been ill-planned yet carefree and, in hindsight, had come to symbolize the vast chasm between being newly married and being parents. These days commitments and responsibility, soccer practice and homework, all the gnawing necessities of raising their kids trumped the ability to pack up and drive in any direction until they ran out of gas or money. In some fleeting moments, when the kids screamed and fought, Dan mourned that absolute freedom that lay behind him in the rearview mirror.

Walking down the aisle, he ran his fingers down the spine of the old books. He paused on another that caught his eye, a collection of paintings by Max Ernst. A tremble started in his finger and ran the length of his arm, all the way up to his head, where it lodged itself in the base of his tongue, merging with the glass behind his eyes, tickling.

That book, the very same edition, had once sat on the shelf in the reading room of the orphanage. He had spent nights, flashlight in hand, flipping through the pages as thunderstorms raged outside. To an audience, he had once described Ernst as if Dali had raped Picasso, a description that earned him a nasty letter from the dean of Women's Studies, but a description he felt valid. Ernst's paintings, those twisted visions of shapes birthing appendages from the ground, growing skyward, wrapped in colorful cloth and stretched skin, how they had saved him from the fear he felt as the lightning flashed and the orphanage shook. How they set him free.

That was a lifetime ago, he thought. How could he have forgotten that? A life in which he had stuttered and been scared of the dark, long before the box and the wood and the trembling tongue were all replaced by that piece of glass and the occasional flash migraine.

He placed the book back on the shelf and felt the tremble float from his mouth, pressure lifting as he walked away.

Thump.

The book fell to the floor.

It had fallen from the shelf and lay open in the middle of the stacks, pages askew. A tremble surged up his arm again, and his tongue grew heavy as the glass itched.

He walked back, looking at the book with caution, as if perhaps it would fly up and attack him. It lay open to a painting, *The Eye of Silence,* a bizarre, intangible mess of impossible columns and mountains carved into intricate shapes like the skin of a slumbering titan. He closed the book and returned it with haste to its place on the shelf. There, a face thrust itself out at him from the void.

"Boo!" said the woman's face.

He stumbled backward, dropping the books with another heavy thump. A few students at distant desks turned their heads in his direction. He collected the books, watching the shadow move behind the shelves, now more annoyed than frightened by her sudden appearance.

"You scared the hell out of me," he said as Karina rounded the corner with a grin.

"I'm sorry. I couldn't help it. You looked so, I dunno, busy. In your own little world."

"Well, I was."

"There room for two in that little world of yours?"

"You wouldn't like it," he said, putting the book back on the shelf.

She approached him, bridging the distance between them with the precision of a siren, and Dan felt an intense need to make the conversation as short as possible. Especially in public. Eyes were on him, and she had all the discretion of a teenager.

"What are you doing here?" he asked.

"I came…" she started, then paused, blinking as her smile faded to something less playful. "I came to apologize. Yesterday, I wasn't myself. The fire, it wasn't your fault, but I took it out on you. And, well… I'm sorry."

"It's okay."

"No, it's not."

"Don't worry about it. We were all, I dunno, in shock. Really, it's okay."

"Shock or not, what I said was wrong."

She drew closer. Her hand fell to his arm, and her fingers ran up it to his elbow. Now that the apology was out and equilibrium was restored, that smile and all that it implied grew across her face until she had to purse her lips to stop it.

"Can I make it up to you?" She leaned in, whispering, "This weekend? Napa? Our favorite place?"

Her smell inebriated him, wrapped him in warmth and offered the touch of skin. He wanted nothing more than to close his eyes, to kiss those lips, feel those fingers touching him. But beneath that, like a faint odor of something teetering on the edge of rot, was a sad sort of desperation to her voice that had grown in the months they spent apart. It was like returning to a childhood playground, once so grand and unending, revealed later in life to be almost pathetic. Despite her scent and sexuality, he thought, time had revealed her to be a shade of what he once desired.

"Karina…"

"You and me, Boo Bear?"

"Stop…" His throat was tight, and he had to swallow to get enough moisture to make the words. "Stop… please."

"I miss that, Dan. I miss us. I miss you. All of you."

He felt her hand running down his arm, tracing the edge of his belt, dipping under and into his pants. Her desperation repulsed him. His words were heavy, and it took all his might to spit them forth, and even then, all he could say was, "I said stop!"

But it wasn't the words that stopped her.

It was the push.

He had meant it to be a nudge, firm and final, hands drawing a line between them, a clear sign to stop. Or at least that was how he pictured it.

Instead, his tongue had fluttered, and the words had rolled back down his own throat into a childish stutter—

"I suh-said-stuh-stop!"

And the pressure exited his hands, pushing her stomach in a sudden jolt, sending her stumbling a good two feet back, slack-jawed and stunned. Her shoulder connected with an oversized book, which fell to the ground with a massive thump, a sound that once again drew the attention of the students at the distant desks.

"I'm sorry, Karina. I didn't mean to—"

"Fuck… you," she said in two bursts, followed by a gasp of air. He had shoved her, hard, the way a detective might shove some unruly dame in a black-and-white movie before kissing her or slapping her or both. And there had been, in that brief void between action and reaction, a realization on both their faces that mirrored each other. Then coldness bled back into her eyes, utter and complete. In a flash, she turned and stormed off, black hair shimmering and satchel swinging as she disappeared beyond the shelves and the curious stares of the students.

Wonderful, Dan thought as he scooped up the books and squeezed his temple, and he wondered, if he squeezed hard enough, could he shatter the glass and forget the whole mess?

ALMOST DAWN

"YOU LOOK TIRED," Tommy said as he climbed into bed and opened his Nintendo.

Various sports figures covered his comforter, all frozen in mid-action. Baseball, football, basketball, even hockey, which Tommy had once shown enough of an interest in for Dan to buy him a pair of rollerblades and a stick, all of which now sat in the closet, unused in over a year. He pulled the comforter up to his son's chest, folding it back and tamping it down.

"Rough day at the office, I suppose."

"What does that mean? Rough day at the office."

"It's an expression."

"An aspression?" asked Jessica from the bunk above.

"It means, I dunno, things at work could've gone better."

"Are you going to the fire?" Jessica asked.

"The fire?"

She nodded. "It's an aspression. Like, not have your job?"

"Oh." Dan laughed. "Am I going to get fired?"

"Yeah, that."

"Highly unlikely," he answered. "But your mom might fire me if I don't get you two to bed. Close it down, Tommy."

Tommy did as he was told and closed the Nintendo, placing it on the shelf next to his soccer trophy. "Night, Dad."

"Night, buddy."

Dan stood up, face-to-face with Jessica's bunk, the dolls and toys all lined up at the foot of her bed. Only Mr. Bun remained, held tight in her hands.

"Sleep tight, angel."

He gave her a kiss. She thrust Mr. Bun out expectantly, its head flopping around like a wilting flower. "Mr. Bun too," she said.

"Mm-hmm." He gave Mr. Bun a kiss, tasting the salt of years of care bestowed on that old rag bunny.

"Goodnight, kids," Dan said, turning off the light as he closed the door.

A few seconds passed before the dim light of the Nintendo grew beneath Tommy's comforter in the darkness.

"Stop that," said Jessica.

Tommy ignored it. He knew how quick she fell asleep. All he had to do was keep the volume down until she did and he could play *Metroid* until the battery ran out. And this time, he had the charger.

"I said stop!"

He turned the Nintendo off and sighed. He didn't hate his sister; he just hated sharing a room with her. It wasn't fair. His parents had a big house, bigger than most of his friends, but they wouldn't let him sleep downstairs. That was Dad's room, where Dad did important stuff like read old books and use the computer and look at stupid paintings.

"Knock it off!"

"I turned it off, you spaz!" Tommy snapped. "Jeez. Go to bed."

"I'm not talking to you," she said, voice shaking in the shadows.

"Who? Mr. Bun?"

"Not him."

"Who?" Tommy asked again. Was she talking in her sleep again? Or to one of her imaginary friends?

"Who?" he asked again, and the bunk bed above shifted and creaked. Annoyed, Tommy climbed out of bed and up the rungs of the ladder until he was looking into her bunk. Jessica sat in a tent beneath the sheets, Mr. Bun stationed outside, staring back like a sentry.

Tommy scanned the bed, top to bottom, but there was no one else there: just a lump beneath the covers and those stupid stuffed toys.

"What are you talking about?" he asked.

Jessica lifted the sheet, peeking out from a small hole, glancing around the darkened room.

"He's gone," she said. "Mr. Bun scared him away. For now."

In the year they had shared the bedroom, Jessica had claimed she'd seen everyone from Santa to the Tooth Fairy and half a dozen cartoon characters, all visiting her between darkness and dawn, but he knew otherwise. There was no Santa or Tooth Fairy or Easter Bunny. All the nocturnal intrusions were parts his parents acted out for her amusement. They were lies to keep her happy, no different than when his grandpa had pretended to pull a coin from behind her ear, the same coin Tommy had caught the glimmer of moments earlier in the old man's wrinkled hands.

"Go to bed," Tommy said, and he pushed Mr. Bun over and climbed down as Jessica whined, "Hey!"

THE LIBRARY WAS WET WITH SHADOWS THAT GLIMMERED LIKE OIL BENEATH the flickering fluorescent lights. It was cold. Far colder than a September morning should be. A distant barking came from deep within the dark rows of bookshelves. Someone had let a dog into the library. Its shrill yips broke his concentration on the book he had been studying. Yet when he closed the book, he noticed the cover was blank and wet and his fingers were stained with paint. Disgusting, he thought as he wiped the paint on his shorts.

His fingers were wrong. They were small and unwrinkled, the fingers of a child. The tips, all ten, were wrapped in gauze bandages stained purple from the paint. Even his legs were short and scrawny, devoid of that thick hair he'd had for years.

The dog barked again, the lights flickered, and he felt a shiver as he tried to remember what book he had been reading but couldn't. He couldn't even remember why he had picked it up, or what time it was, or what had brought him to the library. He had tucked his kids in, brushed his teeth, plucked yet another gray hair from his head, taken his Imitrex, and then what? Was he dreaming again?

Or waking up? Mr. Glass asked as something ran past the stacks of books. It was a dark shape, small and skittering and frantic. It chattered like tumblers in an old lock.

His eyes scanned the rows of books in front of him. Each section sat numbered with the same digits—555—endless in every direction. He stood up, searching for the chattering sound and dropping the book. The book made a metal clang as it landed on the floor, but when he glanced down, it was no longer there. Instead, an old railroad spike rolled around, covered in rust. Another spastic movement followed that rattling sound as he caught a sidelong glimpse of the shape. It was small, like an animal, and yet it didn't move like one. It phased and pulsed, like a stop-motion movie, a special effect from the silent era of film.

His thin legs moved fast, breaking into a sprint. He ran past shelves filled with blank books all bleeding purple. Past those numbers, the triple five, written in a childish scrawl. His feet echoed out on the soft rug, drumbeats beneath the flickering light, and the floor felt like grass. Around the corner, turning past those numbers, and there it was. A brown shape, with hair.

Ginger sat in the middle of a row of books. Her tail wagged across the carpet in an unnatural, epileptic motion. Her teeth chattered, rapid clickity-clacks of fang against fang—and yet she wasn't looking at Dan.

She was sitting at the feet of a woman who stood beneath a pulsing yellow light. A woman whose naked body swam with pictures that dripped fresh ink down bare flesh.

"Karina?" Dan asked, but the woman ignored him. He called her name again, thinking perhaps she hadn't heard him, but she continued thumbing through an old book.

Only when Ginger barked at her did she raise a single finger to her lips before returning to the book.

"Dan," said a voice.

Ginger barked a second time, louder.

"Dan!" said the voice again, but it wasn't Karina's. It came from the floor and the ceiling, from a place a thousand miles away. He knew that voice, but when he tried to name it, words failed him. When he tried to picture it, a featureless mound of flesh floated beyond his vision.

Karina put the book back on the shelf, turned, and walked away from him. The ink from those intricate waves and dragons and chrysanthemums all leaked down her back, down the curve of her ass, down her legs and into a pool on the floor.

"DAN!"

She gave a single glance back at him, and he saw tears flowing from empty eyes.

"Wake up," she whispered.

IT WAS COLD IN THE BEDROOM, MORE SO THAN IT SHOULD'VE BEEN FOR THE first week of September. For a moment he thought he could see his breath in the air and the shape of Tommy standing by the door. Both disappeared as his eyes adjusted to the darkness. Linda was sitting upright in bed, eyes on him.

"Wake up," she whispered.

"What is it?" he mumbled, glancing at the clock. Ten to six. It was early.

"I don't know, but she's been barking for five minutes."

He was going to ask who, but he already knew. Ginger's incessant barking came from somewhere outside in a steady rhythm. Not frantic, but alarmed and loud enough to wake the neighbors. If it wasn't stopped, he'd never hear the end of it from Marty, and a few days later, the homeowners association would send another one of its warning letters. He already had three.

He climbed out of bed, into the cold, in search of his robe.

"GINGER!" HE CALLED, OPENING THE BACK DOOR. SOMEWHERE FAR OFF, HE could hear the whir of a sprinkler. The bricks were wet with dew that made the small patches of moss growing between the cracks as slick as black ice. His foot slipped and he pinwheeled forward, regaining his traction on the edge of the bricks.

Click went the flashlight. Fog hung in clumps throughout the backyard, rendered into glowing orbs like lanterns in the darkness as the flashlight beam passed through them. He scanned the yard, starting to the left by the umbrella and patio table they had their dinners on during the summer. He scanned past the wood hot tub whose water needed to be emptied. Further along, the box hedges, then past the old birdbath that had come with the property.

"Ginger, where are you?" he called in a hushed voice.

The barking, which had been so perfectly timed in five-second intervals, ceased that moment. He knew she was nearby, hiding perhaps. She was a master of silence when it came to trouble, able to stifle her sounds whenever someone was searching for her. Then he heard movement, leaves rustling, the snap of a dry twig followed by growling from along the fence by the rosebushes.

"Ginger?" He swung the flashlight along the fence, drawing closer to the bushes and posts that propped up those roses Linda loved so much. That silly hobby of hers that she slaved away at, season after season.

He saw more movement and homed in on the redwood fencing. A shadow passed by the fence, and Dan swung the flashlight at shoulder height along the damp wood. There, he found the source of the movement. His flashlight fell from his hands as a gasp escaped his throat.

For a moment, he thought he was still dreaming.

A bloodshot eye stared back through a hole in the fence. It blinked and disappeared after the beam crossed the hole. That image that had made him gasp, that old blinking eye glaring through the fence and fog, now made him feel as foolish as a child.

"Sorry, Marty," Dan said, picking up the flashlight.

"Shut that damn dog of yours up or I'm calling the cops," said the shadow beyond the fence. He heard Marty's footsteps moving away from the fence, back to the house next door.

"Working on it," Dan answered with a shake of his head as the shadow left, taking that peering old eye with it. "Hope you break your hip, you old prick," he mumbled but felt little satisfaction as his words hung in the air, like a whispered curse at a teacher's back.

The flashlight fell back to the roses and something white beneath them. Two popsicle sticks sat on the dirt, mudded and broken. More rustling as Ginger emerged from between the rosebushes. Mud clung to her fur in small patches. Her paws were wet and black and glistened in the moonlight. And something else, something on the white and brown fur around her mouth. Something red stained her jowls.

"Ginger, come here, now!"

For once she obeyed, waddling over with a grunt. Her face was spattered in a dark red substance that looked like old paint or—

Blood, he realized.

"Jesus, Ginger, are you all right?" He squatted and lifted her up, carefully avoiding the smear that clung to those long hairs in small candy-like droplets. Ginger tried to lick his face, but he pulled back, inspecting her. Her tail wagged, her fur was intact, and save for the mud and blood on her face, she looked as healthy and stupid as usual.

Another rustle from the bushes in the corner, and a thought cut through his mind like a knife.

Not 'er blood, said Mr. Glass.

No, it's not, Dan thought. *Then whose is it?*

The bush rustled again. A few drops of dew slid down from the roses and some petals dislodged, fluttering down onto the damp earth. A tiny shape fluttered about beneath the fronds and undergrowth. He reached out, flashlight trained on the epicenter of the noise and movement. There he saw something blue, a flower or a leaf perhaps.

No, a feather. It was a blue feather.

He lifted the fronds, his flashlight falling on a hole in the dirt. It was small. The earth around it had been tilled by Linda's hands and then dug up by Ginger's paws. Inside the small hole lay a thrashing shape. A bird fluttered about, half covered in dirt and blood. It hopped up, and for a moment it looked as if it was going to fly away. But it couldn't.

Nearby sat the remains of the bird's wings. They were torn clean from the body, as if surgically removed and stacked for later consumption. No different than when Ginger saved the dried pig ears Linda would buy, leaving them hidden around the house until she forgot them and Dan rediscovered them months later, covered in mold. Only this wasn't a snack bought for a few bucks at Petco, but two wings torn from a living thing.

The bird struggled to climb from the hole, flapping its phantom wings, two raw patches, before collapsing back into the hole to begin the hopeless act all over. Ginger had never chased squirrels, shown only a passing interest in birds. She had fled from every dog at the dog park, whimpering in fear until Dan grew tired of apologizing to other dog owners and stopped taking her. She was an animal without a purpose, an ornament. And yet here, somehow, she had caught, maimed, and toyed with this bird, perhaps intending to go on for hours before she was interrupted.

Dan felt revulsion and pity, but he steeled his stomach. He reached out and took the broken creature in his hands. It pecked at his fingers, the attacks little more than the final, futile actions of an animal that sensed its time had come. Its body disappeared between his hands as he turned away and squeezed.

It was a quick death. The neck broke with a soft pop that offered little more resistance than if he were striking a match. The bird went limp in his hands, thin toes curling around his fingers in a final reflex. Ginger let out a single grunt, perhaps sensing her play toy was no more.

He placed the bird back into the hole where it lay, awkward, like one of his daughter's bean bag dolls. He took what remained of the wings, feathers splayed and loose, and placed them over the bird. White spots marked parts of the wings, and he realized this blue jay was not native to California. The jays here were larger, aggressive; they sometimes came in through the open door to steal Ginger's dried dog food. This blue jay was delicate, with a triangular rim of feathers that sat on top of its limp head like some broken crown.

How far had this bird flown? Hundreds, perhaps thousands of miles, only to end up bested by a dog that had twice chewed through the power cable on the hot tub pump and probably fried what few brain cells remained after generations of inbreeding.

Life was cruel like that, Dan thought, and he pushed the dirt into the hole where the bird's motionless eyes disappeared beneath the cold earth.

CYANOCITTA CRISTATA, MORE COMMONLY KNOWN AS THE BLUE JAY. HE WAS right: it wasn't native. *The Field Guide to North American Birds* placed its range east of the continental divide. He had seen such jays throughout his youth, but never since settling in California. Here, the scrub jays flew about, crestless creatures he regarded as little more than flying rats. His curiosity satisfied, he closed the field guide and put it back on the bookshelf where it lay, out of place, among Jessica's Spongebob books, Tommy's *Illustrated King Arthur* series, and Linda's growing collection of Sue Grafton novels.

He washed his hands twice, first downstairs after giving Ginger a quick rinse and a second time before climbing into bed. Still, the smell of the bird, the dirt, and Ginger all lingered.

"No burglars?" Linda mumbled.

"Two. I fought them off with a chainsaw."

"Liar…" She smiled. "What was it?"

"Just a bird that stupid dog of ours was trying to bury."

"Mmm," Linda said, her toes curling next to his. "A bird?"

"A blue jay. Poor thing. Ginger must've snuck up on it. Honestly, I'm a little impressed."

"We buried a bird yesterday." Linda yawned. "A blue jay." She rolled over, away from him, and pulled the comforter up to her neck.

"Really?"

"Mm-hmm. In the rose garden. Jessica found it at school. Poor dear, she was so shaken up," Linda mumbled.

Dan considered it for a moment. Maybe the dog hadn't caught it. Maybe she had dug it up, just another one of her holes around the yard. "Are you sure it was dead?"

"Positive," Linda whispered as her voice took on that somnolent drawl that blurred the consonants. "Now get some sleep. It's almost dawn."

CHILD CARE

THE SCREAMING STARTED at exactly 7:35 in the morning. Dan knew this because he had just put the coffee pot back beneath the digital clock and thought he needed to hurry. The fire had thrown his lesson plans for a loop, and he needed to revise the remainder of the semester's lessons. Then his daughter's screams had erupted from upstairs, startling him into spilling his coffee on the newspaper.

He didn't bother to clean up the coffee, as the screams were not the usual playful shrieks that had become like white noise to him. Instead, they were piercing, loud and long, the kind parents reacted to out of instinct. He was halfway up the stairs as her lungs gave out. By the time he threw open the door to the kids' bedroom, the screams had resumed.

Jessica sat atop her bunk bed, still in her pajamas, mouth wide open and eyes clamped shut. Tommy stood half dressed, his Nintendo on the floor, covering his ears and shouting, "Shut up! Shut up!"

"Jessica, honey, what is it?" Dan shouted, running his hands over his daughter's face, searching for signs of pain that could prompt such screams.

"Mr. Bun! It's Mr. Bun! He hurt Mr. Bun!"

"What?" Dan shouted as Jessica pointed to the bottom of her bed, where that old stuffed rabbit sat. The damage was immediately apparent. Two holes had replaced its button eyes. White stuffing hung in threads like loose optic cords.

"He hurt Mr. Bun," she screamed again. "He took his eyes!"

"Honey, it's okay. We'll find them," Dan answered and turned his attention to Tommy. "He hurt Mr. Bun," she had said, and Dan knew what had happened. "Thomas, did you do this?"

"No," he said, shaking his head as his eyes darted up to his sister.

"Thomas, tell the truth."

"Dad, I didn't do it, I promise!" he whined, pointing to Jessica. "Maybe she did!"

Dan studied his son's eyes. They were the eyes of a liar. Dan knew them well because they were his own eyes. How many times had he lied to Linda, to her face, to his children? All the seminars, the weekends away, the late-night dinners and scratches on his back. And now those same eyes stared back from a nine-year-old boy, reflecting his own lies like two little mirrors.

"I'm very disappointed in you, Thomas."

"I swear to God!"

"Give me your Nintendo."

"Why?" he whined.

Dan put Mr. Bun back on his daughter's bed, walked over, and reached for the Nintendo on the table. Seeing this, Tommy lunged for it, but Dan was quicker. He held it up while Tommy looked on with a mix of curiosity and horror.

"You can't break your sister's toys, Thomas. You know that."

And he snapped the Nintendo in half.

The glass behind his eyes vibrated white hot. The two halves of the Nintendo buckled and bent until the plastic gave way in a resonating pop and the system folded the wrong way. Just like the bird, only a little harder and not as messy. He dropped the two halves back on the table, eyes never leaving Tommy, whose mouth hung open in shock and betrayal.

"You… always blame me," Tommy gasped, eyes welling with tears. "I hate you!"

"You'll get over it."

Tommy turned and ran to the bathroom, slamming the door so hard that a picture of his second-grade soccer team fell off the shelf and shattered. Like father like son, Dan thought. Even down to the flair for destruction.

TOMMY DIDN'T COME DOWN FOR BREAKFAST, AND LINDA SPENT TWENTY minutes just talking him into going to his soccer game. To Dan, she had seemed less concerned with his lie than Dan's handling of the matter, a fact she had told him after learning he had broken Tommy's Christmas present.

"You could have just taken it away," she had said. "Did that occur to you?"

It hadn't, and in hindsight, he regretted his actions, feeling as if they had belonged to someone else, someone less controlled. Nonetheless, he knew that if Linda had been there, the worst that would have happened would have been a stern warning followed by a hug. Then, when she left, Tommy would have provoked Jessica again for tattling. That had become the pattern these days. Provoke, apologize, wait, and repeat. Always pushing that line in the sand forward, testing the boundaries. All Dan had done was reset the line, but it wouldn't be long before Tommy tried to move it again.

But he wasn't thinking about that anymore.

By noon he had put the fight out of his mind and was focused on the painting that sat at the end of the study. He had a few hours before he needed to pick up the prints at the university, and he was determined to come up with some answers. Jessica was upstairs, having a "tea party," which meant that he could focus on the painting that had been clawing into his thoughts since he woke up this morning, mocking him.

He ran his fingers along the back of the painting, feeling the edge of the frame and the canvas. Strange, he thought. The colors and composition of the image itself continued as if it had been painted on a flat surface and then affixed over the stretcher bars. The paint, as far as he could tell to the touch, was unvarnished. The layers felt thin and fresh beneath his fingers. He began to suspect that the painting was a recent creation, and if so, that eliminated any possibility of the artist being deceased—and with it, any chance for Dan to claim a long-lost discovery.

And the canvas itself, something felt odd about it. He had touched thousands of paintings, could have lost his job a dozen times over if museums had known his fingers had caressed their collections. It was an impulse he couldn't ignore, no different than a chef tasting his own creation. Every time he touched the same paint that had been laid down by the artists, he felt an instant connection, a bond, as if he were the reflection in a mirror and the artists were his true image.

He didn't feel that with this painting.

Instead, the canvas and paint upon it were cold and empty; there was a void where there should have been a mirror, and from that darkness, no artist stared back. Yet everything felt familiar: an unreachable itch, a word on the tip of his tongue that retreated down his throat and sat uneasy in his gut, gnawing like a parasite. After years of study, countless paintings identified by mere smudges of oil and ink and obscure detail alone, this simple, anonymous painting mocked him. "It's got your name written on it," Miguel had said, and Dean Robert had laughed because he had been right, or at least he would've been until tonight. And this, more than anything, embarrassed him: that something that should have taken mere hours to identify still sat incomplete after two days.

There was no signature, nothing hidden along the brown edges and rear frames, no secrets behind it. He felt like a student again. He gave up, stepping back, and when he turned his head away from that frustrating canvas, a shape attacked him. Two buttons floated, inches from his face, connected by a thread to an inanimate form.

"Oh my," he said, smiling.

"Did I scare you, Dad?" Jessica asked, lowering Mr. Bun, who had two buttons sewn to his face, one of which Dan recognized from an old blazer of his.

"No, sweetie, you didn't."

"Mr. Bun says I did. He says I scared you good."

"Mr. Bun has new eyes, I see."

She nodded, chewing on a finger, then reached out to touch the painting.

"Honey, dirty hands."

She stopped, sniffled, and studied the painting. "Whatchya doing?"

"Well," he said, "I'm trying to find out who made this. See, paintings usually have a bit of space on the side or back where there's no paint, right?"

"Why?"

"Because the canvas was pulled over the stretcher frame, and the artist doesn't usually paint all the sides and these folds and stuff."

"Oh. Why not?" she asked.

"Because no one would see those parts of the painting." He reached and touched the seam on the side of her spotted sundress. "Like this."

"Oh." She nodded, and her finger returned to her mouth.

"What's unusual is this one was painted everywhere. Front, back, all those little folds down here. See?" Dan tapped on a loose piece of canvas in the lower-left corner that was painted and stapled. "See?" he asked again, tapping it with the pencil.

Jessica didn't see. She stood before the painting, that same expression of confusion locked on her face as she chewed her finger. A trickle of blood ran down from the corner of her mouth and onto the floor.

"Jessica?" he gasped.

She stood there, eyes staring off at something a thousand miles away. Dan could hear scraping, and as the blood began to trickle down her chin, he realized that sound was tooth on bone. He grabbed her, pulled her hand out of her mouth. She blinked several times.

"Oh. Why not?" she asked, smiling with crimson teeth.

THE CRYING HAD BEGUN, AS IT OFTEN DID WITH CHILDREN, NOT AT THE injury itself but at the discovery that the injury had drawn blood. The screams came in waves. First at the sight of the blood, then as cold water rinsed the wound, and again when Dan disinfected it. The screams subsided while they waited in the pediatrics unit of the medical clinic, Jessica placated by the lollipop Dan had gotten from the reception desk. The crying returned when Dr. Lee produced a needle to anesthetize the wound and persisted after the final stitch, up until Linda arrived and scooped her up in her arms.

"She did a number on her finger," Dr. Lee said. "Had she pressed any harder, she might've caused nerve damage."

Doctors, Dan thought. They always spoke so optimistically around parents. One look at Linda, who appeared on the verge of hysteria herself, and he understood this false confidence wasn't for him but for her. He wondered how Dr. Lee delivered news to terminal children and if he did it with a smile.

"What concerns me isn't necessarily the injury. It'll heal and, most likely, won't scar."

"I don't understand why she did that," Linda asked, and Dan realized she was looking not at the doctor but at him for the answer. Or perhaps for the cause.

"That's what concerns me. Children learn tactile sensation early. Babies grab fingers, toddlers push themselves off the ground, fall over. We've all seen it. Now, some children develop an under-sensitivity to physical contact. They fall over and skin their knee but they don't realize the warning signs or the injuries. Hence childproof scissors. They might be overly physical, too rough with something fragile. Their muscles are still calibrating. Some kids even hurt themselves, accidentally of course. Has she displayed such prior behavior?"

Linda shook her head. "No, no, she's been a normal child in every—"

"Actually," Dan cut her off. "There was an incident today. Earlier."

Linda looked at him, first with confusion, then epiphany. "Mr. Bun," she said.

"Her doll," Dan cut her off again. "Its eyes were pulled out. I discovered it this morning. She said our son did it. I thought he did, but now I'm not so sure."

The doctor clicked his pen several times and studied Jessica as she swung her feet from the chair and whispered to her princess doll. Dan felt a small spike grow from the back of his head and push his eyes forward. He rubbed his temple.

"Could she have done that as well?" Linda asked, head turning between Dan and the doctor as if she were refereeing a tennis game.

"It's possible," said the doctor as he clicked his pen again. "Maybe she's externalizing some stress she feels, a change perhaps. You said she just started school?"

"On Monday," Linda said. "It hasn't gone as smooth as we'd hoped. Should we be worried?"

You're already worried, or were you asking permission to continue? Dan thought as the pressure grew inside his head. His words were becoming sharp, his patience short. The headache was going to be a whopper.

"Jessica, honey?" Linda asked in a soft tone. "Did you hurt Mr. Bun?"

Jessica kept her gaze on her swinging feet. The question hung in the air, unanswered.

"Jessica," Dan barked. "Your mother's asking you a question."

Her feet stopped swinging. "I don't remember," she said in a whispered voice laced with shame. Then her feet resumed their pendulum arc. Back and forth.

"Well, I wouldn't be too concerned," said the doctor as his pen went clickity-clack again, and Dan felt another bolt behind his eyes. That pen, he realized. That sound brought on the discomfort circling behind his sinuses like a low-pressure storm. A whopper of a headache indeed. He thought of the Imitrex, those pink little pizza slices inside the medicine cabinet.

Break glass in case of emergency, Mr. Glass mumbled.

"The important thing," the doctor continued, "is to keep an eye out for any unusual behavior or signs. If they occur, we can run some tests, but I don't think it'll come to that." He flipped to another page in the chart. "How're you doing, Dan? How's the old noggin these days?"

"I'm fine," Dan said as an aura blossomed around the doctor like a gilded halo, and he wanted to leave, soon, or he'd risk losing his lunch.

"Any problems with the medication?"

Dan forced out a smile. "It does the trick."

"Good," the doctor said and closed the chart. "If it's doing the job, then I'm doing mine."

He clicked his pen a final time, then put it down. Dan felt the headache, and the aura that came with it, slither back into silence somewhere behind his eyes.

COMPLICATIONS

COLD LIGHT FLICKERED off Sajid's glasses, coming from the computer screen as he scrolled through the library of photos on Dan's memory card. He shook his head a second time, coming to the end of the thumbnails. Dan saw it now, this "problem" Sajid had emailed him about.

"What time did you say these were taken, Professor?"

"Around seven," Dan said. "Maybe later."

Sajid cycled to another digital photo of the anonymous painting. There it was again: another blur, the same as the others, this time blooming out from the edge of the painting like a glowing spiderweb. Each and every photo displayed a similar result, all thirty-seven of them.

"Can you remove it?" Dan asked.

"What do you mean?"

"Like use a filter or something?"

Sajid laughed. "This isn't CSI. I can't hit enhance and fix it. Besides, there's too much light. Washes out the details. See that?" He stopped on one photo. The glow took up half the painting, casting a shadow across it.

"What is that?" Dan asked.

"Glare from the sun, maybe? Reflection from the flash? A smudge? Heck, could be the CCD in your camera going out. Who knows?"

"That's impossible. It's only a few months old. Besides, I didn't use the flash."

"Well, something washed out the image, like a sun shaft or something."

"These were taken at night," Dan said slowly, as if to a child.

"That's funny," Sajid said, zooming in on a washed-out close-up of the painted field.

"What is?"

"Well, I was just thinking that you're taking a picture of a painted sunset, but it's like you're taking a picture into the sun." Sajid scrolled back to the thumbnails, every one displaying that same defect. Useless, all of them. "Do you still want printouts?"

"No," Dan said. "I'll reshoot."

"You can check out some of our cameras. We've got lights, too. Those'll help. Some of the photos had focus problems. Like this one," Sajid said, clicking another thumbnail. It was a close-up of that little girl in the yellow dress. "See, her face is blurred, but her hand isn't."

Dan studied the picture. Sajid was right. The girl's face was out of focus, like some high-speed object caught mid-motion, but her body and arm were rendered in perfect clarity.

"Did you use a tripod?" Sajid asked.

"No," Dan answered with a spike of frustration, knowing that Sajid would blame the focus issues on an unsteady hand. He sighed and reached for an equipment requisition form.

HIS SMARTPHONE VIBRATED FOR THE EIGHTH TIME IN THIRTY MINUTES. He didn't need to check the message to know who it was. The first two had come five minutes apart and read, *we need 2 talk,* which was followed by, *R u there???*

He hated text messages in general and hated hers even more, how she reduced three-letter words to simple letters, as if spelling the word "are" took Herculean effort. As the messages grew more frequent, he simply stopped checking them altogether, switching his phone to vibrate for fear of irritating that glass that chewed on the gray matter behind his eyes.

He made the mistake of turning on his computer to look up the phone number of an artist he was trying to contact, a possible lead, and his instant messenger automatically loaded. Before he could close the application, a new message bounced on his screen with a cheerful *pling*: *u @ the office?* He ignored her message, knowing that he could say the janitor had turned his computer on. He didn't keep office hours on Thursday.

He began by querying contact information for the artist R.L. Emerson, whose gothic surrealism bore a passing resemblance to the unknown painting sitting at home. He had completed half his query when the instant messenger popped up again and read, *heLLo?*

The thing about computers Dan hated the most was the constant surprises. Sure, they made sending messages and shopping easier, and it was nice to know there was a whole subculture of fetishists out there far kinkier than he'd ever dared to be. But these things weren't important. What was important was that technology worked for him, not against him. And today, it seemed determined to do the latter.

He was almost certain his web browser was the active application, but when the instant message icon plinked a third time, he saw that he had typed his entire search query into the chat box instead. He scrambled to undo his mistake, but it was too late. Wherever Karina was, she had undoubtedly just seen the words *dRineheart is typing a message* appear in her IM client as it did whenever someone started to respond.

Now he couldn't ignore her. He needed to defuse the situation, not detonate it, and given their last encounter, he had to be careful. Why couldn't it be simple with her? Why did every minute of his day carry the constant threat of exposure? A threat she had long ago waved away, saying, "I can be discreet if you can."

i know ur there! read the next message with a cheerful pop, followed by a smiley face that Dan found more insulting than the constant stream of messages.

Discreet. Mr. Glass laughed. *She's about as discreet as a circumcision with pliers.*

Fuck off, Dan typed, finger hovering over the *enter* key when a knock at the door echoed out.

Do it, whispered the glass.

"It's open," Dan called and pressed *delete* until the message was gone.

Dean Robert entered. He looked tired, Dan noted, older than usual. His face didn't stretch into an instant smile and his wrinkled hand didn't drift up into that silly half salute that it often did when he entered Dan's office.

"Hey, Bob, how are things?"

Dean Robert nodded, lips pursed together as his hands sank into his pockets. "We need to talk," he said as he sat down on the couch.

Another instant message chirped out, and Dan muted the computer before pulling up a chair opposite the coffee table and sitting down. "Of course. What is it?"

"I had an interesting morning. Not one I care to repeat." The old man sighed.

He knows, said that lazy piece of glass, and Dan felt his left hand twitch and seize up into a fist. Had Karina told him? Or the students at the library?

"I spent the last two hours with the investigators. Fire and insurance. They were thorough. Very thorough, to say the least."

Dan felt his hand relax. "And?"

"They believe they've found the source of the fire."

"Really?"

"It was arson."

"What?" Dan scoffed. "How can they tell?"

"There were inconsistencies. Their words, not mine. They were vague but insistent that the fire didn't originate from any of the lamps or outlets."

"Where did it come from?"

"They weren't sure. What they're certain of is that negligence didn't play a part. The burn patterns were controlled. Planned." Dean Robert inhaled, his nostrils flaring as his forehead wrinkled. He leaned forward and looked Dan straight in the eyes for the first time in years. "Dan, I need you to be honest with me."

Here it comes, he thought.

"Would any of your students have reason to do such a thing? Any reason at all?"

"To start a fire?"

"Yes."

Dan exhaled, leaned back, and tapped his foot for dramatic effect. He could think of one in particular, but even for her, such an act would be obscene. After all, she had cried, both in the Archive and in his arms on that very couch. Or had it been an act? Another masquerade of hers, one of countless that had driven him to end the affair as quickly as possible. No, she would never. He put the thought out of his mind and filed it away under the absurd.

"No," Dan said. "None that I can think of."

Dean Robert held Dan's stare for as long as he could, then smiled and clapped his hands, ending the discussion.

"Very well," the old man said as he stood up. "And how goes your search for the unknown artist?"

"Bunch of dead ends."

"Well, I'm sure you'll find something. You always do," he said, pausing by the door. "And, um, about this fire. If you think of anything…"

"I'll let you know," Dan answered.

"Of course."

Dean Robert left, and Dan returned to his computer to find five new instant messages, the final one reading, *r we still on 4 the weekend???*

THIRTEEN MILES AND FIVE ZIP CODES AWAY, KARINA SAT IN FRONT OF HER laptop, staring at the blinking cursor, waiting for a response that never came. The apartment was bare, undecorated, having been moved into eight days earlier. It was smaller than her previous place, but then again, she had months to find that apartment last year and only days to find this one. Her sketchbook, camera, her clothes for the day, the necessities, they were the only items she had bothered to unpack. The rest of her bags sat against the wall, claim tags from Italy still wrapped around them, a reminder of the failure that had been her summer abroad.

Downstairs, she could hear the old Jewish couple listening to the news at full volume. That had been their routine for the last week, perhaps the last half century, and she didn't expect it to deviate. They were old and set in their ways, no different from the grooves in the old stone streets she had seen overseas. After the news, they would watch *Jeopardy!* And then *Law & Order* before going to bed. They smiled when she signed the rental agreement, when she got the keys, and when she saw them in the mornings, day after day. Most people would call them kind.

Yet she hated them.

She hated their silver hair, those matching canes, their afternoon walks around the block, how they stopped to marvel at the few trees that changed color this time of year like a pair of toothless kids before a toy store. She hated their smiles. Hated the way the old man shuffled back to the duplex with a grin and a newspaper, as if he'd walked on water, while the crone teetered on the stoop with a cup of coffee in hand, waiting. They reminded her of Italy, of the families smiling and laughing in piazzas as their spawn chased each other beneath the summer sun. Drinking wine and coffee and plucking at bread with sun-spotted talons.

She had studied them, filled pages of her sketchbook with drawings of their happiness until she had drawn them out and replaced them with pictures of herself and her man, hands entwined, old, smiling, sharing coffee and wine and feeding each other bread beneath that same warm sun. It was the future, her future, their future, and the more she drew, the clearer it became.

And then came the doubt, growing like a tumor on her heart, spreading through her veins until it infected everything, even the art she loved. The doubt that they'd ever share those moments, that future. The doubt that he loved her. The doubt that he felt the same emptiness that made her sick, literally, unable to eat the bread or drink the wine and coffee without throwing it up moments later. A sickness, coursing through her. His sickness.

And the doubt that he would leave that family, that burden he had confessed he hated the same way she hated that old couple downstairs. The doubt, it crippled her, made it impossible to do the job he'd fought so hard to get her.

Did he exile you? the doubt asked. *Did he sweep you away like a secret?* In the void that came after each unanswered question, the doubt whispered back. It whispered that she was no different than a mistake, a blemish to him, and the sickness filled her.

The computer chimed, and her eyes refocused on the screen, those cold black pixels that read, *dRineheart has gone offline.*

Exiled indeed, said the doubt.

ENTENTE

"I OWE YOU an apology."

Tommy turned his attention from the TV to his father standing in the doorway of the living room. Tommy's face was cold and annoyed. He blinked, perhaps wondering if he'd misheard his father's words. "What?" he asked.

"Tommy, this morning I made a mistake."

"You broke my Nintendo," Tommy said in a flat voice.

"I know, and I'm sorry."

"I didn't do it."

"I know, and I'm sorry about that, too."

Tommy squinted as if his dad were a desert mirage that at any moment would turn into sand.

"Tommy, I..." Dan started, considering his words. "I never knew my parents. I know it's hard for you to understand what that's like, but try to imagine a hole. You call me Dad, right?"

"Duh," Tommy quipped.

"Who do I call Dad? Who do I learn from if I never had a father?"

"I don't know," Tommy answered.

"Me neither. All I have is a hole there."

"So what?" Tommy asked.

"So what I'm trying to say is, it's not easy being a father if you've never had one. I'm your dad, but I'm human, too. I'm still learning. And sometimes I make mistakes."

"Like breaking my Nintendo?"

"Like breaking your Nintendo." Dan smiled. "And I'm sorry I didn't believe you."

Tommy studied his father. Then, as if realizing some small joke, he smiled. "That's okay, Dad."

Dan smiled back. He took a deep breath and sat down on the old ottoman beside the couch. "Your sister looks up to you. You're kind of a hero to her. Like, I dunno, Superman or something. You know that, right?"

Tommy nodded. "I guess."

"I know she can be annoying, but try to be nicer to her, okay? You're the world to her."

"Did you ever have a… you know, like a brother or sister?"

There were cold nights and thunderstorms. The clack as the old chest slammed shut, and how the darkness and fear had suffocated him. Crying, for what felt like lifetimes. Fists and fingers against wood until every fingernail had come loose and his fingertips were raw and wet. The thought of that darkness sent his stomach into a corkscrew, and he felt the glass vibrate white hot deep between his ears.

"No," Dan said. "I didn't. But if I had, I think I would've wanted one like you."

A smile grew on Tommy's face, and he fought to keep it from spreading. Instead, he simply said, "Thanks, Dad."

"You're a good kid, Tommy," Dan said as he stood up and walked to the door.

"And you're a good dad."

Dan felt his eyes twitch, the corners growing heavy with tears. "And you're a good dad," his son had said. "You're a good man," his wife had said. "You're a good lover," Karina had said.

You're a good liar, the glass said.

He reached around the doorframe, felt the box he'd left on the end table just outside the living room. "And, um, about that Nintendo of yours..." he said, then tossed the box to Tommy, who caught it as his eyes went wide.

"Oh, cool! Nintendo 3D!"

He tore into it with excitement. Several games fell out of the box as well—*Mario Kart, Street Fighter, FIFA Soccer*—games the clerk had assured Dan were must-haves for the system.

"Thanks, Dad!" Tommy said, turning back to the empty doorframe where Dan had been standing until a moment ago.

THE STUDY WAS AWASH IN A THOUSAND WATTS OF WHITE LIGHT. HE HAD spent the last hour setting up the lights and had blown the fuse twice. The wiring was as old as the house, almost eighty years, and he had to unplug the television and computer to keep the circuit from popping again. Tommy didn't mind that the TV was off, as he was immersed in his new toy, an excited "whoa, cool" coming from the room in regular intervals. Jessica was busy practicing her vocabulary and spelling words for the week with Linda in the dining room. He could hear the occasional laugh echoing down the hallway.

He mounted the heavy DSLR camera on the tripod. He'd checked out a few grand's worth of lenses and lighting equipment to go with it, having felt embarrassed the first batch of photos had come out so unprofessionally. He started with another wide shot of the painting. The camera whirred with each click, capturing the composition in twenty-five megapixels of resolution. Then, as he did before, he started from the left, capturing three images and adjusting the F-stop to be safe before moving on to the next invisible grid section.

That bobble-headed girl with her tears and sack-like skin. That brooding boy and his pinhole eyes. The old wallpaper of the house, a small piece of it peeling back. And that spot between the kids and beneath the window. Empty and unbalanced, as if waiting to be filled.

And the window, looking out upon the sunset landscape where that lonely tree stood. Again, the hill looked larger, as if it had grown since he'd last seen it. Impossible, he thought, and when he tried to remember its size, it seemed only natural it had always been that shape. A lump in the middle of the field.

And atop that hill sat the sick tree with the shadow behind it. Dan stopped on that image and lowered his camera. The shadow. Had it moved, too? It was closer than before, as if it had stepped out from behind the tree and taken two steps toward the viewer.

Of course it hadn't really moved; such a thing was impossible. Still, a nagging doubt lingered: if the painting hadn't changed, was it possible his memory had?

He pulled back from the viewfinder and took his compact digital camera from the desk. He scanned through the first set of photos, searching for the tree and the shadow. There they were. He zoomed in on them until the tree filled the LCD screen. Part of the shadow was there, but the rest was washed out by that tendril of light, that artifact that stretched across the hill and masked the contents. If they had changed, he had no evidence. And if he had no evidence, then they couldn't have changed.

Right?

He returned his camera to his desk and continued using the DSLR to capture sections of the painting row by row. That little girl in her yellow dress. That old clock, its three missing numbers, hands stuck at 5:55.

There was a brass engraving on the side of the clock, a nameplate written sideways. The words were illegible, little more than hairlines and too small to read. They formed the shape of two words with what looked like an ampersand between them. Dan blinked, and as he did, in that microsecond that his eyelids flashed blackness, he caught a glimpse, or at least he thought he did, of movement. It had come from the lower-right side of the painting.

His eyes narrowed in on that brooding boy on the left side. There he was, standing, staring with defiance at the viewer as he always had. His right arm, reaching off-canvas—but it wasn't his right arm that had moved, had it?

No, it was his left hand. His fingers were curled into that same familiar half fist, but there was something in them, something black and circular with small white fibers hanging from it.

Look closer, Professor, whispered Mr. Glass.

Dan understood it now. Jessica had seen the painting, had seen the disconsolate boy in it, had seen the torn-out doll eyes clutched in that boy's hands. Those eyes, obviously taken from the dolls at the feet of the painted girl.

Jessica had seen this violation.

Then she had pulled out her own doll's eyes.

That's one way to think of it, mumbled the glass.

That's the only way to think of it, Dan thought. Paintings were color and canvas and not so different than a child's imagination. Jessica had seen the boy in the painting, seen the doll's eyes in his hand. Then she copied it. And when she saw what she had done, how she had destroyed her favorite toy, no different than picking wings off a fly, she cried and she lied. What had the doctor said? She was still adjusting. She could make up anything she wanted. She could blame it on Tommy or any one of her imaginary friends and keep the truth locked away until it was forgotten and the lie itself became the truth.

Unless…

Unless what? he thought.

Unless she didn't copy it, but rather the other way around.

He heard the faint clatter of nails on the hardwood floor behind him, followed by a snort. Ginger stood at the threshold of the room, sniffing out some distant smell, her tail tucked between her legs.

"Come on, girl. Let's go to bed."

He turned off the lights and left the room, whistling for Ginger to follow. She paused, giving the painting a long stare, then lowered her eyes and scampered off after Dan.

AN HOUR BEFORE DAWN, LINDA AWOKE FROM A DREAM CONVINCED THAT she had heard a door slam downstairs, followed by a sound, sudden and sharp, not unlike the scraping of a wet finger against crystal or the yelp of an injured animal. It had lasted for a single second, then ended, leaving not even an echo in the cold morning air.

She sat there for a moment, listening to the darkness, the silence, until her eyes grew heavy and she forgot what had awoken her. She draped her arm over Dan, gave his shoulder a kiss, and fell back to sleep.

HOLES

AFTER HIS SHOWER, he found Linda scrubbing dirty footprints off the stairway rug. "Kids must've tracked dirt inside," she said with a yawn. "I'll tell them to be more careful."

"Good morning to you, too," Dan said and planted a kiss on the top of her head before heading downstairs.

"Breakfast's on the table," she said. "Oh, and your phone rang twice already."

"Thanks, hon," he said, realizing he'd left his cell phone in the study last night.

The newspaper was laid out on the kitchen table, next to the coffee and an omelet. He made it to page three of the business section before Tommy came bounding inside, followed by Jessica. Both were out of breath, and Jessica's face was contorted in distress.

"Dad!" Tommy gasped. "We can't find Ginger."

"Did you try the side yard?" he asked, sipping his coffee and turning the page.

"Yes! And the front yard, and she's not there."

"She's gone!" Jessica added.

"I'm sure she's around here. What about upstairs?"

"We tried everywhere!" Tommy said, raising his voice, and when Dan lowered his newspaper, he saw that Jessica was on the verge of tears.

"She's not in the front yard or inside or anywhere! I can't find her!" Tommy spat out.

"Do something!" Jessica added.

"Okay, okay," Dan said, realizing the situation might be more serious than he had thought. Breakfast and the business section would have to wait.

"What's wrong?" Linda asked, walking in and sizing up the scene.

"Ginger's AWOL again," Dan said.

"What's AWOL?" whined Tommy. "What does that mean?"

"Is it an aspression? Like dead?" asked Jessica.

"It means missing," Dan said, folding the paper. "Okay, Tommy, Jessica, I want you to check each room. Under the beds, closets, everywhere, okay? I'll look for holes in the yard. I dunno, maybe she got under the fence or something."

HOLES INDEED. HE FOUND FOUR ALREADY, ALL ALONG THE WESTERN FENCE that bordered Marty's yard. None, however, were more than a few inches deep, and he suspected that Ginger had given up digging after realizing it required sustained effort for longer than five minutes. She had, on her best days, the attention span of a toddler, something that had made even the most basic dog training classes a nightmare. He made a mental note to fill in the holes and continued to search the backyard.

The box hedges tapered off, replaced by foot-high ferns and patches of mint beneath, which Linda had planted three years back and never seemed to die. The fence grew to a height of eight feet, and Dan stepped over the plants, following that redwood fence where Marty's vulture eye had peered out from the darkness the other night.

He scanned the ground and bushes until he came to Linda's rose garden. The largest rosebush looked sick. It drooped as if tired or unwatered and gave off a sour fragrance. Like some sort of infection, small gray nodules grew along the base of the stalks and tapered off six inches up the plant. The lumps were fattest at the bottom, a few as large as a cherry, all excreting a white foam. At the base, a few small slugs and insects gorged themselves on the foam.

Nearby, fresh dirt sat in small piles beneath the fronds. There was a hole in the ground, in that same spot Ginger had dug the other night, only this time it was no larger than a fist. The dirt was fresh and appeared to have risen out of the ground and then collapsed in on itself, like a gopher mound or a sinkhole filling a void.

He saw tracks in the dirt. They were small, an inch long and three-pronged like a lazy Y with a third line down the middle. They were spread out a few inches from each other, leading away from the hole. They were bird tracks.

He followed them beneath the fronds until they continued on the red brick walkway. There, with each additional step, the tracks faded away on the brick. He glanced around the red brick, following the straight line he predicted the tracks would have made, walking toward the dining room window and the bushes beneath it. Sure enough, the tracks reappeared in the damp earth beneath the window opposite the rose garden, where they were joined by paw prints. He lifted the foliage and saw where they led.

A small air vent led into the basement. Old screening, screws and all, was covered in white paint from when the house had gotten a fresh coat decades ago. A patch of metal had given way to rust and disintegrated.

A patch, Dan thought, just large enough for a small dog to squeeze through.

DUST ROSE FROM THE BASEMENT LIGHT AS IT FLICKERED AND GREW WARM. He hadn't been beneath the house in nine months, not since the boiler burst last winter, and now he remembered why. Every time he ventured down to the basement, the dust and stench of damp earth shook the glass loose and threatened to grow into a full-blown migraine. A category-five tornado.

A real fustercluck, Mr. Glass said.

He turned the flashlight on as the redwood stairs creaked beneath his feet. The new boiler hummed and clicked like a hibernating beast, and all he could think of was how many spiders might be lurking behind the corners or tucked into the holes of the unused wine rack. The basement was, as most basements eventually became, an oubliette, a forgotten tomb from their previous lives before suitcases and souvenirs were replaced by strollers and cribs.

There was a chance, he thought, that if Ginger had gotten through that hole in the screen, then she could be down here. It was a five-foot fall from the ground level into that meter-high crawlspace. A place littered with old mouse traps, an uneven foundation, and a dozen other things that stupid dog could've hurt herself on. She could be injured—or worse.

He took an old golf club from the set Linda's father had passed down to him as a wedding present. "Treat my daughter as good as I treated these," he had said to Dan as he sucked on a cigarette a decade ago. And then, eight years later, in a morphine delirium as the cancer gnawed away at him, he had told Linda to get the clubs back from that cocksucker she was dating.

"I'm sorry, Daddy. I think he sold them," she had said, squeezing Dan's hand as the old man coughed and wheezed.

The crawlspace behind the wine rack tapered to a narrow height of a meter, and Dan wondered what kind of diseases he was breathing in from that stale air. The flashlight beam cut through the shadows, tracing the outline of old boxes and tools. A lawnmower, some folding chairs, a box labeled *broken clock,* and a suitcase, probably now home to a nest of mice. And far off, behind the junk, lay the hole in the vent where a dim shaft of light reached down into the bowels of the foundation.

He wriggled further into the crawlspace. The dust tickled his throat and he felt phlegm building up. He pulled his shirt up over his nose and mouth as he squeezed himself closer to the old suitcase. A brief chill passed through him as footsteps and laughter pounded on the floorboards above. The wood vibrated with each step, sending curls of dust downward.

He coughed again, pulling himself closer to the pile of junk that lay between him and the shaft of light. He put the flashlight in his mouth, between his teeth, coughing and forcing his jaw to hold it steady so he could use his hands to scoot deeper beneath the house.

Then he heard something. A sound came from behind the suitcase. It was wet, that of water dripping, perhaps from one of the old pipes. And behind it, a faint tapping echoed out, something hard clicking against stone. A wounded animal, a dog perhaps, bones broken from the drop.

He extended the golf club, first poking at the suitcase, then hooking onto a strap and sliding it aside in short jerks. There was a shape behind it, an abstract shadow woven into the darkness next to the old folding chairs. *Ginger. Oh, God,* he thought and shined the light on it.

It was not one shape but two, and they separated with a screech and a flutter of movement. Dan shielded his eyes. Something small and wet and dark lay on the ground. The other shape was covered in brown filth and blue spotting, and it moved in frantic, startled spasms. And the smell: the smell was that of rot and warmth. His stomach fluttered and he tasted bile in the back of his throat and bit down on his lip. His fingers seized up, and for a moment they were raw and wet and he was locked away inside that old trunk, screaming into the darkness and clawing at the wood.

No, he told himself. He wasn't there. That had happened long ago to another person in another life. And with that thought, his world swung back into focus. He could see the flashlight beam and hear the shrill sound the shape made.

A grime-encrusted blue jay leaped about in the crawlspace. The creature had no wings, only two broken nubs that protruded from a dirty body and spasmed in useless circles. Its face was matted red and its beak held what looked like a small worm, but Dan knew it wasn't. At its feet lay the sideways body of a bloated dead rat. Its lower half had collapsed inward, forming a raw opening where maggots danced about, fat and happy. The bird let out a feverish squawk and pecked at another maggot.

Dan felt the bile rise again, and he could hear laughter echoing out from three decades back, that same laugh when the old trunk had locked him away, and he wanted to scream out, scream out that he was sorry.

Mr. Glass cackled in the darkness as Dan fought back the filth in his mouth and gave one loud scream—"Fucking die already!"—and swung the golf club into the shrieking bird.

Muddied feathers fluttered about the crawlspace as he silenced that insane shrieking.

He put both the dead animals in double trash bags, dropped them in the garbage can in the garage, and closed the lid on that whole disgusting discovery. He felt filthy. His shirt was ruined, covered in dust and flecks of odorous filth. A total loss, he realized as he washed his hands in the kitchen a second time. When Linda saw it, she asked, "What happened to you?"

"You don't want to know, trust me."

What else could he say? "Sorry, babe, found a twice-dead blue jay having some rat chow-chow beneath the house. Don't worry, third time's a charm." Besides, the other night he was certain he felt its neck break between his hands, but obviously, he'd done it wrong.

Unless…

Unless what? Mr. Glass asked.

No. Any other thought led to the absurd, and he didn't feel like considering Jesus birds at this early hour. Not with one missing dog, two distraught kids, and a semester of lesson plans to take care of.

He drank two glasses of orange juice, one after another, unable to kill the acrid taste in his mouth. By the time he finished and changed shirts, Linda was loading the kids into the car for school. Tommy put up a fight, protesting, eyes red and heavy. Jessica sat in the back seat, whispering to Mr. Bun.

"Don't worry, buddy. I bet she just went for a stroll, like last time, right?" Dan said and smiled.

"I hope so," Tommy mumbled.

Linda started the car, put her sunglasses on, and turned to Dan.

"Will you make up some flyers? The kids have a half day. Maybe we can put them up when you get home."

"Of course," he said, feeling his phone vibrating in his pocket. "Have a good day at school."

HIS CELL PHONE VIBRATED ANOTHER TWO TIMES, AND THEN HIS HOME phone rang, prompting him to answer it without checking the caller ID. He had no reason to suspect she would call his house—she never had before—and his number was unlisted. Yet there it was, Karina's voice, coming from the same phone his wife carried from room to room.

His fury was only overshadowed by his surprise. Yet instead of apologizing, Karina launched into an immediate rage, accusing him of using her, abusing her, lying to her, and exiling her. He found that last accusation rather accurate when he considered it. All the while, he listened, fingers curling into fists until his nails dug into his palm, saying little more than the occasional "I'm sorry." And all the while, the glass grew, barbed and heavy, behind his eyes.

"If you're so sorry, you'll make it up to me this weekend," she snapped.

"I don't know what you want me to say. I can't go to Napa," he said, switching the warm receiver to his left ear. "I'm sorry. I just can't."

"Why not?" she demanded. "Why not?"

Dan sighed. "Something came up. Our dog's missing, but that's not the point—"

A laugh, angry and desperate. "Your dog? Dan, you knew I booked it. I told you on Monday. I can't get a refund now."

"I never asked you to do that," he said, and his eyes fell to the roses above the sink and the murky water in the vase, where a thin layer of foam floated on the surface.

"I don't understand," she whined again. "I came home from Europe for you, for us. Doesn't that mean anything?"

"I never asked you to do that either."

"Of course not. You didn't have to ask because I don't mean anything to you, right? If I did, you would've."

"What?" Her logic confused him, and he had a pressing desire to slam the phone down no different than he had with Tommy's Nintendo.

"You would've asked, Dan," she said, voice taking on a frustrated tone, as if she were talking to a child. "Asked me to come home. But you didn't, did you?"

"Listen, let's talk about this later, okay?"

"Later?" she cut in. "Always later. When? Next weekend? Should I book an appointment? Or will your brats and that bitch have some soccer game?"

He felt the words erupt, yet he didn't even realize he had said them, merely witnessed them coming from deep inside with the same force the bile had surged forth with not an hour ago.

"Listen, you schizoid cunt. Don't you ever disrespect my kids or my wife again. Ever. Not after all I've done for you. Understand?"

There was a long, empty silence on the other end of the phone. He could hear her breathing as Mr. Glass burned white hot, a tiny supernova behind his optic nerves, and the beginning of another aura formed in the corner of his eyes.

"You coward," she hissed. "Fuck your kids, and you know what? Fuck you, Dan. Fuck you. This whole thing was a mistake."

More silence. She might be waiting for a response, he thought, but he was determined not to give her one. Not this time. His harsh words had struck deep, deeper than he'd meant, and he didn't want to let Mr. Glass speak for him a second time. He clenched his fist, and in the silence, he realized why it was so quiet. Somewhere far away, in some dark room of her shitty apartment, she was crying.

For all her maturity and self-confidence, for all her talents and gifts, she was, after all, little more than a girl used to getting her way. And when that failed, she fell back on tears as blackmail. It was pathetic.

"Jeez, Karina, come on."

"No," she said in a soft voice. Then a second time, calmer, collected: "No. You're right. I shouldn't have said that about your family."

He knew the routine. It was her schizophrenic version of good cop bad cop in a single body.

"Don't worry about me, okay?" she said in a numb voice.

He sighed. "Karina, come on."

"I'm fine," she said and repeated it again, as if only to herself. "I'll be fine."

A click signaled the end of the conversation and the line went dead. Dan studied his hand. His fingernails had left four little marks in his palm that were filling up with blood like crescent lakes on the surface of some alien planet.

Your birds, Professor, said Mr. Glass. *Seems they're coming home.*

Keep calm and carry on, Dan thought.

INVERSION

IT TOOK HIM a few minutes to whip up a template for a missing-dog flyer. While Dan felt he was decent with words, he did find it rather difficult to describe their dog without highlighting her shortcomings. Puny, breathes odd, not very intelligent: all words he had started typing but soon deleted.

Instead, he noted that she was friendly and easily attracted to food and that two children dearly missed her. And that there would be a reward. He pondered adding a price but felt it would be easier to negotiate with whatever party found Ginger. More importantly, he knew that whatever price he put, no matter how reasonable it felt, would ultimately result in him being called a cheapskate. "I'm glad their happiness is only worth fifty bucks," he imagined Linda saying in his head among the mumblings of the glass still smelting among his gray matter.

He opened a kitchen drawer containing dozens of photos from over the years. Most of them were of the kids, one parent in the picture and the other behind the lens. Among them were copies of a professional portrait taken of the family two years ago. He studied his hairline, disappointed to find that it had receded further than suspected and had lost its brown undertone.

He hated seeing a picture of himself. Always had. Perhaps, he thought, because it never matched the mental image he had crafted of himself over the years. Like hearing his own voice on the answering machine or reading a quote of his in an art journal. They were distant words by a voice he vaguely recognized as his own. It was why he felt more comfortable behind the lens than in front of it, why few family pictures contained him. Even the few that did, the photos that hung on the walls around the house, assorted celebrations of past activities, holidays, vacations only fun in hindsight, even they had been blocked out of his mind and blurred into the walls no different than the crown molding and wallpaper. They had become decoration and little more.

He flipped through the years, film prints giving way to digital, hairlines disappearing and the occasional wrinkle setting in, until he came upon the batch he was searching for, a series of Christmas photos taken last year. Tommy had his Nintendo and Jessica was holding her dolls up as Ginger sat between them in one of the few shots where she didn't turn and flee at the sight of the flash.

Confused, Dan blinked as he studied the photograph.

It was wrong. Very wrong.

The kids, the presents, the tree, and Linda, they were all just as he'd remembered. But Ginger, she looked different. Her hair, even as a puppy, had been long and straight. It required little grooming, something the breeder had assured them wouldn't bother Linda's allergies.

Yet the dog in that photograph did not have the same hair.

Its hair was wired, unkempt, a seaweed bed that hung in uneven clumps as if it hadn't been washed in years. Ginger's eyes had always been soft and vacant, the glass stare of an imbecile. The eyes of that dog were milky, dark, and cold. Its teeth were uneven and stained brown, a sneer of spotted gums as if it had smelled a horrible odor.

Dan rubbed the photo again, wondering if oil or something sticky had spilled onto it, but it didn't change. The dog in that photo was a husk that bore no more of a resemblance to Ginger than a mummy bore to the living. He flipped through the photos, finding another one taken on a hike in the mountains outside of Santa Cruz last spring. There it was again, tugging on a leash held in Tommy's hand while the green hills and lazy clouds sat frozen in a gray sky. And again, that same sick look on its face. The dog's hair was thinning around its hindquarters, pink skin beneath a patch of fur on its tail. Its face was frozen in a similar sneer, cataract eyes reflecting the light back at the camera like a flash off glass.

He pushed the photos aside, searching for more. And he found it. Another memory, another image of that diseased dog he hardly recognized. He slid that photo aside as well. And another. And another. All absurd and twisted, and he saw the auras, finger-like and jagged, spike out from the corners of his own vision again.

Impossible, he thought. Someone had switched the photos. But who would do that?

Unless…

Unless what?

Unless she had always been like that. Unless he'd misremembered her. The dog that followed him to bed last night, like all the nights prior, was not that dog. *No, there's got to be another explanation,* he thought, ignoring the voice that said the only other explanation was madness.

A sound startled him out of his trance, loud and clear. Running and laughter echoed out behind him, nearby, and he spun his head around. They were the same sounds of giggling and running he had heard in the basement an hour before.

"Hello?" he called out. "Tommy? Jessica?"

He could sense someone there, the way a person knew when someone was staring at them, even from the shadows. A vague energy, a feeling that something had been displaced. A chill passed through him.

"Jessica?"

A low giggle seemed to come from the refrigerator. Then, as it faded, he realized it had come from *behind* the refrigerator. No, not behind it: *beyond* it. It was as if the sound had penetrated the walls, then the plastic and metal of the Samsung fridge, and focused on him like an X-ray. He felt his hair stand on end as one thought rang clearer than all others.

Someone was in the hallway.

"Jessica? Honey, are you playing games?" Dan asked as he

followed the sound, and he could feel his voice tremble. He knew Jessica had walked all the way home from school on the second day; Linda had told him about that incident. He didn't think she would do it again, but he also didn't think she would bite her own finger until it bled or that she would pluck the eyes from her favorite doll. Of the two children, she had become the less predictable one.

But the laughter, it didn't sound like her voice. In fact, it didn't sound like anyone's. Instead, it sounded recorded, old, as if funneled through a telephone from decades ago and finally transmitted.

His fingers curled in as another thought settled into his mind. What if no one was there? What if his mind had slipped sideways and the laughter had not come from without but from within? Was it, like the glass and migraines and auras and perhaps even that diseased dog's photos, simply inside his mind? Was he slipping toward some unknown precipice—or perhaps had he already?

No. He realized what it was, and when he did, he put those dark thoughts out of his mind and stood up.

"Karina? Is that you?"

He followed the giggle into the downstairs hallway. There, framed photos of the family stared back, suffused with a dim glow from the flickering lights above. He wrote off the flicker as a symptom of his migraine, nothing more than the glass simmering behind his eyes. It wasn't those soft, weak colors that bothered him, but the thought that she might be in his house.

"Karina?"

A squeal, rubber soles on the hardwood floor beyond the door. It moved fast, followed by a giggling echo in phasing bursts, in and out. He was almost certain it was Karina. God, what was she doing here? First she had called, and now…

The footsteps came again, now from the dining room. He put his thoughts aside and moved quickly past the family portraits and the bathroom and the door leading to the basement. As he entered the dining room, he saw the other door leading into the kitchen rattle and swing shut, and he swore a shadow moved beneath it.

She was here, that resentful girl. She had come to his house. For what? To play more of her games? He was tired of them, tired of her games, tired of it all. Tired of the control she had over him, the threats of suicide or worse, the discovery of the affair and how she dangled that threat, spoken so casually—"I just think we should come clear"—as if she would have to pick up the pieces of his marriage. That anger pushed him to move, to sprint in a burst across the dining room and toward the kitchen, where he would grab that bitch and scream, "Don't ever come back!"

But he didn't. Instead, he threw the kitchen door open, shouting, "Found you!"

The figure by the sink screamed and leaped back. A brown bag crashed to the floor, contents shattering and spraying across the wood.

Linda covered her mouth in fright, an expression that gave way to rage, and she threw a dishtowel across the room at him, but it fell several feet short. For a split second, he thought her reaction was almost comical and childish.

"What the hell is the matter with you?" she screamed, body seeming to cave in on itself as she caught her breath. "Why would you do that?"

"I'm… I'm sorry," he mumbled. "I thought…"

"What are you, ten years old? Jesus, you scared the hell out of me."

"I'm sorry. I didn't mean to."

"Great. There goes the orange juice." She picked up the leaking grocery bag and placed it in the sink. "I hope you're happy."

"Honey, I'm really sorry. I thought—"

"What, it'd be fun to give your wife a heart attack?"

She reached into the junk drawer, pulled out that pack of cigarettes and her father's silver lighter. She struck the lighter twice, and on the third click, it lit. She took a lungful of smoke, then turned to her husband with raised eyebrows. "I get this one today for that crap you just pulled."

"Fine," he said and repeated it a second time. "Fine."

"And you get to clean up this mess."

"Fair enough, but first you need to see something."

"What now?"

He hurried over to the table where the photos of Ginger lay in a scattered pile. He brought them to Linda, dropping them on the counter like a detective presenting evidence to a suspect.

"Look at these," he said, tapping them. "Look."

She did, lifting them up and thumbing through them while taking a long drag off that cigarette. She blew a jet of smoke from the corner of her mouth and he waved it away. He hated that habit of hers, thinking of all the times she'd promised to quit, but he let it slide today.

"I think we should use the one from the hike," she said.

He scoffed. "You're kidding, right?"

"Well, which one do you want to use?"

"No, honey, look at them! Look at Ginger." He retrieved the photos, pointing at the one by the Christmas tree—but his eyes stopped on it a second time. The kids, their new toys, and Ginger, just as she'd always been.

"How about the other one, by the fountain last spring?" she asked. "It's a close-up."

He studied the pictures, uncomprehending. Each photo showed Ginger as he'd known her, that smooth hair, clean teeth, not a speck of matting or rot. Even those eyes, as vacant and clueless as always, stared back.

"Hello?" she asked. "Everything all right?"

"Yeah," he said under his breath. "I just thought you should choose the photo."

"Are you okay?" she asked, blowing another jet of smoke toward the window.

"Why wouldn't I be?" he said with a smile.

THE TWELFTH STUDENT

HE TAUGHT HIS second and only lecture of the week in Room 17-B, a spare studio on loan while the Archive was under investigation. Eleven students had shown up with eleven somber faces, and Dan did his best to reassure them that their work this semester would continue despite the setback. Only Karina's table sat empty. The sight had relieved him at first. But as his lecture on the variety of solvents and their use in restoring frescoes wound into its second hour, he began to worry about her absence and what it implied.

In over a year, Karina had only missed one class, on a Wednesday in March after a short stay at the hospital. She returned on a Friday, wearing a long-sleeve hoodie that hid the bandages on her wrists. On that day she carried on with her usual studies with no mention of the injuries or the events that led up to them. Instead, she smiled at Dan with her usual knowing grin as the rest of the students listened to his lecture and took notes.

Seventy-two hours earlier, they'd had a fight, a monster of a blowout. He tried to break off their budding affair, she turned abusive, and cruel words were said by both of them. She threw things: an iPod, a vase, books. All crashed off the walls of her crummy apartment as her voice reached such hysterics that he thought she might be possessed. Even the neighbors banged on the door to see if she was still alive. He had a long talk with them, during which he listened to a litany of complaints they had with his "girlfriend." He just nodded, happy to be out of the apartment, where the spring air calmed his mind. In hindsight, he should have known her silence inside harbored no respite, only more horrors.

When he returned inside, he found her in the kitchen, a blank look on her face as she pressed a paring knife into her left wrist. Her right wrist already leaked crimson down her arm, where it cascaded off her elbow in a thin ribbon and pooled on the yellow countertop. Her face was blank, and to him, that was the most haunting image of all. It was a numb mask as she sawed back and forth across her left wrist as if she were cutting a vegetable. When he pulled her hand free, he saw tendons and veins, raw and pink inside the open seam.

She fought him, roaring and shrieking at the interruption, clawing and gnashing her teeth like a feral animal. By the time he wrestled her to the cold tile, her face had grown pale from blood loss. He used his favorite tie, one the kids bought him for Father's Day, to make a tourniquet for her gushing right wrist. As he finished wrapping her left wrist in a dishtowel, she could only put up a weak struggle. Her skin had taken on a blue hue that reminded him of ice, and he thought there was no way she could survive.

The hospital was only a few miles away, and she spent most of the drive lapsing in and out of weak sobs, apologizing for ruining his tie and asking him to close some imaginary door. Traffic was sparse, so he blew through several red lights, one of which snapped a photo of him that he later intercepted in the mail before Linda saw it. He signed the form as they wheeled her into the ER, numb as the nurse asked if she was his daughter.

On Friday, Karina resumed class, smiling, wearing that hoodie that hid the bandages beneath long sleeves. Never so much as a thank-you for saving her life, never so much as an acknowledgment that her hands would have cut to bone had he not stopped them. It was on that day that he realized she needed to be removed from his life, and doing so would require a surgeon's touch.

THE PLAN WAS SIMPLE AND CAME TOGETHER OVER THE COURSE OF A FEW days. He had phoned a former classmate after reading an email calling for applicants to join a handpicked team to spend a year in Italy. He later told Karina that he and Nathaniel were friends, but the truth was they hadn't spoken in years. Nathaniel felt Dan had stolen Linda away from him in grad school, where she had been his date to one of his pretentious fundraisers.

Nathaniel came from money. For him, art was a means to rub elbows with the rich and powerful, a pursuit that Dan believed to be Nathaniel's true and only passion. Yet Nathaniel had made the mistake of bringing a date who came from money herself, as Linda wasn't impressed with it, nor did she enjoy being the trophy to a man who was. They had talked at length, laughing like old friends, ignoring everyone else, including Nathaniel's glare over the guests and champagne glasses, and Dan felt a small sense of victory as he finally had something Nathaniel couldn't buy. To Dan, the contrast between the man she arrived with and the man she left with couldn't have been wider, like some backward Cinderella story.

A year later to the day, Nathaniel wore that same spurious smile as Dan and Linda exchanged vows at a small beachside ceremony.

He had hardly spoken to Nathaniel in the years since, only in a professional capacity, but Dan needed him for the plan. Nathaniel was, even if he didn't know it, a keystone piece, and Dan had to humble himself for it all to come together. It would be worth it, he told himself as he dialed the Caracci Institute.

The apology took thirty minutes as it wove from pleasantries to accusations and tenuous reconciliation. It was further complicated when he learned Nathaniel had filled the final spot the week before. Yet despite the bad blood between them, Nathaniel admitted that he harbored a tremendous respect, professionally at least, for Dan's talents and reputation, even if he freely admitted to thinking he was a rather duplicitous asshole. Despite that, he agreed to create an eleventh spot for Karina, sight unseen, on the condition that Dan return a future favor, a term to which Dan was more than happy to agree.

All that now required his attention was to persuade Karina to make the move, a task he felt certain that he could accomplish, given the right mood and setting. He knew the place before he hung up. And so he booked a weekend at their getaway in Napa, where the idea was presented and, as planned, took hold like a virus. By the end of the weekend, as his car drove south across the Golden Gate Bridge, she turned to him and said, "I think I'm going to go to Italy. Like you said, chance of a lifetime, right?"

"Right," he answered.

THE LECTURE FINISHED A FEW MINUTES BEFORE SIX AND THE STUDENTS filed out of Room 17-B, some pausing to schedule appointments over the next week to discuss new projects. When they left, Dan closed his computer and checked his cell phone. The lack of messages from Karina after three hours and her empty workstation left a confusing void, a hole, and he wondered whether to fill that emptiness with worry or relief.

FATHER & SON

"STRAIGHTEN IT OUT a little. The right side," he said, and Tommy followed, holding the flyer at shoulder height to the trunk of the magnolia tree. The setting sun cast a dappled glow down through the canopy of the trees, painting the quiet, affluent neighborhood in an almost mystical light, not unlike some Romantic-era landscape.

"There you go," Dan said. He lined the staple gun against the flyer and pressed down. It fired twice, small dabs of wetness spotting the corners of the flyer from the sap beneath.

"Think she'll come home tonight?" Tommy asked as they walked to the next tree.

"She's a smart dog," he answered, ignoring the cackle of the glass. "I'm sure she'll find her way back. She's probably out on some doggy adventure right now, you know?"

"Jessica thinks she's dead."

"Well, Jessica also talks to dolls."

Tommy laughed, and hearing it made Dan smile. They'd spent the better part of an hour walking down the quiet side streets of Alder Glen, flyering every oak, elm, and magnolia in the neighborhood between Wildwood Lane and the community gardens at Pardee Park before looping back home, yet not once had Tommy smiled. It was something he did less as he got older, as his laughter gave way to sighs and sarcasm. Dan missed the old days when they kicked the soccer ball around, back before he went from being his son's hero to being "lame," as Tommy had put it.

"Here?" Tommy asked, nodding to a tree.

"Sure. Hold it up for me?"

"How's this?"

"Perfect."

Clack clack. He stapled the flyer in. The rustle of leaves in the wind filled the silence after the stapler fired, and beyond it, something else, a faint electric hum in the evening air. For a moment he caught a glimpse of a young girl with strawberry hair running past the gate of the Salazars' awful McMansion across the street. He thought he saw a firefly hovering in the distance, but when he blinked, it was gone. There were no fireflies. Not here, he thought.

"You're not allowed to do that," a voice said, and Dan knew who it belonged to before turning.

Marty stood at the corner of his yard, leaning on his fence, a pair of garden shears in hand and a loose piece of ivy hanging from his overalls. "Those ads." He nodded. "You're not allowed to post 'em."

"They're not ads, Marty. They're flyers. Ginger got out this morning."

"Doesn't matter what it's for. Can't have people putting signs up willy-nilly. Homeowners association doesn't allow flyers, Daniel. You know that."

Tommy shifted, eyes jumping from Marty to Dan. He could tell by the tone in that old man's voice, and by his father's stiffened posture, that there was a problem. He just didn't understand why.

"Marty, I don't care what the homeowners association allows. It's our dog."

Marty put his hands on the fence and leaned over. It reminded Dan of how his teachers stood over his desk while his mind was far away from the classroom. That old son of a bitch, ruining the one good afternoon he'd had with Tommy in weeks.

"We'll just take 'em down, Daniel," Marty said with a shrug and a smirk. "That clear enough for ya?"

"And I'll just put more up. And if a single one's missing by Monday, you'll be the next thing that's nailed to the fucking tree."

Dan raised the staple gun and fired it at Marty in a quick one-two-three burst. At first Marty lurched back and blocked his face with his gloves and the garden shear, a sight that made Tommy's mouth fall open. As the second volley of staples bounced harmlessly off him, Marty realized not only how foolish he looked but that he wasn't going to win this round.

"That clear enough for you, Marty?"

The old man waved his hand as if swatting a mosquito and mumbled, "Asshole," as he turned and walked off.

Tommy had heard his dad swear before, always on accident and always followed by a scolding from his mom. But he had never, ever heard his dad say a bad word deliberately, let alone the F word. His dad had used it just like those action stars in movies he wasn't supposed to watch. Instead of a real gun, it had been a staple gun, but the effect had been the same. *Adios, fucker.* Problem solved.

"I'm sorry, Tommy. You shouldn't have heard that," Dan said as they resumed walking.

"It's okay."

"No, it wasn't. I lost my cool."

"He deserved it."

Dan laughed, and Tommy studied him, curious why those three words had elicited such a chuckle from his dad.

"Yeah," Dan said. "He's deserved it for a long time."

Dan pointed to another tree. Tommy raised the flyer. His dad lined up the staple gun and fired twice. *Clack clack,* just like an action hero.

"Dad?" Tommy asked.

"What's up?"

"Thanks for doing this."

"Anytime, pal," he said, smiling and rubbing the back of Tommy's neck. "Just don't tell your mom what I said or I'll be in deep... you know?"

"Shit?"

Tommy looked up again, unsure if he'd crossed a line only adults were allowed to cross. His dad just smiled and nodded.

"Yeah," he said. "That."

The two of them, father and son, walked home, smiling in the final rays of daylight.

HAVING FINISHED THE LAST OF THE DISHES, LINDA TURNED THE FAUCET OFF and turned her attention to the vase of sick roses above the sink. A brown discharge drifted from the base of their stalks and reached upward in thin tendrils, like oil in water. Grime layered the surface. A few of the petals had curled in on themselves the way bugs did when they died. Sick or not, the roses were the last vestiges of summer, and she couldn't bring herself to discard them just yet.

"Daddy!" Jessica shouted, turning her attention from her doodles in the margins of her phonics workbook to the back door. Linda felt two arms wrap around her, then lips settling on the back of her neck and a warm embrace that made her close her eyes and smile.

"All done?" she asked.

"Every tree from here to Channing. Half the neighborhood at least," Dan answered. "Any word from the pound?"

"Nothing yet, but they'll call if she turns up."

"What about dinner?" he asked.

"I was waiting until you got home. What do you feel like?"

"No," he said. "I meant, let's go out for dinner."

She raised an eyebrow. "Out? As in—"

"Chairs, a table, someone else cooking. Exotic, right?"

"Indeed, Professor."

"Besides, when was the last time we went out to eat?"

Linda laughed. She really couldn't remember. Six months, a year perhaps. "Our honeymoon?" she joked.

"Probably. It's been a rough day on the kids."

"Well, where should we go?" she asked.

He considered it. "I don't know, but someplace special."

SOMEPLACE SPECIAL

CHUCK E. CHEESE was a chorus of laughter and clattering games, a cavern of sounds and smells that filled the packed restaurant on that Friday night. The wait for a table took thirty minutes, a chore made easier for the kids when Dan gave them twenty dollars to spend on games and rides. Neither he nor Linda had envisioned spending their Friday night surrounded by arcade games and ball pits and families with twice as many screaming kids as theirs, yet once they arrived, it seemed the most logical choice. The adults could eat and talk while the kids bounced off their glucose rush in a child-safe ball pit and mashed video games with greasy fingers.

Back in the kitchen, they had tossed around the idea of Mexican food or a new teppanyaki restaurant downtown, and he was certain the kids would enjoy watching a grilled onion sliced into a flame-spewing volcano. However, once Tommy understood they were going out for dinner, a rare concept with their finances, he refused to go anywhere else and soon found an ally in Jessica by reciting tales of excitement from his friend's birthday party at the mouse house over the summer. The two of them chanted "Chuck-eee Chee-suh" a dozen times, clomping about the kitchen like a marching band until both Linda and Dan gave in.

Twenty minutes after they sat, the pizza arrived. The kids returned with handfuls of tickets and promptly devoured it, turning their napkins into stained rags like some oily crime scene.

"Can we get some more tokens?" Tommy asked with a hiccup that reeked of tomato sauce.

"I suppose," Dan said, giving Tommy another twenty dollars despite Linda's scowl. "Share it with your sister."

Tommy ran off, and Jessica followed behind. She paused as if she'd forgotten something, then doubled back and tugged at her dad's hand.

"Come on, Dad," she said. "Let's play in the ball house."

She raised a finger, pointing at the neon-colored ball pit and the undulating inflatable snake that wound its way into it, depositing screaming kids among the hollow rainbow balls.

"No thanks, sweetie. Let your mom and me have some grown-up fun. Besides, that's only for kids."

"But other dads are in it," Jessica said. "See?"

Sure enough, a bearded, late-twenties guy with a *Tron* T-shirt rolled around in the ball pit and laughed while his son held on to his arm like a rodeo rider.

"A little fun wouldn't hurt you, eh, Professor?" Linda said with a smile and a raised eyebrow. A dare.

"Please, Daddy?" Jessica smiled and blinked with those eyes, the eyes of her mother. They were the same blue eyes he had fallen in love with years ago when Linda glanced past Nathaniel and the rest of the guests at the party and straight at him. He couldn't say no to those eyes. He never could.

"All right, let's go."

Jessica squealed and almost pulled him out of his seat with an energetic tug. He gave a shake of his head back at Linda, an embarrassed shrug, only to be met by her smile. And her blue eyes, glimmering with a sheen of happiness.

Jessica surveyed the inflatable obstacle course leading into the ball pit and nodded like a tiny general preparing for war. "Now we have to go in there," she said, pointing to the giant inflatable snake's mouth. The structure, while large, wasn't made for people of his age and size. It was going to be a very tight fit.

"First the snake eats you. Then you go into his tummy. Then it makes a poop," Jessica said matter-of-factly, tracing the course with an outstretched finger all the way to the snake's tail, where it ended in the ball pit. Dan realized that she was, at least on an anatomical level, correct.

"I'll go first," she said.

"Okay, honey."

She climbed the pink tongue stairs, each flexible step tracked with dirt from countless shoes, and into the cartoon snake's smiling open mouth. There, she pushed aside the inflatable uvula that bounced from side to side.

"Come on!" she called from inside that rubber reptile mouth, and Dan felt his fingers twitch as he thought about climbing into the small space beyond. He stood there, waiting, and would have for hours, but a line of impatient kids was forming behind him.

He stepped into the snake's mouth, pushed aside the uvula, and crouched to his hands and knees. The inside of the throat was pink, decorated with cartoon pictures of things the snake had eaten: cheese-cakes, hotdogs, pizza, a cola, all items that could be bought at the snack bar, and Dan was impressed the company had managed to sneak in such a clever bit of subliminal advertising. No doubt kids would be craving a Coke after a half dozen laps through the digestive tract of some rubber serpent.

"Come on," Jessica called out again and crawled around the bend ahead.

Dan followed, but where she was small and nimble and used to scurrying about on her hands and knees, he was clumsy and awkward. His hands had trouble adjusting to the flexible vinyl walls, and his ankles shifted on the bouncing floor.

"Hurry!" she shouted, and he caught a glimpse of her Pink Princess slippers as another elastic hole swallowed her up.

He surged forward, head rubbing against the inflatable grooves, and he felt sweat forming on his forehead, sticky and wet. He reached the second barrier: two halves of inflatable vinyl with a hole just large enough for a teenager. He wondered how adults, how even some of the heavier kids he saw, could fit through such a passage. Somehow, he thought, they did, and so he dug his hands into the seam, planted his feet into the rubber, and pushed himself into the shadows.

He fell sideways onto a hard surface and felt a sudden burst of pain as his shoulder groaned and throbbed. It was dark, surprisingly darker than the previous section. The floor was not soft and flexible but made of something hard like wood or stone. He blinked several times to check that his eyes were open, but each time the darkness remained, black and vast. Somehow the light didn't penetrate this far in, and he found himself struggling to right himself in the pitch black.

Then everything went sideways.

A distant buzzing filled the shadow, an electric hum, faint and unchanging and whispering of summer. He felt the floor, hard and cold against his body, and pieces of it caught on his shirt like splinters. He stretched his hands out in both directions, shocked to find they couldn't extend further than his waist before running into the same hard obstruction. The corridor was small, too small for him, and when he tried to stand, his knees were cramped and trapped and his head hit something hard only a few inches from his face.

This isn't right, he thought. *This isn't right at all.*

He pushed his feet back against the rubber seam, trying to wriggle back, but found his feet running up against yet another hard obstruction. He kicked it but it just rattled and shook. Had he taken a wrong turn and perhaps ended up in some sort of maintenance section? Was that even possible? He was trapped, alone in that humid shade with that electric hum.

Panic began to grow. He could no longer hear the kids laughing or screaming. He could no longer hear the clatter of air hockey or the beeps of video games. All he could hear was the beat of his own heart and the hollow sound his limbs made as they scraped against the immovable surface. And that electric hum that blanketed the darkness like a chorus of insects.

He tried to focus his thoughts and brushed his hands over the obstructions, feeling for an exit, a hole, anything. He felt spots, small objects beneath his palm that broke loose and fell upon him like leaves. Around them, he felt indentations in the hard surface, slick and wet.

Oh God, please get me out of here, he pleaded. *Think, think, think. Keep it together. Keep calm and—*

He remembered his key light. It was small, no larger than a bottle cap, and it hung from his car keys.

Please…

He pulled it out, fumbling with it.

Please!

Click.

The blue light was overwhelming. His eyes shut on reflex but he forced himself to keep them open.

PLEASE!

The light cast long shadows down the wood, revealing grooves and indentations stained red and smeared like frantic cave paintings an inch from his face. In them he saw splinters, dozens of splinters, some bent at crooked angles, others pulled in long pieces as if the very grains of the wood itself had been stripped with bare hands.

And in those crimson-stained grooves he saw a fingernail, bent and broken. No, not one but several, hanging from the flayed wood grooves like dry leaves. And in that tomb, he felt, above all else, that he was not alone. That something was whispering into his ear from cold lips behind that electric hum.

Dan didn't remember screaming. Only empty sounds came from his mouth. The whole event, the shift as he later remembered it, happened to a different person in another life, one that he'd forgotten.

He felt hands, so many hands, all pulling at his ankles and knees, then a burst of light, like a supernova, a rebirth, and he was greeted by cakes and hotdogs and pizza slices, all flying past on a pink palette. And then more light. Faces swam into view. First the bearded face of the man with the *Tron* shirt, then a woman who kept repeating, "I think he's having a heart attack."

Dan felt his head roll to the side and he saw Linda running through a crowd, kids and adults and a giant mouse with its arms limp at its sides. He heard a kid crying, and somewhere beyond that, someone said, "What have you done?"

He sat on the bench outside, eyes focused on his left hand. It still shook, as it had for the last ten minutes. He didn't hear Linda emerge from the entrance, but when he looked up, there she was. The color had come back to her face, but the worry was etched deep, a worry he'd never seen on her. It was the look of a mother after a child stopped choking on candy, when horror and fear had subsided and left behind relief and distrust.

"The kids are fine. They're playing games now. I don't think they're too worried anymore," she added, eyes falling to his shaking hands. "Do I need to be?"

"No," he whispered.

"Hon, should we go to a hospital?"

"No," he answered again, and his shaking hand went into his pocket. "I'm fine."

The air was silent and charged as Linda sat on the bench beside him and sighed. "Honey, you don't look fine."

"I am," he said. "Really. Trust me, I'm fine."

And he did feel fine, or at least he was driving in that direction. The panic, for now, was in the rearview mirror, safely receding to memory and embarrassment. He wanted nothing more than to put the whole thing behind him, move on, and forget it. It'd been years since he'd had a panic attack, so long he'd forgotten what they were like. Then the fear had turned the world sideways, and only the clattering glass and the darkness had remained, old and familiar.

"Dan," she said in that soft voice that he knew meant she wasn't convinced. It was the voice of a mother getting to the bottom of a mystery: a broken window and a baseball, a crying daughter and a desecrated doll, or a husband screaming in public before a dozen different families. "Honey? What just happened back there?"

"I have a thing about small places," he said.

"Like claustrophobia or something?"

He nodded.

"Really? I never knew that. Since when?"

He glanced up at the flickering lights of the parking lot lamps. A family walked past, toward a minivan. He saw the children turning to stare at him, and he knew that when they got in the car, they'd say, "That was the crazy man!"

"Since when?" she asked again.

Go on, said Mr. Glass. *Lie to her.*

But he couldn't. If only for tonight, there would be no lies.

"Since I was ten," he said, taking a deep breath. "My brother and I, we were playing a game. See, there was this old house down the hill from the orphanage. It was his best hiding spot."

"A game?"

He nodded.

"You mean like hide-and-seek?"

He nodded again. "Anyways, there was this basement inside. A storm cellar. Only a few kids knew about it. In the basement there was this old trunk, you know, like a hundred years old, half rusted but sturdy as hell. Kids would stash their cigarettes and nudie magazines in it."

He waited for a laugh or smile, but none came. All she said was, "Go on," so he did.

"He, umm… he convinced me to climb into it. And I did, you know, to hide."

"Oh gosh." She squeezed his hand.

"Anyways, he closed it on top of me. He said it'd be just for a moment. But it wasn't. See, he slid this old railroad spike into the latch so I couldn't get out."

She gasped. "What? Why would he do that?"

"It was just a stupid kid prank. I dunno. He said…" Dan paused, rubbing his head as the glass grew warm at the memory. "He said, 'I just wanted to scare you. I just wanted to scare you.'"

"Dan, sweetie, that's awful."

He swallowed. "It was the worst thing I can remember. I couldn't hear, I couldn't see, I couldn't move, I couldn't breathe. I scraped my fingers raw on the wood, fighting and screaming for him."

"How long were you in there?"

"I don't know. Hours, maybe? I blacked it out. Even to this day it's just… emptiness, you know? What I do remember is this: it was Father

O'Malley and not David, not my brother, that finally let me out. I never forgot that."

Linda squeezed his hand, and he could feel it was no longer shaking.

"You never mention him, so I never ask."

"What's to mention? He was older. I was smaller. That was that."

"Did he ever apologize or get in trouble?"

"In a way. A few months later some kids made fun of his haircut. He almost beat one of them to death. He got worse, his sickness more…" He trailed off, remembering the lights and the white room, the silence and that shell that sat eternally staring back. "Anyways, they transferred him out of the state, into special care. He bounced around. Different places, different treatments. Nothing worked. I wrote him, but he never wrote back. We drifted, grew up and grew apart."

"Was that where he…" She hesitated, unable to finish the question.

"Died," he said, finishing it for her. "That's where he died. Yes."

"Did you see him before that?"

"Once. On my eighteenth birthday."

The room was white, Dan thought. So white and lonely. Only the buzzing of the overhead light and the psychiatrist's pen, clicking in and out, as they stared at the silent, shackled form of his older brother. A pale visage, deathly so. A form that didn't move but simply existed, staring slack-jawed at the corner of the room. A form that whispered "I'm sorry" in an endless loop. It was a husk, a shade, and whatever lived inside was silent and still.

"He didn't recognize me, or if he did, I couldn't tell. They kept him drugged up, sedated, and the disease did the rest. I knew—somehow I knew—I'd never see him again. And the truth is, I suppose, he died years before. To me, at least, he'd been dead a lot longer." Then he turned to Linda, shrugged as if to close out that forgotten chapter, and said, "And that was that."

PLAN B

BREAKING INTO HIS house was easier than she had imagined. The lights had been off for over a half hour since that liar and his whore had driven away with their crotch goblins in the back of their shitty sedan. In the silence and shadows, she had watched, and now the wait was over. All she needed to do was reach over the side gate, unhook the latch behind it, and slip into the house.

Now to deal with the dog, Karina thought as the gate closed behind her.

She had never been in his house, yet she had seen it dozens of times. First from the maps on the internet where she could zoom in, almost all the way on the front door, and read the brass *NO SOLICITORS* sign above the doorbell. And from the seat of her car, parked in the darkness, where she watched the silhouettes by the windows. Those shadows, large and small, that sometimes kissed and sometimes fought but never invited her into that warm house.

This wasn't her house, a fact she had realized last night. It would never be. She would always find herself outside, looking in on that life. And then this morning, after that unpleasant conversation and its cold words, in the tears and sickness that followed, her ideas turned to crystal and all became so perfectly clear that it spread through her body like the deepest orgasm. With that epiphany, she knew what to do. *Freedom*, she thought. *Free him from them.*

She followed the hedges into the backyard, passing a bird feeder filled with brackish water and some dying rosebushes. The area was lit by yard lights in the shape of small pagodas that she knew were too tacky for someone like Dan. Those kitsch little lights, they spoke of all the compromises and concessions he had made to that whore, each one chipping away at him over the years until he was little more than a shadow of the man Karina knew he wanted to be. She would free him. Yes, she would free him of that whore and those kids and that life he had never wanted.

And if he didn't want to be freed?

Well, there was always plan B, she thought, as she crouched by the doggie door and whistled. She reached into her pocket, past the cold metal, and found the dog treats. She could feel the hard edges of the sedatives that had been pushed into the meat filling. The vet had told her not to give a medium dog more than six a day, two at a time, and so she had stuffed over thirty into the treats, three in each. A final feast to quiet the beast.

She whistled again, louder, waiting for the flap to open and that dog to emerge for its treat. Emptiness answered back, and beyond it, a distant electrical hum from an insect, a cicada perhaps.

"Come here," she called, pursing her lips into another whistle, but realized she'd forgotten the dog's name. Jerry or Jasmine or… whatever. But the black flap of the doggie door remained still.

Then she remembered Dan had said the dog had gone missing. She hadn't believed him at the time—his lies were so numerous these days—but perhaps he had been telling the truth. It was hard telling with him. That family of idiots, they had all looked so happy as they climbed into the car and drove off past her parked car, but then again, they always looked happy.

As she thought about their smiles, she felt the sickness build up above her crotch like a sudden bout of cramps that sent her lurching over to her right side. She grabbed the wrought-iron rail and her stomach folded in on itself as she dry-heaved.

She thought of Italy and those families.

She thought of the old Jewish couple that lived downstairs.

She thought of the liar in his bed with that hag at his side and those spawn she'd squeezed out from the gash between her legs.

The sickness came up a second time, twisting her stomach, yet only gasps of air escaped her lips as if she were a drowning animal. No. She would not let the sickness control her. She had too much work to do, too many mistakes to fix.

She steadied herself and gave a gentle push on the backdoor handle, yet it didn't budge as she had hoped it might. Dan sometimes left his office unlocked, even after he'd gone home, and occasionally she would sneak in and go over his emails and web history. She had thought his carelessness would have carried over to his house; she had planned on it or perhaps just never thought of an alternative. Only hours ago her idea had been so clear, so crystalized, but now she found the details more complicated. For a moment she wondered if the whole plan was worth it.

Yes, she told herself. The whole thing was... Was what? Unbalanced. Yes, it was unbalanced. That word seemed to capture it exactly. It was unbalanced and unfair and they needed to pay. She needed to free him and make them pay. The liar and his cunt wipe wife and those urchins, those parasites he called by names. The mistakes all needed to be fixed so he could be free and they could be together. So all could be balanced.

The doggie door was too small to crawl through but just large enough to reach into. And if the dog wasn't there, she thought, then nothing could bite her. Yes, it was destiny. The dog had gone missing to allow her into the house without a key, all part of some grand plan in which she was the lead character. The clarity chased away the final edges of the sickness and all was right again.

Reaching through, she found the locked doorknob and turned it from the inside. Destiny indeed.

The inside of his house at 3350 Greer Park Lane was not as Karina had expected it. The picture in her mind had been one of tasteful, classical decorations and minor masterpieces lining the walls like a personal museum. A framed Poussin reproduction or perhaps some painted bacchanalia near a rustic gas stove where dried peppers hung by thread. Instead, it was a simple house, no different or more exciting than her relatives had, only this was larger and scattered with occasional toys and books. A worn-out dog bed sat by the corner next to a bowl, the name *GINGER* painted in a child's scrawl. Dead roses sat in a murky vase above the sink, and a wedding photograph of Dan and Linda hung at a crooked angle on the wall, mocking her.

That photograph, she was drawn to it. When her fingers touched the warm glass, the sickness flared up. For a brief second she almost vomited into the sink, but she forced it back inside. That photograph would be the first to go, she thought, and she pulled it free from the wall with a sharp yank that took the nail and a strip of wallpaper with it. She tossed it onto the kitchen table, smiling as the glass cracked.

Filled with a sense of calm, she walked to the drawers and opened them, one at a time, until she found the silverware. Her fingers flitted across them until she came upon a special set, older and nicer than all the others, and she knew these were both wedding presents and family heirlooms. She placed the silverware on the table next to the wedding portrait.

Tonight the house would be her canvas, its contents her paint. Tonight she would bring balance to this whole skewed mess.

She opened the refrigerator, scanned the rows of leftovers, the juice packets, and a re-corked bottle of red wine that would have driven the Italians mad if they saw it chilling inside. She needed something smaller and settled on the condiments: pesto, mustard, and a jar of jalapeños, all good enough to work with, at least to start. She put them, with the silverware, atop the wedding picture. Then she walked to the microwave.

The timer only went as high as fifty-nine minutes and fifty-nine seconds, but that would be plenty of time, she thought. After a few seconds, the metal began sparking. In under a few minutes, the jalapeños were boiling inside the jar. The sound of ruin made her smile.

HER FINGERS TRACED THE COLD TILE SURFACE OF THE KITCHEN countertop, not unlike the frames of the paintings she loved, and came to a stop at the rack of knives sitting in a wooden block. She ran her fingers over the hilt of each, feeling their weight against her fingers. Then she selected a medium-sized paring knife. The stainless-steel tip glistened as she withdrew it. In her hands, it felt good, balanced. As she looked around the room, she found the perfect place to put it.

The whore and her spawn. They were staring back at her from across the room, happy and content. Yes, she would cut them. There were books and notes and newspaper clippings, but most sickening of all was the drawing taped to the wall. It was a horrid mix of crayon and marker that depicted a nauseating and clichéd scene: a father, a mother, two kids, and a dog stood before a house with a chimney and swirls of brown felt-tip smoke. The words *I love mine family!* were written in a clumsy scrawl above the name Jessica, signed with two backward S's.

Karina heaved forward and drove the paring knife deep into the drawing. The blade vibrated and the plaster split as it sank into the wall. She withdrew it and repeated, again and again, feeling the blade loosen the plaster as inch-long gashes turned the childish picture of that bitch into nothing more than loose strands of paper. With a sudden scream, she buried it up to the hilt.

The blade hung from the wall, vibrating from the force of the final blow. She had destroyed that whore, and only then was she satisfied with her work. All that was left of the picture were those two kids, that rat dog, and the liar. If this house of lies was his creation, then its destruction was to be her catharsis.

She would fix them all soon enough, she thought. Balance would be restored.

But for now, there was more work to do.

THE KHMER BUDDHA HEAD ARCED THROUGH THE AIR AND SPLIT THE LED TV screen in two. What remained of his flat-screen TV fell to the floor, followed by the stone head that had, until moments ago, decorated the mantel. Now it lay, like much of the room, in a gutted, broken pile, scattered and shattered. The candles had been cut, the curtains carved until they hung as frayed tinsel. She disemboweled the couches with a serrated knife until their stuffing lay spread about like confetti, and the living room, like much of the house, was reduced to a violent mess. She flipped the glass coffee table onto its side by the fireplace and spent the next fifteen minutes feeding photos to the gas flame. All that remained was that final photo album she'd found on the kitchen table.

As she crossed her legs and sat down, the metal in her pocket pressed deep into her hip. It was uncomfortable, but there was a good chance she'd need it for the finishing touches. If all went sideways, it would be her way out, an insurance plan, a final solution to end all the lies.

She took the gun and placed it on the floor next to that wretched photo album. Then she settled on the first series of photos. They were a disgusting mix of digital printouts and old pictures from a film camera. Each picture showed that liar or the whore and their horrible spawn as they developed and grew over the years like fattening grubs. She cut them to pieces, just as she had cut Jessica's picture, then added them to the fire. The flames flickered and grew as the ink burned, the paper curled, and ash danced in the updraft.

She stopped on a photo of that rat dog and felt the sickness bubble up to chest level. The beast was hideous, far uglier than she'd ever thought, and it made her angry to think that Dan could share a house with such a thing. Its face was little more than matted hair, its eyes two curdled marbles. A spotted tongue hung out of a crooked mouth like a limp, filthy sleeve. Worst of all was the casual way the family sat around the beast, each of them smiling and staring at the camera in front of a glowing Christmas tree.

She pulled the picture from the album and tore it up like a student ripping a failed test. As she tore it a fourth time, she heard something from the other end of the house. A noise, sudden and sharp, over the sound of tearing paper. She swung her head toward the hallway. The air was thick and dust hung in glowing moonbeams around the room. The hallway felt darker, dim and cold.

Far away, an electrical hum grew, seeming to come from within the walls. A vague taste of rot danced on her tongue. Everything felt… off-balance, she thought. Even that word, "balance," seemed foreign and out of place, as if it had been injected into her thoughts, intended for another but intercepted by her. But that wasn't her concern, not now. The end was close, she told herself. She stood up, ready to meet it.

Another sound, louder and longer. It resonated with a frequency that seemed to penetrate her skin and go right to her bone. It was unmistakable. It was a dog, whimpering. That filthy beast, they had found it. Or perhaps never even lost it. The whimpering grew, coming from the room at the end of the hall, behind the closed door. Had the dog been home this whole time? Had they left it locked in there like the monstrosity it was?

Her clarity of mind was fading and she found herself thinking muddied thoughts, small regrets and actions that didn't seem to logically line up yet had somehow brought her here, to this very moment. For the first time tonight, Karina felt genuine doubt in her plan. Past it all, past the torn photos and tears, their dead bodies and the taste of gun smoke in her mouth as she pulled the trigger, a single voice whispered that it was all madness and mistakes on the road ahead.

No, she thought, *don't be distracted. Finish it.*

She fingered the gun, light and warm to the touch, and moved it to the pocket of her sweatshirt. Behind that door at the end of the hall, that same sound ran in a loop. A faint canine yowling and the rattle of metal.

She stepped toward the door, hand inches from the knob. *Finish it*, she thought. *Fix these mistakes, one by one, and if he doesn't savor his freedom, he can be fixed as well.*

Then she opened the door.

THE STUDY WAS DARK AND COLD, SHOCKINGLY SO. A CHILL, LIKE A WALK-in refrigerator, yet behind it hung a damp taste of dry grass and earth. The buzz of insects seemed to fill the darkness, then faded as a passing car lit the study in long shadows. A rectangular object sat at the other end of the room, an unframed painting as large as she was. It seemed to shimmer for a brief moment as if it were beneath glass. She drew closer to the towering shape, intrigued.

It was a simple painting: an empty old room, a grandfather clock, and an open window that looked out onto a small hill with a dead tree atop it. Other than its size, she found the painting unremarkable, devoid of anything that really held her eyes. It was little more than a photorealistic still life with too much empty space on both sides. Unbalanced. Yes, it was all wrong, as if it was unfinished.

That sound returned, the muffled whimpering, and only then did she remember what drew her to the study. Past the painting, off in the left corner of the study, by the bookshelf, sat a small form.

"Hello?" Karina asked as the sickness rose, and she saw that what sat in that corner was no animal. "Jessica?"

A child's shape crouched in the corner, a yellow dress shaking as it cried. Faint, muffled sobs as if it were scared…

… or hiding. *From who?* she wondered. *From the boogeyman.*

Yes, from the boogeyman. *From me,* she thought, fingering the gun as she approached the shape.

"Jessica?" she asked again, and the girl shivered in response. Her hair had small burgundy streaks in it, held up in two pigtails tied with white lace ribbons.

How long had she been hiding here? An hour? Two? Karina had thought the house empty, but in hindsight, she realized she'd always heard the whimpering and crying, just as she'd always heard the hum of insects. From the backyard, into the kitchen, through the halls and into the living room. It had always been there, a white noise, a constant behind all else.

"Jessica!" she snapped a final time as she clenched the gun and raised it.

"I broke it," sobbed the little girl, but it came out as, "Aieee buh-woke eeet," rolling off heavy, trembling lips. And as she said this, Karina saw what the girl held.

A small animal bone, no larger than two fingers spread in a victory sign, was clutched in her hands. One side was dirty, covered in muck and hair. The other had a row of teeth on it: fangs, incisors, and molars. The girl stretched her hands upward, holding a dog's jawbone, raw and wet, like a child asking a parent to fix a toy. As she presented this gruesome artifact, her face passed into a beam of light from the window, and all within Karina's mind went sideways.

The sickness erupted, fast and violent. Karina cupped her hand over her mouth and vomited into it.

The young girl had no face.

Or at least nothing that resembled a human face. It was a mask, but only in the sense that the skin painted on a doll's face was a mask over an abstract shape. Cracked patches of paint hung from bark-like skin, and between the cracks lay wet stitching. Her eyes were empty chasms, not even sockets where eyes had once been, but holes into a dark core that leaked tears of wet paint down cracked cheeks and past cold, quivering lips. Her engorged head rolled around on her neck like a pendulum.

Karina felt a second spasm and covered her mouth, but the sickness escaped between her fingers. Instead of being repulsed, the girl, that doll-headed vagary of a child, shuffled toward Karina. She hadn't stood up, or if she had, the action had taken a mere microsecond to complete. To Karina, the doll-headed girl appeared suddenly upright, as if the movement between squatting and shuffling had been spliced out. Her hands reached out, holding that jawbone—"Aieee buh-woke-eeet"—and behind her, Karina saw what she had broken.

A dog lay on its side in the corner where the girl had just been. The liar's disgusting rat dog. Ginger. It gave Karina a weak glance, like an old mutt greeting its owner on a hot afternoon. A whimper came from a wet hole where its bottom jaw had been removed, and it wagged its tail and farted in spasms.

The sickness gave way to something else, and in the transition between the two, for one clear moment that stretched forever, Karina felt no other feeling than utter and complete regret. She thought of Dan, of the first time they met, how witty and clever he was and yet how awkward and clumsy he came off. She thought of the knife and how she drew it across her wrist, not deep enough to kill but deep enough to keep him there for another hour, another week. And she thought of the smile he gave her as she boarded the plane, the smile that meant a part of him was happy to see her leave, and how she had replayed that smile in her head over the summer months in Italy beneath that sickening sun.

Most of all, she thought of today. Of her plan, her stupid fucking plan to kill them all, one by one, and then finally herself. All those actions and plans, when laid out and played back in that brief ocean of clarity, stood awkward and embarrassing and foreign, and had someone else told them to her, she would have called them insane. But it wasn't someone else: it was her, and for that, she felt absolute shame.

And then the void collapsed, the shame was gone, replaced by a horror so vast her mind reverted to that of a child, and her thoughts became simple.

Not right. Something wrong happen. Move. Away. Go!

She tried to run, but her feet fell out from beneath her and the hardwood floor rose up to catch her. The world went sideways, and a bright pop lit up her senses as the floor connected with her ear. The instant ringing muffled her screams, which came in short, shrill bursts.

The girl drew closer. Her eyes were empty but somehow she saw, and Karina felt that sick child's glance moving up her legs, up her body, up her head, and then beyond.

"Can I keep it?" the doll-faced girl asked with a drawl, then added, "Please?" but it came out as, "Puh-weeeese."

Karina gasped out a single sound, no more than an airy cough, and she realized the girl wasn't asking her, but something behind her.

A shadow fell over her, and from the floor, she looked up to see a boy looming over her with cold pinhole eyes. He sneered with contempt like a prison guard or a child finding an insect and raising a foot. Then he sank his hand into her hair. Cold fingers wrapped around the roots of her scalp. His grip was fast and tight, tighter than she'd ever felt, fingers like hooks that dug into her skin. Then he pulled her with such force that she slid three feet in less than a second.

The friction on the hardwood floor burned the skin from her heels as she was dragged away from the door.

She grabbed the boy's hands, or at least where she thought his hands should have been. Her fingers sank into the skin like it was warm butter, and she saw brown paint coating her fingers as she withdrew them.

Another lurch, another tug, and the floor tore skin from her calves as she slid further away from the door. Her fingers flailed at the floor, clawing, searching for something, anything, but found nothing. Then she found the strength to do one final thing.

She screamed.

And screamed and screamed and screamed.

And as she screamed, the doll-faced girl skipped and clapped her hands and that broken dog with its missing jaw turned in excited little circles as if chasing its tail.

Karina felt two things, and then she felt no more. A final violent yank across the floor, away from the door, toward the edge of the room and that painting. And something wet and old swallowing her, body and soul.

Then all became darkness and anger, utter and complete and devouring, and she knew nothing else.

RUIN

HIS DAUGHTER LAY asleep in his arms, just as she had for most of the trip home. Linda had insisted on driving, allowing Tommy to sit up front. Now Dan carried Jessica across the lawn to the front door as Linda locked the car and followed behind.

"Maybe Ginger came home," Tommy said a little too loud, and Dan raised a finger to his lips as Jessica mumbled and shifted.

"Maybe," Dan whispered, reached for the keys in his pocket, and unlocked the front door. It had been years since they all left the house together, so long that he had forgotten which key opened the door. Two wrong keys and then the tumblers clicked into place and he pressed the handle down.

The first thing he noticed was the smell. A terrible reek of electrical fire and food overwhelmed him. An orange flicker to his right caught his eye. The fireplace was on, small flames licking the bottom of the decorative logs. A thin layer of smoke hung under the ceiling. A faint popping and the sound of a smoke alarm chirping came from the kitchen.

"Why is the fireplace on?" he asked as he turned the entry light on. Linda screamed at what she saw.

The entry light didn't carry all the way into the living room, but the damage was still visible. The couches had been torn to pieces, the television smashed. Glass and papers lay scattered on the rug in a semicircle.

Dan passed Jessica to his wife, and Jessica awoke, mumbling, but his voice cut in over her protests. "Honey, stay with the kids outside."

"What's happening?" asked Jessica.

"Go! Over to the sidewalk, now," Dan shouted. Tommy just stood there, frozen. "Now! All of you!"

Linda pulled them down the walkway as he turned to the house. He saw the smoke coming from the kitchen. Had it been thicker, he would've stayed outside, but it came in small wisps and he felt he had to try and stop it. He had fire insurance, sure, but it never covered the things that mattered. Houses could be rebuilt, but photographs could never be recaptured.

"Be careful," Linda called as he hurried inside.

Coughing, he pulled his shirt over his mouth. He hurried in, through the dining room and to the kitchen, the source of the smoke. His fingers pounded 9-1-1 on his cell phone as the lights flickered on and off. The cell phone rang twice before the operator answered.

"Nine one one emergency," said the voice.

"I'm calling to report a fire and a break-in—my address is 3350 Greer Park Lane. I need police and fire personnel immediately."

"Right away, sir. Please stay on the line."

"Okay," he said, pushing the kitchen door open.

"Are you at the residence?"

"I'm in the residence."

"Sir, are you certain you're alone?"

"No, my wife and kids—"

"The intruders, sir. Are they still on the premises?"

Dan felt his blood chill as he surveyed the kitchen. Paintings were askew, the refrigerator was open, and a picture Jessica had drawn in preschool had been impaled by a knife and hung in tatters.

"Karina?" he said under his breath as his eyes scanned the room for her shape among the chaos. He found nothing, only destruction.

Then a low electric hum filled the room as the lights grew brighter.

The microwave rumbled and exploded in a violent flash behind him, and darkness consumed the house.

"Sir, are you there?" asked the voice on the phone. "Sir?"

THE POLICE ARRIVED FIVE MINUTES LATER.

A patrol car was first on the scene, but the police officer waited for backup before entering. Three of them disappeared into the house, guns and flashlights held high. From the sidewalk, Dan and Linda watched the beams of light as they lit up the rooms from the inside. It was like something out of a movie, and Tommy even pumped his fist in the air as another police car screeched to the curb.

"Think they'll get the bad guys?" Tommy asked, but no one answered.

The fire truck arrived soon after, and it took the firefighters a half hour to clear the house and declare it safe. By then, most of the neighbors stood on the sidewalk, watching the spectacle. Dan felt embarrassment and anger, knowing that Marty was there among the group, probably smiling, as if karma had caught up with Dan for their earlier altercation.

WITH THE POWER WORKING AND THE LIGHTS BACK ON, THE TRUE EXTENT OF the damage became visible. The house hadn't just been vandalized: it'd been desecrated. Ransacked and violated.

"We've checked every room, every closet, basement and attic," said the detective. "Whoever did this, they're gone. Probably have been for a while."

"What about fingerprints?" Linda asked. "Did you get any?"

"A few, some from the photographs in the living room. They'll need to be entered as evidence if that's all right."

"Of course," Dan answered.

The detective noted this in his book, then turned to the wreckage of the living room and nodded. "Most of the damage looks malicious in nature, perhaps some kids having a good time. And you're pretty sure your valuables are accounted for? Jewelry and such?"

"So far," Linda answered.

"Then I have to ask, have either of you made enemies with anyone lately? Anyone with a reason to do this?"

Linda turned to Dan, and he felt his hand vibrate as the glass wiggled and burned. *Tell them,* it said.

"No, sir, none that I'm aware of."

"Why do you ask?" Linda inquired, and Dan wished that she'd let him do the talking.

"Damage of this nature, cut-up photos and such, sometimes it's someone you know. Crime of enmity, we call it. Like the perp wants to prove a point."

"Well, they proved their point," Dan said. "They scared the hell out of my family."

"Like I said, could be some kids. Wouldn't surprise me. We'll know for sure in a few days when we get the prints. In the meantime, we'll keep a car in the neighborhood so you folks can sleep easy."

"Thank you," said Linda.

The detective nodded, tore off a copy of the report, and handed it to Dan, adding, "For your insurance."

"Goodnight, sir," said Jessica, and the detective gave her a tip of the hat before closing the door.

HE TIED OFF THE SECOND GARBAGE BAG, OPENED A THIRD, AND DUMPED A Tupperware full of meatloaf into it. Linda had insisted the fridge be cleared out, food and all, in case any of it had been "tampered with." It was a notion he first thought absurd, but now, after an hour alone with his thoughts while cleaning the kitchen, it was a notion he couldn't ignore.

He knew who had done this, without a doubt.

The cut photos, the knife that had, until the police took it as evidence, been embedded in the wall through a drawing of his family, even the destroyed wedding photo: they were all things that bore the emotional signature of one woman. Enmity indeed. *Hell hath no fury like a woman scorned.* His house was evidence of that.

And now that fury was what he was trying to hide. If Linda cleaned up and saw what he did, a seed of doubt would start to grow, and next would come the questions. He had insisted she put the kids to sleep and leave the cleaning to him. "They need their mother," he had said, but he also needed privacy. While she waited for them to fall asleep, he scoured the house for anything: a note, a picture, a confession, any information that would connect Karina to the vandalism and, ultimately, to him and the affair.

But there was nothing to be found, no incriminating evidence of her in any of the rooms. If she had been here, she had left no trace. And for the moment, the great mistake, the lie, would continue to stay hidden. He could control it, he thought. If nothing else, he was a good liar. He could control it, and in time he could be a good husband again.

His eyes fell on that hole in the wall where the knife had been embedded inches deep until the police removed it. The cracked plaster stuck out like a wound. A pale chunk the size of a golf ball hung by a few loose threads of insulation. Inside the gash was something else, something that glistened and shimmered. A hum, faint and flat, came from inside.

He pushed his index finger into the wall and grimaced as it slid into warmth. The hum faded like a passing train. It was sticky, a honey-like substance, and he wondered if bees or wasps had been nesting inside the walls. He withdrew his finger and recoiled in disgust. It reeked of rot, an acrid stench that made his eyes water. He ran soap and water over it, scrubbing it several times until the stench was gone. Then he made a mental note to have their house examined by pest control on Monday.

"Kids are asleep, finally," Linda said, emerging from the dining room and leaning against the doorframe.

She looked tired, drained, as if she'd aged five years since the day began. Her hair hung down to her shoulders on one side, leaving the other side bare. Dan eyed the curve of her neck and how it met her chin. It was a part of her body he'd always found a curious beauty in. He remembered that same mysterious curve rising from the spaghetti straps of her black cocktail dress as she held a champagne flute and smiled at him years ago.

"Hon?" she asked again, perhaps for the third time. "Are you okay?"

I did this, he thought. *I brought this into the house. The lie, and now the destruction. It's my fault. I'm sorry for so many things,* he wanted to say.

Instead, all he said was, "You look beautiful."

THEY MADE LOVE FOR THE FIRST TIME IN MONTHS THAT NIGHT. Downstairs, he kissed her on her neck, on that spot that turned her breath to a short gasp. She clutched the doorframe as his lips moved down her body and he hiked up her dress. He was clumsy at first, but as he remembered his way between her, she came alive, grasping his hair and moaning. They both felt the charge after the adrenaline had subsided. A distinct arousal, a surge of life and lust and hormones after the evening's fright.

They tiptoed upstairs, past the children's bedroom. As she took his hand and led him to the bed, he felt young again, nervous even. He thought of all the nights he'd snuck out of and back into his dormitory years ago.

By the time he entered her, she was no longer dry, and she found herself, despite the pain, climaxing easily and often. When he could no longer hold back, she whispered his name and pulled him deep inside her and held him there, kissing his neck and smiling in the shadows.

Afterward, she laid her head on his chest, a faint smile on her lips as she traced her finger in small circles from his stomach to his neck. "You're a good man, Dan. I hope you know that," she said in the drowsy quiet that followed.

"Thanks, honey," he said, but she heard the doubt in his voice. She looked over at him and tapped on his heart.

"I mean that. The kids are lucky to have you. I am too."

A good man, murmured the glass. *Or a good salesman?*

He gave her a kiss on her forehead and smiled.

"Love you," he said and closed his eyes.

AFTER THE STORM

HE COULDN'T REMEMBER a single dream he had that night. The house was quiet. The occasional rattle and hum of pipes and settling wood echoed out like whispers in the night, no different than usual.

There was barking, a faint breeze that passed through the kids' room, and shortly before dawn, Tommy awoke, certain that Ginger was pawing at the bedroom door. When he opened it, nothing was there, and he returned to bed and forgot all about it.

The next morning Dan and Linda finished the last of the cleaning. By the afternoon she turned her attention to the rose garden outside, and he watched her pulling handfuls of weeds from the ground in wet clumps as he itemized the insurance claim. He called the humane society twice, but they still had no sign of Ginger, and he found himself thankful the kids' minds were elsewhere.

That Saturday Tommy had friends over for the afternoon and they sat around the kitchen, playing their Nintendos. It amused Dan to see three silent kids mere feet away from each other yet all in their own handheld worlds.

Jessica kept to her room, and he could hear her talking to her dolls in a raised voice, occasionally shouting. When he opened the door and stuck his head in to check on her, she simply raised a finger to her lips, as if quieting an invisible class of students. She spoke of Ginger only once that weekend, at lunch, and when she did, it was in the past tense.

They spent the afternoon at the Junior Museum, where Tommy played with pneumatic tubes and water-pressure mazes in the science section. Jessica wandered about the small zoo, laughing at geese and raccoons, wrinkling her nose at the bats, and staring at a pair of sleeping bobcats. When he tried to take a picture of his daughter near the cats, they awoke with a start and hissed at him before scurrying off.

Tommy's soccer team lost their game on Sunday by two points, one of which Tommy gave the other team by hand-balling a shot on his side's box. Some parents shouted and jeered, even a few on Tommy's own team. Dan just gave his son a shrug and a grin that made Tommy smile as the players took their places for another kickoff. With eight minutes left in the game, a Bearded Collie broke free from its leash and bounded onto the field where, to the amusement of some and the annoyance of others, it herded the soccer ball around and brought the game to a standstill. Eventually, its owner coaxed it away with some apple slices. Tommy laughed, loudest of all, and Dan joined in.

There by that soccer field, he thought that for all these years, he had been only acting, only pretending to be interested, only pretending to be a good parent and a good husband. But even if he was pretending, even if it was a mask he wore and a role he acted, it felt warm and wonderful, and if he kept wearing it long enough, if he kept pretending to be something he wasn't, could he forget what he really was?

Yes, he thought. Yes he could.

He would smile and laugh and wear that mask until he forgot it was there. He would be all those things: a father, a friend, a teacher, and a husband. And as he thought about that future he would make, he felt, for a moment, truly happy.

It would be the last time he would ever feel that way.

TWO

"Whoever wants to know something about me, they should look attentively at my pictures, and there seek to recognize what I am… and what I want."

—*Gustav Klimt*

GHOST IN THE MACHINE

"HOW LONG WILL this take?" he asked Sajid, who sat before the computer and tapped the mouse. It was a Monday afternoon, and Dan had just finished his graduate class, where Karina had again failed to show up. Much like the way Jessica spoke of Ginger in the past tense, he hoped he could soon do the same with her. The idea had grown on him. Now he sat with Sajid in the back of the digital lab, poring over a second set of photos of that painting.

"How long? Well, that depends on the weather," Sajid answered.

"The weather?"

"Whether the database has any other works like it," he answered with a smug smile. "Whether… weather… never mind."

"Cute, but what does that mean?"

"Well, the software's still in beta, but it works. Most of the time. If there's a Van Gogh, it recognizes the swirls inherent to the style. A Lichtenstein, maybe it's the lips and tears. More common works, it could take as little as a few minutes. But this, who knows?" He tapped the screen, which showed a well-lit master shot of the painting beneath a superimposed grid as the hard drive clicked and chattered and the progress bar read zero percent. "Maybe a few hours, maybe a few days, maybe never."

"Maybe never?"

"It all depends on the whether," Sajid said again with a grin.

"Really?" Dan sighed.

"Sorry, couldn't help it. You know, if you could get a sample to the lab, they could date it. That'd give us a range, which would narrow the search."

Dan considered that very course of action last week but then decided against it. Dean Robert was a stickler for expensive lab tests, and Dan didn't want to further strain the pittance his department had for discretionary research. However, the project had been the dean's idea, and seeing the unmoving progress bar at the bottom of the computer screen made Dan decide to roll the dice on this one.

"How far away were you when you took this?" Sajid asked.

"Ten feet, give or take," Dan said.

"Sure about that?"

"Positive. What's wrong this time?"

Sajid stopped tapping the mouse and zoomed in on the lower-left quadrant of the grid near that boy's hair. He highlighted a box and zoomed in again. "Nothing's really wrong. It's just…" He squinted. "And you used the Mark Six we lent you?"

"Yep," Dan answered again. "And the tripod, and the lights."

Sajid chewed on the end of his pen, studying the screen, then said, "Well, that just doesn't make sense."

"Why's that?"

"Look, that's a twenty-five-megapixel camera. Its resolution tops out at seven thousand by five and some change."

"You're losing me," Dan said. He hated when Sajid spoke in jargon, like some TV scientist spouting off knowledge in some arcane area of expertise. It had taken Dan countless hours to study the digital side of his profession, and that was almost a decade ago, back before Google became a verb and tablets were still something the doctor prescribed. These days he considered fumbling his way through PowerPoint an accomplishment in its own right.

"Okay, Prof, think of it like this. It's the amount of clarity an image has. The higher the resolution, the more you can zoom in, like this."

Sajid clicked the mouse and opened up another file. It was a portrait: seventeenth century, French, Dan guessed from the clothes and muted color tones. Sajid zoomed in on a somber face of an aristocrat staring at the viewer.

"At four hundred percent, it gets blurry. We see the pixels and artifacts." Sajid adjusted the zoom until it read 1600 percent. The picture lost all clarity and became a series of colored pixels. "Now it's like Tetris. See what I mean?"

"Yeah. Megabytes."

"Megapixels."

"Right."

"Anyways, this picture of yours," Sajid said, switching back to the painting. "Notice anything?"

Now Dan understood it. "His hair..."

"Exactly!" Sajid cut in. On-screen, he had zoomed in on that brooding boy's hair, and yet it was still perfectly clear. There were no pixels, no artifacts, no Tetris blocks. Just dark brown strands of hair greased and combed to the side. He tapped the screen with his pen where the zoom level read 3200 percent. "This shouldn't even be possible. Not with the Hubble telescope, and definitely not with that Mark Six."

"I don't understand," Dan said.

"I don't either. I really don't," Sajid answered with genuine confusion and took a deep breath. "I'll get some coffee and we'll dive into this. Sugar?"

"Black," Dan answered and reached for the mouse. "May I?"

"Be my guest," Sajid answered and got up.

Dan scooted his stool closer to the computer, hand falling on the mouse, which gave off a small static shock. He zoomed back out until the zoom level read zero and the painting filled the screen. That whole unbalanced composition: the window, the field, the two little kids.

He focused on a new area, highlighting the clock and zooming in. It had always bothered him for a reason that sat on the tip of his tongue like a drunk memory. The painting had been rendered very realistic, and while he knew that the living subjects, the boy and girl, were figments of the artist's imagination, he held a suspicion that the clock had been drawn from reality.

He zoomed further in on the clock face, those two brass gilded hands bisecting the face at 5:55 with the missing numbers from nine to eleven o'clock. Centered above the twelve was a crescent slit that displayed a small picture that Dan suspected changed based on the time of day. The current picture, a lazy yellow sunset, displayed the silhouette of a dog leaping in the air after a bird that had just taken flight.

The coffee pot gurgled. Somewhere else in the lab, Sajid spoke on the phone with who Dan assumed was his girlfriend based on the hushed whispers and repeated mumblings of, "Mmm, baby."

Dan scrolled down the image of the clock, stopping on the left side where he'd seen the brass plate and those indecipherable markings. At home, they were mere hairlines of paint on the canvas. Yet on the screen, at that clarity, they appeared cleaner and more three-dimensional than when he'd stood an inch away from the paint. It was impossible, as Sajid had said, and Dan now agreed. Impossible, yet there it was in front of him, an undeniable glitch.

He zoomed in further on the writing etched into the brass. Two words with something between them. An ampersand, just as he thought.

Cobald & Sons.

It was a name. He took out his notepad and wrote it down. As he closed the notepad, the screen shimmered for a second and the hard drive emitted a furious clacking. He zoomed out until the whole clock filled the screen and clicked *print*. Nearby, a photo printer hummed to life, grinding out the selection. If the clock had a name, it would take him one step closer to finding the artist, if indeed that was the intention of the donor.

And if it wasn't, then what?

He put that thought out of his mind as he scrolled around the image, settling on the open window and the hill beyond. He zoomed in on that hill. Again, it seemed even larger, as if the earth had grown. Another click and he was zooming in until he saw tall blades of green grass, overgrown and wild, yet the clarity of the image never changed. It was like seeing the world through a perfect pair of glasses.

As he scrolled up the hill, the blades of grass changed, growing browner, lifeless, until scattered patches of dead grass and weeds surrounded that lonely tree. From afar, the tree had looked healthy, but when it was magnified, another reality emerged. It was sick and dying. A dark moss engulfed the right side of it, spreading downward to the trunk and upward to the branches. Leaves hung wilted and curled like a thousand dead insects. In the center of the moss, where it was darkest and most gangrene, lay a single handprint.

The shadow stood, frozen in motion. Like the hill, Dan was certain it, too, had changed since he last saw it. It was no longer behind the tree but in front of it, as if it had taken another few steps toward the viewer. The form was not just dark: it was devoid of light, an absolute black. There were no subtle transitions, no careful shades or blends or brush lines where the shadow met the colors of the landscape it was painted on. Instead, only a sharp divide, a razor's edge between the browns and greens of the hillside and the consuming darkness of the shadow.

Dan scrolled up the shadow further. The elongated arms disproportionate to its body, the thin waist line that hinted at nudity or starvation, and the gumdrop bump atop its shoulders that suggested its head was hunched forward. He clicked the mouse again, zooming in on that darkened lump until it didn't so much as fill the screen but swallowed all the color from the world around it.

Staring into that shadow, that perfect black, Dan thought of an ocean, endless and deep. Not an ocean of water but an ocean of time. Where dense kelp forests of memory and emotion shimmered. Where abstract shapes lay dormant and asleep like bugs that waited a dozen cycles of the seasons before waking.

Found you, the broken glass said as it rattled and hummed.

Dan didn't know how long he stared at the void, but at some point, minutes or seconds ago, it had shifted. The darkness bled apart like a child's book of tricks, an optical illusion, and between the shadows, two shapes emerged.

A pair of eyes.

The computer screen flickered, the hard drive stuttered, and a pop echoed out. For a second the darkness bled out of the computer screen like a flower blossoming. It broke the two-dimensional borders of the monitor as it unfolded like ink on cotton.

The pop was the sound of the hard drive dying, followed by a flash of light from inside the computer tower. Then the lights in the lab died, and in the darkness, Dan smelled smoke, the faint odor of burnt metal. A dim blue light cut through the darkness.

"Not again," said Sajid as he held up his cell phone and walked over to the cabinet. "Call you back, babe."

He produced a flashlight, tapped it a few times, and then clicked it on. The beam cut through the darkness in clear, crisp light and pointed at a nearby breaker box, already open.

"Sorry, Professor, this sometimes happens. Bleeding-edge hardware and they have us on Edison's own circuit. We've learned to set the auto-save to every other minute. Okay, here we go."

Sajid counted down three switches, then flipped the breaker back on. A spring-loaded click rang out and the darkness was chased off by the cold white of fluorescent lights. Sajid pointed to the computer. "Turn her back on, will you?"

Dan pressed the power button on the computer tower. It emitted three distinct beeps and flashed a red light. The monitor read *NO INPUT*.

"Nothing's happening," Dan said.

"That's not good," Sajid grumbled, and he pressed the button again, receiving the same series of three beeps and a red light. "Huh." He frowned. "That's not good at all."

THE SURGE, AS SAJID HAD CALLED IT, FRIED THE COMPUTER AND everything in it, including Dan's memory stick. The contents, once a list of photos, now showed only an unreadable folder and a list of random file names, each only 555 bytes in size. When pressed, Sajid explained that Dan's data was still on the memory stick; it had just forgotten where it was since its table of contents had been damaged.

"Sort of like amnesia," he had said before mumbling, "Fucking piece of shit," and slapping the computer tower.

It wasn't a total loss. Dan still had the printout of the clock and the name Cobald & Sons, which raised more questions than it answered. But the day was over and those questions would have to wait.

He left the printout on his office desk, then locked the door. He stopped before the Turtle and pressed the call button several times until it lit up. The gears groaned in protest as the old elevator awakened. Waiting there, he thought of that image he'd seen in the shadow before the surge. Had there really been eyes in the darkness? Or had they been his own, reflected back in a trick of light?

There was an explanation, a reason behind it. Computers didn't bleed darkness, and eyes didn't open from shadows. They were machines made by men, and men were imperfect. There were always glitches, he thought, and it was silly to think otherwise, considering it had taken a two-hour class at the Apple Store just to teach him how to use his smartphone.

The elevator gave another sound, a rusty, rumbling belch from that old, cold shaft. He thought of the circuit breaker and the darkness, of men and their imperfect machines. One power failure was enough for the day. One too many, especially with a whopper of a migraine brewing.

He decided to take the stairs.

SPECIAL NEEDS

IT WAS A BEAUTIFUL day, seventy-three degrees with a slight breeze and the occasional fat cloud drifting across the sun. The kind of day that had made Linda fall in love with Northern California over a decade ago.

She spent the better part of the afternoon pulling dead weeds and grass from the backyard gardens. Most of the roses had some strange form of rose canker that had spread faster than she'd ever seen. To fight it, she bought several bags of compost and some Osmocote and spent the late afternoon on her hands and knees, mixing the two into the soil until her back throbbed and her thoughts drifted to the cigarettes.

Pleased with her work and hopeful it would save the rose garden, she returned to the house to check on Jessica. A half hour earlier, she had sent her off to start on her homework and review her vocabulary. Her teacher, a petite girl hardly in her twenties, had said Jessica was a respectful student who never misbehaved yet hardly ever spoke in class. She asked if Jessica had had any schooling before kindergarten, a question that upset Linda when she thought about all the hours they'd spent reading and preparing during the summer.

Then she dropped the real bomb.

"I hope this doesn't come off the wrong way," she had said in the parking lot, "but has she ever been tested for learning disabilities?"

"What?" Linda laughed, studying that presumptuous young girl, no more than a kid, really. "No, of course not. Why? Do you think..."

"I'm sorry. I shouldn't have thrown that out there so lightly. I was just curious."

"Curious? Should she be tested? Do you think she has—"

"No, no, of course not. She's probably just a little shy, that's all. Forget I said anything, okay?"

"Mm-hmm." Linda nodded, annoyed and already watering that seed of doubt that girl had carelessly planted.

She spent the remainder of the afternoon bouncing between gardening and Googling early childhood learning disabilities, wondering what signs she should be looking for. As Jessica finished her snack and got ready for her afternoon studies, Linda analyzed each of her actions.

"Need some help?" she asked Jessica.

"No thanks, Mommy. If I get stuck, I'll ask you for help, okay?" Jessica answered before clomping off upstairs.

"Good girl," Linda said.

This week her phonics words included consonant-U-consonant-E patterns, words like "tube" and "cube." After a half hour, Linda expected to find Jessica seated at her table upstairs, surrounded by her toys and busy with her spelling practice. Instead, she found a darkened bedroom and her daughter at the window, standing on a chair and drawing on the glass.

"Jessica, be careful, honey!" Linda gasped. "Don't do that!"

Jessica didn't respond, only continued scribbling against the glass, her blue felt-tip marker squeaking.

"Jessica! Listen to me!" Linda shouted.

But she didn't listen, a defiance that made Linda flush with anger. She crossed the room, noticing pages of drawings on the children's table, and knew that not only was Jessica disobeying her now but that she had disobeyed her earlier. She had hardly begun her homework.

"Jessica!" Linda said, hands falling on her daughter's shoulder, yanking the felt marker from her hand. "Honey, why aren't you listening—"

Linda stopped mid-sentence. Jessica stared back at her with glazed eyes as tears ran down her cheeks and pooled on the fabric collar of her dress. Linda went from fury to worry in an instant.

"Oh my god, honey, what's wrong?"

Jessica stared at her mother through empty eyes, no different than a lifeless doll. Linda checked her for signs of injury, running her hands over her daughter's tear-streaked cheeks.

Then, at her mother's touch, a broad smile spread across Jessica's face and she said, "No thanks, Mommy. If I get stuck, I'll ask you for help, okay?"

She hopped down from the chair, dragged it over to the table, pushed the drawings aside, and resumed her workbook lesson. Linda watched, perplexed, as her daughter picked up where she had left off in her phonics work.

"Jessica," Linda asked and picked up the stack of drawings. "Honey? What were you doing?"

"Drawing, silly."

Linda studied the drawings. They were all the same general composition: a dog, a bird, and a woman with black hair, all playing on a hilltop by a tree. Linda understood it at once. She crouched next to her daughter and held the pictures out.

"Sweetie, is this the bird you found at school?"

Jessica nodded without looking at the picture.

"And is this Ginger?"

Jessica nodded again, filling in question five in her workbook.

Linda pointed to the woman with black hair. "Who's this, honey? Is this your teacher?"

Jessica shook her head.

"No? Who is it?"

"That was Daddy's friend," Jessica said with a smile. "Now she's my friend." She then held out her hand and counted, "Rhymes with 'at.' Bat, cat, fat, hat… mat!" She filled in question seven with a smile.

Linda turned back to the window streaked with blue felt lines like half-finished stained glass. A single figure, nothing more than a shadow made of uneasy blue scribbles, stared back at her from the glass.

"I'M WORRIED ABOUT OUR DAUGHTER," LINDA LATER SAID AS DAN LAY ON the ground, legs protruding from the side of the painting in the study. He pushed further behind the canvas, an X-Acto knife in his hand and a small pen light in his mouth. Linda had worries. It seemed like she often did. He learned long ago to tell the difference between when she wanted his opinion and wanted to decompress.

"Would you tilt the light over?" he asked, and she felt a spike of frustration but tilted the light closer to that hideous painting of his.

"Perfect," he said from behind it. He ran his fingers along the inner rim of the painting, feeling the seams along the stretcher's edge.

"Did you hear what I said?"

"Of course," he lied. "What about it?"

"She's acting odd. Daydreaming more than usual."

"Well, what's an appropriate amount of daydreaming for a six-year-old?"

"I don't know. Her teacher thinks..." Linda said, then decided against passing the speculation on, knowing how it had infected her thoughts all afternoon. "I think she's having trouble dealing with Ginger's disappearance."

"Really?" Dan asked to buy more time. He ran his fingers over the nails. They were evenly spaced, holding the canvas to the simple wooden stretcher in precise half-inch gaps that kept it taut. He found a spot in the lower-left corner where one of the nails had come loose. He wedged a screwdriver beneath it and pried it upward. The paint gave a hissing crack as the nail popped free.

"Dan, are you even listening?"

"Of course I'm listening. I just... I don't know what you want me to say, hon. She's six years old. Losing a dog, it's a big hit to take at any age. But it's part of life. And it's been, what, five days? We need to come to terms with the fact that Ginger, you know, might not be coming home."

"So that's it? We should all just move on?"

He shifted onto his side and used his left hand to hold the screwdriver up, freeing his right hand. He began to cut a stamp-sized square from the lower fold of canvas with the X-Acto knife.

"I'm not saying that, honey," he said as the knife caught on a tough thread of canvas like a tendon in meat. He sawed the knife back and forth, clenching his teeth and increasing the pressure.

"So what are you saying? Because, frankly, our daughter's like a stranger at times, and I'm all out of ideas."

"What I'm saying is—"

The X-Acto burst through the thread of canvas with sudden force. Dan felt it arc inward, shaving under flesh from wrist to thumb. He clamped down on the wound instantly as his hand snapped back and burned.

"Fuck!" he shouted, dropping the knife as blood and warmth rushed to his head. An inch-long curl of skin hung from the outside of his left thumb, flopping back all the way to where it met his palm. For a brief second he saw pink muscle beneath the peel before the blood pooled in like a red tide. He clutched the wound, forcing the loose skin back against his thumb. Wetness ran down his fingers and out the bottom of his other hand. It already hurt like hell.

"What's wrong?" Linda asked and gasped when he emerged from behind the painting. His sleeve was already stained crimson. What the fabric didn't absorb dripped off his elbow and onto the hardwood floor. More than the pain, he felt embarrassed and helpless, like a kid.

"Oh my god, honey, that's really bad!" she said, wide-eyed at the sight of so much red.

"No shit," he snapped, storming toward the door. "So where's the fucking Bactine?"

Linda insisted that he go to intensive care to have the wound looked at, but he would hear nothing of it. Two sets of stitches for the same family in less than two weeks was not a precedent he wanted to set. Instead, Dan dressed the wound himself, wincing first at the sight of that flap of skin shifting about on the pool of red, then at the burst of pain as the Bactine coated the raw tissue.

He kept pressure on it for a good twenty minutes before the bleeding finally slowed. The adult bandages were old and stiff, so he settled on two of Jessica's Hello Kitty bandages. Even with the wound cleansed and dressed, he still saw crimson beneath the white and pink bandage and knew that Linda was probably right: he should have gone to intensive care.

He returned to the study with several paper towels and cleaning spray. When he searched the hardwood floor around the painting, he found no traces of blood. Only that piece of cut canvas remained on the floor where it had fallen. Perhaps Linda had cleaned the blood, he thought, although he was certain he had heard her go upstairs. Or perhaps he hadn't dripped any on the floor. He felt it drip, but he hadn't seen it.

He took the piece of cut canvas and dropped it into a small plastic sample bag from the university labs. He labeled it *Anonymous – D. Rineheart,* then turned off the lights in the study. For a brief second, as the darkness took over, he swore he heard a dog bark. When he listened again, only silence answered him.

GATES OF HELL

SHE TOOK THE sample bag, clipped it to the requisition form, tore the barcoded receipt off, and handed it back to him.

"We should have preliminary results in a few days, Professor," Denise said with a smile that hinted at more than just professional courtesy. He only saw her once or twice a semester, when some side project brought him to the museum's lab, and every time her hair was a different color. Today it was a shade of lavender over silver. Karina had never liked her, and Dan realized it was, perhaps, because she, too, recognized a flirt when she saw one.

"Thanks, Denise. Take care," he said and walked out.

"You too," she called out, and he heard her popping her bubble gum and knew she was grinning.

IT WAS A SUNNY AFTERNOON. A SLIGHT BREEZE BLEW THROUGH THE eucalyptus trees that lined the walk from the museum back to the Fine Arts Building. Students sat on the grass of the quad, studying or tossing Frisbees or just enjoying summer's dying grasp into autumn.

He fell in love with the university on a day like today, a decade ago when Dean Robert escorted him and Linda around, stopping at the sculpture garden outside the museum. The offer had been ten grand less than what Chicago had offered for an associate professorship, a significant difference. Yet it was the laughing voices and the warm breeze through the trees that had sold him. He accepted the job on the spot with a handshake as they laughed before Rodin's Gates of Hell. Even today he could still hear the laughing voices and see that sculpture garden from his office window, and he knew that for all the mistakes he had made, that one decision years ago was not one of them.

Back in the office, he spent almost an hour looking up any information he could find on Cobald & Sons but found little other than a dozen dead ends. Then, on a hobbyist forum, he found a reference to a clock manufacturer in Monterey by the same name. His heart jumped when he saw the 831 area code, despite the decade-old copyright at the bottom of the webpage.

The phone rang six times and he was about to hang up when a breathless old voice answered with a cheerful, "Hyello."

When Dan asked if he'd dialed Cobald & Sons, the voice gave an affirmation, correcting his pronunciation. "*Ka-buld*, like a stone road," the voice said.

"Right. I know this sounds odd, but I'm trying to track down any information on a specific model of clock you might have made."

The cheerful voice asked for a model number.

"That's the problem," Dan said. "I have a photograph. Would that help?"

"Perhaps it might," said the cheerful voice.

"Could I fax you a copy?" Dan asked.

The voice laughed back. "Only if you want to buy us a fax machine."

"I guess email's out of the question."

"And you'd have guessed right," the voice answered with a laugh that turned into a cough.

Dan glanced at his watch. "What time do you close?"

THEY CLOSED AT SIX, WHICH GAVE HIM JUST UNDER FOUR HOURS TO DRIVE to Monterey. Plenty of time, he thought, and he could even stop in Gilroy for a burger. The last time he'd passed through had been with his kids on the retreat from their ill-fated Disneyland trip. A trip that included Jessica getting pink eye from the swimming pool and Tommy throwing a tantrum after discovering he'd left his Nintendo charger at home halfway to L.A. The whole drive back, all he had looked forward to was that garlic mushroom burger, most of which ended up in his lap as Linda yelled at him for trying to eat and drive at the same time. "No, he didn't want to kill the family," he answered, but he was quickly changing his mind. They both vowed never to take another road trip until they were driving their kids to college.

He studied the photo printout one last time, fixating on the painted clock and the time its hands were frozen at: 5:55. The number held no special meaning, at least none in the academic world he was familiar with. Yet he felt he should know it, like an old friend's birthday or the lyrics to a pop song he hadn't heard since the eighties. Five fifty-five. It rolled off his tongue, maddening, and the more he thought of those three numbers, the more he looped back to the realization that he was chasing a phantom. He filed it away further down his mental to-do list, then put the photo into his briefcase, took the directions, and shut off his office lights.

The office hallway was dark, unusually so for the afternoon. The air held a chill and lingering dust, perhaps from the repair work two floors up in the Archive. The door handle gave him a static shock as he locked it. Down the hall, the overhead light closest to the Turtle flickered on and off, then died with a faint hum. A second later the elevator doors opened with a ding and a groan.

Then something poured out of the elevator.

Or at least Dan perceived it to have poured out. As the light inside the elevator dimmed, he realized it might have just fallen from the old doors as if it had been leaning against them. There it lay, an androgynous lump on the dark ground at the end of the hallway. Behind it sat a rectangular object, blocking the door. As the elevator doors closed and opened on it, he saw something glimmer in its shape, like brass buttons or metal.

"Hello?" he called, and he noticed another overhead light, closer, flickering on and off in rapid succession. The thing on the floor writhed as if it had been jolted with electricity. Then it did the impossible.

It vanished.

The elevator doors closed with a ding.

And Dan blinked in disbelief, mouthing, "What the fuck?" as his mind rewound what he had just seen.

The elevator doors had opened.

A shape had fallen inward.

And then it had vanished into the floor.

One, two, three, rattled the glass as faint auras sprouted like flowers from the corners of his vision. Another overhead light gave a final hiss and dimmed. In an instant, the shape was rising beneath it, followed by a sucking sound and a low-level ultrasonic pop like a change in air pressure. The shape didn't so much as reappear but unfold from the dark floor the moment the light faded, as if the two points of darkness were connected by some subterranean tunnel.

Four, five, six, clacked the glass as the writhing shape crawled out of the ground inside the darkness.

A grinding sound came from the shadow. Metal clattered against linoleum flooring as something heavy scraped across the floor in slow, clumsy movements. At the edge of the darkness, a lurching, humanoid shape drew closer to the light. Dan squinted, and for a second he could see the frame of a small boy, sunken pinhole eyes and a cruel sneer, pulling a rattling object behind him.

Another overhead light flickered on and off two doors down from Dan's office. That lumbering shape unfolded in that new pocket of shadow. Another wet slurp and a pop in his ears followed the jump from shadow to shadow as the shape grew closer.

Seven, eight, nine, said the glass inside his head, drowned out by a rattling noise, a loose lock against metal.

Another hum as a filament in the hallway light burned bright and then faded, first to a small orange ember, then to darkness. The shape unfolded a third time, spanning the gap between the lights with a wet smack. Something wretched filled his nose, like that of a corpse or the stench that came off Linda's father in the moments after he sputtered forth his final incoherent words—"open the door"—and then expired.

A single light remained between him and the lumbering thing, that child-sized shape dragging the clattering, abstract block, and he saw something wet and glistening connecting them.

Ten, eleven, twelve, said the glass, and Dan realized he was counting the number of steps the child-thing took. The moment this epiphany struck him, the child-thing paused, its hidden, slouching form quivering and growing erect. It extended its right arm to point at Dan from the shadow.

A noise filled the hallway, growing like a midnight train, and Dan recognized it. It was the rattling sound of the dying, the final breath as life left the lips of the dead. He had heard it when Linda's father died. He had been the only one there to hear it when that old salesman gave up the ghost. Yet Dan didn't believe in the supernatural, nor did he put any stock in the final words of a cancer-stricken old man who had lied for half his life to his family. There were explanations behind everything, even the apparition that now moved toward him.

And until that sound, that rattle, he hadn't felt scared, only confused by the image that his mind was unable to perceive or understand. It was as if he were numbly watching a contortionist or a magician perform a trick. The rattling sound, it sharpened his senses, and at once a panic, not unlike what he'd felt on that ill-fated dinner with the kids, seized his body and sobered his thoughts.

Run, he thought.

Where? Doesn't matter. Run and hide.

The light outside his door blinked above him, and the death rattle grew louder.

Run and hide and never ever look back.

Ready or not, said Mr. Glass.

He crashed into his office, slammed the door behind him, and locked it. Outside, through the open window, he saw daylight, a shocking contrast to the dim hallway where that thing had crawled between shadows. He closed his eyes and counted backward. *Ten, nine, eight.*

Rewinding the events of the last minute, he found there was a sharp divide between them, not unlike the curtain between fading dreams and waking realities. And his dreams had always been dark for as long as he could remember.

Seven, six, five.

Had this been a waking dream? Had he been daydreaming, no different than Jessica or even himself when he spent all those years staring out a window over the midwestern plains? A scared little kid, listening to his brother's ghost stories, then taking them to bed with him, where the demons and monsters lurked, waiting just beyond the light? There was nothing to be afraid of, he had thought once and now found himself thinking again. The light of dawn always came, revealing those monsters to be lies, revenants conjured by his mind, banished back to imagination.

Four, three, two.

Yes, there had been nothing in the hallway, only a brief power outage and the residual effects of the panic attack from the other night. That was it, he thought. Things did not crawl forth and warp from shadow to shadow. And painted boys did not stalk him. To think otherwise was…

What? Mr. Glass asked. *To think otherwise was what?*

"One," Dan said aloud.

He listened to the silence. A breeze wafted through the window and he could smell a faint trace of marijuana in it. Some of the fine arts students were probably outside in the cloisters below, smoking a fatty before Professor Schoeder's lecture on surrealism. And if there were students downstairs, then whatever had fallen out of the elevator must have passed them earlier. Yet instead of screams, he heard only hushed laughter.

He exhaled and shook his head in private embarrassment. *Keep calm and carry on,* he thought.

Then the whole door buckled and rocked. His heart leaped into his throat as his hand curled in on itself. He tasted an earthy odor, rancid and vile, that stuck to the roof of his mouth like bad medicine. He wanted to spit but he couldn't. The door shook against his back, and the doorknob rotated.

The thing was there, pushing its way in, and in his fear, Dan did the only thing he could think of. He grabbed the absurd Thinker bookend, a gift some forgotten undergrad advisee had given him a few years back, and gripped it by its head. He cocked the weapon back, ready to swing it in a wild arc at whatever was coming through as the door opened.

A wrinkled face peered in with a smile and asked, "Dan, are you in?"

Dean Robert didn't quite know what to make of the sight of his colleague, pale, wide-eyed and perspiring, primed and ready to crush his skull with a Rodin. He had only caught the image from the corner of his eye, and by the time he gasped, Dan took a step back and lowered the bookend.

"My god," the old man exclaimed. "You scared me half to death. Are you all right?"

Dan fumbled with the sculpture, let out an awkward, delirious laugh, and shook his head. "I was cleaning. You startled me," Dan answered, and Dean Robert blinked as if the excuse was both absurd and insulting.

"You… Never mind. I'm not sure I want to know."

"Sorry, Bob," Dan said, feeling the need to add something.

Dean Robert decided to let it pass, not because he believed Dan's excuse but because he simply had no idea how to press the matter further without embarrassing him. And besides, he wasn't alone.

"Dan, there are some gentlemen here to see you," he said, opening the door.

A SMALL DELAY

HE DIDN'T LIKE the detectives from the moment they stepped into his office. Not because they were impolite or rude, as television shows had conditioned him to expect, but because they were an obstacle between him and his business that afternoon in Monterey. The longer they stayed, the worse traffic would be on the southbound 101.

When they identified themselves as detectives, he assumed they wanted to interview him about the fire and he could brush them off with a quick statement and reschedule for a better time. Then they dropped the bomb and he had to sit behind his desk as the piece of glass slid through his gray matter.

"No one has seen her in five days," said Detective Barton, who sat in the chair opposite Dan's desk. Dan placed him a few years younger than himself due to the smooth face beneath thin stubble that gave him the look of a man trying to appear older. He spoke in an effeminate voice and rarely made eye contact, instead keeping his gaze locked on his leather-bound notepad.

"Now, traditionally, we wait a little longer on missing person reports, but the, uh, circumstances in this case—"

"These particular circumstances warranted our prompt attention," said the other man in a Southern drawl, who had identified himself as Detective Cooper. He was taller, pushing six feet, with a stocky frame and gray complexion that made Dan think of those vets that came back from wars, packed on the pounds, but kept the attitude of a soldier. Dan couldn't place his age other than to guess somewhere between his late forties to early sixties.

"I don't understand. What circumstance?" Dan asked.

"We can't elaborate," Cooper said and turned his attention back to the bookshelf.

Dan felt a tremendous dislike for him, in particular the way he nosed about the office, picking up each object as if it were evidence in some crime.

"Well, what can I do to help?" Dan asked.

Cooper smirked at the answer. Barton clicked his pen several times. "When was the last time you were in contact with Ms. Calloway?"

Dan felt his hand shake at the sound of the pen and her name. He clenched his fist.

"Karina?" he asked. Of course Karina. They could have referred to her by her middle name, Francis, or KFC, the nickname she said kids called her in middle school, and he would've known who they were talking about. He just needed them to think he didn't know these things.

"Karina, yes," Barton answered.

"Last time I spoke to her…" Dan said, clicking his tongue. "That would have to have been Friday, around ten in the morning."

Detective Barton didn't write anything. Instead, he flipped back to another page as if confirming something, his eyes never meeting Dan's. Dean Robert shifted on the couch, and Dan could see his forehead wrinkle as he tried to read the detective's notepad.

"What was the nature of the conversation?" Barton asked.

Dan laughed. "Should I have my lawyer present?"

Cold stares from the detectives. "Should you?" asked Cooper.

"It was a joke," Dan said. "Forget it."

"Your conversation on Friday," Barton reminded him.

"Right. We talked about the usual stuff: her project, what she was going to do for her thesis. I'm her advisor, and I had some ideas I wanted to go over. Before the fire she was restoring a Verduchi," Dan said, realizing they probably had no idea what that was, so he added, "That's a painting—"

"I know that," Cooper said, thumbing through a book on contemporary Iranian art.

"So you didn't see her that day?" asked Barton.

"See her? No. We had an appointment that afternoon, but I had to cancel."

Barton jotted something down on the pad and, as if sensing Dean Robert's wandering eyes, shifted his body so the pad sat in his lap, obscured. "Why is that?" he asked. "Why'd you cancel?"

"Family emergency," Dan answered. "Our dog went missing."

"Sorry to hear that," said Barton.

"Were you fucking her?" Cooper said without looking up from the book. Dean Robert and Dan exchanged a stunned glance, but Barton continued to stare at Dan and click his pen as if nothing unusual had been asked.

"Excuse me?" Dan asked.

"Were you... fucking her?" Cooper asked again in that slow Southern drawl, as if speaking to someone hard of hearing.

"What kind of question is that?" Dan snapped back.

Cooper returned the art book to the shelf as a look of contemplation passed over his face. "I suppose it's a simple question, really. Yes-or-no kind. Ain't illegal, least not in this state."

"Bob," Dan said, turning to his old friend. "I don't have to listen to this."

"Gentlemen," Dean Robert cut in. "Please."

Barton waved his hand, perhaps dismissing the other detective and his tactics for the time being. Cooper just shrugged as Barton continued. "Her neighbors called in a noise complaint, said the TV had been on for days. Officers investigated and found the apartment in a state of disarray. They found an overnight bag, clothes, reservation for a hotel in Napa."

"Well, there you go," Dan said. The two detectives glanced at each other, and Dan felt his hand shake. "I don't understand. What's the problem?"

"She never checked in," Barton said.

"Well, where'd she go?" Dan asked.

Barton's head lowered again as he flipped to another page in the notepad and continued. "Would it surprise you if I told you her car was found parked around the corner from your house?"

"Absolutely. Of course it would," Dan said, regretting how quickly he answered the question. "Well, was it?"

Again, the notepad and no answer. He was starting to sense a pattern, some sort of verbal guerrilla warfare. Attack and retreat.

"Her phone records indicate that she placed several calls to you last week. Seventeen texts on Thursday alone. Don't you think that's a little unusual?"

For most people, sure. Mr. Glass laughed. *But Karina, about par for the course.*

"You have to understand, some of our students spend upwards of two years working on their projects. Hell, we just had that fire. She was devastated. Bob, you remember her reaction?"

Dean Robert gave a weak nod, not one of support but of resignation. He knew that old man's trust in him had taken a heavy blow this afternoon.

"We're aware of the fire," Barton said and folded the notepad over. "In fact, her prints were found at the scene of the fire."

"Of course they were. She's one of my students."

"Her prints were also found at your house."

Dan put on his best look of disbelief. "What?"

"Last Friday you reported a break-in. Officers found two distinct sets of prints. Hers, and another we've yet to identify. They were small, a kid's print, but they weren't found at her apartment, so I have to ask, have you ever brought your children to work?"

"No," Dan answered. "No, never."

"I don't understand," Dean Robert cut in. "You gentlemen, you think Ms. Calloway might have set the fire? And broke into Dan's house? Why?"

"We were hoping he could fill that in for us," Cooper said.

"I..." Dan stuttered and laughed. "I have no idea. She hasn't been to class all week."

Barton took that down in his notepad. "We ran her passport number to see if she might've gone abroad. She hasn't, but it turns out the Italians have her flagged on Interpol. An assault charge from July. Claim is, she got into a scrap with another student, sent him to the hospital, if you can believe it."

Dan could believe it indeed.

"Only reason she wasn't detained is she pressed rape charges, which have since been thrown out."

"Jesus," Dan said under his breath.

"We also checked the hospitals. No sign of her presently, but we did come across something from March 21st. She was admitted on a 5150—a seventy-two-hour psychiatric hold—with lacerations to her wrists. I don't need to tell you who signed her in, do I?"

"No, you don't," Dan mumbled. He remembered signing the form like it was yesterday, but it couldn't have felt further away. As his pen scrawled his name, he had wondered if the whole thing wouldn't come back to haunt him.

The glass laughed. *Your birds, Professor. Seems they're coming home.*

"So, Professor," said Cooper. "You still maintain that your relationship with Ms. Calloway was, how should I say, purely academic?"

"Absolutely," Dan said with a nod. "Absolutely."

"And in light of these coincidences..." A smile crossed Cooper's face. "You're certain you don't know where she could be?"

"No," Dan said. "I mean, gentlemen, if I had any idea, I would have told you."

"Well," said Barton, closing his notepad. "As they say, if you think of anything..." He handed Dan a business card. His name and phone number sat beneath a gold badge and an embossed title: *Investigator.*

"Anything at all, I should call, right?" Dan asked as he took the card.

Barton's eyes hung on the Hello Kitty bandages adorning Dan's left hand. His eyes narrowed, if only for a second. Then he nodded and hiked up his belt. "Yes, please do," he said.

Cooper stood, staring at a framed painting next to Dan's framed degrees. "That a real Heimdell?" he asked.

"Sure is," Dan answered, and Cooper nodded at the answer as if it had passed some internal sniff test. Dan felt his distaste for that man grow. He was testing Dan, both showing off his own keen eye for obscure art and belittling Dan's exclusive knowledge, as if the job was something any hobbyist could do. When they left, Dan could hear them talking and laughing in a low murmur from the hallway, like a pair of students that had stifled giggles for the last twenty minutes.

"Dan," said Dean Robert, "I think we should have a long talk about Ms. Calloway."

CREATIVE TYPES

"UN-FUCKING-BELIEVABLE!" he said for the third time in as many minutes as he pounded his fist on the steering wheel. The horn gave a reflexive honk that made the woman in the hybrid in front of him glare into her rearview mirror.

He had meant to avoid rush hour and had instead wound up in the middle of it. Without traffic, it was an hour and a half at best to Monterey. But today, like most, the traffic stretched for miles on the 101, past the houses and mansions of Alder Glen, almost to the gates of the university itself. It had taken him the better part of an hour to drive fifteen miles to the San Jose airport exit, where the stop-and-go traffic had finally stopped altogether.

Dan rewound the day's conversation in his head. The detectives knew about the affair; that much was obvious. If Karina really had disappeared or, worse, finally made good on her promise to "end it," as she often said, he would become what was referred to on TV shows as a "person of interest." And on TV shows, people of interest ended up having their whole lives dissected in front of their families. Business trips revealed to be trysts, secret bank accounts exposed, reputations ruined. And the paper, that local rag, would love nothing more than to take another whack at the university. It could be Scandal of the Year for a fourth one straight. Buy three, get one free.

The phone call with Nathaniel that followed that grilling had been equally as lousy. At first he swore at Dan in Italian simply for waking him up. Then he confirmed everything the detectives said and more. His complaints about Karina read like a bad reference letter. Her work was shoddy at best. She was unprepared and often late. She didn't get along with the rest of the team and she made inappropriate passes at Nathaniel, a married man. By mid-July she had deteriorated to the point of open instability. The other students grew worried and Nathaniel was swamped with complaints.

He heard that she had become obsessed with a student from Salerno. They had some sort of violent altercation when the student's girlfriend visited on a Friday. The police were called, reports were filed, and Nathaniel was forced to get involved. He gave her a week off, a grave mistake, he said in hindsight. She never showed up the following Monday. Instead, she disappeared, but not without a final dramatic exit.

"Nathaniel didn't tell you?" Dan remembered her saying back in his office almost two weeks ago.

"The piece was ruined. Four hundred and twenty-two years of history, gone. She even left the muriatic acid at the scene. Can you believe that? Of course, it's still 'speculation' to the *polizia*, but to me, Daniel, to me, there's no other explanation. She destroyed it out of spite, pure and simple. Now go ahead and tell me this was your best student, Daniel. I want to hear it. Tell me you didn't know she was a liability."

He told Nathaniel he was sorry. That it was all a misunderstanding and he had no reason to suspect his sponsored student would turn out to be such a grade-A fustercluck. He did what the little piece of glass said he did best: he lied.

And by the time Nathaniel hung up, he believed it because, well, why wouldn't he? Why would Dan have sent him a student primed for a nervous breakdown? Artists were, of course, always a bit strange, something Nathaniel agreed with. And this strangeness seeped over to the people who worked with art as well. It came with the trade. The poets and the musicians, of course, they were truly in the deep end, but there was oddity among those who spent hours staring at paintings. A creative tax that made them less likely to be at the center of a conversation than on the edge of it, smiling and nodding and taking an extra-long gulp of the champagne. But in regard to her professional ability, he had, of course, no reason to suspect that Karina would have done anything less than a flawless job. That was why he fought for her spot, he told Nathaniel. Because he believed in her, believed she held more talent than he ever would. And that was his job: spot the talent, nurture it, and let it go. Then, like any teacher, hope that she struck gold and made a name for herself. Maybe he had, somehow, missed the mark on this one. Bet on the wrong horse. The signs were all there, but maybe there was something else, an unseen variable that had festered and, triggered by stress, sprung out to everyone's surprise.

Yes, there was no way to predict such a thing, and he was sorry that it happened, but people were hard to read. Like the paintings they worked with, the whole story was often hidden.

They were, after all, unpredictable people.

MONTEREY

THE CLOCK STORE was a relic of the past, a craftsman's shop that he guessed saw no more than a handful of customers a month. A single sign above the dusty counter proclaimed in gilded letters, *Veritum Dies Asperit*. And beneath it: *Time Discovers the Truth*.

The counter was unmanned, probably had been for the majority of the day. Even the cash register was old-fashioned: an engraved metal box carved with vines and flowers that danced up it in columns. He guessed it had seen at least both world wars and, like the clocks lining the walls, required tender care to keep in working order. A bell sat beside it. He tapped it twice and it gave a cheerful ding in response. Somewhere from a back office beyond the counter, he heard movement and the sound of metal scraping.

"Gimme a moment," a scratchy voice called out.

"Take your time," Dan replied.

He paced around the store, taking in the merchandise. The clocks echoed throughout the old store, pendulums swinging like a dozen dead men from the gallows. Some towered almost to the ceiling itself. Others, shorter, hung on walls and sat on dusty mantels, all clicking away in perfect unison.

All except one.

He paused before a redwood mantle clock and squinted. At the top sat that familiar logo he'd seen in the photo: a dog leaping through the air after a bird in flight. Below that, the hands were stuck at 5:55. Odd, he thought. With all the clocks in perfect synch down to the very swing of the pendulum, that one would have fallen out of synch moments ago, perhaps around the time he stepped into the store.

He reached out, hands drawn to the knob on the side, wanting to turn it and correct this oversight when the clock suddenly clattered. The hands spun, clicking up five minutes in five rapid movements that made him take a step back. For a brief second he thought he'd broken the clock.

Then a stamp-sized door sprung open and the metal logo, that bird and the dog, split into two equal pieces. A thimble-sized bird popped out and bobbed its head up and down. The clock chimed off six cuckoos, joined by the sound of all the other clocks gonging, chiming, and clattering like a wooden choir. After six nods of the head, the bird disappeared back into the door as silence fell over the room.

"Never did like that one," said an old man in a wheelchair, emerging from the back office and eyeing Dan through thick spectacles. His face was unshaven, not out of style but of age and laziness. His hair was little more than a few white cotton balls on the side of a liver-spotted head. He struck Dan as appearing almost cartoonish, as if he should be in some hand-drawn apothecary, drying herbs and distilling slimy parts of fungi.

"Always thought they were silly," he said, pointing at the clock. "Little doors with those odd birds bouncing out every hour like sugared-up retards. But families love 'em, so we made 'em. Customer's king, after all. S'what can I do for you, son?"

"We spoke on the phone earlier about a—"

"Ah, I remember now," he cut in with a smile that seemed to stretch every wrinkle in an opposite direction. "Fella with the photo and fax machines."

"Yes," Dan said, withdrawing the very photo from his case.

"Lemme take a look at her," the clockmaker said, switching one pair of glasses for a thinner pair. Dan handed him the photo and noticed the old man was missing half of his right ring finger.

The old clockmaker held the photo, scowling at it, perhaps locked in some personal battle with his own memory. His tongue clicked as his face kept that same frustrated expression for almost a minute. Then he smiled, placed the photo on the counter, and slid it back toward Dan with a hooked finger.

"This is a painting," he said.

"Is that a problem?"

"Most folks bring a photo or a photocopy. Some even bring the whole dang clock. First time anyone's ever brought me a painting of a clock. Or a photo of a painting of a clock, I suppose."

"It's an unusual situation."

"Ain't it always? Still, I know this clock."

"You do?"

"Sure enough. That's why you're here, ain't it?"

"What can you tell me about it?"

"Well, see the sloped crown at the top? This curved ridge on the corners?" The clockmaker pointed to the top of the grandfather clock, where it rose like a double mountain adorned with twin castles in the center. "My father made this. Forty-eight or forty-nine, most likely."

"You can tell that from a picture?"

The clockmaker raised an eyebrow as if Dan were asking him to perform basic arithmetic. "Sign on the door reads Cobald & Sons. Now, my father was the son in that name, which makes me a third-generation clockmaker. My memory's fickle but my hands are steady. They remember every clock out that door, 'cluding this one." He slapped a hand on his useless legs. "I was standing when I helped him make that style of crown. Then I went to Korea. I didn't stand so much after that, nor did I do these crowns."

"I didn't mean to offend you," Dan said.

"Facts don't offend, so none taken. Take a peek at the face, will you?"

Dan studied the face of the clock. That dog leaping through the air after the bird, those hands stuck at 5:55.

"Anything seem askew to you?" the old man asked.

"It's missing three numbers. Nine, ten, and eleven."

"Sure, but that ain't all it's missing. What else?"

Dan shook his head. "I don't know."

"Take a look behind you, 'round the room."

Dan turned his attention from the picture to the clocks surrounding the small shop, all their pendulums and machinery clattering away in the last light of day. Relics, really. And then he saw it.

"The numbers—"

"Bingo," said the old clockmaker with a pop of the mouth. "That painting of yours, they're numbers on the face, most of 'em at least. We only use Roman numerals. Always have."

He was right. Those clacking and chiming relics around the room were all emblazoned with Roman numerals across their faces. But the clock in the picture was marked with numbers, except one. The five o'clock mark was a simple V, and Dan felt a spike of stupidity for not noticing this discrepancy. Clocks were not his specialty, but art was, and there had sat such an obvious yet overlooked clue that he wondered if he wasn't losing his touch.

"So they changed it? Why would they do that?"

"Who knows? Maybe they drew it from memory," said the old clockmaker.

Dan told him about the painting, filling him in on key details, trying to read him for any signs of recognition, but aside from the clock, there was no familiarity on his face. The old man shrugged with indifference that some anonymous artist had chosen his clock to occupy a part of a painting no different than someone might care that a Coke can turned up in the background of a sports photo.

"As to why it ended up in that painting of yours, I haven't the foggiest," he said. "Same for why they changed all the numbers but the five. What I can tell you is this: almost every clock we did back then were custom orders, this being one of them. Gimme a minute an' I'll find out who bought it."

"Take your time," Dan said.

The old clockmaker laughed as he turned around and opened the cabinets behind the counter. "We don't take time, son. Time takes us."

His old fingers ran across dozens of ledger books with a precision honed over decades and more accurate than a laser. The more Dan watched this old man, the more he respected him, and even though their careers were different, he recognized a true artist when he saw one. He hoped there would be another to take his place, another son to tack onto the sign and keep the craft alive, but he suspected it was a hopeless wish. His son, if he had one, was probably off foreclosing on a house or running some dot com, wondering whether to put Pops in a rest home before selling the silly business.

"There she is," said the clockmaker as he blew dust off the ledger. The spine gave a crack as it opened. Each turn of the yellow pages seemed to strain the book to the point of breaking.

"Here we go," he said, putting his glasses back on. "Spring of forty-nine, right on the money."

"Who owns it?" Dan asked.

"Can't say who owns it now. Could be halfway to Tibet. But says here it was bought by a Mr. and Mrs. O'Donnel. Route 71, outside Crawford, Nebraska." He closed the ledger. "Might want to start there."

Dan felt his fingers begin to rattle. "No," he said. "No one's there anymore."

ECHOES

THE SUN LAY just beyond the Pacific, an afterglow behind a vague fog wall, drenching the oceanside highway in a lazy amber light. Pines and redwoods cast long shadows that reached across the highway like the fingers of a banshee. Night was coming, and Dan turned his headlights on as the car hugged yet another turn on the drive home. He rolled down the window, the ocean air sobering and sharpening his thoughts.

He hadn't thought about that clock in thirty years. On that day, the sun had seemed almost like it did now. Long shadows and lazy light, and how it all fell through the loose holes and slats in the old house as his brother looked for the hidden passage into the storm cellar.

There had been dust and drawers and an old calendar that read *Firestone 1952*.

And there had been the old clock and the startled bird that flew from it.

"Zip it, you idiot!" David had shouted when Daniel gasped at that bird.

"Sorry," Daniel said as his eyes rose to the old clock hands, but they were at 4:47.

He wasn't even certain there had ever been a clock in that old house, but when he focused on his thoughts, he was unable to ignore it. It was as if the clock had been drawn onto his memory by some invisible artist repainting his past. Superimposed, like a bad effect added to a DVD on its twenty-fifth anniversary.

"WAKE UP, LITTLE BRO," DAVID WHISPERED AS HE STOOD OVER THE bottom bunk. The room was dark and the children were sleeping in their bunk beds while the moon watched over them all through the wide windows of the second-floor dorm.

"Hey." He nudged the shape in the bottom bunk again and clicked on his survival flashlight. "Wake up."

The shape moved in the darkness until David saw the pale face of his younger brother, eyes blinking as he yawned. "What time is it?" Daniel asked.

"Late. I brought you something," he whispered, and he reached beneath the bed as Daniel stared back with a bewildered expression. "Here, take a look."

David pulled out a worn old art book. The cover had come off in small patches, but the author was still clear: Max Ernst. Daniel looked at his brother with apprehension, unsure if there was some hidden trick to it, like a dog fed by the same hand that beat it. Then Daniel smiled and took the book, and David winced when he saw the bandages covering his younger brother's fingers.

"I thought you luh-law-lost it?" Daniel said, opening the heavy volume.

"I lied," said David with a sigh. "I hid it from you."

Daniel's eyes drifted back to his older brother, and David could see the wrinkles that always formed on Daniel's forehead when he thought of something sad.

"I'm sorry," David said again.

"Go to bed, schitzo," said a voice from the far end of the room.

David snapped his head in that direction like a snake ready to strike.

"Who fucking said that?" he demanded, his loud voice cutting through the silence. A challenge hinting at violence, as his voice often did these days. A few bodies stirred, perhaps waking up, perhaps trying to fall asleep, or perhaps just trying to ignore another one of his confrontations.

"Don't worry," said Daniel, closing the book. "I'll look at it tomorrow. It's okay."

David nodded but didn't move. He wanted to say something but instead just gave a deep wheeze and scowled. He wanted to say so much, but it never came out. Somewhere between his brain and his mouth, his words tangled up, and he lacked the wit to unwind them. Instead, they slid back down his throat and sat in his stomach, heavy with regret.

"Thanks, big bro," said Daniel, and he reached out and turned off the light in David's hand before rolling over and closing his eyes. "Go to sleep," he said with a yawn.

And if Daniel had been awake, he would have seen David wipe tears from his eyes and say, "I'm sorry."

But he didn't.

THE FOG PARTED AND THE HEADLIGHTS TRACED THE BROWN AND WHITE form of the deer rushing at the car. Instinct took over, and Dan slammed on the brakes, twisting the wheel to the left. The median rattled beneath the wheels, and he smelled the stench of rubber as the car came to a stop halfway between the oncoming lanes.

He glanced back through the passenger window and saw the deer standing there, proud and unmoving, as if it'd just won a game of chicken. It held something in its mouth, a shape, like a brown lunch bag or a small animal. Thick strands of dark liquid dripped from it. What he had thought were white spots on its fur he now saw to be scabby mange. He slammed his fist on the horn, holding it on the second honk until the sick deer trotted away, off the road and into the foggy hills.

LINDA HUNG UP THE TELEPHONE AND RUBBED HER EAR, STILL WARM AND ringing from the hour-long conversation. Her mother had called to discuss her aunt's thyroid cancer and the latest results, which were the same as the previous results and the ones before that. It was, as the doctor had said and her mother repeated, like a cat sleeping on a fence: it could fall either way or it could stay where it was.

Her mother's drinking, however, had fallen off that fence headfirst and came through the phone line in a slurred voice and the occasional giggle. The combination of antidepressants, anti-anxiety medications, downers, and diet pills she took daily to keep her perky and functioning numbered over a dozen when Linda had last checked. On top of that, the wine, which she often got into by the afternoon these days, had the effect of turning her into an intelligent zombie, a friendly husk that mashed her words together and always steered the conversation back to the latest family gossip. Linda dreaded another Thanksgiving, her mother spilling chardonnay from a glass held in a limp hand as the kids asked why Grandma talked funny.

It made her sad to see her mother reduced to little more than the mumbling dead. Her mother who had raised her while her father was off at conventions and having affairs, who went back to get her MBA at fifty, whom Linda had modeled her own idea of family upon. It made her mad that her father had smoked and drank his way to an early grave, leaving his wife alone in a house far too large for her needs when she was far too stubborn to leave it.

"She could move in with us," Dan had said after the cleaning crew found her mother halfway beneath the coffee table with a fractured hip and a broken brandy glass. "Maybe a little sun will do her good."

It had been an idea Linda had never considered and an idea her mother rejected. "A silly idea, Linda, truly. I just don't have time for such things," she had answered, and Linda wanted to ask her if falling down the hardwood staircase in a barbiturate haze was on her schedule, but she bit her tongue.

Yes, her father had died and Linda realized that her mother was, in her own way, following him faithfully into destruction, same as she'd done during all his lies and secrecy.

Linda opened the junk drawer, reached deep in, and felt the pack.

Tommy was on the couch in the living room, playing Nintendo, and Jessica was upstairs. If she was quick, she could step out onto the back porch and smoke before they noticed. Five minutes alone to clear her mind, that was all she wanted. She thought she deserved that.

Then she heard a whimper.

It seemed to come from all around. She recoiled her hand from the drawer on instinct, thinking perhaps a mouse had made its way in there. Then the sound came again, low and faint, in three quick bursts like Morse code in an old newsreel.

It was a dog, whimpering. "Ginger?" she asked.

It had come from the hallway. No, it had come through the hallway, like a vapor bending and twisting in a current of air.

It had come, she realized, from Dan's study.

The air inside was cold, and as she turned on the lights, she looked for an open window but found none. She had heard it again, moments ago, a faint whimpering behind the door to the study. She opened it quickly, ignoring the shock of static electricity, and she half expected to see Ginger sitting there in the study, wagging her tail.

Instead, the darkness greeted her, cold and enveloping, and she felt a tremendous sadness. She thought of her father on that hospital bed, damp with sweat, talking to no one and shouting for someone to close the door. And her mother, in that massive house that her only child had grown up in and left behind, asleep on the couch while some late-night talk show gave way to infomercials and, eventually, static.

"Ginger?" Linda called again, looking around the room for a shape of any sort. The painting loomed, and she remembered how Ginger had scratched at the door when Dan was off at work, trying to get inside. Maybe Ginger was behind the painting, she thought and crossed the room toward it.

She had never liked that painting. Those two children, born from a dark mind, standing and staring. Yet she felt drawn to them, and she squinted and studied their bodies. The girl in the yellow dress was holding a naked plastic doll with a pair of blue bird wings affixed to its headless torso. All across the tan plastic of the doll's body were small, colorful tattoos of waves and blossoms and dragons, stenciled on like a painted egg.

She shuddered, sickened to be sharing the house with even a remnant of a mind that could create such a thing. It seemed to stare back at her like a murderer behind bars, restrained yet thinking only of violence. She wanted it out of the house tonight. Now. Yet she knew how important it was to Dan, so she would tolerate it, just as she had tolerated his many eccentricities: his nightmares, his nervous tics, and that stutter that came out once or twice a year when he was frustrated. And that night at Chuck E. Cheese and how he had screamed louder than the roar of the music and games.

She heard another whimper, one that came from everywhere, even inside of her. She thought of phantom limbs and how amputees felt pain in fingers and arms they'd lost long ago. Could owners hear the phantom sounds of runaway pets?

She walked around the painting, hoping to peer behind it and see the form of their dog. Yes, if she only had one wish, then it would be for Ginger to return, happy, perhaps a little filthy from a weeklong adventure beyond the fence. Little miracles did happen, she told herself as the sound of that whimper faded. Wishes were granted, dogs returned home, and children smiled again at the sound of their mother's voice. These little miracles weren't too much to wish for.

She peered behind the painting, into the shadow it made as it leaned against the wall, but there was nothing. No dog, no sound, and no little miracle. Only emptiness and a lingering doubt that she'd heard anything at all. Sadness grew in her as she realized Ginger and all the happiness she had brought was now gone, perhaps forever. A void in the house, an empty dog bed and a water bowl sitting beside it, both waiting to be filled.

What had Dan said? "We need to come to terms with the fact that she's not coming back."

Yes, Linda thought, she did need to come to terms with this. That the dog—like her father and perhaps soon her mother, too—was among the departing or departed. She needed to come to terms with the fact that only she remained to mourn their void.

A small hand wrapped around her wrist and tugged. She didn't so much as scream but let out a frightened chirp, like a smoke detector on its last battery. Jessica pulled on her wrist again, and Linda felt fury. "Honey, don't sneak up on me!" she scolded.

Jessica gave a numb nod in return. Her eyes were focused not at the painting but through it, as if her real target lay a mile away. Then she blinked as if coming out of a deep thought, the same way she'd blinked upstairs when she had been doodling instead of studying. "Sorry, Mommy," she said. "But this room is for Daddy."

"I know, honey. I'm…" Linda hesitated; the faint suspicion that she might've heard Ginger whimpering now sounded absurd in her own mind. "I was cleaning," she said instead.

"That's okay, Mommy," Jessica said, and for some reason, Linda felt her daughter knew she was lying.

"Homework help?" Jessica asked, and her eyes rose to meet her mother's. They were the eyes of a smiling child.

"Of course, honey," Linda answered and led her daughter out of the study.

MR. BUN

SUMMER'S LONG REACH into September finally grew weak, and for the first time since spring, Linda had to wear her flannel gardening jacket to fend off the chill in the breeze. The wind picked up last night, not long after Dan came home, and howled well into the morning. They awoke to find leaves scattered about the yard and an overturned umbrella by the old hot tub.

The front yard had fared even worse. Dan left the gate open last night, and by morning leaves were scattered around the lawn and driveway. Across the street, a fallen oak branch left a wide gash across the mansard of the Salazars' absurd McMansion. As he swept the leaves from the driveway, Dan felt a surge of satisfaction watching the Salazars shake their heads in dismay as the offending branch was dismembered and loaded into a tree shredder.

By noon the leaves sat in a large pile in the driveway, and Dan retired to the study, coffee in hand, to read over proposals his students had submitted for their revised fall projects. Jessica stopped by the office, standing at the threshold and staring at the painting, and when he asked her what she was doing, she told him she was looking for Mr. Bun.

"Have you tried the laundry hamper?" he asked.

She shook her head and meandered off to the den, where Tommy and Sam were playing their Nintendos and eating popcorn. When she asked if they had seen her stuffed toy, Tommy threw a piece of popcorn and called her a nasty name. Sam laughed, and she left the room.

Last night she felt something during the windstorm. Something cold had tugged at her feet beneath the sheets and clicked its tongue, and she had clutched her rabbit and told it to go away and counted to 150, and then it was gone.

When she awoke, Mr. Bun was by her pillow, but after she ate breakfast and brushed her teeth fifty times top and bottom with her favorite Barbie Burstin' Bubblegum toothpaste, she saw Mr. Bun was gone and was replaced by a single dried leaf on her pillow. It was a deciduous leaf, which meant it fell off the tree about every three-quarters of the year, but she didn't know how to spell it so she couldn't look it up in the encyclopedia.

She opened the back door and looked out into the backyard for the old rabbit but only saw Mommy cutting pieces off those sharp bushes. Mommy had told her to finish her homework. It was important that she didn't "fall behind" the other students, which, she knew, meant she was "not smart" and had to work extra hard. If Mommy saw her playing, she would get mad and speak in the Slow Voice while she helped her finish the pages. She hated the Slow Voice because Mommy only used it for her, and it meant the words would be small and easy to understand and not big words like "hippopotamus" and "investigation." The Slow Voice was for stupid girls, and she wasn't stupid. No, she was special and smart and she had found the door and opened it before anyone else. That was why she had magic friends who lived in the dark.

Maybe they had taken Mr. Bun.

Yes, that was it. It was a game and they wanted to play with her. They were always playing games, counting to fifty and running between the walls right before dawn. They didn't need to sleep, but she did.

Jessica giggled and ran back into the house. Later, Linda would recall through tears that she thought she had heard Jessica at the doorway, talking to herself, but when Linda turned around, the door to the house was open and empty.

Everything clicked into place when Jessica saw the pile of leaves in the driveway. They were piled next to Daddy's car, half as high as she stood. They were maple leaves, which were also deciduous and the same shape as the leaf on her bed. She knew the front yard was "off-limits," but maybe Daddy had swept Mr. Bun up in the leaves by accident. He had, after all, thrown out her favorite blanket last year by accident, and Mommy had yelled at him. That was not a Happy Day.

She would have to be quiet, but she was good at that. The front door was easy to open; she had seen Mommy and Daddy open it before, and they let her do it when they ordered pizza or food from China that burned her mouth and came with funny spaghetti. She closed the door, making sure the lock was turned so she could get back in. Then she ran across the grass to the pile of leaves. Across the street, people were cutting branches off the tree by that ugly house Daddy hated, and it made a loud noise like the machine in the sink that ate the vegetables.

The pile of leaves smelled nice and wet, and she remembered how Daddy would, when she was younger, sweep them up as big as a mountain and she and Tommy would jump into it. They had laughed and thrown the leaves at each other, and then she found a slug on her arm and she realized there were icky things hidden in the leaves and she cried. But she was a baby then and now she was a big girl and icky things didn't scare her anymore.

Then something moved inside the pile of leaves and she stopped a few feet short of it and waited. It moved again, a few wet leaves tumbling down as the pile shifted. The slugs and snails and worms were small and they couldn't hurt her, but whatever was inside the leaf pile was large and big and looked like it was breathing. Leaves were vegetables, and if the slugs ate a lot of them, they could be big and strong, big enough to gobble her up.

The leaves rustled and moved a third time, and the strangest thing happened. A hand reached out. Jessica whimpered and stepped back as if the hand would keep growing until it stretched all the way across the driveway and grabbed her. But it didn't. It was a small hand, and behind it, she could see the face of the boy and his little black raisin eyes inside the pile of leaves. His hand was balled in a fist, and when it opened, she saw something glimmering and shiny in his gray palm.

Her six-year-old mind tried to comprehend what she saw. The boy in the pile of leaves held a key in his outstretched hand. A few icky things clung to his arm, but they didn't seem to bother him. Perhaps they were baby slugs with baby teeth, like hers, and didn't bite. Then his arm disappeared back into the pile of leaves, taking the key with it.

It was a game. She knew it!

He had taken Mr. Bun and left the leaf there for her to find. The leaf had led her outside to the pile where he was waiting, and inside, he held the next clue: a shiny key! But to get the key, she would have to reach into the leaves and take it from the icky things. She glanced back at the house and thought about asking Mommy or Daddy for help, but she knew they would be angry that she went off-limits, and then she couldn't get the key and find Mr. Bun.

And that was a Bad Thing.

No, she was a big girl, and big girls weren't afraid of icky things. She rolled up her sleeves and crouched in front of the pile of leaves and reached into that spot the boy's hand had protruded from. It was wet and warm and she felt her knees shake as she thought of giant slugs and grown-up teeth chewing on the leaves, then turning their pincers onto her intruding arm.

But there were no pincers, only the metal of the key, slick and cold, waiting deep inside the pile where the boy had been. Her fingers grasped it, and she pulled her hand from the pile in a flash and wiped the muck and yellow leaves from her sleeve.

She knew the key the moment she opened her hands. Daddy used it during the summer to open the old lock on the hot tub outside. They had played in the warm water and she had worn her inflatable Learn2swim armbands, and they had all laughed when Ginger scampered up and jumped in with them. It had been a Happy Day, and maybe that was where Mr. Bun was now, with Ginger, playing in the warm water. Another Happy Day waiting for her, and she had the key to it all!

She ran as quick as her feet could take her, closing the front door and turning the lock so no one knew she had been off-limits. Then she ran out to the backyard, but Mommy wasn't there, and her gardening tools, that big spoon and the hand fork and those small scissors, all sat in the grass by the sick roses. It was good, she thought, that Mommy wasn't there. If she was playing a game and not working, then Mommy would use the Slow Voice and be sad and wouldn't let her look for Mr. Bun and Ginger.

She ran around to the side yard, by the umbrella, and there it was: the wooden hot tub. It made funny noises at night, like it was having a bad dream or choking on something, but in the daytime, it slept beneath the plastic cover. She gave a look over her shoulder, and when she saw no one was watching, she took the key from her pocket and put it in the old lock on the big lid.

The lock clicked and sprang open and fell to the ground. She pushed against the big lid but it only buckled as the plastic gave a groan. It was heavy, maybe too heavy for her, and she knew that Tommy wouldn't help. He would throw popcorn or call her a bad word and tell on her. If only she was strong and smart and big like Daddy or Mommy, then maybe she could open it and find Mr. Bun.

Something glimmered to her right and her eyes snapped toward it. A quarter of the way around the heavy lid sat a metal bolt latch that held the lid to the wood body. The sunlight seemed to bounce off it even though the sun was behind gray clouds above. The latch, that was how it opened. The lock and the latches. She remembered helping Daddy open them on the Happy Day in the summer. There were three of them and a lock, like the four points of a compass, and only when they were all opened would the lid fold back. She smiled with excitement. She wasn't a stupid girl. A "retard," as Tommy had called her. She was smart and clever and she would solve this problem and find Mr. Bun.

The bolt latches slid open easily and she saw specks of rust fall off. Then, remembering how the two halves of the plastic lid folded together like a giant taco, she put her arms under the lip and pushed it up. It was heavy, heavier than anything she had ever lifted, and she could only hold it for a moment, but in that brief time, she had seen him. Mr. Bun was down there! Then she had to let go and drop the heavy lid.

Mr. Bun was in there, but he was in trouble. He was down at the bottom of the dark water beneath leaves and sticks and some icky oil. He was old and weak and she had to save him because the water would hurt him, make him into a raisin like the bathtub did to her skin. He had watched over her at night and kept the monsters away, but now he was in trouble and she had to be a big girl and save him. She had to lift the lid by herself.

She dug her heels into the wood step and pushed against the lid with all the might her little body could muster. The lid buckled and popped up again, and she used one hand to hold it at an angle. She looked down into the brackish water where the old rabbit had been. For a brief second she saw him staring back up from the bottom of the water, heavy and helpless, floating up toward her.

"Found you!" she said with a giggle.

But it wasn't Mr. Bun. The water shimmered and his face blurred and became that of the boy's face, and he was sneering with anger as if he'd been woken from sleep. His fingers broke the surface, then his face, and his rattling tongue filled her ears. She felt his fingers wrap around her neck, and they were cold and sticky and strong, stronger even than Daddy's.

Then those fingers pulled her and she felt the cold slap of water, first on her face and then down her whole body. She saw, for a fleeting second, the light from the lid disappear as it slammed shut and the world went to shadow and ice.

Of the endless terrors born of becoming a parent, the nightmares of kidnappings and accidents and broken bones, the worst-case scenarios that haunted their minds, finding their own daughter floating inside an old hot tub lay among the dark recesses of unconsidered horrors. There were crooked stairs behind the basement door, chemical cleaners beneath the sink, even Jessica's own bunk bed, which she had insisted on sleeping atop. Yet those dangers had all been safeguarded behind locks and railings, their children given countless lectures about safety. There were places that were off-limits, actions ingrained into their kids' heads—"look both ways," "don't put that in your mouth"—and before that afternoon Dan and Linda had felt their children could be trusted not to put themselves in harm's way.

The murky water of the old hot tub did not factor into their horror the same way some parents described with confusion how a faithful and gentle family dog snapped one day and mauled a child to death. There had been no warnings of the hot tub because, to them, it was impossible for their children to access. There were three bolt latches and a padlock. The key was kept on a ring in the garage above the mess of tools that Dan told himself he would one day organize. The key hadn't even been labeled, only affixed with a small yellow dot that matched the yellow dot on the back of the padlock. It was only when Linda unleashed a banshee wail that sent him running to the backyard, when he saw the padlock and key together on the ground next to one of Jessica's Pink Princess shoes, that he realized he had forgotten to drain the hot tub.

The shape hung wet and limp in Linda's arms, and when he saw it, his mind seized up. The thing looked inhuman. Golden hair clung to its face like a dirt-sullied veil. For a brief point in time, he saw his child self, not in Linda's arms but rather in the tender embrace of Father O'Malley as he carried him through that dark basement after hours in the trunk.

The second scream brought reality crashing back, and it was his daughter's body held by Linda that drove him across the chasm between the door and the hot tub. Time distorted and seemed to exist at two speeds, both in fast-forward and slow motion.

"Do something!" Linda screamed and lowered his daughter's body to the bricks. "Oh, God, please do something!"

He brushed the hair from Jessica's face, and when he saw her eyes were closed, his heart sank—*Please, oh please,* he begged—as he felt for a pulse on her neck and tilted her head back and opened her mouth and listened. He saw Tommy and Sam standing at the doorway, frozen in terror, and he heard Linda shouting for them to call 9-1-1, but the words were muffled and quiet. He thought back to a CPR class he had taken on a Saturday in college, but the actions and their order made no sense. Something yellow and thick covered her tongue, and he dug his fingers into her mouth. He withdrew a moist leaf and threw it to the ground, screaming her name.

Then a sound came from between her lips, a sound he knew and dreaded. It was a low liquid rattle that hung in the air of the hospital when his father-in-law expired. A rattle that came from that shadow child who stalked him in his hallucinations. A rattle that now came from his own daughter.

It was the rattle of the dead.

No, no it wasn't.

It was the sound of water burbling forth, first in weak gasps and then exploding from her lips in a violent fountain. She convulsed and he lifted her forward, slapping her back as her body bent in on itself and she let out a wail. It was the scream of life, the scream of a newborn baby, the scream of their daughter who had almost drowned in that fetid water he had forgotten to drain. It was heartbreaking and beautiful, and when he heard it, he cried.

She coughed again, her tiny hands clutching his biceps, her eyes open and weak. Those eyes, those beautiful eyes of her mother, now leaking pathetic little tears as they blinked and looked up at him. He saw them and he knew she would be all right, so he hugged her as tight as he'd ever hugged her before.

IT WAS THE SECOND TIME IN TWO WEEKS THAT EMERGENCY VEHICLES SAT outside their house. The paramedics examined Jessica and said she was lucky to be alive, that they'd had situations similar to this that didn't end well. They listened to her lungs, took her blood pressure, and said both seemed all right. They asked her questions and she stared back at them, uncomprehending. They even shined a flashlight in her eyes and said her pupil dilation was slow and asked to take her to the hospital for further checkup.

"You did good. Probably saved her life," one of the paramedics told

Dan with a slap on the shoulder like a boss congratulating an employee on clinching a business deal. Dan wondered what they said in the situations that ended in tears.

"Tough break. Should've drained the tub."

"MY GUESS IS SHE'S GOING THROUGH A BIT OF PTS," SAID DOCTOR LEE with a nod. "Post-traumatic stress. It's not uncommon for children to sort of shut down. Temporarily, of course."

"I don't understand," Linda said, glancing at Dan as if perhaps she had misunderstood the answer. "She's hardly said a word."

"None, actually," Dan added. "Not a peep."

"And she might not. At least not right away. Not until she's ready."

In the two hours between the paramedics and the ambulance and the scans, she hadn't said a single word, hadn't done much of anything except follow the nurse's directions and stare at her feet. When Linda asked her a question, she replied with a nod or a shake of her head, then reset her glance back to her shoes.

"You have to understand," said the doctor. "She had a terrible experience, easily the most frightening of her life. She's probably still processing it."

"What can we do?" asked Linda.

"Same thing you always do: be loving parents and let the healing process take place. When she's ready, I'm sure she'll let you know."

"You don't think she has, I don't know, brain damage or anything?" asked Linda, looking at Dan as if the words themselves were cursed and capable of harm.

"Very unlikely. The scans didn't show anything unusual. Physically, she's fine. Mentally, it might take a little longer. Consider that she, on a very real and tangible level, just learned about her own mortality. For most children, this is a very complicated issue, one that takes them years to fully grasp."

Years, Dan thought, or lifetimes.

"I wouldn't be surprised if she has trouble sleeping or even displays some deviant behavior. Children often block out trauma, or change it, all so they can come to terms with it. But besides today's little mishap, she's a perfectly healthy young girl. And such a pretty one, too," he added, poking her in the shoulder and smiling at her, but she returned only a blank gaze.

THE DOCTOR WAS WRONG ABOUT ONE THING: SHE HAD NO TROUBLE falling asleep that night. They both tucked her into bed, mother and father arranging her dolls, and she smiled upon seeing Mr. Bun sitting at the top of her bed, waiting on her pillow. Within minutes she was fast asleep, that old rabbit held tight in her arms.

THE LOST COAST

IT WAS 10:00 A.M. when Dan smelled Denise's cotton candy bubble gum, the same kind that Tommy chewed, coming from her lips not far from his face. She slid the lab results across the counter to him.

"We ran the sample through two spectrometry tests to determine the paints used. Based on the additives, we have a winner."

"Really?"

"Mm-hmm," she said and leaned further over the counter. He noticed the top three buttons on her blouse were open. He could make out the form of her generous cleavage as she flipped through the last few pages of the results. The fact that her blouse was open, he suspected, was not a mistake. When he was waiting in line earlier, he had only noticed one button open.

"Okay, here we are," she said. At the top of the list, next to a rating of ninety-nine percent accuracy, sat one name. "Yuray Arts," she said.

"Never heard of them."

"I hadn't either. They're pretty popular with the twig and granola crowd, but they only sell regionally, so—"

"Whoever painted this bought it there," he cut in.

"Exactly," she said with a smile, as if he was a smart kid and might get a treat.

His eyes fell back to the results. "Were you able to generate a list of pigments?"

"Already done," she said, flipping to the fourth page that listed eight different colors. "Sample size wasn't big enough to get a full list, but it's a start."

He cleared his throat and looked at the results. "What about the canvas?"

"That was another can of worms," she said. "We had some funky results, so we sent it up to the city for further tests. Should have the results anytime now."

He smiled and took the lab results. "You're a superstar, Denise."

"That's why they pay me the big bucks, Prof," she said with a smile, and he saw brown streaks along the base of her teeth.

"You've…" He pointed to his teeth. "Something in them."

She blushed and turned away, picking at her teeth with her blue fingernail, and he caught a glimpse of gray, scabby gums inside her mouth.

His car crossed the Golden Gate Bridge on the northbound 101 shortly before two. He picked at the remains of a Zippy Burger and Cheesy Shock fries while listening to a congested woman on NPR discuss a new David Sedaris book with the author. He had to turn off the interview for fear of falling asleep.

Outside, it was a clear, blue, and crisp day. To his right, he could see Alcatraz, Marin, Angel Island, and all the tourists standing along the edge of that giant red bridge and taking photos. To his left, the sun hung high over the endless Pacific, above the whitecaps of waves that dotted dark waters. He thought about the various creatures lurking just beneath that black water and the time he took the kids to see the humpback whale migrations. Tommy had cheered and Jessica had screamed and Linda had spent the afternoon seasick, vomiting below deck.

He stretched his shoulders and rolled down the window, smelling the crisp ocean air. It woke him up. It always had. Half a lifetime ago, when he left the plains and red dirt of the Midwest behind, the Pacific greeted him without question, only acceptance, ending the eighteen years of dreams that had come before. He had no money then, only a name and a backpack full of art books and an ambition to build a new future in a new place. It had worked out pretty well, he thought. These old Nebraska bones hadn't just built a future: they'd built a whole new life.

The GPS listed eighty-four miles before his next turn, another fifty-five miles past that, and then thirty more, for a total time just under three hours. He pushed the pedal down, hoping to make it up the coast in two hours and change.

HE MADE IT IN JUST OVER TWO HOURS, CROSSING THE OLD TRUSS BRIDGE that spanned the Greywood River where it emptied into a lazy cove beneath towering sea cliffs. Driftwood lined the flat, drab beaches. A faint marine layer hung over the horizon. A single fisherman slept in a distant chair as his fishing pole stood watch over the cove.

The town was small and quiet, a sleepy getaway where families vacationed in the summer, then forgot about in the off-seasons. It seemed to exist in a different country, where time stood frozen in a glacial decay of post-war industry and spotted tourism. Where every store sold the same knickknacks made by a few local artists and all the postcards were from a decade ago.

He had little trouble finding Yuray Arts. It was an unmissable building, a converted barn flanked on the sides by a market and the local post office. He pulled into a parking space, stepped out and stretched his body, nodding to a boy walking his dog, who stared at him with a mix of curiosity and suspicion.

Denise had called the supply store a mom-and-pop operation, but when he stepped in, he realized she'd been way off the mark. The store was larger than most craft stores, even larger than the university supply store back in Alder Glen, which served a student population ten times this town's size. Hand-carved driftwood signs hung above each section of the store. Even the door was decorated in the style of the sixties, fluorescent paints and endless spirals like a silkscreened poster of some Haight-Ashbury folk band. Bells clattered as the door closed.

"Be down there on the dub," said a voice from above, and Dan craned his neck upward, surprised to find a loft area that contained even more supplies. The man upstairs was tall, easily over six and a half feet. A salt and pepper beard hung in two braids halfway down his chest. Dan couldn't decide whether he looked like he belonged behind the handlebars of a Harley or beneath a protest banner, waving a piece sign.

"What can I do you for, chief?" the tall man asked.

"I have sort of an odd request," Dan answered as he took out the lab report.

"Long as it ain't a blowjob, I'm all ears."

Dan laughed. "No, I can't say it is."

"Then we're good. What's hurting ya?"

"I'm working on tracking down the artist of a painting I received."

"Collector?"

"Professor, actually. Down in Alder Glen."

"Ah. Go Oaks," the man said with a weak pump of the fist.

"What?"

"Football team. You got a solid lineup this year."

"Right, yeah. Anyway, this is sort of a side project," Dan said as he slid the lab report and a photograph of the painting to the tall man. He studied the painting, muttered, "Far out," and turned to the lab report while Dan continued. "We ran an analysis of the paints used, and they were mixed here."

"Been selling paints since '78. That's a lot of ground to cover."

"Here's a partial list of the pigments used. I feel stupid asking this, but you're the only lead we have. You wouldn't happen to remember selling them, would you?"

The tall man stared at the page. His blue eyes squinted and created even more wrinkles that ran across his face like folds on a blanket. Then he nodded. "Yep. Yep. Lucky day, chief."

"Really?" Dan asked, embarrassed by how enthusiastic he sounded. Like a kid getting a new toy.

"Came in over the phone about, oh, two months back. I remember it 'cause I drove out to deliver it. We do that with all orders over a hundred."

"Who was it?"

"The artist or who ordered it?"

"Both."

"Well, I can't be sure about the artist, but it was Halgrove," he said and handed the sheet back to Dan. "Old Mabel Halgrove. She ordered this batch specifically, in this order, plus maybe a dozen others, I suppose. I remember thinking it kind of odd but par for the course with her."

"Why would that be that odd?"

The tall man smiled. "We've got some interesting folk around here. Real characters, if you catch my drift. And Mabel, she's in a class all her own. That's not a bad thing. It is what it is. But I will tell you there is no way on God's green earth Old Mabel painted this."

"Why not?" Dan asked.

"'Cause, chief," the tall man said with a smile. "She's as blind as a bat."

THE CAT LADY

THE HOUSE WAS small, a single-story ranch home set a half mile down a dirt driveway that took Dan an hour to find. The GPS had led him off the highway to the access road and then flashed *No Map Data Available* after a mile. It took two trips up and down the bumpy access roads until he saw a hand-painted sign by an old metal gate that read *MABEL HALGROVE*.

Twice he called the number the tall man had given him, and twice it went straight to voicemail. He pondered his options, not wanting to drive onto her property without her consent, considering a man with a double-braided beard had described her as eccentric. Blind or not, she could still point a shotgun in the direction of a sound, and Dan suspected the type of people who lived on these distant ranches and painted boys with pinhole eyes might be the type to be well-armed.

The sun descended, giving the sky an amaranthine and tangerine hue, and Dan decided he'd already driven too far to turn around. He made the decision, opened the gate, and drove a half mile up the dusty road toward the small ranch house atop the hill.

The first thing he noticed was the cats. There were at least a dozen outside the porch. They darted about, half feral and wild, scattering as his car came to a standstill on the gravel. A few brave ones approached, and one even slithered under the car to seek warmth.

"Hello?" Dan called out to the house. Lights were on, both inside the house and outside on the porch, where more lazy cats milled about like a backwoods swamp family. Inside, he was able to make out vague movement through the thin patterned curtain. Feline shadows watched from the window.

"Hello? Ms. Halgrove, are you home?" he asked again, and the only answer was the sudden hissing and screech of two cats fighting beneath his car, the loser darting off into the bushes to lick its wounds.

The porch groaned under his feet, and he tried not to think about how many cats were beneath it, endlessly humping and birthing offspring and fighting over scraps. He had disliked Ginger—this much was true—but she had a certain pathetic affection, a need to be taken care of that kept his hate at bay. There was none of that to be found in these cats. Any affection displayed, he thought, was a means to an end. He felt momentary satisfaction as he gave one of the braver beasts a sharp punt that cleared it off the step.

"Hello? Ms. Halgrove?" he called out again, hoping for some sort of answer or sound from behind the window, but no such response came. The door was ajar, no more than a few inches. The screen in front lay torn and frayed at ankle height, loose strands of metal and hair hanging, evidence of some battle it had lost against paws and claws.

He knocked on the doorframe. While he waited, he watched with amusement as a fat striped cat pushed its way past him and into the house with a lazy hiss like an ornery old man. He knocked again, and again there was no answer.

Two thoughts crossed his mind at almost the same time. The first was that the sun had finally set, it was past six, and he was two hundred miles from home on a ranch, trying to contact a blind cat hoarder who might or might not also be an incredible artist. The second thought was that he wanted to open the door and look inside. If he didn't, this whole absurd question would go forever unanswered. He wasn't sure which idea was more irrational.

Deciding he'd come too far, he called her name one last time, and when no one answered, he opened the door.

The smell was the first thing to hit him. It was a sour reek of gas and excrement. Piles of cat shit lay about the floor. Paw prints led through the occasional filth like dirt tracks at a murder scene. Pieces of the couch and armchair hung in fibrous clumps, clawed down to the wood. Balls of fur lay like tumbleweeds against the walls. If Linda were here, he thought, she would be in the throes of an allergic reaction at the sight of it all.

"Ms. Halgrove, hello?" he called out again, but after seeing the state of her house, he hoped nothing would answer back. If it did, it might be little more than a shambling mess, a long-haired monstrosity like something from a Japanese horror film.

The living room was decorated with an assortment of trinkets that looked like they'd been raided from a sorcerer's tower. Dreamcatchers made of dyed thread and oiled twigs swayed in the cool breeze. Crystals and gems wrapped in twine were nailed to the walls like vines on a forgotten jungle ruin. A dozen different idols and figurines all sat on shelves: some were Mayan representing death, or Balinese depicting the afterlife, and a few others that he wasn't familiar with.

Those heads, he had seen them before, all of them. In that anonymous painting, a shard of mirror had reflected a row of doll heads. But they weren't dolls, he realized. They were figurines. A surge of excitement built up as he realized the painting was tied to this house. He was on the right track.

The floor creaked with each footstep he took. The air was thick with cat dander, the occasional hair floating past in some micro-current like a boat in an invisible river. And the smell. It made his stomach tighten. He had smelled it before, in the basement, when he found that bird and that rat. He had smelled it in the hallway, outside his office, when he'd hallucinated that shadow child. He had smelled it years ago, but he couldn't remember where. Perhaps, he thought, when Linda's father had expired.

Another cat pushed past his feet, startling him. The creature meandered toward an adjoining room, followed by two others. From further inside the house, he heard the distant chattering of their feral brethren, as if they were carrying on a conversation. He followed their mewling voices around the corner, deeper into the house.

"Hello?" he called out, hoping nothing answered.

The drawing room was spacious and picturesque. A wide window looked out upon the rolling hills, where the distant vineyards intersected a highway lit by the glow of distant cars.

And there it was.

A massive table sat before the window with a single overturned chair. Torn canvas, wood bars, and nails and knives and brushes covered one end. Tubes of paint lay about the table, each stamped with that familiar Y symbol of Yuray Paints. Those colors, he recognized them from the canvas back at his house. A palette sat nearby, covered in paints and a layer of white mold from where a cat had defecated on it. This spot, overlooking the hills, had once been a place of creation. Now it sat in decay.

Next to the mess sat several pieces of paper and an old black fountain pen. The words *HERE IN ART, DENIAL* were written dozens of times in a haphazard scrawl and then crossed out. The variations changed, the word "here" becoming "her" and the missing E finding itself in front of "art," spelling "eart." Some letters were written larger than others, circled and refined, D's and A's and I's all bearing different strokes as if practiced in the dark.

He dropped the papers as a sudden discomfort washed over him. A feeling, an epiphany, that he had wandered far off the lit path and deep into the forest. This woman and this house, he thought, were not right. Not right at all.

"Ms. Halgrove," he called out a final time.

The cats continued their chattering in the nearby kitchen. One hissed and ran past him with something wet in its mouth, and the smell made him gag. He turned his attention past the darting feline and to the kitchen beyond.

Then his mind went blank.

The first thing he saw was the shoes. One was angled upright, toes pointed at the ceiling. The other shoe was twisted on its side. The brown leather was speckled with bits of a dark substance that caught the light like oil at night. The socks that rose out of the shoes had probably been white, once long ago, but were now stained brown and green and crusted over as if embalmed in scabs. What remained of the legs was discolored and yellow, swollen in places, raw in others. Sprouts of dark hair adorned the pieces that hadn't been consumed, and only bone remained of what had.

His mind went over the images—the shoes, the socks, the patchwork flesh—until he comprehended what he saw. And when he did, he ran through the house and out into the front yard, where he threw up in the bush.

THE POLICE AND PARAMEDICS TOOK OVER A HALF HOUR TO ARRIVE. IN THAT time Dan ventured back into the house to verify that what he had seen had been real, not another illusion of his mind, like the belly of the inflatable snake or the dark child in the hallway. He steeled his stomach for the sight, but upon a second viewing, he didn't fare much better, and his throat soured yet again.

He was only able to look at the lower half of the body from the other room. Its upper half was obscured by the kitchen counter, but even that, he knew, would be seared into his mind for life. The old woman's body had been stripped almost to the bone in small, haphazard mouthfuls. The remaining parts, pieces really, were discolored and alternated between an olive green and a mustard yellow. It had bloated, grown in mass, and its skin had cracked in places, not unlike an old painting.

In the sunset light that poured through the window, one thing stood out on her. A fold of white paper sat tucked into her blouse pocket. Compared to the mess, it was clean. If she had painted that thing that sat in his house, had scribbled the note and sent it to him, perhaps she still held one more clue, folded and close to her heart.

He eyed that paper, focusing only on it, not the shape beneath it or the mewling beasts gathered about and feeding. He took a deep breath, an explorer pushing into the abyss, a deep sea diver, and then he entered the kitchen. He looked away, beyond the corpse and the old house, to a place far off and peaceful and clean. He knew what was there but he didn't have to see it.

A cat hissed as his hand lowered closer to her shape, closer to that pocket and the fold of paper. Inches, really. That was how far away his fingers were when he caught the reflection off the window. His blood went cold, his feet refused to move, and he found himself unable to turn away. Most of the old woman's face had been left intact, other than the lips, which had been pulled free in strands like a starfish stripping the paint off the hull of a boat. She stared at the window, her final lipless sneer reflected off the glass and straight at him, waiting, perhaps for him to stand right there and see her reflection. As if she was just another subject in a painting guiding the viewer's eyes.

He grabbed the piece of paper from her blouse pocket. Then he ran, backward through the house, and once again, his stomach emptied itself.

He wiped his lips, tasting bitter, and shooed off a cat that'd come to inspect his mess. Then he opened the piece of paper. Scribbled in that shimmering ink in delicate, almost imperceptible scratches, sat the following:

XII:4 I:1 II:9 III:18
IV:14 VI:5 VII:8 VIII:20
V is the key to the door.

THE PARAMEDICS HAD STRONG STOMACHS, BUT EVEN THEY HAD TROUBLE bagging the body, and he heard them debating how to remove the corpse without it falling apart. Only the sheriff, an old man well past retirement, seemed indifferent. He took down Dan's story without any suspicion, recording how he had found her, why he was looking for her, and little else. Dan left out a few details—the note in her blouse pocket and how he'd disturbed a crime scene—feeling they'd only raise more questions—questions he didn't have answers for. Satisfied, the sheriff scratched his mustache, snapped his notepad closed, and spat on the ground.

"Helluva thing," he said.

"How long do they think she's, you know, been dead?" Dan asked.

"Hard to say. I'd figure on a few weeks at least."

"A few weeks? That long?"

He nodded. "Takes a body a while to bloat up with all the gasses inside. Lucky you found her. That many cats, this far out, might not have been much left in another few weeks."

"What was she like?" Dan found himself asking. For the first time since he'd started to look for her, he realized she had been a human, had lived and breathed, and had a whole life prior to his discovery. That he had, in his fear and shock, reduced her to a grotesque story made him feel a pang of guilt.

"Wh'was she like?" repeated the sheriff with a smile. "Well, Old Mabel was, I suppose, same as a lot of folk out here."

"How so?"

"Get," he said and buried his boot into the side of a cat trying to sneak back into the house for another serving. "Look around, son. We've got two types of people out here: those born here and those who move here."

"So she wasn't a local?"

The sheriff laughed. "Sure, but that's not the point. See, no one moves out here without wanting to leave something behind. Ex-artists and ex-hippies and ex-cons, all looking for some piece of land and some peace and quiet. As long as they keep quiet and peaceful, they're fine in my books. And Old Mabel was as quiet as they come."

"Did she have any family?"

The sheriff raised an eyebrow. "You her biographer or something?"

"I'm starting to feel like it." Dan laughed. "I know this sounds crazy, but I think she sent this to me. I just need to find out who painted it."

He handed the sheriff the photo of the painting. The man gave it only a momentary glance, uninterested.

"Yep, that does sound crazy. Gonna be hard to confirm it now, too. No family that I've heard of, but I'm sure she didn't just crawl out of the soil an eighty-year-old shut-in. As for friends, closest thing to that would be Madame Tamara."

"Madame Tamara?"

He nodded. "Yep."

"Does this Madame Tamara have an address?"

"Follow the highway south and look for her sign. You can't miss it," he said, spitting on the ground again. "Just look for the sign."

THE PROTÉGÉ

TAMARA'S SIGN WAS, indeed, hard to miss. He half remembered passing it earlier before pulling into Greywood Bay. Neon depicted a red triangle with a blue eye set flush in the center. A yellow sun surrounded it all. The name *MADAME TAMARA* was emblazoned beneath it in glowing white. Dusty windows advertised various services from Tarot cards to palm reading and crystal gazing. Below them sat credit card decals, most of which had been scraped off.

"Unbelievable," Dan mumbled as he closed the car door.

He had seen plenty of businesses like this spread across forgotten highways and rural areas, places where people turned to preachers and mysticism instead of reason and logic. He paid them little more attention than he did the magician who guessed someone's weight at a circus. Another car sat in the otherwise empty front lot, a recent-model German import, and he doubted it belonged to the same person who owned the old house.

The door jingled as he opened it and stepped into the waiting room. Like Mabel's house, the room was decorated with dreamcatchers, crystals, and small idols. Three framed photos of Indian holy men hung on the wall opposite the couch. A jeweled frog that doubled as an incense holder belched streams of smoke. A Tibetan mandala adorned the wall, and he pegged it as a hackneyed Chinese knockoff.

The waiting room was a converted foyer with a curtain of beads dividing it from a room behind, through which he saw three shapes sitting around a table. He walked over, pushed several beads aside, and stood there in silence, observing the scene in the interior. A middle-aged woman, whom he assumed to be Madame Tamara, sat on one side of a table and rocked back and forth like a palm tree in a tropical breeze. Her eyes were rolled back and her mouth was open, lips quivering in a whisper.

Across from her sat a couple around Dan's age. One glance at their clothes and he knew they owned the car out front. The woman was dressed in a power suit and the man had a gold watch. They held hands, as if in a slight trance themselves, and Dan watched as the husband bit his lip and fought back tears.

"He says he loves you," said Madame Tamara, as if the words were heavy and took all her energy to cough up. "He says, don't be angry, don't be sad… about…" She paused, blinking her eyes in quick succession, and for a brief moment, she made eye contact with Dan. Then she returned to the couple. "Don't be angry about a thing, a gift he wanted… something he asked for."

"A bicycle," said the husband, and he turned to his wife. She gave a desperate nod, an affirmation, and turned back to Tamara.

"That's it, a bicycle. It was a present," Madame Tamara continued.

"He wanted a bike for his birthday, but…" The wife trailed off.

Then the husband cut in. "I thought it was too dangerous. There were so many accidents in our neighborhood. He could have hurt himself and I…" The man swallowed hard and blinked. "It was all he talked about."

"He says don't worry. He's happy now. It doesn't hurt," the psychic continued, eyes fluttering. "He says…" She paused and drew in a deep breath. "He says you were the best gifts of all. And he'll always be thankful for the time he had."

She exhaled and her whole body seemed to shrink, like an animal deflating after a predator had left. Or a cat, Dan thought. Then she blinked again, glancing once again to Dan, then back to the couple as she shook her head.

"I'm so sorry. But sometimes, if the spirit is strong and at peace, the connection can't be held for long. And his was as strong as any I've ever known."

With those words, the businesswoman burst into tears and fell into the comfort of her husband's embrace. Madame Tamara slid the box of tissues to her. She took them, two at a time, wiping her eyes while her husband rubbed her neck and smiled. Dan realized there sat two broken people, two parents—or former parents. Had the other day's events in the hot tub turned out different… Well, he didn't want to go there.

"Thank you so much," said the businesswoman between sobs. "I can't explain—"

"I know," said Madame Tamara with a kind smile. "You don't have to try. It's my job, and tonight it was an honor."

It took several minutes for the woman to compose herself. Madame Tamara just sat there, smiling, offering her tissue after tissue, nodding and waving off the stream of gratitude. The husband handed her several hundred dollars but she didn't count it. Instead, she placed it on the table next to a string of prayer beads and smiled at them as they got their coats and mumbled a final thank-you.

Dan held the bead curtain open for them, and the husband gave him a smile, a small nod of appreciation. In his eyes, Dan saw a deep sadness that betrayed his stoic exterior. Hours earlier, Dan thought, he'd probably been knee-deep in equity trading, but now, after hours, he was a thrall to some off-ramp psychic in a no-name town.

After they left, Madame Tamara put the money inside a small box next to a deep blue crystal globe, then looked at Dan with puzzlement. "It's a little late for a reading, hon. 'Fraid I'm about spent for the night."

"Actually," Dan said, and he stepped into the reading room. "I'm not here for that."

Madame Tamara studied him for a moment, and he wondered if she already knew why he was here. *Of course she doesn't,* he thought.

She's just good at reading body language. A charlatan peddling fake souls to the bereaved.

"I see." She nodded. "Well, in that case, I'll let my hair down. Come on into the kitchen."

WHATEVER AURA OF MYSTICISM THE DIM LIGHTS OF THE READING ROOM gave her faded in the kitchen. Beneath the harsh light, her thinning gray hair and freckled skin seemed to age with each minute she took in the news. He told her everything he knew about Mabel Halgrove, starting with the painting, his drive to Yuray Arts, and his discovery of her body a few hours ago. She never spoke, only listened while she boiled water, put tea bags in separate cups, poured hot water in, and sat across from him as he finished. He left out the gruesome details of her friend's demise, opting simply to say that she had been dead for a while.

"That much I guessed," she said, nodding at the news as if it were no worse than a parking ticket. "I'm sorry to hear that, and I appreciate you telling me. But I'm not all that surprised."

"Not surprised? About what?"

"Her death, the painting, that creation. I've heard it already. She said it'd been… How'd she put it? Fermenting. Yes, that was the word. She said it'd been fermenting for a long time. And somehow, I knew, after she finished it, it'd be the last time I saw her."

"I'm sorry," Dan said, smiling at the absurd idea. "You sound like you actually think she painted it."

"I don't think she did: I know she did. Last two times I saw her, it was all she ever talked about."

"So you saw her, I mean physically saw her, put that paint on the canvas?"

"Didn't need to. Ol' Mabel was powerful, and so was our bond. I didn't need to be beside her to know what she was birthing."

Dan scoffed, a wide smile crossing his face. He felt like he was talking to Tommy or, worse, Jessica and explaining that the closet wasn't full of monsters and dolls didn't talk.

"I'm sorry, but you do realize there is no way, I mean no physical way, a blind person could paint a picture with that level of detail, right? It's impossible. Physically impossible."

"Hon," she said with a smile that only elevated his frustration. "I've seen things that would turn your hair as white as ash. Thirty years now I've watched Old Mabel reach into the nether and channel the dead. She taught me everything I know. And compared to her, I'm not even an opening act."

"You really expect me to believe this?" he said, feeling the glass buzz behind his eyes, annoyed at her theatrical words.

"I don't really care what you believe. World's round or the world's flat. It's all the same to me," she said, blowing into her hands and then opening them as if releasing an invisible bird. "But the point remains: you're sitting in a psychic's kitchen, so a part of you must wonder as well."

"Look, I just watched you fleece those folks. That couple back there? The bicycle? They told you everything. Anyone with a basic understanding of psychology could see that."

"Ah, the Thompsons, lovely people. Tragic about their son, but those things do happen. Tell me, did they look like they felt fleeced to you? Or did they look happy?"

"That's not the point."

"No, Mr. Rineheart, that is the point. What you want and what you need, they ain't the same. Those two, they didn't need a séance, and I probably couldn't have given it to them. Their boy was far beyond the sight of my shores. What they needed, really, was a little sense of peace and hope after a tragedy, a chance to say they were sorry. That, I could give them. Cheaper than therapy, and it doesn't drag on for months. Try getting that from someone with a basic understanding of psychology."

"But you lied to them."

"They lied to themselves. We all do. Why? Because the truth, Mr. Rineheart, it doesn't always give us the closure we need. Is that so bad?"

The chair squeaked as Dan leaned back and sipped the tea. "Okay, back to Mabel," he said. "So was she like… How would you say? Possessed or something?"

"Possessed? No, no more so than a magnifying glass is possessed by the light that passes through it."

"What does that mean?"

"It means she was special. Touched. Words only reduce her gift to vagaries."

"Enlighten me."

She sighed, tapped her fingers on the table, and swirled her tea, and Dan thought for a moment that maybe she was looking for answers at the bottom of the cup.

"Well, what are we doing here? Right now?" she asked and waved her hand, pointing to the corners of the room.

"I don't know. Talking? Drinking tea? I'm getting a migraine."

"You get many of those?" she asked, tapping her fingers on the table.

"I don't know. At times, sure. Are you reading my fortune?"

"I'm not so sure I'd like what I saw," she said. "But back to the question: what are we doing here? We're existing, Dan. Existing. You, me, this table, these old chairs. It all exists here, in this room, in this world, in this reality that we all agree on, correct?"

"I suppose," Dan said with a smirk.

"Uh-uh. There is no 'I suppose.' We're dealing in absolutes because, as sane individuals, assuming you are sane—"

"Or you," he added.

"Or myself," she agreed. "Assuming we're sane, we both agree that when I hold out this cup of tea"—she held out her cup of tea, swirling it around as she continued—"it is in fact a cup of tea we both perceive, not a snake or a ball of spiders or a burning bush. Sound fair?" She raised an eyebrow and waited.

"Yeah, sounds fair," he answered.

"Good. Now consider this cup of tea. Let's say the tea's the spirit and the cup's the body, and for argument's sake, we continue to agree. Spirit and body."

"That's a big leap for an atheist."

"Even atheists put their faith in something. They just call it science."

She smiled at him, then released the cup. Instinct kicked in and he reached out to catch it, but he was too slow. It hit the kitchen tile and shattered. Several large pieces spun across the floor and rattled. The rest sat in a starburst semicircle around the puddle of tea.

"Now tell me, where's the soul?"

"Well," he said, smiling at her theatrics. "It's on your floor, that's where."

She got up, took a dishtowel from the sink, and crouched over the mess, dabbing at it with the towel.

"Not just on the floor, but everywhere. In me, when I drank it. In the air, evaporating. And yes, on the floor."

She wiped up a large pool of tea and held out the wet dishtowel.

"And sometimes, places or objects or people themselves, they act like a sponge. Spirits cling to them, get into their fabric. Using them to move from one place to the other, like tea from a bag to a cup to the floor and now into the sink."

She twisted the dishtowel, beads of tea dripping between her knuckles and into the sink.

"And Mabel… oh, the spirits did cling to her. If I were a candle, she was the sun."

He bent down and scooped up a few remaining pieces of the broken cup. Tamara took them with a smile and dropped them in the garbage bin.

"I still don't understand, physically, how she could have painted that picture."

Tamara studied him for a moment, then let out a disappointed sigh the same way Linda did with Jessica after hours of studying only to find her unable to remember a single word.

"Dan, you haven't been listening. It wasn't Mabel that painted it. She was just a medium, a conduit for the dead." She lifted her fingers, tapping her freckled cheeks just beneath each eye. "And the dead, they aren't blind."

BLEED-THROUGH

HE DIDN'T REMEMBER much of the drive home. He left Madame Tamara's not long after nine and crossed back over the southbound Golden Gate before midnight, his FasTrak box chirping as he sped through the toll lane. He had spent the drive rewinding the day's events in his mind. They felt distant, detached, as if they'd happened to someone else, some character in a movie. He refused to believe that the painting sitting in his house right now was made by a blind lady who had ended up as food for half the cats in the county. A blind lady who channeled the dead and, if Tamara was to be believed, poured it out onto canvas like a human photo-printer.

It had to be a scam, a rouse, just like the one he'd seen Tamara pull on the couple who'd lost their child. An elaborate stunt to build a mythology around a single obscure painting. It wouldn't have been the first. There were stories, countless tales of cursed paintings or forbidden objects stolen from the tombs of pharaohs or the coffers of dead Jews during wars. Unholy reliquaries and haunted wine boxes and paintings sold on eBay with warnings that said *BUYER BEWARE!* Sometimes they even fetched incredible prices in private auctions. But in the end, the stories were always revealed to be hoaxes and the sellers exposed as scam artists playing on people's obsession with the supernatural.

But if it was a scam, he thought, it was an elaborate one. One that involved a dead body and a clock that tied it directly to him. And two notes, both written in that childlike scrawl. Had it been a child's hand that wrote it or the hand of a blind old woman? A woman whose hands, if Tamara's madness was to be believed, had jerked about between canvas and palette like the limbs of a marionette guided by an unseen master. A conduit, she had said. A conduit for the dead.

And what did the dead want?

He thought of his lecture, of the script he had memorized and recited with little thought. *To be remembered,* answered Mr. Glass, throbbing deep inside his gray matter. *To be pulled through the fog of time and decay and neglect, pulled to the surface and shown to the world.*

THE ALARM, NOW ALWAYS ON AFTER DARK, BEGAN ITS TWENTY-SECOND countdown by the back door. He put the combination in and pressed the star button, and the blinking red light turned green. Upstairs, footsteps echoed out, fast and hard, like a child out past his bedtime and sneaking back in. Tommy perhaps, playing his video games well into the night. Dan crossed through the dark kitchen, pausing for a moment as something gleamed off the wall in the moonlight. It was a firefly, flickering in the darkness. No, it wasn't. It was something else.

That hole in the wall, the one made by the knife, had grown larger. Fissures had sprouted out of it like cobwebs, leaving wrinkles in the wallpaper. An electrical hum came from within the hole. Dan touched it, wet and soft, then peeled a chunk of loose plaster out.

An insect wriggled forth, buzzing like a high-voltage power line. He gasped, repulsed, as the thing clicked and buzzed, emitting that same high-frequency noise and fluttering veiny, transparent wings. He recognized the insect, though he hadn't seen one in years.

It was a cicada.

He didn't kill it, though he wanted to. Instead, he wrapped it in a tissue, put it inside a jam jar, and left it on the sill by Linda's wilted roses. He tried not to think about how many more might be between the walls. Tomorrow he would call the exterminator and have them bug-bomb the whole kitchen if need be.

He tiptoed up the stairs, passing through a cold draft that made him shiver, and as he reached the hallway, the sound of a door shutting downstairs made him pause for a moment. He didn't remember if he'd left the kitchen door open or not and decided he must've left it ajar. The house was old, after all, and it was only at night, when everything was silent, that its old bones creaked as it settled into sleep.

He stuck his head inside the kids' room. Tommy was curled up on his side in the fetal position, the pillow over his head as if he had fallen asleep trying to block out some noise. Only his lower half stuck out from beneath that sports comforter.

Above him, Jessica slept in the middle of her bed. Her pillow was empty, and her body lay curled and hidden beneath the sheets. Her stuffed toys and dolls were all lined up at the foot of her bed like little soldiers facing their commanding officer. Yet something was wrong with them.

All of her dolls and toys were missing their eyes. Some had empty holes in the fabric where buttons had been torn out, leaving behind torn thread or stuffing. Others, with hard plastic faces, had their eyes simply scratched off, as if by some sharp instrument. Dan gave the shape beneath the covers a gentle pat, felt it shift, and tiptoed out of the room, wincing at the static shock from the doorknob.

He entered his bedroom, took off his shoes, and placed them next to the wall, glancing at the shape of his wife asleep on her side beneath the covers. When he turned on the bathroom light, the reflection in the mirror startled him. He looked older, more so than he remembered. In the overhead light, dark circles beneath his eyes made his face seem like a mask or the corpse of a stranger. He didn't often feel on the cusp of forty, but tonight he thought he looked the part.

He opened the medicine cabinet, finding the Imitrex in its plastic and foil sheet next to the Motrin and Tums. Those pink little pizza slices that silenced the tornado inside his mind. *Break glass in case of emergency,* he thought as he popped two bitter pills, considered a third, but decided against it. The only thing worse than a migraine was a rebound migraine, when the mind grew immune to the medicine and diminishing returns kicked in. That was a road he didn't want to go down, one that he imagined would end with Mr. Glass shouting and growing to tumorous sizes and Dan spending his day with the curtains drawn.

Five minutes later, as he crawled into bed, the glass had withered back to a manageable size, a pea inside his skull. The sheets were cold to the touch, as if they hadn't been warm in months. He glanced at the windows, checking to see if they were open, but they weren't. Dust hung in the moonbeams between the glass and the floor, and the HEPA cleaner hummed nearby.

"I think our daughter needs therapy," he said with a smile. "After today, me too."

He closed his eyes, rolled onto his side, and as he gave Linda's shoulder a gentle kiss, the skin on his back burst into goosebumps. Instead of being warm and soft, her shoulder was cold and had an unpleasant texture to it, a firmness that felt like the husk of a hard fruit. He wondered if he wasn't touching the headboard.

"Honey?" he asked, running his fingers down her shoulder to the back of her neck in the same way that always made her purr with ecstasy, but no such response came this time. And then he saw it, on her neck, and he sucked air in between his teeth as his fingers recoiled from her skin.

A black and red tattoo was etched on her skin where her shoulder blades met the base of her neck. Linda didn't have a single tattoo on her body.

"Karina?" escaped his lips.

The thing in bed rattled out a long, wet response that penetrated the very bone of his head, as if it were coming from inside his skull. His vision shook as that piece of glass vibrated and he felt the migraine erupt. The rattle grew as the shape in bed rolled over, silky black hair glimmering in the moonlight.

That thing was not his wife.

It was an abstraction, a vaguely feminine form that resembled Karina insomuch as a Picasso resembled a real person. Its eyes were empty black pits, as if giant thumbs had pushed them inward, leaving stretched skin sockets and shadow.

There was a moment, a brief negative space between the emergence of the thing and the comprehension and horror of what it was, when the world swam in perfect clarity. To a person behind the wheel of a car, it was that silent second before glass and metal shattered and buckled. To a condemned man, that final click of the lever before the gallows dropped and the rope snapped taut.

To Dan, it was the last bit of light being swallowed by the darkness as that old trunk slammed shut.

Then it was over and he was in his bedroom and the wet thing that lay beside him opened a painted maw. The death rattle that came from the Karina-thing raised to a crescendo. He felt himself falling backward into darkness as it reached out for him with sticky hands.

The impact of the floor and the rug beneath it sent a surge up his spine that snapped his mouth shut and jolted his nerves. The rug scraped against his boxers as he scurried back, away from that thing, that vague, naked form he'd once found so beautiful. Its flesh was covered in shifting, shimmering tattoos that consumed each other. Its skinny hands gripped the edge of the bed like those of a feral animal, a tiger about to leap from the trees, to pounce on him.

It rattled off words in a chattering voice that rose and fell in pitch. "What have you done?" it squealed, gray breasts heaving and twitching. "What have you done?"

Frantic, he slid back further, the fibers of the rug chafing his thighs. To his left, another shape emerged. Yellow was the first color to bleed into the world, followed by a patch of rust-colored hair atop a swollen head. The girl from the painting cowered in the corner, not five feet away from him, whimpering and crying. Her hands kneaded a moist shape. Small fingers over blue feathers where a dog collar with a brass tag dangled from the wet filth.

"Answer me! What have you done?" the Karina-thing clacked, perching on the bed.

"I just wanted to scare him," the girl from the painting sobbed.

He felt his bladder empty warmth down his leg, and his fingers burned as if the skin had been peeled back and every nerve was being pulled by tweezers. *Move,* he thought. *Run away.*

A light appeared at the doorway. Then a shadow crossed before it, eclipsing the warmth and safety of the hallway. A boy stood there, that very same boy from the painting. His clothes were filthy and wet, as if he'd been playing in a slaughterhouse. His eyes, if they could even be called that, were simple blots of darkness that stared straight at Dan.

And his right arm, that twisted texture like leather or the roots of an old tree, was not an arm at all but an obscene appendage. It was old skin pulled taut like thin rubber stretched over moving organs, a swollen umbilical cord. The skin glistened beneath the hallway light, all the way from the shoulder down to where it connected to a rectangular shape. The shape it was fused to gleamed with brass and metal.

It was the shape of the familiar old trunk.

The kid took another step, passing through the threshold of the door in a sudden flicker. The appendage stretched, and the tension pulled the trunk across the floor, bouncing and rattling and leaving a crimson trail in its wake.

"Dan!" the voice called, blending between that of his wife and Karina's and a thousand others, and all he could do in that moment of madness was cover his eyes and scream.

He felt their hands. One at first, then two, warm and strong, grabbing his own hands. The light was so bright, and behind it, he heard an old voice ask, "What have you done?"

The hands pulled at his fingers with ferocious strength, and someone shouted his name again. He didn't want to open his eyes, didn't want to let in whatever lay in the darkness beyond, but it was overpowering, a tidal surge between the cracks of his hand. Fingers pulled at his, cold and strong, breaking through his grasp, and he screamed and lashed out.

Linda fell backward onto the bedroom floor. Her back connected with the edge of the bed, knocking the box spring and mattress crooked. Her nightgown was askew, hiked up above her hips from the force of the fall, her underwear exposed between splayed legs. Her face was a mask of horror.

Tommy stood at the edge of the bed, just where that dark boy had stood, only Tommy was crying and covering his mouth. "You're scaring us! Stop, please!" he gulped again and again in run-on sentences.

Only Jessica was silent, unaffected by what Dan realized had been a nightmare. She combed the hair of her doll softly, as if ready to fall back asleep.

"Goddammit, Dan," Linda said, her words spat out with an indignant rage. "What's the matter with you?"

THAT QUESTION LINGERED IN HIS MIND FOR THE REST OF THE NIGHT AS HE tucked the kids back into bed. To his surprise, Jessica had simply crawled to the top bunk and required no more attention than a simple hug. It was Tommy that, despite his outward strength, had been most affected by seeing his father caught in the grips of a waking nightmare, and Dan knew nothing he could say would erase it. The kid would carry that memory for years. The best he could do, the best he could hope for, would be to minimize the damage.

"What were you dreaming?" Tommy asked.

"You know, I honestly don't remember," Dan answered with a smile and a nod, pulling the sheet up to his son's neck.

"Was it scary?" he asked.

Dan nodded.

"I don't understand. Why do we dream?"

"That's a good question, but I don't know. No one really does for sure. Some people, scientists and stuff, they think our dreams are a way to work out our problems. Kind of like thinking while we're asleep."

Tommy's eyebrows dropped and he squinted, pondering the thought. "So if we have a nightmare, then we're thinking of a really bad problem?"

Dan smiled. "I don't know, Tommy. Maybe. The important thing is, they aren't real. They can't hurt us."

Tommy nodded and smiled. Dan could see he felt reassured, and if it took lying to his son so he could sleep that night after what he'd seen and heard, Dan thought that was an easy price to pay.

"Yes they are," said a flat voice from above. Dan stood up, looking at the top bunk, where Jessica lay with her back to the room. He wasn't sure if she had spoken since the accident, but it was the first time she had spoken to him. Her voice lingered in the air, a hoarse echo, a shell of the sweetness it had once contained.

"What was that, honey?" he asked.

She rolled over, looking him straight in the eyes. He felt for a moment that he was not gazing into the face of a six-year-old girl but into the eyes of something far wiser. And something far more truthful.

"They're real," she said again in that hoarse voice. "They can hurt us."

"What are, sweetie? Bad dreams?"

She shook her head and pointed a finger at the floor. Somehow Dan knew she wasn't just pointing at the floor but beyond it, and the only thing he knew that lay beneath the boards of the bedroom floor was the study below. But she wasn't pointing to the room, he thought. No, she was pointing to something in the room.

She leaned in close and whispered, "First they took the old woman. Then they took Ginger. And then the girl with the skin pictures."

"Skin pictures?"

"On her back," Jessica said, and Dan felt his blood run cold.

"Who? Who told you that?"

"The man with the broken name," she said as she turned over and hugged Mr. Bun. Then, as if she had answered a simple math question, she whispered, "Goodnight, Daddy."

LINDA LEFT THE LAMP ON HIS SIDE OF THE BED ON, PERHAPS, HE THOUGHT, to ward away any further nightmares, no different than when the kids asked him to leave the closet light on. He turned off the light and climbed back into bed. Her skin was warm as he slid in next to her, her back spotless of ink. He shut his eyes and touched her skin, and as he did, he heard her voice, soft but clear and precise. Two words.

"Who's Karina?"

He hesitated, fingers trembling on the skin of her back.

"What?" he asked.

"You said a name," she said in a flat voice.

"Did I?"

"Mm-hmm," she said again.

He took a deep breath, considering all the possibilities, all the ways he'd planned to broach the topic with her, one day, if he had to. But now, he thought, now wasn't the time.

"I don't know. Name doesn't ring a bell," he said to the darkness.

Beneath the sheets, her feet moved away from his. "Liar," she said.

SCRYING THE NETHER

TAMARA AGREED TO visit that afternoon.

He needed to get Linda out of the house. The idea, the fact that he called Tamara, embarrassed him, and he didn't want to stack his wife's doubt onto his own. He told her he had to go to the university and couldn't pick up the kids from school. He also knew Tommy had soccer practice and that Linda would have to bring Jessica along to that since Dan, in theory, wouldn't be home. That left him with two hours of alone time at home, and to buy a little more, he asked Linda to pick up Chinese for dinner, knowing it was over in Menlo Park. Despite her insistence they had enough leftovers, she agreed, as long as he phoned in the order before six. Then he canceled class for the second time that week.

It worked out perfectly.

Linda pulled out of the driveway just before three. Not thirty minutes later Tamara pulled in, driving an old Buick that belched out smog as it settled in the driveway. Dan caught a glimpse of Marty peering over the fence like a kid watching the circus come to town.

He didn't know what he expected from Tamara: perhaps some grand arrival, a flock of ravens unfolding to reveal her form, or a hearse with tinted windows and a pentacle for a hood ornament. He found himself disappointed. In the light of the day, she looked no different than anyone else he'd come across at one of the local organic grocery stores or DMVs, going about their daily chores and paying their bills. The peninsula was filled with enough odd people, and compared to some of the students he'd seen around campus, Tamara wasn't that outrageous.

"Thanks for coming," he said, reaching out to shake her hand. She gave him a gentle shake but didn't answer. Instead, she studied the house, her eyes tracing its form like an architect surveying a construction site. She nodded, not at him but at the task ahead.

"I don't mean to rush you, but my wife comes home in a few hours. I don't think she'll be too happy about this."

"Say no more." She smiled and hoisted a worn leather bag from the trunk. "Now, about the fee we discussed. I feel uncomfortable asking for payment upfront," she said, letting it hang in the air.

"Don't," he said, opening his wallet and removing eight crisp fifties. She had agreed to come down in part, she said, because she wanted to see firsthand what Old Mabel had created. However, business was business, and she required a full day's fee, quoted at four hundred dollars. "Just be honest, okay? That's all I ask."

"Of course, hon." She smiled, taking the money and tucking it into the pocket of her old coat. Then she clapped her hands and said, "Now, let's get down to business."

SHE PAUSED BEFORE CROSSING THE THRESHOLD INTO THE HOUSE. He noticed that same small set of prayer beads clutched in her hands. They were dark, made from some soft wood and adorned with symbols he didn't recognize. They could just as well be some prop from Harry Potter, but he suspected they weren't. She thumbed over thirteen of them, then nodded and stepped inside.

"I can definitely feel a presence," she said in a slow voice as her eyes traced the contours of the entryway, same as they had outside.

"Sure it's not the wind?" he asked.

She gave him a glance that lasted only a second but said it all: his humor wasn't welcome while she was working. "Whatever it is, it's old. And it's angry."

She walked over to the window, staring at a small crack that had formed around the crown molding. She reached a finger out to touch it, then paused, thinking against it.

"Tell me about the child, your daughter."

On the phone, he had told her about Jessica and her words that had chilled him. He left out the details of the nightmare and the shifting woman with the "skin pictures," as his daughter had called them. Hallucinating a painting was one thing. Hallucinating a missing woman he'd had an affair with was a whole new problem.

"What do you want to know about her?"

"Well, how old is she?"

"Six. She's in kindergarten."

"Was she an orphan? Adopted?"

"No," Dan said. "Why do you ask?"

She didn't answer. Instead, she nodded, as if some private curiosity had been satisfied. She walked into the living room, giving slow, thoughtful glances at the couches and the stitching that ran down the pillows. Her lips moved with faint whispers.

"Your son, he doesn't believe in Santa Claus, does he?"

Dan laughed. "Tommy? No, he believes in sports. Soccer, basketball in the winter, baseball in the spring, video games in between."

"But your daughter does. She has imaginary friends, I'm guessing."

"She's six. Of course she does."

Tamara bent down by the fireplace and reached her hand over the decorative logs. A second later she pulled away, as if burned by an invisible flame. A good actress indeed, he thought.

"So, what, you think she's being haunted by the ghost of Saint Nick?" he asked.

"Did I say that?"

"No, but come on. What kind of question is that?"

"Remember the tea, Dan? Children, sometimes the elderly, sometimes even people of great faith, they act like conduits. Why? 'Cause they believe. Much easier to pass through a door that's open than one that's locked."

"What if someone doesn't believe?"

"There's always more than one way into a house. And more than one—"

Tamara snapped her head back to the foyer. Her eyes scanned the stairs, as if something silent and unseen had just run down them and into the hallway. He felt a chill pass behind him.

"The painting," she said, reaching out an arthritic finger that pointed past Dan, to the door at the end of the hallway. "It's there, isn't it?"

DAN ENTERED THE STUDY FIRST AND TURNED ON THE LIGHT. AGAIN, Tamara paused before the threshold, thumbing another thirteen beads before entering. Her eyes bulged as they fell upon the painting at the other end of the room.

"Heavens!" she said. "It's like Ol' Mabel described."

Tamara studied it, a small smile crossing her lips as if she were seeing a photo of a long-dead friend. Then the smile faded and she pulled her hand away from the painting.

"Something's wrong. Something's missing."

"What?" he asked. "What's missing?"

"I don't know, but it's unfinished. Like something's just a bit—"

"Off-balance?"

"Yeah," she said, nodding. "That's the word."

She squatted on the floor, placing the duffel bag down and running her fingers along the floorboards.

"What are you doing?"

"Shh," she quieted him and put her ear to the floor like a child listening for a distant train, ear to a rail. Then she stood up. "It's everywhere."

"What is?"

"I don't know what it is, but it's everywhere."

"In the floor?"

"No, everywhere. Like the tea, it's moving from place to place. Growing like an infection, a sickness."

He thought of Linda's rose bushes and how sick they had looked. That crack in the wall, how the very plaster had grown moist with something foul and rotten inside. The cicada, the photos of the dog, the blue jay, even his dark dreams these last few days.

"I sense memories. Sorrow and rage, like a… a voice crying out from the nether, not for justice… but something darker."

"Back up," he said. "What do you mean 'memories'?"

"Some spirits are shades, traces of negative emotions left behind by an incomplete life, an injustice. A stain, if you will, unable or unwilling to be washed away and forgotten. Over time, they grow, distorting, fermenting, transforming, like an organism in hibernation, until they're strong enough to emerge from the cold nether."

"What's the nether?"

"It's the negative space. The void between life and absence. To cross back, they need a conduit, a hole between this world and the nether."

"And then what? Old Mabel found it?"

"Or maybe it found her."

She bent down and opened her bag. He caught a glimpse of several woolen-wrapped objects and the glint of metal. She removed a wooden bowl with an inlaid layer of metal and glass.

"What is that?" he asked.

"It has many names, but most call it a scrying bowl. Those older and wiser than I believed silver to harbor special properties when dealing with the metaphysical."

"Vampires and such, right?"

"Not quite. Silver conducts energy and reflects light better than any other metal. As a man of science, I'm sure you knew that." She winked at him, reached into her bag, and pulled out a bottle of water. She shook it several times.

"Holy water?" asked Dan.

"Blessed by a virgin priestess of the Oakland tribe." She took a sip and swallowed it. "It's tap water, Dan."

He smiled as she poured it into the bowl, lifted the bowl up, and swirled it around until a small whirlpool pierced the surface. Then she placed it back on the floor and waited for the water to settle. Beneath it, the silver acted as a mirror where Dan saw his own distorted reflection.

"Please, step back while the water settles," she said, and he took three large steps back toward his desk. "Try not to make any vibrations."

"What are we supposed to see?"

"Extra-dimensional entities—spirits, if you will—are often dormant, invisible to our spectrum of light. It takes a lot of energy to manifest in our dimension. That's why, some believe, hauntings happen in waves. Phases, they call them. Like the moon."

"So it's a ghost camera," he said with a smile.

"In a sense. The water and the silver distort this residual energy, like a crystal or a camera lens, bending it into our dimension, where its shadow becomes visible."

She bent down, looking at the clear, motionless surface of the water.

"Here we go," she said and picked up the bowl.

She began by walking around the room, holding the scrying bowl close to her chest like it were a hot bowl of soup. Each step was careful, precise, and she moved with a grace he'd thought impossible for someone of her weight and age. Her face held a focused, concerned expression as she took two steps closer to the painting. Her bottom lip quivered, and a slight gasp of air escaped her nose as her nostrils flared.

"What do you see?" he asked, thinking for a moment that a small part of him was beginning to believe the theatrics, if only out of morbid curiosity. What had she said? Open the door? Yes, he was opening it, but only a crack. And what he saw inside seemed like bullshit.

"I…" she said in a quiver.

"What?" he asked.

"I… I don't…" She peered closer, face wrinkling.

Spit it out, you old kook, he wanted to say.

"I don't see anything," she said, turning to the left, angling the bowl at the painting again and craning her neck sideways. She did the same to her right and took another large step back.

"Nothing?"

"I don't understand. I felt a presence," she said, her face filled with confusion. "I'm sure of it."

Dan stepped toward her, making sure his footsteps were light and soft. He peered into the bowl, his back to the painting, and as he did this, Tamara screamed.

The bowl fell from her hands, clattered, and rolled across the floor, leaving a trail of water behind. She leaped backward, and her face changed in an instant from confusion to horror and repulsion. She covered her mouth as she stared at Dan with wide eyes. His heart pounded, ears ringing and flushed with warmth.

"What was it? What duh-du…" he stuttered, words like glue in his throat, and he could feel his fingers curling. "What did you see?"

"I need to go," she said, and there was no sense of calm or kindness in her voice anymore. Instead, she sounded like a scared child. "I'm sorry, but there's nothing I can do here and I really need to leave."

She left the bowl on the floor, broken and wet, and by the time he caught up to her, the front door was closing.

"Tamara," he called out as he hurried to the driveway. She slammed the trunk and made for the driver's side door before he could intercept her. "Tamara, please, wait. I don't understand—"

He grabbed her shoulder and she shrieked again, sliding away, down the length of the car as if he were about to stab her.

"Don't touch me!" she gasped. Her hands dug into her pockets and she took out the money he'd given her. Four hundred dollars, eight fifties, and she didn't so much hand it to him as toss it on the ground at his feet. "Take it back. I don't want it."

"What did you see? Tell me!" he demanded, and she took another step back like a kid about to be whipped by a belt.

"The hell is going on there?" shouted a voice that he knew belonged to Marty. Dan snapped his head around, saw that old bastard by the fence, a hose in his hand.

"Not now, Marty!" Dan shouted and turned back to her. "Tamara, what was it? Please!"

Her eyes were filled with tears and her lips trembled as something resembling sadness settled across her face. She shook her head and opened the door to her car. Then she looked him in the eyes for the first time since she'd run out of the house.

"I saw everything," she said in a voice laced with pity. "I saw it all, and there's nothing I can do to fix this. I'm sorry—I'm so very sorry—but I can't help you."

"What? I thought you said—"

"I was wrong. Your family, get them away. Get them far away from all this."

"What? Where?"

"Anywhere!" she screamed, then covered her mouth. Sadness washed over her again, and her lips trembled. "There's no happy ending here, nothing. I'm sorry, but I need to go."

And she closed the car door, started the engine, and drove off down the street, leaving Dan alone on that driveway. Far away, a cicada hummed in the breeze of the late afternoon.

HARD EVIDENCE

"LISTEN TO YOURSELF. I implore you, Daniel. Listen to what you're saying."

He drew a breath in between his teeth as he paced before Dean Robert's desk. The office was clean, unlike Dan's, more of a museum than an extension of the classroom. Dean Robert leaned back in his expensive chair, the kind the university only supplied to its eldest and most respected faculty. The chair squeaked and broke the silence as Dean Robert thumbed through Dan's report.

"I can hardly believe I'm saying it either. Trust me, there's something wrong with that painting. Something off."

Dean Robert tossed the report onto his desk as if it were something disgusting, something beneath contempt. It was so unlike his usual calm that the action struck Dan as vaguely comical.

"Something off?" the old man asked. "You're basing this, this absurd conclusion, on what, exactly? One, some fairy tale your daughter told you. Two, a string of coincidences, half of which you admit were dreams. Not exactly irrefutable proof given your behavior as of late."

Dan cut in. "My behavior is not the issue—"

"I'm not finished." Dean Robert slammed his fist on the desk, rattling his gold-plated business card holder. This time the action wasn't comical but sobering. "And three, and I want you to pay attention to this part: the fact that it gave some psychic, of all people, the heebie-jeebies?"

"I think it killed the artist that made it. Or played a part in her death."

Dean Robert shook his head, opening the report to the third page.

"Ah, right," he said in that condescending tone that made the glass behind Dan's eyes swell. "The so-called artist. An elderly ghost whisperer who, according to this, was blind. And ignoring that minor detail, she was also best friends with the very psychic who sold you on this crazy idea in the first place. This is how people join cults or… or… or lose their life savings."

"She didn't want my money. She gave it back."

"Sure, and she'll be back next week for ten times the price! How do you not see this?"

Dan stopped in his tracks, eyes darting about the floor as another idea came to him. "The fire."

"What of it?"

"Maybe Karina didn't set it."

"I don't follow."

"The fire happened the night we got that painting."

"We received three others that day."

"But it wasn't burnt."

"And neither were they! Not because they're supernatural. Because when the warehouse moves a painting to the Archive, they go in the first available space, and that space was next to the sprinkler!" Dean Robert took a deep breath. "My god, I feel like I'm talking to a child."

A child? The glass behind Dan's eyes slid back and forth in precise slashes at those words. Fireworks lit up when he closed his eyes and rubbed his temples. He had to sit on the couch to get his balance. Dean Robert let out a disappointed sigh, as if his own son had been sent to a gulag.

"I know what this sounds like," Dan said with a sheepish grin.

"No, Daniel, you don't. Madness wouldn't even begin to describe the way you've been acting this semester. We're all on thin ice, what with the fire, now this whole Karina thing—"

Dan felt his fists curl into tight balls. "I didn't have anything to do—"

"I don't want to hear it. I'm too old and too tired for lies. Now, I encourage you, one friend to another, go home. You want to take on this side project? Fine. Trace it all the way back to Vlad the Impaler, but get hard evidence, okay? Not some silly story that destroys your reputation."

Dan felt his fingers stop moving. An idea, as bright as a flashbulb exploding, swam into his head and the glass stopped moving.

"Hard evidence," he said. "You're right, Bob. I'm sorry. I don't know what I was thinking."

"Just do your job," the old man said, and Dan could see disappointment in his eyes. "That's all I ask."

Dan nodded. "I will."

"THAT SHOULD BE THE LAST OF IT," SAJID SAID, SCREWING THE VIDEO camera into the tripod. They stepped back and studied their work.

It had taken two hours to set up the equipment, and now half the photography lab sat in Dan's study, pointed toward that giant painting. Tamara had her scrying bowl and he had Sajid, who hadn't required as much convincing as he thought he would. In fact, he took a particular interest in the technical side of the plan.

The only promise Sajid had required was that the equipment be returned by seven in the morning so it wouldn't be labeled as missing when inventory was taken. The university had strict protocols and limits on how much equipment could be checked out, and Dan knew he had gone above and beyond that. He also knew that if he put in the proper requisition forms and filed the necessary paperwork, they would make their way to Dean Robert's desk during one of his mid-semester budgetary reviews. And there was no way he could justify over forty thousand dollars of equipment used on a project that, hours before, he had scoffed at. But in the end, he would have his hard evidence and Dan would have his apology.

Sajid pointed at the camera on the left, the first of three. "This is the primary video. It'll always be running. Should be able to store at least twelve hours at broadcast quality. It's not the best, but it'll do for a master shot. Next to it, we've got the thermal passive imaging camera, this little toy."

He waved his hand in front of the large camera that looked like something seen at an airport. Dan noted a dark blue rendering of four fingers and a thumb on the display screen. Sajid flexed his hand, and orange and purple ripples of heat emanated from it in waves.

"It captures anything with a temperature. It's calibrated to room temp, so if something's hotter or colder, it'll show up. Like the *Predator* movies. Follow?"

"What about this?" Dan asked, pointing to the back of the camera array. A large DSLR camera sat at waist height with a white ping-pong-ball-sized half circle mounted above it.

"That's set up with motion sensors, no different than an automatic door, just a whole lot more sensitive."

Sajid pressed the *standby* button, then snapped his finger in front of the camera. The two studio flashbulbs popped without delay. Blinding light bounced off the silver umbrellas, bathing the room in momentary white as the camera clicked several times. Dan blinked, trying to wash out the spots burned into his eyes.

"Now, once you start it all up, it's like home security: you don't need to touch a thing. To turn it off, flip the switch." Sajid tapped on the industrial power strip on the floor. "Any questions, Professor?"

"Yeah," Dan said. "Do you think it'll work?"

Sajid studied the setup, nodding with a proud smirk.

"In theory, absolutely it will, no doubt."

His gaze fell to the painting, the centerpiece of the setup. The girl, the boy, the room, the window, and that distant tree atop the hill, all frozen and silent as if posing for some surrealist photoshoot.

"Personally, I hope it doesn't. That's the creepiest fucking painting I've ever seen. And if that thing moves, you've got bigger problems."

"If that thing moves, I may not be as crazy as I feel."

"Or, you know… crazier," Sajid said with a nervous laugh.

TICKTOCK

"ARE YOU FINISHED?" Linda asked. Her presence brought him back to the present, away from the paper and those words he'd spent the evening studying. She stood at the door, sweatpants rolled up and the remnants of the evening's cleaning on her terrycloth sweatshirt.

"Yeah, I'm done," he answered, and she took the plate of cold lasagna from the desk where it sat uneaten for the last two hours. Her actions were muted, annoyed, like when she shunned Tommy or Jessica for saying something impolite or cruel to her. The only sound was the clatter of the fork and knife.

"This too?" she asked, pointing to the wineglass where the red wine had settled and left a layer of sediment at the bottom. He swirled it, watching the ruby maelstrom engulf the tannins.

"Cheers," he said with a smile that she didn't return. The mere fact that he smiled made her squint, as if he'd somehow slapped her with his behavior over the last twenty-four hours. He had forgotten to order the Chinese food and she had called him, furious, wondering why she was at the restaurant, trying to pick up an order that had never been phoned in. Italian was the fallback, and her mood sank further when she returned to find him and Sajid setting up the camera array. She wanted that painting out, not because she believed it to be any more than canvas and paint, but because her husband had changed with it around. His eccentricities grew, his stutter was more frequent, and his words were charged with an intensity that made her want to take a step back from him.

He gulped the wine down in one sip, smacking his lips and licking the dry bitterness that coated his cheeks. She took the glass and walked out, adding, "We're going to bed," in a flat voice.

"Okay, goodnight," he called out, but she had left, and some part of his mind remembered it had not been a minute ago but perhaps several. Perhaps an hour, even.

He returned his gaze to the notepad spread out on the desk, his nemesis, the thing he'd stared at so long that his lasagna had dried and his wine had settled. Old Mabel's note contained cryptic scribblings, but he was beginning to feel that her madness had a method—or at least a shadow of it.

The note read,

XII:4 I:1 II:9 III:18
IV:14 VI:5 VII:8 VIII:20
V is the key to the door.

The Roman numerals had numbers next to them, eight in total. The painted clock had nine numbers, minus one for the V at five o'clock. Yet when he paired them up, all he came up with was a series of numbers that made no sense. And that final hint, *V is the key to the door*, ambiguous and maddening. The more he focused on the numbers and their sums, the more the glass burned behind his eyes. Like the painting, it was a puzzle without enough pieces to solve it.

He crumpled the note, buried his head in his hands, and pushed his thumbs into his temples. Minutes passed in slow beats, during which the glass simmered and cooled. He could hear the ticktock of the clock down the hall, like a metronome, counting every second. He tried to make it to one hundred without blinking and found it easier than he'd imagined. After all, he'd always kept great time. Down the hall, the clock chimed twelve times at the exact second he knew it would.

Dan blinked, and in that brief second as his eyelids descended and a single frame of shadow took over, he felt as if he could see that boy in the overalls blinking with him.

But the boy hadn't, of course. And this whole idea, the absurdity of it, made his lips draw up into a cynical smirk. He felt like a kid trying to draw shapes out of a passing cloud in the vast fields beside the orphanage.

"DOG," DAVID HAD SAID AS DANIEL SCANNED THAT BOUNDLESS MIDWEST sky filled with countless clouds. "Dog with three legs," he added.

"There." Daniel pointed above them, his fingertips no longer wrapped in bandages but now dotted with small scabs.

"Not bad," David said as something wriggled in the grass nearby. A bug, perhaps a rollie-pollie. He might try to find it and feed it to the geckos in the science room. No, that would be a mean thing. He didn't do mean things anymore. Instead, he'd rather sit with his little brother.

"My turn," Daniel said, eyes scanning the sky. "Okay, the thinking man."

"Like the statue?"

"Yep," Daniel answered. David studied the tapestry of the cloud, the puffs of white shifting at the ends as lazy winds tugged them over the Great Plains. One cloud stuck out, a shape closer to a rectangle with a small protrusion that seemed to reach out and curl back, and he could see blue sky through the errant wisp.

"There," David said, pointing straight up, and as he did, the shape emerged from the cloud and he saw with precision what Daniel had wanted him to see. The vague form of the upper half of a man, his arm curled back, hand resting beneath a head that hung downward in contemplation. *The Thinker.*

"Found it," he gloated. "Okay, my turn. How about…"

He scanned the clouds. So many possibilities, so many pictures, and one even looked like a rabbit.

"Bugs Bunny. See if you can find that," David said, nodding and turning to his younger brother, but Daniel wasn't there any longer, and only an empty spot of flat grass remained.

THE CLOCK DOWN THE HALL CHIMED AGAIN AND DAN BLINKED, UNSURE OF how long he'd held his stare on the painting. He tried to remember how high he'd counted. Had it been two hundred? Three hundred? He had lost count, and no matter how hard he tried, he couldn't recall what benchmark he'd passed.

His eyes were dry, and the piece of glass behind them throbbed in low, dull bursts that left a sour, dirt-like taste in the back of his throat. And his legs, they lacked feeling. When he tried to flex his toes, a pain shot upward from his feet and ended at his waist, half asleep and buzzing with phantom beestings.

And over all of this, the painting still loomed, staring back through three sets of eyes: the boy, the girl, and the shadow, closer still. As he blinked, he sensed they were blinking in time with him, no different from his own reflection when he combed his hair in the mirror. As he took a breath, it seemed, so did they.

That frustration, that impotence of being unable to catch them in the act, grew like a rash screaming to be scratched. The more he stared, the more still they remained. And yet, like a trick of light, out of the corner of his eyes, he could see dust particles floating in that old room behind the layer of paint and a distant firefly flickering in the twilight field.

"Come on," he said, feeling his fists ball up.

"Come on," he said, standing up.

"Come on!" His voice rose as he took several steps forward, closer to the ring of cameras pointed at the painting. Only the mocking tick-tock of the clock down the hall was brave enough to answer him.

And the painting remained as it always had, still and quiet.

His eyes scanned around the picture, starting with that boy, across the room to the girl, and then between them, rising upward, like he'd found the tip of an invisible triangle between them. His glare stopped on that hill with the single sick tree, its leaves now gone, its branches like a thousand broken fingers reaching to a blue sky filled with clouds.

Clouds, he thought. Perhaps even Bugs Bunny. Those clouds hadn't been there before, had they? Yes, the sky had been empty, rendered with a western glow; this he knew. But now it was deeper, the shadows were longer, and the clouds had bled in as if they'd always been just beneath the surface, emerging like water stains.

And the shadow atop the hill. That abstract form of vague, human semblance. It was larger, closer, as if it'd taken yet another four steps toward the viewer. Yet Dan couldn't imagine the painting any other way. He knew it had changed, but it seemed to have always been this way, as if this were its natural state of existence and the change had taken place not on the canvas but in his memory.

Funny thought, said Mr. Glass, and he felt it slide upward through his brain and come to rest directly on the bone of his forehead.

"Come on," he said one last time, willing the painting to do something, anything, to prove that part of him that thought this madness incorrect was indeed neither mad nor incorrect. A part that said it would be easier to follow the madness, to give in to it rather than to step back and think, for one clear second, that this fact was true: he was in his house, talking to a painting, and daring it to move.

The clarity of that one thought was sobering. It was as if the manic energy that had kept him focused on that painting for the last three and a half hours had, in mere seconds, revealed itself as a symptom of something far darker.

David finally lost it, Mr. Glass mumbled. *Went away and never came back. Care to keep going down the rabbit hole?*

"Cowards," Dan found himself saying, not just to the painting but to himself. He had allowed Tamara to infect him with her ideas and superstitions, just like his brother's scary stories that had lingered with him until dawn.

Chicken, Mr. Glass replied, but the only sound that answered back was the distant metronome of the clock down the hall as Dan switched off the light.

He poured himself a glass of pomegranate juice and swallowed it in a half dozen gulps. His eyes stung, his throat felt parched, and his thirst was bottomless. He poured another glass and did the same, wiping his mouth and licking a small splotch of the ruby juice off his hand like a vampire.

The last several hours had passed in a blur, a splice cut from his life. Despite having remained as focused and motionless as a monk, he felt exhausted to his core, as if he'd run a marathon or been locked in another all-nighter with Karina at the Chateau Adultery. His hands danced and shook when he held them out in the glow of the refrigerator light. He put the juice away for fear of dropping it.

He placed the cup by the sink, eyes falling to that jam jar on the sill next to the wilted roses. Inside sat the tissue—and something else. It wasn't the cicada he had found the other night but something brown and old. He opened the jam jar and fished it out.

It was a piece of leather. It was old and cracked, covered in stitching from where it had been attached to something. It looked as if it had dried and fallen off a suitcase from a century ago. Or something larger.

No, it had come from the inside of the wall, he told himself. The house was old, and beneath the layers of paint and wallpaper lay things that even he didn't know about. Not bugs but physical things, remnants of its previous lives with previous families no different from fossils. There were no cicadas, and any other explanation led back to Tamara and her infectious ideas and this whole stupid plan.

He would go to bed, he thought. Go upstairs, lie down next to his wife, and fall fast asleep without brushing his teeth. His body would welcome the warm bed, and before he could count to fifty, he would fall asleep.

Then, as he threw away that piece of leather, a realization washed over him: an electric arc between two related thoughts, a connection that made his body grow cold.

He had thought of falling asleep before he counted to fifty, and he'd been counting the clock for the past several hours.

But now the clock was silent.

No, said Mr. Glass, *it's always been silent. Or did you forget?*

Yes, he thought. It had always been silent and he had forgotten.

The clock was a gift from Linda's parents, and it sat in the hallway for eight years. But that was until two years ago, when Tommy and Sam knocked it over, splintering it beyond repair. Not even the faint spot on the wall where it hung for years now remained. It was boxed up, put in the basement long ago, swallowed by time and memory along with all the other forsaken things that lay beneath the floorboards.

Something popped like a single kernel of corn, and while he was pondering the clock, it popped again. A third time, and he smelled a faint odor, as if a fine layer of dust had been burned.

And then he saw it. In the hallway, beneath the door to the study, came a flash of white light followed by the sound of a camera clicking away.

THE DOORKNOB TO THE STUDY WAS COLD TO THE TOUCH, AND HE hesitated, listening as the camera whirred in a rapid one-two-three click on the other side. Pulses of light reached out beneath the door. He braced himself, turning the knob, and the door didn't so much as open as seem to melt away into the walls and the shadow.

The room was as dark as he'd left it, yet it felt larger, cavernous. The overhead lights gave a dim flicker as their power was redrawn to the flashbulbs aimed at the painting. A half second after they pulsed, the room dropped back into shadow, the coils of the flashbulbs fading from a brilliant white to a faint amber. In that half-second explosion of light, that blinding freeze-frame where all was visible, he could see the air thick with dust motes that danced like fireflies. A few pieces of dust landed on the hot flashbulbs and were vaporized into wisps of smoke.

In the center of it all sat the painting, motionless and still. Nervous, Dan approached the circle of cameras, looking for movement within that forlorn canvas but finding none. His glance dropped to the three cameras, one capturing three still frames in rapid succession and the other two recording video. The video camera's display jumped between shadow and blinding light, catching only brief glimpses of the painting before the pixels bled white from the flash and the autofocus readjusted. The thermal imaging camera display showed the painting in that same cool color as the rest of the room, deep blues and turquoises giving way to faint wisps of red from an outside streetlight. There was no movement in either of them.

"Come on," Dan said, staring back at the painting, and a second later, he felt a chill, as if a pocket of cold air had passed through him.

It started, first as an imperceptible shift. Darkness grew, no more than an inkblot on the thermal imaging viewfinder, and for a moment Dan thought the camera itself was malfunctioning, like an antique movie projector burning a reel of film. The inkblot bled across the display, outward in symmetrical directions from the point on the painting where the shadow stood. It unfolded, as if a line had divided it and the halves were mirror images of each other. It grew into a viscous stain of darkness, swallowing the amber and purple-heated hues of the thermal display, two lines protruding like long ears. He heard a voice say, "Found Bugs Bunny!"

But it wasn't a cloud or a rabbit on that liquid crystal display, rather a hole opening, a shadowy orifice that swallowed the rest of the picture's heat signature like invisible flames consuming the canvas. His eyes left the viewfinder and fell on the painting itself, scanning it in the brief light between the darkness, but nothing was amiss. Everything stood where it should: the boy, the girl, the clock, the room, even the shadow. There was no change, only an evanescent feeling that things were not as they should be.

The thermal viewfinder showed a different reality, one beyond his vision. In that dimension, the inkblot grew larger, like a cancer attacking healthy cells, consuming them and turning them to shadow. It rippled as it grew, repainting the canvas not in a single shade of darkness but in an undulating abyss of black, colors impossible to isolate from each other. A shimmering oil slick of emptiness.

And it grew larger.

A pop, a flash, and three clicks.

The shadow reached the edge of the painting.

Another pop, another flash, and three clicks.

He took the thermal camera and zoomed out until the canvas

shared the viewfinder's space with the study and the room around the painting. Through the LCD, the shadow bled over the edges of the painting, and he felt his mouth dry up. The darkness was cascading from the borders like vines, climbing the wall behind the painting. Blackness dripped out onto the floor and crawled up the bookshelf until the camera could zoom out no more and cold shadow devoured it all.

Another pop, another flash, and three more clicks.

Movement caught his eyes and he looked up from the now-black thermal display. He heard a distant ticktock as the clock in the painting began to swing its pendulum. At first the motions were rigid and strained, like a flip-book animation or an old movie effect. It swung in three frames—left, right, center—and repeated. Then it added a fourth and a fifth frame until its motions grew as smooth as any other clock. He no longer saw the layer of paint on the canvas. It had vanished. Or perhaps it had simply never been there at all.

Another pop, another flash, and three more clicks.

The clouds came next. They shifted and moved away from the viewer, giving that painted window a feeling of endless depth. Long shadows passed over that grassy hill with that rotten tree atop it.

Another pop, another flash, and three final clicks.

Then the thermal viewfinder changed and his eye fell from the painting back to the LCD screen. The darkness remained, but a new color grew from it. Blue. The coldest color the camera could capture. Two blue figures emerged from that black void.

A boy and a girl.

Dan's eyes snapped back to the painting, and there they were, staring back at him. The painted girl stood up and the boy smiled through brown teeth.

And they both blinked. He'd finally caught them.

Then, in the four-second space that it took the flashbulbs to cool down and fire up again, both the painted children traversed a great distance. They moved out of the painting and appeared less than a foot away from Dan, no longer flat but fully spatial and moving. He saw the top of the boy's head, his hair parted over a gray scalp. And the girl's yellow dress, billowing as if made from paper.

And in that brief flash, the room became terror.

The boy let out a rattle as he lugged that fleshy trunk-arm behind him. His one gray hand, as cold as the deep ocean, grabbed at Dan's arm. The girl belched forth a backward laugh as she held a deformed object in her arms like a Madonna with child. It was a twisted canine shape of animal hair and blue feathers sewn together. It wore Ginger's glittering collar and stared out through button eyes, tongue hanging from where a jaw should have been.

The images overwhelmed his senses. As that flash faded, he saw with utter clarity that he was no longer standing in his study at home but inside the very room of the canvas overlooking that hill as the shadow walked toward him through the field, and he felt, more than anything, utter and complete regret. He opened his mouth and screamed.

Then the flashbulb faded, the darkness embraced him, and endless winds extinguished his screams.

OFF SITE

HER FACE EMERGED from the nimbus of light, wrapped in a hood of golden hair, smiling and reaching out for him. Light bled in around her, and he saw the chandelier of the study ceiling and the crown molding behind her gentle face.

"Dad?" she asked, her warm hands touching his forehead. "Dad? Are you okay?"

Jessica was clutching Mr. Bun and wearing her pajamas. Behind her, the light of dawn crept into the study. He could hear a bird chirping through the window and the distant sound of garbagemen as their truck beeped and backed into reverse.

His words were heavy and thick. He tried to answer, but his vocal cords burned as if he'd spent the last few hours screaming, and he thought he just might have. There was no vast gulf between the events and the morning, only another splice and a splitting headache in the form of the glass, swollen and sharp. He swallowed and answered, "I'm okay, honey."

She knew it was a lie, and her smile seemed to fade a little as he said it.

"What time is it?" he asked.

"Early," she said. "Mommy's still asleep."

"What…" He coughed. "What are you doing up?"

"I had a bad dream," she said.

"Me too." He laughed. "Me too."

"I know," she said and wrapped her arms around his neck in a hug. She held that child's embrace, her fingers petting the back of his head with the same tenderness she showed her dolls, and Dan felt warmth surge through his body.

"I forgive you," she whispered and released her grasp. Then, without any further explanation, she turned and shuffled out of the room, dragging a now-eyeless Mr. Bun behind her.

Dan rose to a sitting position and surveyed the study. He had lapsed into unconsciousness halfway between the door and the ring of cameras. His neck popped as he sat up and his right ear throbbed as if it had broken his fall.

The painting sat where he had last seen it, the various artifacts and occupants reset to their original positions like some sort of demonic Disney ride. The camera equipment and lights, however, were not as he had left them. Both the thermal camera and the DSLR had fallen over. Pieces of their bodies and lenses lay scattered about like broken teeth. The two work lights had fallen backward and lay shattered on the floor beside scorch marks. Only the video camera remained upright, its display blinking with a red low-battery icon.

HE DIDN'T WAIT FOR LINDA TO WAKE UP OR MAKE BREAKFAST. HE DIDN'T even shower or brush his teeth. Instead, he did what he felt was the first smart thing he'd done in weeks: he hauled that evil fucking painting out of the house and stuffed it in the back of his car. All six feet of it went in, back seats folded beneath it. The camera equipment went next to it, broken pieces rattling in the metal cases.

He sat behind the wheel and took a deep breath, trying to shake the chill that had settled upon him after he awoke. It wasn't even seven and the harsh morning light bloomed off the silver hood of his car and burrowed through his eyes, into that piece of glass behind them, hitting it like a prism that scattered his thoughts.

One, two, three, he thought. *Focus on the task at hand. Keep calm and carry on.*

His fingers reached into his pocket, feeling the memory cards inside. When he got to school, he would, of course, make copies, but not until Dean Robert had seen their contents. There would be apologies, of course, directed at him. There would be speculation and verification and the video would be analyzed until the old man had nothing to do but turn to Dan and say, "My god, you were right."

Yes, that's how it would go, he thought.

But that was hours away. For now, there were more pressing matters. The painting had to go. Another hour in the house was another hour of infection, another hour for those things to step out of the frame again. If it was up to him, the whole thing would burn, but this was bigger than him, bigger than one dead psychic and another who had fled. This thing, he realized, changed everything he believed in. If paintings could move, then, well, there were other roads to go down. Roads that led to answers to questions he had yet to consider.

Chicken. Yes, Tamara had been a chicken, but he wasn't.

The wretched painting seemed to know his intentions, and from the back seat, he heard a dog whimpering and a clock ticking. They would be silenced shortly, he thought as he turned on the engine. He had just the place for them.

HE PULLED INTO THE STORAGE FACILITY FIVE MINUTES AFTER IT OPENED, driving through the gate and down the rows of endless orange storage sheds until he found unit G-22. He did his best to focus on the crappy pop music. He had to. The voices started shortly after he left his house. An incessant whispering and counting, like children playing hide-and-seek behind him. He half expected to look in the rearview mirror and see their ashen, painted faces looking back, but they never appeared. Still, their words lingered, distracting, and he drowned out their counting and laughter with bad radio.

His tires squealed as he pulled up sharp to the curb and popped the trunk. He paused before the digital lock to the storage unit, struggling to remember the combination. It was rented in the university's name, paid for on his faculty credit card, and its contents were mostly old student projects and furniture of little value from his previous office. He had also stored some of Karina's belongings in there when she moved apartments in March.

That was it; he remembered the combination. It was her birthday—day, month, and year, in that order. He had changed it so she could get in and had forgotten to change it back.

He punched the eight digits in. The display chirped and the metal shutter rumbled upward, dropping small plumes of dust.

"In you go," he said to the painting, placing it against an old bookshelf that had sat in his office until last winter. The fluorescent bulb above flickered twice, one-two, bathing the interior in a lazy yellow glow.

He gave the painting a final glance and thought of Ginger and how she'd whined at the kennel, literally screaming and throwing herself about the cage, all over a week-long vacation they took to Hawaii that had cost him a month's salary. He caught a whiff of Karina's fragrance and heard a faint buzz of a summer cicada.

"Don't go anywhere," he said and pressed the close button.

MELT DOWN

"JESUS, DANIEL, YOU look awful," said Dean Robert, mouth hanging wider than usual. Sajid turned, having been in whispered conversation with the old man when Dan had burst forth from the stairwell. His eyes opened so wide that his tan forehead became a creased sheet of wrinkles.

"Bob, you nuh-nuh, you nuh..." Dan struggled as the words caught on his tongue, thick as clay and tasting of salt. He tried again, slower, holding up the memory card. "You need to see this."

"I DON'T FOLLOW. WHAT AM I SUPPOSED TO SEE?" DEAN ROBERT ASKED, squinting through his glasses at the image on the screen. Sajid had imported all the photos from the camera memory card and was scanning through them like a flip-book on the monitor. They started with the test photo, where Sajid had tripped the motion sensor and it captured the painting in perfect clarity in three separate snapshots. The timestamp read 8:22pm.

The next set of photos came at 10:24pm, another series of three depicting Dan waving his hand before the camera and studying it with disdain. He remembered taking those when he tested the set up a second time.

"First two sets were good," Sajid said. "But after that, it's corrupt."

The remainder of the memory card, 185 sets of three photos each, were all indeed corrupt. Each photo was little more than an inverted mosaic of dark pixels that matched the color palette of the painting. On some photos entire sections were simply black patches where no image had been recorded. Others captured brown and black static or mirror image pixel-blots like some low resolution Rorschach print.

"That's not right," Dan said. "Something's wrong."

"It's what's on the card," Sajid shrugged. "User error maybe, I don't know."

"I saw it, there was no user error," Dan said and reached into his pocket, finding the memory card with the video on it.

"Here, try this one," he said, and Dean Robert watched his trembling hands pass it to Sajid, who ejected the first card from the computer and inserted the second with a sigh. It took the computer several seconds to read the contents of the card and in that silence Dan could hear Dean Robert's teeth grinding.

"Don't worry, Bob," Dan said with a smile that the old man ignored.

"Okay, here we go," Sajid mumbled, clicking on the video files. The screen dimmed for a moment and the video began playing. Like a surveillance video, it showed a jerky still frame every half second above audio. In the center sat the painting. At the bottom of the image, in the timeline slider, waveforms depicting recorded sound rose and fell like small mountains.

"Here?" Sajid asked.

"No, keep going."

Sajid sped through the thumbnails of the video, pausing over a set of audio waveforms rising around an hour in. He slowed the video down again, still centered on that unmoving painting.

"We're going to bed," said Linda's voice off screen. A break of thirteen minutes of silence in the audio waveforms was depicted as a plateau, then another wave rose up and Sajid played that.

"Okay," said Dan's recorded voice said off camera. "Goodnight."

Dean Robert fidgeted in his seat as Sajid scrubbed through another two hours of video footage, the sound waveforms little more than a flat line, the thumbnail images unchanging.

Then, at 2:25am, the thumbnails showed a dramatic change. They depicted darkness, single frames of shadow. The waveforms rose in steady peaks that reminded Dan of a heart rate monitor.

"There," Dan said. "Play that."

"Okay, here we go," Sajid said, and he tapped the space bar that started the video in real time.

Darkness then light, alternating. The painting and the flashbulb. The audio played the rising whine of the flash charging in the darkness. As it hit its crescendo the painting appeared again, bathed in light before receding into shadow.

"Here, watch!" Dan pointed at the screen with crooked fingers.

Onscreen, the cycle continued.

Darkness.

The rising whine of the flash.

A pop of white and the painting staring back.

And darkness again.

The same pattern continued for thirty seconds until another voice emerged behind the sound of the whine.

"Come on," Dan's voice mumbled on screen.

"Come on," he repeated, sitting before the computer.

The pattern continued.

Darkness...

The whine of the flash...

The pop...

Overwhelming brightness...

And the painting: unmoving. Same as it had always been.

The three men watched the cycle continue and in that time no one said a thing.

"Skip ahead," Dan said, wondering if last night's timeline had been altered in his head. Thinking back, even less than ten hours later, he couldn't pinpoint when the painting had moved. Had it been three o'clock? Four? Five? Any of them seemed possible.

Then the computer speakers blared out a horrible screech! Dean

Robert's hands grasped the arms of the office chair. Sajid's fingers leapt together over his lips as if he were in wide eyed prayer. Only Dan hadn't flinched.

The screech exploded again, the camera convulsed, and the screen became a mosaic of green and pink pixels. For a moment the pixels cleared and the camera auto-focused on the grains of the wood floor, first in perfect clarity, then a blur. Back and forth it went for five silent seconds. Then all went black. The audio continued with a third violent screech, but this time it was recognizable. It was human.

It was the sound of a person screaming.

"No no no no no no," Dan's voice stuttered over the darkness on screen. "Don't pu-pu-put me in da-Da-THA-THERE!" it whimpered, rising into hysterics.

"I'M SORRY I'M SORRY I'M SORRY" his voice cackled, seeming to reverse backwards on itself in an instant, like a child who had cried so long his voice had given out. Then it continued again in a loop as he alternated between begging and screaming.

He didn't want to believe it was his own voice. Sure it sounded the same, perhaps even came from the same lips, but he did not remember saying those words. He couldn't have. That voice answering his screams was as alien as the words coming out of it.

"Please," his voice begged from the dark video frame. "Please don't put me in there."

"Here in art, denial," it said.

"My name is Daniel Rineheart!" he cried out.

"Here, in art, denial!" it spat back, louder.

"My name is Daniel Rineheart!" he cried out again.

"Here! In art! Denial!" it called back.

"MY NAME... IS DANIEL... RINEHEART!" he screamed.

Then it all stopped. Only the rising whine and pop of the flash in the dark video frames. The room was as quiet as a crypt.

"Enough," Dean Robert said, and air escaped from Sajid's mouth as if he'd been holding his breath for minutes.

"Wait, there's more—" Dan said.

"Enough, Daniel," Dean Robert repeated, firm voice cracking as he added a whispered "Please."

Dan saw in his old friend's eyes that same sadness he'd seen before, when he'd lied about the affair, when the investigators named him as a person of interest, and when he had pitched this whole idea to the old man not a day ago.

"Enough," the old man whispered.

SEASON'S END

THEY FINALLY DIED.

The roses, all six bushes, had succumbed to the canker sometime over the last twenty-four hours. In the afternoon light, the once-green stalks now sagged, bare of petals or color, little more than thorny sticks in a bed of mud. Those petals that had held a pastel hue even up until a day ago now sat in the damp mud, color bleeding out as rot took over. Linda clipped a few branches one at a time, top to bottom, until they were reduced to gray stumps, indistinguishable from the surrounding foliage. There was nothing she could do, nothing to do, but mourn their loss and remove them.

Move on, like Dan had said about the dog. Move on, from eight years of work in the garden, from seedling to bush and now to dead stick.

"Move on," she said to herself, taking the trowel and working it into the soil around the root ball of the smallest plant.

"Move on, why? Why? Why did you move on?" she said, feeling the earth split beneath that trowel as she forced it deep into the moist, sick soil.

"Why did you die? Why? I did everything for you. I did everything you needed, everything I could," she said, sweat forming on her brow as she felt the roots snapping and breaking beneath the metal. Her hand drove the trowel into the soil, no longer digging but stabbing the poisoned earth that had killed her garden.

"It wasn't enough! It wasn't enough! It wasn't enough!" she screamed, burying that metal trowel deep into the ground and then releasing it. She could feel sweat flowing down her face and something else dripping. Tears perhaps? No matter. She released the trowel and grabbed the base of the dead bush. The thorns dug in through the thick leather gloves, and it felt nice, that biting pain in her hands. She let out a scream, and as the thorns broke through leather and skin, she pulled the stalk back and forth, feeling the earth and roots beneath it come loose.

"Why did you die? Why?" she shouted, and she found strength in that pain, feeling those roots grow weak in the old soil. Those roots that had born petals she'd nurtured season after season. Those roots that'd born colors she'd placed on the windowsill and her father's grave. Those roots, once strong and alive, now lifeless and limp.

Pulling, screaming, and in an eruption of dirt, she fell backward, clutching the stalk of the bush, its moist root ball hanging limp at the end of that pathetic stalk. She gasped, looking at the hole in the soil, letting the dead bush fall from her hands, back to that tainted earth. It was done.

She felt, for the first time in years, something. Not a numb void but rather a pain, searing and torn, in the palm of her hands. A glorious hurt beneath the leather gloves, ripped skin and blood and feeling. Yes, a feeling of life, of something that told her, yes, she was alive and those roses, like her father, could hurt, even after they'd died. That they would always hurt, but the pain they left behind only meant she was alive and that she had cared.

There, in that dead garden, she realized that despite the tears coming down her cheeks, she was not crying but smiling and laughing.

LINDA TOOK A FINAL DRAG, THEN TWISTED THE EMBER CHERRY OF THE cigarette, flicking it toward the dense patch of ivy. She wrapped the butt in a tissue, depositing it, along with the remaining pack of cigarettes, into the garbage. She no longer needed them, no longer even wanted them. They were, as they had always been, nothing other than a hollow way to commune with her father. And like the roses, he too was gone, never to return. All that remained was the lighter, which she placed back into the junk drawer, knowing that in months or years, on one of her cleaning purges, she would find it there and smile at it. Time would relegate it to a happy souvenir, a token from a different life, a memento, and nothing else.

The footsteps came from above, thick and heavy, echoing down into the kitchen. She could almost see the ceiling bending, as if something was running in the very fabric of the house.

"Jessica?" Linda called out as the footsteps faded.

Jessica, she knew, was upstairs, but she had remained quiet for most of the early afternoon, content to doodle and have another tea party with her toys. But now she was banging about as if chasing Tommy. But Tommy was off at soccer practice, and the footsteps that rang out upstairs seemed to come from several sets of feet, not one.

Linda took the stairs one at a time, listening as the sounds of footsteps continued to bang out from the upstairs hallway. As she rounded the corner, she caught a scent, a distinct whiff, of wet fur and something else, something old and rotten, not unlike the same stench that came off the roses. No, she thought, something deeper. The air smelled of wet earth, pure, like a storm had scoured the interior of the house. Yet outside, there was only fog.

Then a distinct chill passed over her, and she had, for a brief moment, the sensation that she wasn't alone in that upstairs hallway but rather surrounded by others. She felt her skin go cold, and her eyes scanned around, but there was nothing. Only her footsteps and the voice coming from the kids' bedroom down the hall.

She lingered outside the door, listening. From within came a cacophony of voices. Not one but several, all talking over each other like some childish poker game, and beneath it all, she heard a clock ticking and a dog barking, as if coming from a great distance away. It didn't sound like a tea party but a full-blown event, voices fighting over each other and laughter beneath it. All from a room divided by mere inches of wood.

She ignored the pop of static as she turned the doorknob, driven by a curiosity and a fear that beyond that wood separation lay another horrible discovery: her daughter, face-down in the brackish water of the old hot tub, or her father's revenant, pulling a dirty coin from Jessica's ear. As the door swung open and her eyes took in the room, she gasped, and her equilibrium fell away.

"My god," she whispered, unable to find any further words.

Jessica stood in the center of the room, smiling at her mother. In her hand hung the nub of a crayon, worn down to little more than the size of a fingernail. The box of crayons sat on the kids' table, torn to shreds, splayed open like a dead animal. A pile of worn-down crayons, perhaps all sixty-four, sat like discarded cigarettes around the dismembered box.

For a moment, Linda lost all spatial perception and bearings, and she felt as if she'd stepped not into a room in her house but into another dimension. It was an ocean of color. The walls, the window, the floor, even the ceiling itself had all been scribbled over in spastic crayon marks. The floor and walls were rendered dark and brown, slashes and circles like old wood. The two walls to Linda's left and right were covered in jagged sketches of decayed objects: an old bookshelf, a broken mirror, an old sink and what looked like a calendar bearing the year 1952. Opposite Linda, the furthest wall bore an angular grandfather clock. To its left, centered, just as it had been in the painting that was downstairs, sat the children's window, again covered in felt-tip marker. Drawn on the glass, and bleeding out from it to the walls in colored tendrils, was a scribbled landscape: a distant sunset over a dead field with a single tree atop a hill.

That window, now covered in marker and crayon, sat more ominous than all the other colors and images. At its center, frozen like a burglar climbing into the house, stood a drawn shadow as large as Linda herself. The dark form was scribbled as if climbing into the children's bedroom, fingers clutching the windowsill.

There were no words that Linda could find to express her utter shock at Jessica's creation. The room had been transformed, rendered into three dimensions like a funhouse trick. The bunk bed, the table, the shelves, each object felt foreign and detached from the tone and images that now covered every inch of the walls. It was as if she were standing within a painting.

"What have you done?" Linda whispered.

Jessica smiled, still clutching the nub of the black crayon, proud of her creation. Then she pointed to the window and said, "We have visitors."

DENIAL

THE OLD SCHOLAR closed the door to his office and motioned for Dan to sit on the couch. He did, unable to keep his foot from tapping on the rug.

"Bob, I don't know what to say—"

"Don't say anything," Dean Robert said, but it came out in three separate words, each pronounced with force. *Don't. Say. Anything.*

The dean opened his bottom desk drawer and removed a bottle of Johnnie Walker Blue, a present that Dan and Linda bought him years ago before they discovered he had quit drinking. The seal cracked as he opened it and poured two glasses, one into a proper snifter glass and the other into a coffee cup. He gave Dan the glass and kept the cup, taking a slow sip of the amber liquid and turning his attention to the window overlooking the quad.

Outside, students went about their mornings beneath the cold autumn air. Not far off sat the sculpture garden and the Gates of Hell, and on a good day, he could see it. But today there was a faint fog and those statues lay out of sight. Dan sucked the whole drink down and it settled in his stomach. He needed the warmth for what was coming next.

"You've put us all in an awkward position here, Daniel," said the old man.

"I didn't mean to," Dan answered.

"Of course not. No one means to make a mess, but the results are one and the same."

"Bob, please," Dan found himself saying, begging almost. "I don't know what happened on that tape, but—"

"Stop," Dean Robert cut in, cold and sharp. It was business now. It had always been. Somewhere along the line, Dan thought, he had gone off the rails, confused the two. Their friendship could only go so far.

"I won't pretend to know or understand whatever it is you're going through. That would be dishonest. You are, obviously, having some sort of crisis. That much is clear."

"It's not a crisis," Dan mumbled.

"Whatever it is, it's affecting your judgment. And your professional behavior. Do you agree?" he asked.

"I..." Dan said, thinking about Linda and the kids. Oh God, what was he going to tell them? Dan couldn't bear to look Dean Robert in his eyes. That man, that kind old man who had hired him a decade ago, had seen such promise in him, had even treated him, at times, like a son.

"I agree... It looks a little strange," Dan answered.

"A little strange? Your behavior has been erratic, to say the least, and frankly discomforting. Look at you. You're unkempt. You obviously haven't showered or taken any interest in your appearance."

"I had a rough night."

"I saw. I wish to God I hadn't, but I did."

"Bob," Dan said, and he could feel tears in his eyes. "Please don't do this."

"I'm retiring this year."

"What?"

"That was the plan. I'm retiring, and I was going to recommend you chair the department. I'm not sure I can do either."

"Bob, I... I don't know what to say."

The old man took a long sip of the whiskey, savoring it. Then he turned to Dan. "I'm suspending you from further academic responsibilities for the remainder of the semester. I could have you fired on multiple causes this very minute. Improper ethics, dereliction of duties, rumored sexual trysts with students—"

The glass hummed. "I didn't have—"

"You stole photography equipment."

"I didn't steal it."

"No, you just bribed some grad student on work-study to do it for you. And you returned it in pieces. For what? What were you hoping to accomplish? A photo of some ghost?"

"Bob, that painting is fucking evil!"

Dean Robert's voice cut in like a cannon. "It's just paint and canvas! That's it!"

"No." Dan shook his head. "No, it's not just that."

Dean Robert leaned back, chair squeaking as he took a deep sip from his mug and closed his eyes. "I want you to listen to yourself, take a second and really listen, then tell me: were the roles reversed, would you not be saying the same to me?"

"I..." Dan started, but he felt the lie, thick and dry. It was stuck in the back of his throat, too heavy to expel. "I know how it looks," he said instead.

"My point, Daniel, is that I could have you terminated. But I'm not going to. You know why? Because I know just how much it would rip your family apart."

All Dan could do was nod. He knew Linda would have to go back to work, and in the current economy, with an eight-year gap, she would be lucky to land at Starbucks. The house, of course, would be impossible to pay off. There would be late payments, and they would lie to each other, trying to catch up as the envelopes got thicker. A few months later they'd receive a notice of default, and then, not long after that, a half season at school at most, the house would be sold out from under them. They'd find themselves standing on the sidewalk, handing over the keys to someone else, another family perhaps, two kids and a dog, and Marty would smile as they drove away from that little side street for the last time.

"Are you listening to me, Daniel?" Dean Robert asked.

"Yes," he answered in a soft voice, eyeing a blue jay as it landed on the windowsill and cocked its head sideways at him.

"You need help. I'm saying that as your friend because I've known you for a decade, but these days I hardly even recognize you. These little tics you get?" He held out his hand and shook it in the air. "The constant lies? Your students, they whisper about your conduct, and these whispers get back to me. And this obsession with that painting of yours, my god. Why I let you take a personal project on, I don't know, but it ends now."

Dan blinked and the blue jay flew away.

"What do you mean?" he asked.

"I mean, I never want to hear about it again," Dean Robert answered.

"You told me to track down its owner."

"No, I told you to figure out what to do with it."

"You told me to find out who painted it."

"What? Of course I didn't." Dean Robert laughed, and Dan felt his fingers curl into balls again. "I don't care who the artist is. That's your affair."

Dan leaned forward, staring into the old man's eyes for the first time since they'd stepped into that office. "You said it yourself downstairs: find out if it's an anonymous donation. It has your name written all over it. That ring a bell?"

"My god," said Dean Robert, and his face darkened. "Is that what you thought I meant?"

"What the fuck else should I think?"

The old dean's voice was slow and low, as if he were speaking to someone learning the language for the first time. "Miguel said, 'It has your name written all over it.' I laughed, because he was right. You understand art like that. Now, if you thought I was insinuating something else, I apologize."

"Bob, you told me it was my problem."

"It is your problem. It's your painting."

"It's not mine."

"It was sent to you. It belongs to you."

"It wasn't sent to me."

"Who else…" The old man paused, eyes narrowing. "Do you have the card that came with it?"

"Of course," Dan answered, fishing the card from his briefcase.

"Tell me, what does it say on there? Who's it for?"

"I don't…" Dan turned the card over in his hand. The same fifteen letters were there in that same scrawl. Only the order was different.

"Read it to me, Daniel. Please," the old man asked.

Dan wiped a piece of dirt off the card and read it aloud.

"It's my name," he said. "Daniel Rineheart."

"Of course it's your name. It's always had your name on it."

PUBLIC SPECTACLE

HIS FINGERS DRUMMED the steering wheel as he drove away from the university for the last time. The old man's words still rang in his ear, mocking. It has your name written all over it. He rewound the conversation in his head a dozen times, furious with himself for not having caught the anagram sooner.

His name: Daniel Rineheart.

The title: Here in art, denial.

Daniel.

Denial.

Rineheart.

Here in art.

They were the words he had shouted from inside the darkness of that video, the words written on those pieces of paper at Old Mabel's house. Those shimmering letters that, like the clock from the painting, now seemed different when he remembered them, as if they'd always shimmered and changed, just out of focus. Had the card really held his name this whole time? Had the painting changed his memory, or had the opposite occurred?

Regardless, he thought, it was a stupid trick, and if that piece of glass behind his eyes hadn't dulled his senses, he would've discovered it sooner. The painting was covered in symbols that spoke to him, and if he'd missed one as simple as his name, what other clues had he overlooked?

Stop calling it that, said Mr. Glass.

"Not now," Dan mumbled.

Not now, not never, Mr. Glass whispered, and Dan thought of the Imitrex back at home and how it would soon silence that jagged headache so he could focus. Yes, there were other clues, many others to be found. And he would find them, he told himself, like finding animals in clouds.

But for now he was exhausted. His neck hurt from the few hours of sleep he had gotten on the floor, if sleep was what that splice in time could be called. His bed—he thought of his bed and his wife and how soft and warm they both were. He would sleep for a week and he would tell her he loved her and then, maybe a day or a week later, he would tell her his job was at risk. Or perhaps he didn't need to tell her at all.

Perhaps, Mr. Glass agreed.

He turned left, blowing through the stop sign a block from his house. Red and blue lights flashed, not behind him but in front. For a moment he thought he might have driven into a speed trap, but no. The red and blue came from outside a house he recognized as his own.

Fancy that, mumbled Mr. Glass.

Two patrol cars idled curbside. Neighbors were gathered, a dozen at least, their attention directed at several men wearing chemical suits and carrying boxes of equipment up the pathway to the front door of his house. He could hear the commotion through the window, and he felt his throat tense up. A truck, like an armored car used at banks, sat behind the patrol cars. The words *MOBILE CRIME LAB* were emblazoned in gold and black lettering.

"Linda?" Dan shouted out as he slammed the car door. The neighbors swung their heads in his direction. The world swam in a surreal thickness; the seconds felt heavy, as if they were happening elsewhere, beneath magnolias in some distant town with its quiet side streets. *Not here,* he told himself. *Not my house. Not my family.*

"Linda," he called again, and then there she was, Jessica in her arms, rushing over. Her face was scrunched, and he couldn't tell whether she was worried or confused or crying or perhaps all three.

"I tried to call you," she said. "I'm so glad you're all right."

"Is everyone okay?" he asked, searching for Tommy and spotting him standing at the edge of the fence like a stranger to his own house. His wife, his family, they were all here, and for a fleeting second he felt relief.

"What the hell's happening?" he asked.

"Professor," a voice said, and he recognized that smug drawl in an instant. "Glad you could join us."

Detective Cooper appeared from the crowd, heads turning and following him. Dan saw the bulge of a gun and a radio beneath his button-down shirt and gray blazer. He wore a smirk, like a playground bully finding the weakest kid alone and with a pocket full of lunch money.

"What's going on?" Dan demanded. "What is this?"

"This is a search," he said and held out a pink piece of carbon copy paper. "And this is the search warrant. Join us inside when you get a chance."

Dan snatched the warrant and glanced over it. His name and address were listed along a column to the left, and next to it, a box labeled *REASON FOR SEARCH* read *MISSING PERSONS CASE ID: BG2210-KFC*. He recognized the KFC as standing for Karina Francis Calloway. At the bottom sat a lazy signature on a line labeled *MAGISTRATE*.

They had arrived an hour ago, lights and sirens flashing. They had knocked and escorted his family out without an explanation. When Linda described it all, she teetered on the verge of tears. Her bottom lip quivered, her words were jagged, and she gave sidelong glances to the crowd. Helpless, he thought, a house cat that found itself deep in the jungle.

"Wait here. I'll take care of this," he said, but he didn't know how he could take care of it, only that he had to try.

He caught up with Detective Cooper in the foyer of his own house, now almost unrecognizable. Several men, perhaps a dozen in total, all dressed in chemical coats and jumpsuits, were in the process of affixing black tarps to the windows. The absence of light made the entryway feel subterranean, as if he were descending into a cave.

"That's close enough," said Detective Barton, flashlight in hand as he took heavy steps down the stairs.

"What are you doing to my house?"

"Luminol," answered Cooper as he picked up a spray bottle. "It's remarkable stuff, really. Picks up any trace of blood, no matter how hard it's been scrubbed. Here, put this on."

He handed Dan a disposable dust mask and cupped his own against his mouth.

"I'm curious, Professor," Cooper said, sliding the mask aside to speak. "That Heimdell, back in your office, how'd you come across it?"

"What the hell does that have to do with this?"

"Edify me. I'm curious."

"I don't..." Dan started, words heavy and thick, heart racing as the technicians sprayed the walls and shelves with that chemical mist. "It was a wedding present. From the in-laws."

"Hell of a gift."

"They were generous. Look, I don't understand—"

"Sure it's real?"

"What?" Dan studied the detective. Was this a joke or a test?

"The painting," Cooper said. "Sure it's authentic?"

"Of course."

"How do you know?"

"How do I..." Dan scoffed. "It's my job. Instinct. I don't know. Call it a hunch."

"A hunch?" Cooper raised an eyebrow as if he found the answer insulting.

Dan felt the glass grow. "There are things the artist did, ways he painted, colors he used and ones he avoided. He did the broad swaths right-handed but the details with his left hand because he had a stroke by that period. Details. It's like apples to oranges if you know where to look."

"The gap," Cooper said, nodding.

"What?"

"The gap between artist and amateur. Like a satellite photo of the Mississippi. Only a blue wiggle unless you're on its shores."

"Sure, I don't know. Look, what's this about?"

Cooper studied his watch and let out a sigh as if late to some important meeting.

"Faith, Professor," Cooper said in that slow drawl. "Would you describe yourself as a man of faith?"

"What the hell does that have to do with this?"

"It's an honest question. Heck, it's one of the oldest. These days, we get all upset. Like someone's trying to peek into our pants and see if we've got foreskin or not. But there's nothing private about faith. We just pretend there is. Step back please."

Barton's hand landed on Dan's shoulder, thick fingers digging in like the claws of a mother bear. He pulled him back as the technicians taped off the window. Dan's fingers curled into fists.

"You didn't answer my question," Dan snapped.

"And you didn't answer mine." Cooper smiled.

"I'm an atheist," he said between gritted teeth, realizing that he was starting to doubt even that these days.

"I didn't ask about religion. I asked about faith. They're different, the two of them."

"How so?"

"Faith's what you double down on when your hand's hot. What you hope has your back when you're boxed in. What drives you. Religion's just whose name you call out. See, we all put our faith in something. All of us. Some even put their faith in deception. Little half-truths here and there. Distortions, if you will, masked with smiles. Some might think themselves clever, twisting the truth around 'til it fits in whatever hole's the easiest. And others might ignore it, like a rat in a wall or some strange lump beneath your skin. Like a dinner party tale, changing a little each time. But me, you know what I put my faith in?"

"Cheap shirts and bad ties. I don't know."

Cooper laughed, slow and low, mask inflating with each chuckle.

"Truth," he said. "With a capital T. It's a powerful thing, don't you think?"

"Can't say I've noticed."

"Sure you have. Look around you. Your faith brought mine. That's what we're doing, Professor. We're chasing shadows."

"You calling me a liar?"

"Call it a hunch." Cooper smiled, dark eyes narrowing. "We're old enemies, you and I. Our faiths, they've been having at each other since the dawn of time. Reckon they will 'til the Rapture. Liars and the filth they spew don't change. They just think they do. Now the question remains: how wide's the gap between artist and amateur?"

He put the radio to his mouth, eyes never leaving Dan, and spoke into it. "We're ready."

The house grew quiet. From distant rooms, Dan heard the sound of work lights snapping on and warming up. A dim blue UV glow bounced off the dark tarps, giving the house a freak-show feel. Voices, faint and muffled.

"We've got something," the radio buzzed. "Southeast room, first floor." Several people snapped their heads in the direction of the hallway like dogs to a dinner whistle.

"Details, Professor," Cooper said as he removed his mask and followed the crowd into the hallway.

Flashbulbs strobed from the study, and Dan felt Barton pushing him to follow Cooper. No longer a viewer, he thought. Now part of the show.

The door to the study was open, the room darkened. A pop of flashbulbs and murmuring voices echoed out from within. Somewhere among the crowd, he could hear Cooper mumble, "Well, well," in that lazy drawl.

Dan continued, pushing his way in as several technicians stepped aside, their brown-stained teeth grinning in amusement. The study was bathed in a UV glow, the corners almost imperceivable in the shadow. His heart drummed and his throat grew dry and narrow in the hushed silence. The rhythmic flash of the camera and the whirring motor of the shutter were the only other sounds as a photographer kneeled and snapped picture after picture.

Then he saw the luminescent smear of blue light.

It started on the hardwood floor in the center of the room, a few simple splotches no larger than pennies. Six inches away, it grew. First in a single line, like a paint stroke, and then another line. Two more joined it and he could make out a vague shape, a handprint where the lines intersected. Four fingers and a thumb.

Like someone had been scratching at the floor.

The blue luminescence was thickest in the center of the room, emanating outward from a single massive stain that bore the impression of another hand, as if paint had been poured over a still subject.

But it wasn't paint. Or at least not paint that came from the end of a brush. It had come from someone, and he knew that the blood he lost when he cut his thumb was a drop by comparison. It was like the floor of a slaughterhouse.

The third segment of the stain was the most abstract and violent. Frantic handprints left small splotches behind, as if fingers had clawed and fought at some invisible wall. Two wide smears merged into a single twisted line like some lazy Rorschach print. Jutting out from the center was a single circle of small paw prints that Dan recognized. He'd seen them before, in the damp grass outside, in the mud, and all about the house over the last two years.

They were Ginger's.

Then the smear ended.

Not at the wall but several feet before it. The trails all coalesced into a single giant brushstroke that accelerated with a final lash of fury and vanished. A single flat line, five feet wide, ended the glowing trail like skid marks ending in a brick wall. But there was no wall, no object to collide with. There was nothing, only a void. Yet something had been there, he thought. Yes, something had stood there for the last several weeks until this very morning.

The luminance ended where the painting had been.

"What is that?" Dan whispered, and he realized the whole room was now staring at him.

"That, Professor," Cooper answered with a smile, "is my faith devouring yours."

INTERROGATION

THE INTERVIEW ROOM at the Alder Glen police station was warm, perhaps a bit too warm. He had expected stone walls, a single mirror, and an empty table with a recorder. The room had all these, but it felt less like a dungeon and more like a conference room where PowerPoint presentations were given to the presumed guilty. A water cooler sat in the corner, humming and burping the occasional bubble.

Dan ran his fingers through his hair. The situation had been a nightmare. The neighbors had stared, gawked, and mumbled as he stepped into the back seat of the unmarked patrol car. Tommy had cried, and when Linda hugged him, Dan saw tears in her eyes as well. Only Jessica had remained unfazed, smiling as the car pulled away, waving to him as officers unraveled yellow police tape across the wrought-iron gate of his home.

He hadn't been handcuffed or read his rights. He wasn't being detained, not yet, merely asked to explain the situation, as Detective Barton had put it. And now, waiting in that room, he realized there was little keeping him there other than his own fear of what would happen if he left. Outside the interview room, the moon hung low in the gray sky through a large window that could just as easily be broken as it could be slid open.

And if he did run, what then? How far could he get? Mexico, perhaps, or further south. What little money they had wouldn't last long, but dollars did stretch further south of the border, and perhaps it could buy him a fresh start. He could learn Spanish, take a job restoring art south of the equator. Linda could teach English and they could save their money day by day, building a new life in a new land with a new name.

He had done it before, he thought.

A new name. The glass laughed, and Dan rubbed his temples, trying to squeeze that little shard between his thumb and index finger, yet no matter how hard he pressed, it slipped away.

A new name. Wouldn't that be a riot? Mr. Glass giggled.

Dan studied that window, so easy to open. *Guilty men run,* he thought, *but the innocent stay. And sometimes the innocent even hang.*

"You're a real piece of work, Professor," said the drawl that he despised as Detective Cooper opened the squeaky door.

Detective Barton filed in after, stopping to fill up his mug with hot water from the cooler and take a sideline seat further away, dipping a bag of tea into the mug like a one-man jury.

Cooper nodded to the mirror. A few seconds later a red light appeared next to the lens of the surveillance camera. The glass laughed again. *Lights, camera, action.*

"I must say, when we first met, I sort of pegged you for the button-down weasel type. But this." Cooper tapped a folder as he sat down across from him, uncomfortably close. "This is quite a revelation."

"Gentlemen, I have no idea what you're talking about, okay?" Dan sighed.

Cooper smiled, as if he expected that sort of answer. He eyed Barton, who stirred his tea with a plastic spoon.

"You're here because of her."

He withdrew a small plastic bag from the folder and slid it to the center of the table. A photo of Karina stared back from inside the bag. That windswept black hair, the hint of a smile on her face, sunlight off her soft cheeks. Dan recognized the picture. He had deleted it and dozens of others on one of his Sunday night camera purges after they returned from Napa. But there it was, staring back at him, and he realized she must've copied it from his camera when he wasn't around.

"What about her?" he asked.

"What about her?" Cooper echoed with a laugh, then tapped the photo again as if Dan hadn't caught something in it. "Professor, you're a suspect in her disappearance. Her car, as I told you, was parked two houses down from yours. Her emails, well, we've read all those. Your name was all over them. Her fingerprints and maybe even her blood: both found in your house. Photos, dozens of them like this, were on her computer. And you say, 'What about her?'"

Barton let out a low chuckle, sipped his tea.

"Look again." Cooper tapped the photo. "Look closely. You remember this."

It wasn't a question but a statement. Dan did remember it. But what he said was, "Why would I?"

"Because you took it."

"No, I didn't."

"Of course not. You're right. It just happens to be the same make and model of a camera you own."

"They sell 'em by the millions. That's hardly proof."

"You're right. It's a coincidence, of course."

Barton laughed. "A coinkydink."

"And see, that's what I keep finding. So many coincidences. Here's another one."

He tapped that photo again, his finger falling on a distant object: a vineyard set on a rolling hill.

"See, I collect wine. I find it a good investment. Maybe 'investment' is a poor choice of words. I find it enjoyable."

"That's nice for you," Dan said.

"It is, actually," Cooper answered. "And I've been here. This little hill looking westward from the Rosinni vineyards. Took the ex-wife to this very spot myself. I remember driving back across the Golden Gate, paying the toll, stuck in traffic. Let me ask you: how much is the toll these days?"

"I don't know. Three bucks."

Another chuckle from Cooper. "Six, actually. But you only pay five. See, you've got one of those automatic FasTrak boxes in your car. Just drive on through, no slowing down. I keep meaning to get one but I always forget. Thing is, your FasTrak ID came up a day after this photo was taken. Southbound, back into the bay. Coincidence, of course."

"Another coinkydink," Barton quipped.

"I go to conferences there all the time—"

"Right. Conferences in Napa. The kind between two people, one of whom's married."

"This is absurd—"

"Is it now? Her emails didn't say the same thing. See, they sort of painted a very specific picture. A mentor and his student. A shared passion for art. Maybe it all started out a secret, something hidden, exciting. Something different. We're human, Professor, flesh and blood. Adultery ain't illegal, least not in California. So when you say 'absurd,' all I hear is a man trying to keep a secret from his family. Or a few secrets."

Cooper clicked his pen. Just once. But when he did, Dan saw the light overhead flicker for a moment and felt his left hand shake. He rubbed it with his right hand and saw Cooper's eyes flick downward for a moment.

"Look, I didn't have anything—"

"This affair, of course, is all hypothetical."

He double-clicked his pen again, eyes shooting down to Dan's hands as he made the connection. Somewhere, not far away, Dan heard a dog whimpering. "Please stop that," Dan said.

Cooper leaned closer. "People change. We all know that. Heck, woman I married wasn't the same as I divorced, and I'd be lying if I said I was the same man. Time changes everything, even secrets. And maybe this secret wanted more. Maybe she starts asking for things. Presents, like a custom bag with her initials on it."

Dan opened his mouth but Cooper smiled, perhaps anticipating it, perhaps hoping for a denial. Somehow they'd connected the custom satchel to his credit card. He held his tongue as Cooper continued.

"Maybe she wants more time with you, another weekend in Napa. Thing is, this kind of change is slow, like a glacier, inch by inch. Then one day you wake up and it's on the doorstep and there's no ignoring it. She doesn't want to be 'the other woman' so she gets more demanding. The calls aren't fun anymore. Meeting her is a chore. Maybe she goes a little Glenn Close and tries to kill herself. Of course, she doesn't say it was her fault. No, no, she says, 'You made me do it.' But we both know the truth: it was a calculated risk. That's why she did it when you were there."

"She did it because I was her only friend."

"You were more than that."

"No, I wasn't—"

"Yes, you were, but that don't make you a bad person. You know why? Because you took her to the hospital. You signed her in, came to visit. We both know a bad person doesn't do that. You cared about her."

"As a friend."

The pen clicked again. One-two-three in quick succession, and in the silence that followed, Dan could hear Barton slurping away at the last of his tea.

"So you took a stroll with this little Betty? So what? It's not like you tossed away the kids' college savings. You had no idea she was dangerous, did you?"

"Protecting his family," Barton said, and Dan saw the light flicker for a second. "Family first," Barton added with brown teeth.

"Exactly. Family first," continued Cooper. "So you call in a favor. You get an old friend to take her to Europe."

Dan felt his heart skip a beat. Cooper smiled and clicked the pen a few more times.

"That was her idea," Dan said.

"Not according to Nathaniel Spinozza," Cooper said, withdrawing a transcript from the folder. "He says, and I quote, 'Professor Rineheart practically begged me to take Ms. Calloway on as a student, a favor that turned out to be a terrible mistake. She was unfocused, unprofessional, and did irreparable harm not only to the project she was tasked with but to the program I started.' It's all here, this so-called idea of hers."

"No, no, no, he asked me. He asked a dozen others. Everyone knew about the program."

Cooper waved the lie away like a fart in the air. "But it wasn't about that, Professor. It was about her. Getting rid of her. Out of sight—"

"Out of mind," Barton added, and Cooper glanced at him like an actor whose precious line had been stolen.

"This whole thing—" Dan paused, clearing his throat as the words stuck. "You've got the wrong idea. Karina was, like you say, unstable. I don't deny that. She, I don't know, grew obsessed. She thought it was something it wasn't."

"Like love?" asked Cooper in a soft drawl.

"I don't know. But I did my best to help her find opportunities appropriate for her skills."

"Maybe she thought if she came back, you'd change your mind. But let's be honest: I've seen your wife, your family. Why give up all that for some girl?"

"Exactly," Dan said. "I wouldn't."

"That's why she didn't give you a choice, did she? No, her threats became worse. Students started talking. Your own boss, even he suspected. I know her type. The more you push away, the more her obsession turns to anger, resentment. Even violence."

"No," Dan said. "She wasn't violent."

"You sure? See, her father claims one of his guns went missing after she visited. We found his lockbox in her apartment, a case of nine millimeters inside. Only five were missing. Why only five?"

"I have no idea. I didn't even know she had a gun."

Cooper clicked his pen again. Dan clenched his fist, and for a second he imagined burying that pen in the smug man's throat.

"Five bullets. Four plus one. I think you know why."

"No."

"You knew what she was capable of."

"No."

"What she might have done—"

"No, you're wrong."

"—to your family—"

"No she wouldn't."

"—then to you—"

"You're so wrong."

"—and then to herself. One, two, three, four, five."

"She wasn't a killer."

"But you thought she was. Deep down, you knew. You knew there would be no happy ending to this."

Dan felt a chill as the detective spat out those three words: "no happy ending."

"So you did what you had to do to protect your family. Because family's what matters. She was going to hurt them and you stopped her."

"No," Dan said. "No, I didn't stop her."

Click-click-click went the pen.

"You protected your family. That's what a man does. She was going to hurt them and you stopped her. It was self-defense, after all. Ease your mind. All this, all these lies, we know the truth."

Click-click-click, again and again. Dan clenched his hands together and thought of distant fields and laughing voices. Of a dark old house and a hidden basement. Of going south and new lives with new names.

"You're wrong," he said. "You're wrong about everything."

"Am I?" Detective Cooper said with a smile as he clicked that pen again and again.

Dan closed his eyes. For a moment he wasn't in that warm room. He was far away, where the walls were white and tall and covered in soft fabric and a woman with a clipboard and a white coat clicked her pen as that ghoulish shape of his brother sat motionless in the middle of it all. And when he had tried to look into those eyes, they looked back, through him, beyond him, and he was nothing but vapor.

"David?" the shrink asked, but he said nothing in return.

"David?" Daniel asked as she clicked her pen, and when she did, he blinked, as if coming out of a trance.

"Are you there, David?" the shrink asked, but David just stared through the woman, through the walls and stone, to someplace far away. The overhead light flickered and his eyes drifted toward it.

"Am I wrong?" she asked again, clicking that pen, but her hands were large and calloused and they belonged to Cooper and the walls were now lined with a large window and a distant moon.

"Yes, you're wrong," said Dan as the room shifted back to that warm police room. He felt the lies grow within, a familiar calm washing over him, and in seconds all became transparent and simple and Mr. Glass grew heavy and hot.

They were clutching at straws. They had loose connections—circumstantial evidence, sure—and all they needed was a confession. A confession for something he hadn't done. *Guilty men run, but the innocent stay.*

"Gentlemen," Dan said with a broad smile that lit a fire in Cooper's otherwise calm eyes. "You want a confession? Here it is. You have nothing. You claim I had an affair? So what. You imply, you actually imply, I might've hurt her? Where's the evidence? This whole charade is bullshit. You have nothing on me. And you know it."

Cooper sucked air in through his teeth and his eyebrows danced upward. He held that look, as if he'd bitten into something wretched and the taste was stuck in his mouth.

"You're wrong about one thing, Professor," he said, opening the folder. He took out a small plastic bag no larger than a business card, and Dan saw Denise's familiar scrawl across the receipt at the top. In the bag sat that small stamp-sized piece of the painted canvas. "You gave us all the evidence we needed."

Dan scoffed. "What is this?"

"You tell us. You recognize it, don't you?"

"Of course."

"Lab said you gave it to them to test. Said it was canvas, but none they'd ever seen. Of course, we both know that's not canvas, is it?"

"What are you talking about?"

"It's skin," he said with a smile that extended across his face as wide as it could, and for a brief second his tongue was black. "Mostly human, from the preliminary results. But we did pick up traces of canine mixed in there, too."

"That's impossible."

"Not according to forensics. Look close enough and you can see a few little hairs. Right there."

Dan turned the bag over. On the unpainted side, he saw a small hair, a mole, and the faint trace of ink beneath skin.

"Get that fucking thing away from me!" Dan spat out, and his chair squealed on the linoleum as he shot back. His mind ran over the possibilities. The blood from his thumb, it had vanished when he returned. Cleaned up, he had thought. Or had it been consumed? And if so, what else could have been consumed?

"We've got you, pal," Barton said with a smile.

"Now," Cooper said in his slow drawl, "why don't you tell us what you did with the rest of her?"

Dan took a deep breath and rubbed his eyes.

"I want..." he started, pushing his eyelids until sparks grew in the darkness and each word felt as heavy as stone. "I want to speak to my lawyer."

LEGAL ADVICE

A FIREFLY APPEARED, drifting down from the ceiling vent in a small figure eight. At first he mistook it for a trick of light, a spot left burned into his vision by the headache and the fluorescent lighting. A gift from the piece of glass that still resonated white hot and mocked him for being so far from his pills. Yet the firefly moved in short, erratic spirals, too quick to be a migraine aura. He watched it flicker about the otherwise empty interview room, a dim yellow-green glow smacking against the wall and ceiling as a thought crossed his mind.

He had never seen a firefly in California.

"Daniel, my god," a voice said behind him, and he turned to find Mr. Cohen closing the door. He was dressed well—he always was—but his chestnut hair had become peppered with gray since Dan last saw him executing his father-in-law's will after the funeral.

"Thanks for coming," Dan said as they shook hands.

"Of course. How are you? Hanging in there?"

"I don't know. How's Linda? How're the kids?"

"I spoke to her and she's fine. She's coming to pick you up, so don't worry about them, okay?"

"They aren't holding me?"

"No, no, of course not," he said, placing his briefcase atop the table, brass buckles clattering in the hollow room. "They haven't charged you, and you haven't confessed to anything. Frankly, you should've never consented to an interview without my presence. Daniel, what the hell were you thinking?"

"I don't know. This whole thing, it's absurd. I haven't even had time to process it."

"I understand. I truly do."

"So what do I do? Tell me."

"Well, you have to understand, they're building a case. And they feel it's pretty solid."

"A case? I didn't… kill or do anything—"

"Daniel, please, just listen. I know you didn't, of course not. But to them, that doesn't matter. They think you did. And frankly, from what I've been told, they've got some fairly solid evidence to support that conclusion, however misguided it might be."

"I don't care. I know what I did."

Mr. Cohen took a deep breath. "They're considering a plea deal."

"Whu… what?" Dan stammered.

"I'd be remiss in my duty not to bring it up."

"A plea deal? What does that mean?"

"It means it's an option."

"An option? That's not an option."

"It's one they're willing to consider and one they're pushing hard. This city, they get something like this once a decade. The place becomes a circus. The whole town gets involved. I know the DA—hell, our kids go to school together—and I'm sure she doesn't want this thing going off the rails."

"Off the rails, huh?"

Mr. Cohen nodded. "No one wants that."

"I get hauled down here, in front of my neighbors. My house, my fucking house, is a crime scene, okay? I can't go back there. And my kids? Oh God, what do you think they're saying about them right now? Their friends? Classmates? What whispers will they hear at school tomorrow?"

Mr. Cohen took a deep breath, nodding at each point until Dan had finished. "I understand, truly, but Daniel, listen to me, please. One, they have motive." And he held up a finger as Dan opened his mouth. "Two, they have witnesses: from your work, from the hotel in Napa."

Another finger.

"Emails from your work computer, text messages. My god, they say they have forensic evidence pending results."

Two more fingers.

"All they need is a hole in your alibi and a body, and this whole thing goes from a missing person to a capital crime. Death penalty, Daniel. Do you understand?"

Death penalty. Those two words hung in the air like a toxic fog, a tasteless joke. Dan felt as if the room had grown larger, unending and vast, and that he was no more significant than that very firefly he'd seen moments ago. *Death penalty, Daniel. Go south. Get a new name.*

"Jesus," was all he could say as he closed his eyes and rubbed them.

"I would be negligent in my duties, professionally and personally, and I stress that latter part as a favor to your father-in-law, who was as close a friend as any, to not suggest you at least consider their proposal and the magnitude of this situation. It would be unwise. You do understand me, don't you?"

"Yes," Dan said and pushed his thumbs against his eyes until he saw supernovas.

Go south. Get a new name. The glass laughed, and Dan opened his eyes to see another firefly fluttering down from the ceiling.

THE WORLD OUTSIDE HAD BEEN REDUCED TO A DREAM. A THICK FOG HUNG in the air, lampposts rising from the parking lot like masts in a cold sea. Within that gray, he saw his wife waiting behind the wheel of their car like a ferryman ready to take him across some stygian river. The only other sounds were the doors of the police station creaking shut and the clomp of Mr. Cohen's expensive shoes on the steps behind him.

"Goodnight, Daniel," the lawyer said. Dan nodded, eyes drifting back to Linda as she stepped out of the car. Behind her, the glow of Tommy's Nintendo bounced off the car windows. He knew Jessica was somewhere inside as well, and he wanted to climb into the warm car and drive far, far away. Somewhere new and open and warm, where the fog and rot and blue jays and fireflies dared not follow.

"And please think about what we discussed," Mr. Cohen added, giving his temple a one-two tap and beeping his own car remote.

Linda broke into a half jog toward Dan, emerging from the fog. Her eyes were wet and puffy and she looked older, more unkempt than he'd ever imagined possible. Her makeup, what remained on, was applied in liberal and pathetic splashes, as if she'd had minutes to prepare. Instead of hiding her fear, it amplified it.

"Honey, are you all right?" she half gasped and wrapped her arms around him. It was the first bit of human warmth he'd felt since the morning, since he'd awoken to that angelic visage of his daughter staring down at him. He realized that he hadn't hugged his wife in days. Not just touched her—there had been many of those moments—but hugged her close enough to feel her heart beating inside her chest.

Tonight it was racing.

"I'm okay. It's..." he started.

"Oh my god, I don't know what's happening. They won't let us into our house—"

"I know, I know," he said. "Honey, you have to understand, whatever they say, this whole thing: it's a big mistake. It's all lies."

"What are they saying?" she asked, those big blue eyes he'd never seen so full of fear. Those eyes. How many lies had he spoken while staring into them, only to be met by trust unconditional?

He couldn't look at them any longer.

Not far off, the headlights of the lawyer's car cut through the fog of the parking lot. Fireflies lit up the mist, and the distant buzz of cicadas in the air drew his mind far away, to wide-open fields beneath an endless summer sky.

"What are they saying?" she asked again.

"Nothing," he answered. "It's all lies."

THE KEY

THE MOTEL ROOM was modest and depressing, little more than two beds, a television, and a view through the third-floor window of a billboard for an airline and the freeway beneath. It was a traveler's motel, a place to rest a head before a meeting in the morning or a predawn flight. It was also the only vacancy in the area, a fact Linda learned while Dan was at the police station.

The investigators had allowed her inside the house, but only under supervision and only to collect a few belongings. Those meager items, a suitcase at most, lay scattered about the motel like refugee artifacts. Jessica's coloring books and homework and Tommy's Nintendo sat atop a few sweatshirts and socks by the double beds. A few dolls lay at the foot next to Dan's folded shirt and a pair of pants. And that tie, that crimson gift from the missing and presumed deceased, sat atop his fold of clothes, mocking him.

The kids hadn't eaten since school and had whined the whole way to the motel, a drive that seemed distant and hazy when Dan tried to remember it. Linda had promised them room service only to discover that it had closed at nine and the only other options were the rows of fast food they'd passed on their drive.

"Tommy, Jessica, let's go. Don't make me ask again," Linda said as she jingled the car keys.

"Why can't we stay?" whined Tommy.

"Do you want dinner? Yes or no?" Linda barked.

"Yes," Tommy answered.

"Then get in the car," she snapped. The kids filed toward the door, Tommy shouting, "Shotgun!" as he pushed past Jessica.

Linda waited until the kids were out of the room, then turned to Dan. "We need to talk," she said. "After dinner, I need to know everything. I need to understand what's happening."

"Of course," he said.

"Your family needs to know the truth. You owe us that."

"I promise. We'll talk about everything when you get back," he said.

"Are you going to be all right by yourself?" she asked.

"Why wouldn't I be?" he said, flashing a salesman's smile, and for a moment she caught the scent of whiskey and old cigarettes. It wasn't her husband smiling back, but her father.

And then he was gone, and Dan gave her a kiss on the cheek that made her flinch.

"Love you," he said.

"Love you too." She smiled, then closed the door.

IN THE SILENCE THAT FOLLOWED THEIR DEPARTURE, THE DAY'S EVENTS crashed down upon him, one after another. He found that, as he thought back, the past twenty-four hours were laced with a haze, moments recalled like snapshots from a drunken night that bore little connection to the person he was. His job, his house, his family, the whole life that he'd built, all reduced to the silence of that crummy motel room overlooking the freeway. How had it come to this?

It started with her, he thought. *That's how.* It started the moment he followed Karina out of his office. That mistake, that stupid indiscretion that now, truth or not, would be revealed like some sick punchline for his family to endure. There would be tears and an end to all laughter, and nothing would be the same. It had all started with her, and now it ended with her absence.

No, whispered the glass. *It started with you.*

Yes, Dan thought. *It did start with me. And since I started it, I have to finish it.*

Finish it, Mr. Glass said. *Open the door.*

A new place with a new name, Dan thought. The family could come, but would they? Would they follow his lead? Would Linda forsake her mother, her few friends, her life, and her roses, all to follow him south toward the warm sun? Or would he have to go ahead to get his bearings and then send for them once it was safe? Yes, that might be possible. Easier for one to disappear than four.

A new name. A new life.

And the old one would be purged by fire. A blaze of chemicals and solvents in which he saw the hallway consumed by flames, the family photos rippling as orange glimmered off the heat-cracked glass. Yes, that would work. It had worked before, for others, and it could work for him. A new name and a new life.

He opened his eyes.

The blank future of his imagination gave him an energy he hadn't felt in years, a youthful excitement to see what lay at the end of the path he was driving toward. Of course, there would always be things in the rearview mirror, just like his brother had once been, but in time they, too, would either catch up or recede, a choice that was theirs and not his.

And he thought of Linda and those three words she had said before closing the door.

"Love you too."

And he believed her, believed that she loved him, or the construction that he was, the thing he masqueraded as. The father, the husband, the lover of art. She loved the lie he lived. In time, perhaps, she could love who he really was.

A new name and a new life. That was what lay ahead of him.

He would need his passport. Linda hadn't packed that, which meant he would need to go back home. He would need to be quiet, perhaps even sneak through Marty's yard and vault the fence, but it could be done. It would have to be. There was nothing here for him, nothing in this motel room, nothing in this city but ghosts and false accusations.

He would have to leave a note. Something small and cryptic. If this plan was to work, Linda couldn't know. Investigators would pore over his words, analyzing them. It would be a lie, yes, but it would be the final lie, and after that, there would be only warm skies and blue waters.

He scanned the hotel room for something to write on. And then he saw it: a wire-bound artist's sketchpad, glitter and glue stains and the wide careless strokes of crayon that only a child could make. It was Jessica's sketchpad, one they bought a month ago on their back-to-school shopping trip. He had seen it at home, sitting on the children's table in her room, seen her working in it with that vague smile and the crayons in her clumsy hands. He had even stolen glances at her pictures, wondering if she perhaps held talent. She didn't, but the pictures made him feel warm—or at least they had before this night.

Now, in that empty hotel room, as he turned the pages, the drawings gave him no warmth.

The pictures started out scattered and scrawled in crayon, figures with great loose circles for eyes and squares for bodies. Dan was little more than a pear-shaped form with four toothpicks for limbs and an unsmiling circle for a head. Linda was radiant, her blond hair rendered as a warm series of squiggles. Standard fare for a child of six. At least the first half dozen were.

But they changed as he turned the pages.

Each picture grew dissimilar, darker, and yet more refined. The crayon swirls and lines of the bodies were no longer vague abstractions but actual shapes. Breasts were drawn on Linda, her form growing more realistic in whatever activity she was depicted—cutting brown flowers, holding Tommy's hand, walking Ginger—and even the dog was drawn in stunning realism, shaded in places, depicting the varied color of her hair and those beady, clueless eyes.

Another picture depicted the family sitting by the fireplace, and she had drawn wrinkles on the fabric of the clothes and shaded in the orange glow on the carpet from the gas flame. Each member was staring straight at the viewer, except Dan, whose face was distorted and crossed out, as if she'd had a moment of frustration and abandoned the picture. The more pages he turned, the stranger her pictures grew. Abstract images, like a sketchbook of an artist studying shapes and anatomy. One depicted a dead blue jay. Another, an animal's jawbone beside a rusty railroad spike.

They unsettled him like crime scene photos, and he knew no child of six could have the dexterity and coordination to draw such things. Unless… he thought. Unless what?

What did Tamara say?

Conduits, whispered the glass.

Who?

The sick, the faithful, the gifted.

Who else?

Children.

Why?

Because they believed.

They left the door open to mystery and enigma. Their imaginations were untainted, still feeling for the edges and shapes inside the shadows. Unfettered by rules and dogma. Exploring the infinite. Because they believed in anything, even Santa and the Tooth Fairy and Bugs Bunny in clouds. Because it was easier to pass through an open door than one that was locked long ago.

The thing, the infection, as Tamara had called it, had found an open door already. It had found Old Mabel in the nether, had used the blind old woman to take shape, like a virus. It had guided her hands, and then it had killed her. No, he thought. Not killed: consumed. Fed off her until it saw no more use for her. A blood-gorged tick taking over its host until it could find another.

And now it had found new hands to guide.

Jessica, who used to run in the front yard and chase the dog into piles of leaves. Jessica, who had always been eager to ask him about his day at work and what he did, even when Linda and Tommy no longer asked or cared. Jessica, who for the last few weeks sat quietly in her room every time Dan passed, staring out the window or talking to friends who weren't there.

But maybe they were there. Maybe they were growing stronger, fermenting, spreading. Tainting the garden and the soil and the things buried in it. Living in the very fabric of the house like rats brought in by some plague ship.

Brought in, he thought, *by me.*

That painting, he had brought it into the house no different than he had brought home the lies and affair. That painting had sat in the study, below the children's bedroom, below their very bed. That wretched thing that whispered in the night and blurred the lines between sanity and darkness now moved through his daughter. His innocent little girl. Jessica, who believed in Santa not just out of a childish simplicity but because she wanted to believe in the surreal and magical and wonderful. She had left the door open to the unknown like a child trusting a stranger, and through that door, a darkness had seeped in.

He wiped away a tear and turned to the final page in her notebook. The picture was simple, more so than any of the others she had made. It was a crayon drawing of the old wooden clock, half finished. She had drawn the form, the face, even a few of the numbers starting at twelve. It wasn't the picture that held his attention for those quiet moments, but what sat underneath.

Jessica's phonics workbook lay beneath the sketchbook, open to an activity page. A child's cryptogram was filled in, boxes of numbers representing letters that formed a simple sentence:

The Fat Cat Ate the Rat

Dan felt the glass hum to life. "There is, at some level, a narrative happening," he had told Dean Robert as they stood before the painting half a lifetime ago. "As if the artist is challenging the viewer to—"

Solve it, said the glass.

He opened his wallet, fishing out that piece of paper he'd found on Old Mabel's body.

XII:4 I:1 II:9 III:18
IV:14 VI:5 VII:8 VIII:20

V is the key to the door.

He turned back to Jessica's phonics book, to that cryptogram, easy enough for a child to solve. The numbers each sat next to a letter, beginning with A:1, B:2, C:3, and on and on, twenty-six in all.

Was it really that easy?

Easier, said Mr. Glass. *Always has been.*

He began at the top of the clock, finding twelve o'clock and the number next to it: four. He counted in is head. *A, B, C…*

He wrote D next to twelve. The fourth letter of the alphabet.

One, that was easy. It was the first letter, A.

"G, H, I," he said, counting the ninth letter and filling in I at two o'clock.

R went in at three o'clock. N, the fourteenth letter, filled in four o'clock. Five o'clock troubled him because it was the missing letter, the key to the door, as the note said. He skipped it and went to six o'clock, a five, E.

Seven o'clock, H, the eighth letter.

Eight o'clock, Q, R, S…

T, he thought. Twenty.

It's a start, whispered Mr. Glass.

He looked at what he'd written around the clock, starting from twelve and moving clockwise: D, A, I, R, N, where it skipped the five and began at six, E, H, T, finishing at nine o'clock.

D-A-I-R-N-E-H-T

It made no sense. There was no such word, or if there was, it existed in a language he didn't know. Frustration washed over him at this endeavor, this insane idea he had followed into another dead end.

Mr. Glass laughed. *Easy enough for a child to solve.*

"Not now," Dan mumbled, staring at that jumble of letters. There was something in them, just as there had been on the card that came with the painting. Yes, the letters were right; it was their order that was wrong.

Bingo, whispered the glass as Dan rearranged the letters on the paper.

R-I-N-E-H-E-A-R-T

His name. Rineheart.

He had used the E twice, but it felt right. After all, clocks didn't have one hand; they had two. Both of these hands could use the same numbers, just as he could use the same letters again. If he used the N and the A twice, he could even spell his name.

D-A-N.

"Dan Rineheart," he said.

No, your real name, Mr. Glass said.

"I hate that name," Dan answered.

You're scared of it, Mr. Glass corrected.

"I'm not scared of it," he answered.

You've always been scared of it, the glass whispered. *You've always been chicken.*

"Never," Dan said, eyeing that empty spot between four and six o'clock. *V is the key to the door,* the note said.

Your real name, Mr. Glass asked again.

Dan's finger scribbled a single letter in over that roman numeral at five o'clock. A single L.

D-A-N-I-E-L

"Daniel Rineheart," he answered, counting up the letters. There were fifteen of them. Fifteen letters in his name.

"Three times five," he said to Mr. Glass.

Those two hands on the clock, the minute and the hour hand that pointed at 5:55, had, after all, been right all along.

"Not quite," said a voice he hadn't heard in thirty years.

BREAK GLASS IN CASE OF EMERGENCY

THE MIGRAINE WAS instant and engulfing, a sea of light. Within it, there was a distinct snap, a tangible noise, the feeling of an ultrasonic pulse. As the auras receded, the lines of his daughter's drawing, of that clock, of the motel room, and, by extension, even the world around him all vibrated like strings on a violin playing a single sharp note. And in that sharp note, a feeling grew, a small spatial distortion, a brief moment of tumbling, and a distant voice saying, "What have you done?"

Then it was gone. And perhaps, he thought, it had never happened.

The noise had been a knock at the door. They were coming home, and his time to run, the dream of the new life and the new name, would have to wait until morning. He stood up and walked to the door as laughter beyond it echoed out and the knocking resumed.

"Did you kids have fun?" he asked as he opened the door.

But no one was there. Instead, a giggle of laughter answered him. Then he caught a glimpse of a yellow dress flapping around the corner and into the stairwell. At the foot of the door sat a dull object no larger than two fingers.

It was a rusty railroad spike.

At the end of the empty hallway, past the amber track lighting and the exit sign where the yellow dress had vanished, the lights began flickering.

A sliver of light grew in a vertical line, up from the floor as the elevator rose. Then the light within flickered and faded and the elevator doors opened with a pleasant ding. Inside lay darkness. And something stirring. A small, moist form spilled out into the hallway. A tentacle of skin stretched behind it, connected to an old wooden trunk.

The track lighting flickered and dimmed. Creaking wood and rattling metal followed behind the shuffling, shambling form of that wretched boy. A cackle from the shadow as the shape took another step toward the light, brown overalls wet and glistening.

"One... two... three," he whispered in a voice that seemed to penetrate Dan's skull and rattle the glass inside it. His pinhole eyes glimmered in the darkness.

Closer to Dan, another patch of track lighting buzzed, flickered, and dimmed. Then the shape collapsed into the ground and reemerged from the new shadow, connected by the darkness. The wood and metal rumbled and clattered as the chest was pulled up through the darkness and clattered onto the rug behind it.

"Four... five... six." The distorted shape cackled, rattling the glass like an approaching train. Inside the darkness, the boy, that evil fucking kid, was looking at him through dark eyes. His own little army of the dead, coming for Dan step by step. Like that game of hide-and-seek long ago, the only way out was in.

He slammed the door shut and slid the latch across it, but he knew it would do no good. The thing in the hallway, that wretched child that spoke with that old voice, it could span shadows like a snake in a hole, and if the room was dark enough, it would enter.

More clattering came from the window. The billboard outside flickered and dimmed, darkening the room save for the bedside lamps. Bone rubbed against glass. That blue jay, wingless bones and dirty beak, thrashed about on the sill, smearing brown filth and decay across the glass. Cicadas hummed from within the walls, and fireflies lit up the air like motes of dust.

Ticktock, ticktock, went the digital alarm clock, and from far away, a dog yelped in pain.

"Seven… eight… nine." That boy's voice laughed. On the other side of the door, the light flickered and died. A bedside lamp buzzed and grew dim. The shadow reached beneath the door.

No way out, he thought. Only further in. The bathroom: the final hiding spot.

The lamp died as he raced toward the bathroom door, casting a final panicked look back at the madness in that room. The walls dissolved like wet paint. The fibers of the rug bent and swayed like a dry field. That blue bird slammed itself against the window and squawked. A rattling child-shape rose from beneath the sheets on the bed, metal clattering behind it.

Gasping, he threw himself into the bathroom and slammed the door. The fan hummed as light filled the small, tiled room. Four white walls, a mirror, and a shower with a vinyl curtain. This would be his final stand. There would be no south, no new life with no new name. There would be only this crummy bathroom, the migraine splitting the glass in two, and the madness banging at the door.

His mind raced and his eyes caught something. A black bag and a zipper. Linda's emergency kit. It had sat in their downstairs bathroom, refilled every six months or so with ointments and Band-Aids and… his Imitrex. Those migraine pills. *Break glass in case of emergency,* he had always told himself, and tonight was the mother of all emergencies.

He tore into the medicine bag, Bactine and gauze and scissors all clattering to the floor, and then there it was, a little pink triangle, his Imitrex. She had brought it. A single wrapped pill sat next to eleven empty holes in the glimmering foil and plastic. His heart leaped as he fumbled for that final pill, pushing it through the foil.

The door rattled, the mirror shimmered, and his fingers, fat and clumsy and filled with fear, slipped on the foil. He pushed too hard. The pink triangle, his little piece of pizza, slid across the counter, clattered twice in the sink, then disappeared into the drain.

"No no no no no oh please no!" he screamed as his fingers dug into the drain stopper, ripping it free. He scoured the muck and hair, but there was nothing, no pink pill caught in the stopper. It was gone, dissolving somewhere in the belly of the plumbing.

He cried out, turning the empty plastic and foil over in his hands, searching for something, a piece of a pill, dust, crumbs, anything to make the door stop shaking and the glass stop breaking deep in his brain.

Then the foil wrapper shimmered. The black lettering glistened in the dim light. The words bled in and out of focus, and for a brief second he felt that same ultrasonic pop he'd heard earlier before the boy arrived. A feeling, far away and remembered, that something small had shifted and changed.

No, not changed, Mr. Glass said. *Never been.*

"What… the fuck?" Dan mumbled.

The back of the pill packet read *RISPERIDONE 4mg.*

It was wrong. The missing pill holes were egg-shaped indentations, a few coated with green dusting. His pills, they were never green and never oval-shaped. The Imitrex, they were pink triangles, his little pizza slices that came in a dosage of twenty-five milligrams. Those pills were not his. And yet they were familiar, as if he had seen them once in a dream.

Water, cold and sobering. He slapped water on his face, staring at his own reflection in the mirror. That face of his, distant and distorted, unfamiliar.

"What do you want?" he screamed to the mirror as the lights flickered and a shadow grew outside the door.

"What do you want?" he screamed again, but this time his reflection did not scream back. As he stood there, staring slack-jawed, he saw that there was no reflection, no Dan staring back from the other side of the glass.

There was only the shadow.

What I've always wanted, answered Mr. Glass through a lipless mouth. *To hear you suffer. To hear you scream.*

Another snap as the world tilted sideways. Hours ago, had Dan thought he would be talking to his own void, begging it, he would have called himself mad. But now, in that cold room, the shadow of the dark child looming outside the door and his own reflection wiped out and replaced by darkness, he did the only thing he could think of.

He screamed and thrust his fist into the mirror.

The first blow shook the entire mirror from top to bottom. His knuckles bent inward as a searing pain shot up his arm. A crack, a small spiderweb spotted with blood, grew from where his fist connected. Dan clutched his hand, and the shadow that spoke in Mr. Glass's voice clutched its own. As he winced, he knew, deep within that dark reflection, it was laughing, mocking his own pain.

The glass cackled. *What beautiful lives we've made with our lies.*

The reflected world beyond the shadow shimmered and melted away, and in it lay a sunset landscape. A small hill, a single tree, and the twilight sun of a vast sky.

Dan screamed again at that taunting image, his fist connecting with the mirror a second time. Cracks shot out like fireworks across the glass. Blood blossomed from his knuckles. And behind the searing pain, the shadow's hand lowered, fingers wrapped in bandages.

But it was no longer a shadow reflected beyond the glass, but himself, his small, scrawny form from three decades ago, hands swollen and red, eyes filled with contempt. That reflected child, that distorted memory, mocked his suffering with a cackle, its own movements mirroring his. There was no shadow, no distant landscape behind it, only a boy of ten named Daniel Rineheart.

And at this image, the glass behind his eyes burned white hot, a supernova, a ticktocking clock waiting decades to chime. His fists balled into tight stones of rage, and as he raised them, that boy he once was raised his own bandaged hands.

Ready or not, Mr. Glass said.

"Here I come," Dan answered.

Their fists swung through the air and connected in the mirror. A sudden crack echoed out in Dan's ears as white-hot pain shot up his entire arm, and his balled fist bent in on itself. Blood spattered like twisted clock hands along the mirror and cracks shot out to every corner.

Then the shards fell, piece by piece, cracking like a thousand icicles in a sudden thaw, taking the image with it and leaving only the dented wood backing. A single, final shard of mirror clung to the frame like a reflective tooth, loose and ready to fall out. In that reflection sat a boy of thirteen in an infinite white room.

The pain in his hand was, for a brief second, distant and irrelevant. Then it came, crashing like a bomb into his nervous system, and he fell backward, away from that shattered mirror and that tainted memory, and felt a slick blanket envelope him.

The light over the sink gave a final blink and all grew dark.

DARKEST BEFORE DAWN

HE AWOKE WITH a spasm, his chest heavy, skin dotted with sweat that left a salty taste in the cool breeze of the autumn air. The last words of his nightmare hung in the darkness of his bedroom. They had been screams for a boy forgotten long ago, echoing backward through time, unanswered for decades. But now, in the cool air, they echoed no more.

He rubbed his forehead, feeling that piece of glass. The wounds of that day had faded in time, but the glass remained, warm and sharp to the touch. That souvenir from the shadow, still whispering and heralding the fog of a migraine after all these years. His old visitor, Mr. Glass. But tonight it seemed Mr. Glass was drifting back to sleep, and that was a good thing.

Dan looked around the bedroom. In his dream, he had been locked in a room, trapped by ghosts and mocked by memories. Chased by twisted children and resurrected birds. Haunted by an image of paint and canvas. And in that room, he had called out for help, but no one had answered.

"Mmm… bad dream?"

The voice came from his left side, beneath the slick sheets of the cold bed. It was kind and loving, and it anchored him back to reality, filling in the corners of the darkness and sending the sharp edges of the dream curling back like rotted wallpaper.

It was the voice of his wife, Linda. Her warm hand found his among the shadows of the sheets.

"Yeah, bad dream…" he answered with a soft chuckle.

As he studied the darkness, he remembered: this was real. The room, the woman at his side, the late-September breeze through the open window. All of it: real.

This was his life. He was thirty-nine years old, married, and at home.

"Want to talk about it?" she mumbled.

"Huh?"

"Your dream. You were shouting."

"Was I?"

"Mm-hmm. Kept saying your brother's name."

"No, I…" Dan thought about it. Then, "I dreamt I cheated on you."

A small laugh from her side of the bed. "Sounds like a nightmare."

"It was," he answered, and he found himself laughing at the thought. "With a grad student. It was awful. She went missing, and there was…"

"There was what?"

"A painting," he said, trying to remember what had been in it. Something old and forgotten. Something that moved through the house at night. "It was… following me."

"Come here," she said, rolling over and running her fingers down his chest. Those warm fingers, soft, always soft to the touch. Always calming. "You're safe now."

He felt those fingers trace down his chest, felt her smile in the darkness. Ten years of marriage and he knew these things, knew the sounds her body made, even in the shadows. Her body pressed up to his, her fingers sliding further beneath the sheets.

"Babe… what are you doing?" he asked.

"Shh…" she said, her lips finding his in a kiss, and he felt her smile.

"It's early…" he said.

"It's never too early," she replied, kissing him deeper, feeling her dry lips against his as her fingers slid down the curve of his hip, as her body pushed against his.

There, in his wife's arms, he felt safe and wonderful. Her tenderness washed away the vestiges of that fear that had awoken him. Her lips and fingers soothed his skin. She pulled him close, her hands on his hips, feet wrapping around his. Her lips kissed his neck, and from the corners of his eyes, he saw a shape in the doorway as the clock downstairs chimed five times.

"Tommy?" Dan called to the shadow as the two adults paused, frozen against each other in the darkness.

"That you, buddy?" he asked, and the boy's shape scratched its head in the doorway. In an instant, the adults decoupled. Dan reached for the bedside lamp and turned it on.

The pain in his hand was instant and electric. When the light fell upon it, he saw glass and bent fingers and blood pouring down his arm. His hand was a broken claw.

It was not his son that stood in the doorway, but the dark child that had stalked him in the dreams of the past weeks, dreams of a lifetime he thought false. A wet rattle escaped the boy's blue lips, those pinhole eyes flaring in the shadows. His arm was fused to a shaking old trunk.

His wife, that form he had been in nude embrace with, now rippled with tattoos and jet-black hair. Her smiling mouth: a toothless chasm of gore.

Ticktock, ticktock, went the phantom clock as a dog yelped out in pain.

There was no anchor to reality, no safe warmth in that room, no respite or calm. Only madness and chaos and his fingers grabbing at the cold, slick bedsheets as he tumbled backward, away from the twisted shade at his side that screamed his name.

"Daaaaaaaaaaan!"

He fell backward, hands grabbing the flower-patterned bedsheets that felt of plastic and water, screaming, back into the darkness as the world shook and that voice called his name.

CONFESSION

FLOWERS IN THE darkness, his fingers tearing at them, a scream, and he ripped himself free from the shower curtain as the bathtub rose up to catch him. Water and porcelain and a flash of pain in his mangled hand all overlapped. The broken bathroom mirror, the shaking door, the cheap floral shower curtain all rounded out the scene. The final shard of the broken mirror rattled and fell, shattering among the others on the counter.

"Dan," screamed that voice as the bathroom door shook again, buckled, then snapped off its top hinge and swung inward. Light flooded in, burning his eyes.

Linda fell halfway into the bathroom. The broken doorknob clattered to the floor, and the bent remains of the laptop she had busted it in with fell from her hands.

"Dan, what are you doing?" she coughed forth. Her eyes searched the bathroom, the broken mirror, the swollen and twisted remains of his right hand, blood leaking down the tangled shower curtain. She found no answer in anything, only fear and confusion.

"I can't do this anymore," he gasped, and he realized that he was crying. Tears poured down his cheeks, warm and heavy.

"Are you all right? Honey? My god, you're scaring us—" And she covered her mouth with her hand as her eyes sprang leaks. "Please stop. Please," she begged.

For the first time in ages, for the first time in his life perhaps, his thoughts were clear and his course of action was laid out like a straight path before him. He saw the end game, saw what needed to be done. It would hurt; this he knew. It would hurt unbearably so, and those who had loved him and trusted him would find their hearts broken. He would shatter it all, this house of lies he had built.

All he needed to do was open the door.

"I lied," he said in a whisper so quiet that he had to say it again to make sure it had even come out. "I lied to you. I lied to the family. I lied to myself."

And all she could say was, "What?"

"This whole time… I've been lying, and I'm sorry. I'm so sorry."

Silence. Her face melted from disbelief to a worry so deep she seemed to become a different person, a woman he'd never seen.

"What are you talking about?" she whispered. "Did you… did you hurt someone?"

He nodded. "I did."

"That girl?"

"No," he answered. "I hurt you."

"I don't understand. How? How did you…" Epiphany flickered and grew in her eyes.

His voice was calm and lucid. It didn't even seem to come from him, but from someplace long ago, forgotten and buried. *Keep calm and carry on.*

"I've been having an affair."

The words slipped out like a vapor, easier to say than he had ever imagined. They hung there in the silence of the room, and she didn't even react for what seemed like an eternity. Every inch of her skin was unmoving. It wasn't her husband standing there, broken and bleeding in that bathroom. No, it was someone else, something old and cold, wearing the false skin and name of her husband. It wasn't Daniel but her father she saw in that dim room. That old smile, the reek of cigarettes and scotch on his breath as he shrugged and said, "Thought it about time you knew the truth, princess."

But the old salesman was dead and buried, and it wasn't her father but her husband, that man she'd locked eyes with one night over champagne flutes and shared walks with back when they lived in a crummy apartment on the bad side of the bay. That man, that liar. No different than the only other man she'd loved and trusted.

"I've been having an affair and I'm so, so sorry," he said.

In that silence, there was nothing, no action or reaction, only an understanding and a subtle glimmer in her eyes. Then her face wrinkled in on itself, and for a moment it looked like she was going to smile, but he knew she wouldn't. She had made that very expression after her father died. It was the look of denial giving way to realization as it swept through her body.

"What?" she choked out.

"With one of my students. I was stupid—"

"No," she whispered. "Please, Dan, no..."

"I was weak. I was so fucking stupid—"

"No, no, no," she said again and took a step back.

"I'm so sorry. I didn't mean to. I didn't want to. I didn't want it to come to this," he said and took a step toward her. "Princess, I'm so sorry," he said, voice again laced with scotch and cigarettes. No, it wasn't her husband or her father, but perhaps she had confused the two and put all her hope in a man who was now revealing his grand masquerade to be a wretched lie.

"No," she said, voice growing stronger. "No, you... you stay there. Don't move. Don't come any closer." Her eyes darted about the floor, scanning the broken glass and blood as if it held some answer. Her husband had gone into this room, but now something else lay inside, and she refused to believe it was the same man. It couldn't be...

"Linda, please." He reached out, but she recoiled as if he were a snake ready to lash out and strike her. "I didn't want it to come to this. I didn't want to hurt you."

"Come to this?" Her voice cracked, hand covering her mouth. She felt sick. "Hurt me? Oh God, how could you? Our family, our children. I trusted—"

"I know."

"We trusted you, Dan. We trusted you!"

"I know," he sobbed.

"You…" she said, words failing her as her hands wrapped around her chest, the sickness threatening to leap out of her stomach at any second. "How could you?"

"I'm so sorry."

"Tommy, Jessica, get your things," she whispered.

"Go," he said.

"Tommy, Jessica!" she screamed into the motel room, surprised at the sharpness that came from her own lips. "We're going."

"Mommy?" Jessica's voice answered back.

"Get your things!" Linda snarled. "Do it!"

"Go, please…" Dan sobbed. "Don't come near me."

"GET DRESSED, TOMMY!" she shouted again, then turned her anger, her rage, back toward Dan.

"I didn't want to hurt you," was all he could say.

"You…" She pointed a shaking finger at him. "You stay there, right there. Don't come any closer."

"Get out of here," Dan said as he slid down to the cold tiles.

"TOMMY! JESSICA! NOW!" she screamed, and Jessica appeared at the doorway, clutching Mr. Bun. Tears streamed down her face and she hung her head low, unable to look at her father. Tommy joined them and took in Dan's shape through confused eyes.

"Dad?" he gasped.

"Go. Get out of here," Dan said as he wiped tears away. "I'll be fine, buddy," he said, voice cracking.

In that doorway, his family looked broken, like refugees from a disaster. And then he realized he'd seen this same image before, the same composition dozens of times. It had sat in his study, painted on canvas, only the subjects had been different. The girl had been crying and the boy had been staring straight at the viewer. But this was no painting: this was his family.

Staring at them, only now, once the paint of his deeds and deceptions had dried, did he understand that he was the artist. This moment, he had painted it long ago, when he followed that young girl out of his office, when he lied into his wife's eyes every day since.

He thought of Tamara and her final words, how sad she looked, and what she told him to do. To get his family far, far away.

She was right. There would be no trip south, no midnight run across the border, no new life and no new names. She had always been right.

There would be no happy ending.

LAST CALL

HE NEVER SAW his family again.

Words were spoken as they left, but he didn't remember them. They were distant, whispers in a hurricane. Then the door closed, and between his tears and sobs, the room grew cold and empty. What had started as sorrow, a vast pain that curled him in on himself, gave way to an overwhelming sense of relief and joy, and he found himself on the cold floor, laughing.

He had saved them.

He pulled himself up and washed his face. The cold water brought an instant clarity to his thoughts. He had things to do and undo before dawn broke.

Linda had left the car keys on the end table by the bed, most likely by mistake. Whether she had called a cab or booked another room just down the hall, or taken the children and fled into the night, was now irrelevant. Those things were part of another life, one he had only borrowed.

He opened his wallet, took out Tamara's business card, and dialed the number. In two rings, her voice answered, groggy and full of sleep.

"Mr. Rineheart," she said with a great sadness before he had a chance to speak. A firefly landed on the telephone cord.

"They're gone," he said in a voice he no longer recognized as his own.

"I'm so sorry," she answered, and he believed her. He had lost the three most important things in his life, and alone, he already felt the void. He knew, somehow, that she did, too.

"Are they safe?" he asked.

"I think so."

"How do I stop it?"

There was a long silence at the other end and the hum of cicadas. He heard a sigh, and when he looked at the telephone, it was beginning to rot.

"You can't. The painting, it was just a doorway. And it's been open for too long."

"I don't understand. I did what it wanted. I..." He hesitated, then added, "They're gone."

Another long silence. The plastic telephone was turning a sickly yellow. Small flakes of plastic broke off the cord as he stretched it.

"I know they are, but you're mistaken. It's you," she said.

"Me?"

"You, Mr. Rineheart. You're what's dangerous."

The receiver grew old and light, his thumb scraping away the plastic as it corroded. On the other end of the line, her voice quivered and distorted as the connection faltered.

"Hello?" he asked.

Her voice cut in and out. "—will always be with you—"

"I don't... I don't understand."

"—wants to be remembered—"

For a second, fleeting really, her clear voice cut through the static of the rotting phone and the frayed cords and he heard her, as clear as he had ever heard Mr. Glass inside his mind. "It's you, Mr. Rineheart. You're the curse," she said. "You're what's haunted."

The line went dead.

THREE

"There is just one difference between a madman and me. The madman thinks he is sane. I know I am mad."

—Salvador Dali

HOMECOMING

THE WORLD WAS fog and memory, and within it, the city slept in blind silence. A hundred houses passed by, vague frames and cold trees in a sea of white. Each streetlight flickered and died as Dan drove all twelve miles to the storage locker in the quiet. There were no cars on that drive, save for one, a pair of headlights that had lingered behind him for a few blocks before receding back into the mist.

The orange metal shutter of the locker showed signs of rust and decay, even from the outside. When he put the code in the keypad, it simply blinked 5:55 before opening halfway and lurching to a stop.

What lay inside looked nothing like it had the day before. The painting had infected the whole unit. The boxes, shelves, the old dresser, and books from his former office all hung in various states of decay. Wood shelves sagged with rot. Damp mold grew over the floor, crunching beneath his feet like dry grass. Gray cicadas buzzed about on wet wings.

The painting, however, was untouched. If anything, it had grown clearer than he had ever seen it. The brush strokes were gone, and what remained was a two-dimensional still frame of a surreal image, and he felt that he could step into it, but he dared not try.

"You and me," he said to the painting, and he knew that it agreed. It was time to make terrible and beautiful art.

The painting went into the back seat. He didn't bother closing the storage unit. Even if the lock worked again, he saw no point now. His course was clear, laid out before him in a single homeward line, and there would be no return trips, only one last stop along the way.

He emptied out the plastic jug from the trunk onto the concrete lot of the Chevron station. Then he filled it up with gasoline from the number two pump. In a small grass lot beyond the empty gas station, fireflies, thousands of them, flickered above the layer of fog. It had been years since he ran in the fields as they flew about in the twilight world. They were beautiful, he thought, and he wished that when this night was all over, he could hear the cicadas and watch the fireflies dance and not be afraid of what they heralded.

He screwed the cap on the container and wiped his hands on his pants. They reeked of gasoline, a smell that stuck with him for the final leg of his silent drive home. The clock blinked 5:55, but he no longer cared what time it really was. Such a thing, he knew, didn't exist. There was only him, the painting, and his final chore, his final work. The world outside was dead.

He pulled into his driveway and turned the car off. Had it not been for the police tape strung across the door, he might've missed his house. It was unrecognizable. The hedges had died out since he'd last seen them only half a day ago. The grass, once verdant and green and carefully cut, was now little more than plagued patches of muck. That once-vibrant maple that Linda had so loved was now sick and corrupted. Damp strands of moss hung from branches, flayed and raw.

He kicked the wrought-iron gate. It fell inward with a rusty groan, clattering onto the brick walkway. He would have cared about the noise, about Marty and the homeowners association, but he no longer did. In minutes he would no longer even have a home. Only the painting and the gasoline mattered now.

The contents of the container sloshed and dripped onto his broken hand, stinging his cuts as he dragged the canvas behind him like a corpse to the furnace. The police tape was stretched across the front door in four diagonal lines that formed two X's. He smiled at the words *CRIME SCENE – DO NOT CROSS,* as if those hollow letters held any true threat. He tore them from the doorframe and threw them to the ground like wrapping paper. He paused at the threshold of his house, his home, a place he no longer recognized.

Then he opened the door.

OLD BOY

THE DETECTIVE'S UNMARKED police sedan drifted through the fog and came to a halt behind another car, one he recognized as belonging to the primary suspect in this homicide investigation.

A call had gone out earlier, a noise complaint over the general radio. Someone was trashing a room at the Terrace Motel, and it sounded violent. A woman and two children had fled the scene, and Detective Cooper felt an immediate surge. He had been waiting for this. Waiting all night.

Suspects, he knew, often made their greatest mistakes in the hours after an interrogation. Something about the surge of fear and the inability to sleep clouded their judgment, and a paranoid compulsion seemed to drive them to cover their tracks. The irony, of course, was that this same compulsion to conceal their mistakes often took them back to some vital clue or the scene of the crime. Instead of concealing, they were revealing. He had bet it all on this one night, bet that it would all come together.

The last day had been a waiting game, really. Baiting and waiting. He'd spent the better part of the interrogation baiting that button-down psychopath, and now he was waiting for the call, gun and badge sitting on his coffee table as he played solitaire and listened to the police radio. And when it finally came in, it was like his prayers had been answered.

He put his faith in Jesus but drove as fast as H-E-L-L. Still, he had arrived too late. The motel room was in a revolting state of disarray. The bathroom door hung slanted and broken at the handle, the mirror shattered, blood and shards of glass scattered every which way. The cheap paintings were all askew. The phone had been melted, perhaps with a blowtorch. Even the window was covered with splotches of some brown filth, and when he rubbed his finger over the glass, he was surprised to discover it was on the outside of the window. He told the patrolmen who had responded to call forensics.

Then he left as fast as he had arrived.

The fog outside was thicker than he'd ever seen in the eleven years he'd lived in the Bay Area, as if someone had poured cotton over the world. It seemed to lull the city into a sleep, something he was thankful for, as it gave him fewer cars to look out for as he sped down East Charleston and called in the APB on the suspect's silver family sedan.

He was tired and the fog didn't help. The last forty-eight hours had been a blur of surveillance and paperwork, forensics and phone calls, and favors called in, all so he could get that search warrant. But he was still missing the final piece, the evidence that would make this case a sure shot, and so he had staked it all on this one gambit. The playbook in his mind nudged him in a clear direction that led all the way back to those side streets and that crime scene of a house. He tried to focus through the fog, and once, for only a block, he came upon a pair of taillights in the distance, so certain they were the ones he was after, but he lost them in the fog.

Then he also lost his way. In the fog, the quiet residential streets lay in a twisting gray void of shapes and trees and nothing else. The town was a labyrinth of shadows and mansions just beyond a white veil, and he felt like a ship's captain trying to navigate a rocky strait between abandoned lighthouses. Every turn was a mistake that could spell ruin.

"Please, Lord," he mumbled as he came to a cul-de-sac and turned back, eyes scanning for house numbers but finding none among the mist.

Then he saw them. A pair of taillights, pinpoints among the fog. Fireflies, really. Another ship in the misty straits between rock and ruin. He followed them until they turned bright red and slowed to a stop by the curb.

He switched his headlights off, watching that parked sedan in the fog. A shape emerged from the car, a shambling mess of a form with a hand that curled in on itself as if broken and useless. The form stopped by a familiar maple that he recognized even among the fog. It stood like a sentinel in front of that psychopath's house.

He had come home.

The form carried something enormous, a large, rectangular object. Cooper felt his heart leap and sing when he realized what it was. The painting, the skin, the evidence. The fool had brought it back to the scene of the crime. Bait and wait, his faith had said, and it had led him true.

Yet there was something else carried in that hook-like hand, and Cooper understood at once what was unfolding before him. The fool carried a plastic canister, wet and dripping. He had returned home, just as Cooper suspected, for a clear purpose. He was going to burn the evidence. The painting, that skin and oil, would go up in flames, and with it the entire house and perhaps even himself.

Yes, Cooper thought. There had been a sort of sick, suicidal gleam in the perp's eye back in the interrogation room, and Cooper knew there was a strong chance he would be using his gun before dawn. Death by cop. He imagined that would be how it went down if it came to it.

And if it did? So what. There would be awards and handshakes and people would say, "Lucky you stopped him, Detective."

No, not luck, he thought. Luck was just another name for the intersection between talent and timing and faith. And it was finally his time. He had waited a lifetime for this. He had followed his faith when everyone else had faltered, and now it had led him to this moment.

He threw the brakes on and came to a stop just behind that silver sedan. He opened the door and his feet glided out across the wet cement and sidewalk, and he noted that the whole world shook like footage in a war movie as he ran toward the house. His approach was silent and fast. It surprised even him that at sixty-four, he could cover the distance so quickly. It was the adrenaline. It spiked everything, tinting his vision brown, no different than the mold and decay hanging from the trees.

The perp hadn't heard a thing. He disappeared into the house and left the front door wide open, and through it, Cooper could see his back exposed inside the foyer.

Then, beyond everything, in the silence before action, a niggling doubt asked, *Sure you want to go through with this, old bones? That house and that fella, they don't look right. And in there may be the stuff left out of last Sunday's sermon. It may not be the starring role you've always wanted, Coops. May not be much of anything inside that door. Sure you want to cross through?*

More sure than ever, he told himself. Then, as quick as they had come, the thoughts vanished.

Now or never, into the open door.

He unbuckled his gun and rushed forward, crossing the threshold to the house and shouting, "Freeze!"

The shadow inside the foyer paused, and Cooper knew in an instant his orders had been heard. It was dark in that foyer, too dark to see anything other than the vague form of the perp and that giant painting. *Weapons*, he thought. *What if he has a weapon?*

Cooper fumbled for his flashlight, raised it, and shouted, "I said don't fucking move!"

The beam of light fell on the back of the perp's head, who gave a slow turn back to regard Cooper's intrusion as if it were one of only minor inconvenience.

Cooper's hands went numb, and he heard, as if from a great distance, the clang of metal as the flashlight and the gun in his hands clattered together. He felt his mouth drop open, limp and slack, and a sudden relaxation grew in his bowels. He knew, but didn't seem to care, not in the slightest, that he had just shit himself.

He held his flashlight on the man and that painting for only a moment, but it was enough—far too much, in fact.

The weathered and aged face of the perp stared back from the darkness, a face that Cooper no longer recognized. His face appeared as if a hundred years old, and yet, beneath it, like a backlit mask, the face of a young boy stared back. Yet it was not the man but the object he carried that bore out a great cavern in Anthony Martin Cooper's mind. A shifting, painted thing, endless and awful. A truth that would haunt his dreams until the end of his days.

The detective felt for a second, but would never be able to recall, a brief snap deep within himself as the beam of light scanned that canvas and revealed only a glimpse of its contents. Then his hands dropped to his sides like two dead kites, and he turned and ran, shrieking, into the fog.

In the hours that follow, Detective Cooper is found wandering among the community gardens, his gun and flashlight still held in his hands. A college student, awoken by the sounds of fire trucks, finds herself unable to fall back asleep and decides to lace up and go for a jog. She cuts through the community gardens by the park and comes to a halt before the stiff form of what she believes to be a homeless man due to the reek of piss and shit emanating from him. He spins toward her with a gun in his hand and mumbles, "Freeze, don't move," but she does neither. Instead, she breaks into a sprint, her fastest ever, and, upon arriving home in record time, she calls the police.

Later, at the hospital, Barton will have trouble recognizing his partner of four years, and his partner won't even recognize him. Instead, Cooper will stare through him, beyond, as if to something distant and shattering. He will laugh and cackle and shout for doors to be closed and ask for jars he can use to catch fireflies. Later, Barton will walk among the still-warm coals of that house and wonder, what was it inside that reduced that once-proud man to a husk?

A stroke, the doctors will guess, admitting there's little evidence. Months later they will discharge him into an empty parking lot where a social worker will take him back to his house and he'll sit at his coffee table, listening to a police radio for a call that will never come.

There will be no awards and no handshakes and no one will say, "Lucky you stopped him, Detective." His pension will only cover a portion of his medical and psychological expenses, and on some rare nights, when the fog is thick, he will find himself screaming at paintings that do not exist and looking for doors that need to be shut.

Then one day, years later, after he bags her groceries at the local Whole Foods, a woman will thank him for helping carry her groceries to the car. His mind will struggle to remember her face, and where his memory was once clear, there will only be a hole, a void. Where things had once been easy, they will now be hard, and the words will come slow. And for a moment, in that parking lot, that kind woman will seem to recognize him and he'll wonder if they had perhaps worked together, long ago, before the coming of the void and the words that now hang in his throat, as thick as mud. Then she'll offer a sad smile and pass him a large tip while a polite teenage boy takes the groceries from him and packs them into the trunk of an old sedan, where a girl with strikingly golden hair will call out, "Shotgun!" as she races her brother to the front seat.

THE OPEN DOOR

IN ANOTHER LIFE, his brother had chased him through the fields of Nebraska beneath the late-afternoon sun.

In another life, they had found an old house and hidden away inside while the other kids had searched for them.

And in that other life, they had found a secret hiding spot in a dark place that had sat forgotten for years.

"Inside?" Daniel had asked.

"Mmm-hmm." David had nodded. "Come on in. The door's open."

THE INSIDE OF DAN'S HOUSE ON THAT QUIET SIDE STREET OF GREER PARK Lane was unrecognizable. It had, at some point, shifted through time and memory and become a distortion, a place that he knew existed with all the clarity of a dream consigned to oblivion. The walls were crumbling. Wallpaper hung in large clumps where a dozen dirty little hands had pulled away at it. The house was dying a rapid death, the decay of decades in minutes.

Somewhere upstairs, a girl with strawberry hair pressed her face against a crayon drawing of a tree and started to count.

"One, two, three," she called out.

He swung the canister of gasoline, splashing a wide arc across the entryway like an abstract expressionist before an empty canvas.

"Four, five, six," he called back as he flung gasoline across the entryway. The wallpaper curled and fell from where the gasoline spattered.

Footsteps echoed out upstairs. Childish laughter hung in the air, and he heard cicadas and birds and a voice that shouted, "I'm not chicken."

In the living room, the couches collapsed in on themselves like rotten fruit. The fireplace belched green flames, and from it, fireflies fluttered out and danced in the air. The mantlepiece sagged and swung downward at a crooked angle like an old porch swing hanging from a single chain.

"Seven, eight, nine," the girl called out.

Dan lugged the painting behind him. From it, from somewhere through it and perhaps beyond, a dog whimpered in pain. As he pulled the frame of the canvas into the hallway, it grew heavy and howled in protest. The edges scraped against the walls, leaving smears of filth and muck that spread out in cancerous tendrils. Every framed photograph that hung from the wall swayed in the dusty air, color fading into sepia tones as he lugged the heavy painting past them.

"Ten, eleven, twelve." He laughed and splashed gasoline into the coat closet. The jackets and scarves, the rollerblades and helmets, the towels for guests who would never again visit all turned brown as their fabric frayed and mold blossomed out from beneath.

The painting grew heavier as he gave it a fierce tug and yanked it further down the hallway. He gave a sidelong glance into the kitchen. The windows were covered in a layer of dust, the yard beyond muted and vague. The vase that had once held his wife's roses was now a fountain of gore. Ill veins hung from dead flowers, cascading off the shelf and into the sink.

He threw the painting against the hallway wall and crossed into the kitchen, the floorboards bending and buckling beneath his feet. He opened that drawer of Linda's and reached deep inside. It was wet and warm and reeked of filth and disease as his fingers dug around inside it. His broken hand cried out in pain as his fingers wrapped around the silver lighter. With a searing tug, he pulled it free from the muck.

Then he flicked it twice. Sparks erupted, but no flame grew from the perforated tip. He shook it and tried again. Nothing. A third time brought sparks and a flame, and he smiled at this small victory.

A wet gagging noise came from the corner. There, on the rotted remains of her once-white doggie bed, sat Ginger. Her form quivered, and what remained of her hair hung in small clumps over bald mange. Her back arched violently as she whimpered, heaved, and belched, brown teeth chattering with each convulsion. Her stomach distended and then, a second later, collapsed inward as another wet belch erupted from her snout. She whimpered and repeated that sick act a third time, those milky, rueful eyes never leaving her former master.

A lump appeared in her throat, long and wide, like the bones she had once chewed on. She let out a shrill rattle and a final belch folded her body inward so hard it looked like she would split in two.

But she didn't.

Thick strands of brown filth poured from her snout as a metal object clattered to the floor. She sniffed at it, sneering, and Dan saw rust and iron beneath the wetness.

It was a railroad spike.

Far away through time, that young girl's voice called out, "Thirteen, fourteen, fifteen."

Dan rushed back into the hallway and grabbed the painting. "Sixteen, seventeen, eighteen," he shouted back.

The house shuddered and bent to the side. Footsteps rang out above and dust motes fell from the ceiling. Another tug on that heavy painting, another shudder, and the house fought him again. The hallway stretched on, almost infinite, and the door to his study seemed to recede to a pinpoint.

"Nineteen, twenty, twenty-one," her distant voice shouted as he lugged the painting further down the hallway, deeper into the bowels of the house.

A light flickered behind him in the hallway as a cold presence passed through him. He turned his head, back toward the living room, where a wet shape climbed from a shadow. That dark boy from the painting writhed upward, glistening and shivering like a newborn animal. One hand clutched the wall, fingers digging deep into it as if into clay. The other arm stretched back, that leathery appendage pulsating and fused with that old wooden trunk. The pinhole eyes stared into Dan, and he felt as cold as he'd ever felt in his life. In those two vacant holes, he saw nothing but emptiness and anger, and he desired nothing more than to stand there forever, until they swallowed what little remained of his sanity.

No, he thought. *Time to open the door.* "Twenty-two, twenty-three, twenty-four," he shouted out.

The boy smiled, then opened his mouth, and a blue jay emerged from between his brown teeth. The bird squawked and flapped its wings, taking flight down the hallway.

"I'm not finished yet, you little shit," Dan said, and the boy gnashed his brown teeth and unleashed a death rattle.

Dan yanked the painting again, and the canvas grew even more burdensome and corpulent, as if something were growing inside it. He had the distinct feeling of not only pulling pieces of wood and fabric and paint but of pulling lives and memories and all the moments contained within. Of pulling the clock and the window and even the fields beyond it.

The door grew closer.

The painting protested and fought, and as he glanced back, he saw hands and arms reaching out from the frame and grasping at the walls.

"Twenty-five, twenty-six, twenty-seven!" the girl called out as the hallway shook and the old pictures crashed to the floor.

"Twenty-eight, twenty-nine, thirty," he answered, and the painting released its grip on the wall and sent him stumbling forward.

The door was so close.

Behind him, that rotten boy skittered along the wall, anchored only to the floor by that leathery appendage, cinched to the trunk like a dog on a rope. And in the bathroom, a woman with tattoos combed her shimmering black hair.

"Thirty-one, thirty-two, thirty-three," the girl with strawberry hair called out.

The study door stood mere feet from him. He reached out for the brass doorknob, straining to pull the painting and all its contents, that whole world within it.

"Thirty-four, thirty-five, thirty-six," he shouted between teeth pressed so tight he thought they might snap.

"Thirty-seven, thirty-eight, thirty-nine," the girl answered, and he felt fluttering wings and feathers on his neck and a dull beak pecking at his flesh.

He heard the death rattle of that boy whispering in his ear through sickly lips, "Forty, forty-one, forty-two."

And Ginger's cold teeth, sinking into his ankle, chattering and chewing with rotten gums.

"Forty-three, forty-four, forty-five," Dan screamed.

And Karina's touch, a single finger sliding down his stomach as she licked at his neck, moaning, "Forty-six, forty-seven, forty-eight."

And he shouted, "Forty-nine!" His mangled hand grasped the cold doorknob, and everything grew heavy and sideways as a voice whispered, "She's almost to fifty."

As he twisted that doorknob, he felt all those things release him: the whispers and feathers and teeth all vanished. His body surged forward, as if he had stepped through an invisible film, a layer of skin that had stretched too far and had finally torn. He screamed and threw himself into the study, collapsing onto the hardwood floor, dropping the painting and the container of gasoline.

"Fifty," he said, voice echoing in the quiet, empty study. There was no decay, no mold or infection. Everything was as the police had left it, even the white grid markings left by forensics where the Luminol had revealed something sinister in the wood.

For the first time since he'd returned home, he could hear himself breathe, could hear his heart beating beneath his ribs. He listened as the plastic jug burbled gasoline onto the floor and the cap rolled away. He listened as his ears rang and buzzed. Then he pushed himself up, his hand screaming out in a sharp pain that shot all the way up his arm and into his brain.

He took the painting with one hand, and in the other, still throbbing and near useless, he took the container of gasoline. He hauled them both to the other end of the study. The only sound was the scraping of the painting along the hardwood floor.

"Ready or not," he said, "here I come."

He hefted the painting up, pushing it back against that wall where it had sat for the last two weeks. It crashed and groaned and all six feet of it stared back at him.

The canvas was blank.

NEGATIVE SPACE

"NO NO NO!" he screamed at the empty white canvas.

His voice echoed back from the solitude of the room. He ran his hands across the white canvas, the smooth fabric, the edges, the places where nails had once held the fabric to wood, but there were no nails, and even the wood felt flimsy and old.

"Where are you?" he screamed and banged his hands against the canvas, feeling it sink inward. Once, twice, three times. Again and again, and each time the fabric stretched, the smooth canvas grew thin and began to give way.

"Where are you?" he screamed again, and he reached both of his hands back, fingers stretching into open claws, and if he had to tear the fucking painting apart strand by cursed strand, he would.

His hands swung toward the painting with all the force he could muster, and he screamed at that mocking white emptiness until his fists connected with the fabric.

But they didn't break through.

Instead, they sank into the canvas.

Ripples shot outward across the white canvas as if he were reaching into something wet and warm and liquid. His arms sank further into the white canvas, and he felt warm shapes swimming past his fingers in a great emptiness.

"Where are you?" he shouted again, sinking his arms up to his elbows in the whiteness. He felt something large and unmoving in the nether beyond. His fingers wrapped around it and he pulled.

The pain was instant and unbearable and unlike anything he had ever felt. White-hot light shot out from behind his eyes. Fingers penetrated into his own skull, deep into his brain, squeezing and tugging the very strings of his fabric.

There had been fireflies and an old house and so many steps into a dark basement. There had been lies, mountains of them, and a girl with strawberry hair had cried into the arms of an old man with a white collar.

Dan screamed, releasing his grip on the object inside the white canvas, and as he did, the pain that had torn into his skull and brain, those fingers inside his own head, loosened and receded and color bled back into his world.

No, no no no, he thought. He had come so far. He had opened the door and taken this curse upon himself, and even if it meant tearing his own sanity out, he couldn't turn back.

Again, he thought. *Do it Do It DO IT!*

He screamed and thrust his arms through the canvas and into the nether beyond. He felt that same shape in the white void, his fingers wrapped around it, and again he felt that pain behind his eyes, unbearable beyond any pain he'd ever imagined. Flesh tore and bone cracked as that piece of glass deep within his skull vibrated white hot and the world turned to light.

Karina lay on a bed of feathers, and he choked her.

"No!" he screamed, and she disappeared and he was choking a woman in a white uniform as rough hands held him down and drew a needle from the brightness.

"No!" he screamed again and squeezed, and from the brightness, thunderclouds formed in symmetrical patterns until they bled black with rain and became inkblots spreading across a gray sky over dead fields.

He squeezed the object inside the white nether again, and electricity arched through his body. He now held wires and paddles to a faceless head as a static hum of a million cicadas exploded and a shaking body arched off the bed, only now there weren't paddles and wires in his hands but the staple gun, and Tommy was staring in wide amusement as Marty shielded his face. But Marty was no longer there, and Dan's own paint-soaked hands were holding Jessica's newborn shape as Linda looked on with tired and proud eyes. Then that newborn baby barked twice and his hands were empty and bandages lined his fingers and the walls and the floor were white and soft and in the center of the room sat David, hands outstretched, reaching forward through time.

As Dan clasped David's hands in his own, Mr. Glass screamed and shook as hooks tore into that tiny shard deep inside his own gray matter. His eyes swelled as they were pulled back into his head, as if something were yanking his very optic nerves down into the base of his mind. Fingers twisted and tugged deep inside his head, and his whole brain shifted and rattled, swelling and thrashing itself against his skull. His bladder boiled, warmth spilling down his legs as the brightness overtook him, but he never let go.

He screamed. Into the endless void, into the negative space, into that world of light. And as he screamed, his brother's hands tugged back, fingers clasping his own as that piece of glass sliced through time and memory and his body spasmed in pain.

And he gave a final tug, pulling on that white-hot object inside the canvas. He felt the shape within the canvas snap and shatter and break free, and all inside him went numb. At the same time as it emerged from the liquid canvas, the very glass behind his own eyes, the very source of his headaches and whispers, exploded into a billion soft shards, and he gasped and cried out as the negative space unraveled.

Color grew, slow at first. Starting from the corners of his vision, the scarlet faded back into that wallpaper that he and Linda had chosen years ago when they moved in. Then oak bookshelves materialized in brown, followed by the polished hardwood floor and the cream-colored ceiling.

The blue drapes that hung over the windows.

The photographs.

His own arms.

The overwhelming whiteness of the canvas before him, rippling like a pond of light.

And in the center, held between his wet hands, lay the thing he had pulled from the canvas.

It was a child of ten years old. He knew this because, for the first time in years, he recognized the face.

It was the face of his younger brother.

It was the face of Daniel Rineheart.

MY BROTHER'S KEEPER

THE GIRL WITH strawberry hair cried softly, clutching that same doll she carried every day at the orphanage. Her legs were splayed from where she had fallen backward and collapsed on the old wood steps. Only a half hour ago, she had been laughing and chasing shadows after she had counted to fifty, and now she wept in a forgotten basement.

Father O'Malley stood over the old wooden trunk, and with a grunt, he pried the rusty railroad spike from the latch that had held it closed. There was a hiss of air and dust, and as he opened the lid, his hand rose to his mouth, covering it.

"My god," he whispered. "What have you done?"

David shook his head, unable to answer, and even that action felt loose and surreal. From somewhere, deep behind his eyes, he felt a strange pinch, as if somehow, curiously, a small piece of glass had become lodged inside his head over the last hour. The pain grew as he approached the old wooden trunk.

He saw bloodstains on the inside of the lid. Splinters ripped from the very wood itself in thin strands. Handprints and fingernails and long lines like some horrible, final painting.

The old railroad spike clattered beside his feet as he took another step forward. He saw fingertips and knees, some of them raw and ground to the bone. He saw hair, black and matted with sweat and little pieces of wood.

And he saw the face of his brother.

Daniel's face was frozen in a final mask of terror and betrayal. His mouth hung wide open, his jaw cocked to one side, swollen and dislocated. One eye had filled with blood and was rolled back into his skull like a scarlet marble. The other eye stared straight at David, as if Daniel had been waiting in that exact pose in all the hours since his older brother had left him locked in that chest. Waiting to see him one last time.

"What have you done?" Father O'Malley asked again, but David couldn't stop staring at that final look of horror on his brother's face. For a brief second, he thought he could hear Daniel speaking, as if somehow there was still breath coming from between those chewed lips.

But it wasn't the breath of life.

It was a slow hiss, a burbling sound of liquid escaping from deep in Daniel's body. A sound, years later, he would hear again as Linda's father died in the hospital by his side.

"What have you done?" Father O'Malley cried out.

"I just..." David whispered. "I just wanted to scare him."

HERE IN ART, DENIAL

DANIEL DIED SOMETIME between 5:30 and 6:30, according to the doctor, but David knew better. It was at five 'til six when his heart stopped beating, the same time that David felt the glass, sharp and warm, crystallizing behind his eyes for the first time.

He never recovered from the death of his younger brother, nor would the children at the orphanage let him.

"Crazy Davey," the kids called him until he beat one so bad that he would never walk without leg braces. After that, the orphans left him alone, as did the faculty, Father O'Malley, and any prospective family once they learned of his past. He was tainted, he thought. Contagious.

He preferred it that way. Alone.

He kept his brother's bunk bed the way it had been before the accident, and he guarded it with a feral ferocity against anyone who would disturb the pile of art books and paints his brother had always loved.

Daniel, who had been meek and weak and born sickly to parents that had forgotten them both. Daniel, who had always tried to keep up, too slow to keep pace, too timid to stand up to the bullies, too scared to sleep during the thunderstorms that scoured the plains during the summer. His little brother, who had looked to him perhaps as if to God: to protect him, to care for him, to even love him. And whom, in turn, David had forsaken in one cruel prank.

And David thought, if their parents had forgotten about them, written them off like a bad mistake and moved on, could he, too, forget what he had done? If Daniel had once thought of him as a god, could he, perhaps, bring back the departed? Could he undo the past?

The glass grew bigger.

And he thought of the tornados and how Daniel had cried every summer when the distant sirens rang out. Or when the storms swept across the dark fields and shook the old building with thunder and lightning and how Daniel, too, had shaken and whimpered. And on nights like those, when the air was charged, he went to his brother's empty bed and left books that he had found from the library, hoping that one day, perhaps, the bed wouldn't be empty and the conversations he imagined in his head would soon be real.

And the glass grew warm and sharp.

And then, one night, Daniel was there, waiting.

In David's mind, of course, there remained that nagging doubt, that little piece of glass behind his eyes that shook when his brother appeared, healthy and happy, his fingers wrapped in bandages, his scars healing.

They counted shapes in the clouds and chased fireflies in the fields together. They talked into the night, and all the while, the glass grew. But he didn't care if he kept the other kids awake because his brother forgave him and all was right again and he was no longer alone.

But all wasn't right.

And one day he came back from class to find his brother's bunk bed gone and several doctors waiting there for him. And when they called him a liar and a killer, he felt the glass behind his eyes vibrate and the world went white hot. When his vision returned, his fists were shaking and covered in blood and cuts and he was being held down as one of the nurses produced a needle. When he struggled, he felt the metal break off in his arm and there was another needle and then a brightness that lasted for years.

In that brightness, there were dreams and voices.

Dreams of rooms and tests and pieces of paper that held mirror images of black and white ink with butterflies and rabbits and voices asking what he saw within them. There was the incessant clicking of pens as they filled out forms and tests, the cold metal on his temples as the electricity hummed like summer cicadas. The mumblings of a dozen different doctors all talking through him, but all the while, he only saw his brother standing behind them, silent and sad.

The room remained the same. Only the doctors changed, and on some days they brought things for him. Books on art from a library they said he could see one day if only he talked and opened up, but whenever he wanted to, his tongue grew heavy and his fingertips burned and the migraines grew until the brightness overwhelmed him and that shard spoke to him from behind his eyes. And when the doctors asked, "Who is Mr. Glass?" he never told them what it held within.

Doors opened and doors closed until the face he saw in the mirror when the men with the white coats shaved him grew foreign and absurd. And he remembered thinking, if he didn't remember his own face, his own reflection, if he had forgotten what he looked like, what else could he forget?

And he felt that piece of glass growing again, day by day.

And his brother stopped visiting, so he began talking, first in grunts and then in sentences and finally in elaborate stories, but every time they wanted to discuss that old house in the field and the basement beneath it, he grew sick. He smelled rot and heard a distant girl sobbing, and that piece of glass vibrated until the headaches took hold and the world went white.

And he remembered words spoken at him, words like "transfer" and "further treatment." Then they were replaced with words like "budget cuts," and he knew that if he lied and smiled and said he was sorry for something he couldn't remember, the doctors would sign the forms on his eighteenth birthday.

So he talked, telling himself it was all a lie, and they listened, telling him he was healing.

And on his eighteenth birthday, he thought of his brother and wondered what had happened to him and realized he was gone, that he had been transferred to another institution, far away, and perhaps he'd see him again. That he was sick with disease and he had to let go and move on.

And he felt sorry for David. He forgave him, years ago, for what he had done. But David was gone, and these days only Daniel remained. And when he signed that name on the check-out form at the hospital, the nurse gave him a sad smile, but he didn't care.

There was no David, only Daniel who walked out through that open door, with a new life and a new name, into a future of his own making.

THE NETHER

IN THE DARKNESS of that locked chest, Daniel had cried out and no one had answered.

He had called out for his brother, the only family he knew, and he kept calling out long after his body had gasped and the color of the world had parted and the wet nether beyond had swallowed him.

There, among the darkness, he felt rage and sorrow. Rage at his hero, his older brother, the one who abandoned him to that tomb. The one who erased him, smudged him from his memory, chipping away at the only evidence that he had existed. The coward who forgave himself for something he had forgotten.

In that dark sea where so many swam past in peace, he found himself unable to let go, unable to forget, even though, over time, he had been forgotten by the only person he had loved. And in that darkness, his sorrow and rage transformed him into something else, something he no longer understood. His name became a hollow construction, a sound spoken by a tongue he no longer possessed, whispered by children as a warning to never hide in dark places. A name now carried by that traitor who left him to die, forsaken and alone.

In that great rift beyond existence, he watched as the last light faded, that brother, that beacon that connected him to the world he had known so briefly yet loved so dearly. That warm tether and all memory of him was severed by the only blood he had.

The years moved on. Others swam past but he remained. The world existed without him. The world didn't need him. The world erased every trace of his small, happy, pathetic little existence like an indifferent wave wiping footprints from the sand.

The quiet of that vast nether no longer sustained him, only fueled his loathing, his sorrow, and his rage. It transformed him into something else, moments caught in memory, flashes of a life cut short, scattered and twisted. And when he remembered those moments of life, they shifted and changed. He no longer saw the world that he had so briefly lived among but only a perversion of it, an abstraction infected with sorrow. He no longer saw himself or remembered what he had once been. All he felt was an endless hole, a void, as if all was unbalanced and wrong.

And then there was another beacon among the great darkness, a vast light, and the closer the entity that had once called itself Daniel swam to that light, the brighter and warmer it became. It spoke in an old woman's voice as it reached into the nether with blind eyes that saw far beyond the living curtain. She found him lost and hurt among the nether and opened the door for him to spill back into the world.

The birth was not without pain, as all births were, and he had spilled forth in broken patches, in emotions and memories and wet colors. Moments from an ill-remembered life, distorted and tainted with spite. A girl with hair the color of strawberries who had cried out. A boy, featureless and forgotten with a stolen name. A room, old and brown that reeked of earth. A clock he had once seen, hands now frozen at the moment his mortal body had broken. Trees and wide-open skies and those shrill blue jays and the hum of cicadas on a summer night. Every image emerged twisted and changed from the nether, and when he tried to re-create them, all he heard was his name being used by another man, a faceless shadow who had once called him brother and yet now had forgotten his very memory.

Yes, the birth had been painful, and he had hurt the old woman, no different than a child pulling the wings from an insect. He was growing strong now, focused, and his memories were growing clearer. As he continued to spill back into a world rife with color and sound and emotion and taste, his rage grew and he felt those weak bones of the old blind woman, that heart so frail. The more of him she pulled from the nether, the more he wanted to hurt her, to feel his power.

And when she was finished, when his second mother bore him forth unto the world and there was little more of herself to give, he whispered a name to her. A name once his own, now stolen and tainted. She was finished with him, and he was finished with her. He had guided those weak hands of hers as she birthed him in something he had once loved, color and paints, something he had marveled at and hoped one day, long ago, to create.

A gift for his brother.

BALANCE

THE GLASS BEHIND his eye no longer hurt, no longer even existed. From the place it had sat for all those years, a warm calm now spread from his head to his toes. He stared into the white canvas that contained the body of his dead brother, hands still gently wrapped around that small, pathetic head.

"I'm so sorry," he said as tears rolled down his cheek. The face was the same face he had seen years ago in that cold, empty trunk, staring back, and he knew it had been waiting for him all that time, watching with that one open eye.

He pulled the rest of Daniel's small body from the wet canvas, that broken frame that was his doing, his creation, a result of a stupid prank and a lifetime of denial. He saw it all now, no longer dulled by the glass. Even that painted clock held his true name. It was not a Roman numeral that stood at five o'clock, but a **V**.

A **V** for David.

The letters had not spelled his brother's name, but rather his own. It was his signature. He was, after all, the artist. He had always been.

He felt movement in the study behind him, and when he turned, he saw them.

The boy from the painting, flesh born of his brother's, lugged that wooden chest with its leathery arm.

Yet David felt no fear.

"I just wanted to scare you," he said to his brother's frail body.

And the girl, his brother's sorrow, no longer crying but simply walking beside the boy with the hint of a smile on her warped face.

"I just wanted to scare you," he said again to his brother.

And he turned around to face the two children.

They looked up at him. The boy's arm distended from its elbow and the leathery tentacle separated from the old wooden trunk like an umbilical cord. Fingers formed from the protrusion as he turned to the girl and nodded.

The two children reached down, taking opposite corners of the old trunk. Beyond them, Ginger emerged from the hallway, her fur golden and lush, every bit as radiant as it had ever looked. She carried the rusty railroad spike between her teeth, wagging her tail the same way she had done when she first learned to fetch the newspaper. She ran up to him, pushing between his legs in a figure eight, her old snail dance.

"I just wanted to scare him," he said to himself.

The two children opened the trunk and a hiss of air escaped, as if it'd waited thirty years, hungering for this moment.

Inside lay darkness eternal. And just enough room for two.

David placed his brother's body into the cold trunk, where it settled into place, the final piece of a puzzle lost for too long. Then he reached into his pocket and removed the lighter, staring at it. That lighter, it had cost Linda's father his life, but it still had more work to do.

"Okay," he said. Then he kicked over the jug of gasoline and flicked the lighter.

The flame ignited, racing across the room in a crescent before zigzagging out and into the hallway. The wallpaper, the couch, the desk, and the bookshelf danced beneath the orange and yellow flames, and he felt warmth all around him like the final rays of a summer sun.

Ginger brought the railroad spike to the boy, and he bent down and took it from her and gave her a gentle pat on her head.

The two kids stared at David expectantly.

He bent over his brother's body inside the trunk, touched its forehead, and closed that single, sad open eye.

"I just wanted to scare you," he said a final time to that frail, weak body of Daniel's.

The eyes opened.

And within them, there was no warmth. Cold hands grasped David's wrist as a wicked smile spread across his brother's face from within that small trunk.

"My turn," said Daniel.

David felt himself pulled fiercely, a single tug that lifted him off his feet and spun the world sideways. He felt his brother's embrace, a cold hug around him in the tightness and damp wood of the chest. He felt those dry lips against his ears, whispering, "Welcome home."

And David screamed.

He screamed as the lid of the old trunk slammed closed.

Screamed as the boy drove the railroad spike through the latch that locked the trunk.

Screamed as the boy and girl dragged the trunk forward, across the floor, into the empty white canvas.

The painting shifted and rippled as they passed into it, and their colors spread out, merging back into their two-dimensional places, that five-foot-by-six-foot prison. The images bled back into view: the clock, the bookshelf, the children, only they were no longer frowning. The girl was petting a dog, and the boy smiled as he held a blue jay in his hand. Between them, beneath that window and that open field, in that empty space that had once seemed unbalanced, now sat the old trunk, forever locked and quiet.

Fire licked at the edges of the painting, but the children made no motion, no protest, as the canvas began to curl and burn and the oils bubbled and cracked.

And should someone have been there to see that painting, they might have remarked it was rather peaceful. It was rather serene.

In an old room, two children framed an old trunk closed tight by a railroad spike, beneath an open window looking out upon a verdant field, where a lush tree sat atop a distant hill, soft clouds above, backlit by an amaranthine glow.

The fire warped the image, and in that moment before it swallowed the painting, should someone have peered close enough, peered through that painted window, across those green fields lit by fireflies, should they have peered all the way out to that distant hill with its solitary tree in bloom beneath a twilight sky, should they have peered close enough, they would have seen two figures, two silhouettes, two boys running hand in hand before the warmth of a summer sunset.

And should they have seen those two boys running hand in hand, they might have remarked that they felt, for a fleeting second, before the fire consumed the image, a sense of peace.

That all within that painting was balanced and right.

AFTERWORD

WELL, YOU MADE IT.

Thank you for following along with Professor Rineheart on his dark journey. Not every ending is happy, and about the only thing we are guaranteed to succeed at accomplishing in life… is death. However, that doesn't mean there can't be a bit of sweet among the bitterness, a bit of happiness among the sorrow. The journey within this story represents—to me at least—an atonement at the fundamental, core part of a human being. We all live in various states of denial, and we all construct our own mythologies and paint them backward onto our past. Professor Rineheart's journey may not have been pleasant (and he wasn't entirely likable, was he?) but he did something that's very difficult for many of us to do: he made his peace with his past, offered himself for judgment, and accepted the verdict. Although his ending wasn't happy, I hope it was at least satisfying.

Forsaken has its roots in a screenplay I wrote long ago and attained about the most possible success while still managing to never get made. It garnered meetings, praise, and a few collaborations. The most frequent comment, however, was that the ending needed to be lightened up. Audiences wouldn't like to walk out of a movie theater feeling sad. Also, "The protagonist is a bit of a prick. Can we make him more likable?" And, "What about Karina? Can we just merge her character with Dean Roberts?" "Instead of a painting, could we make it a haunted smartphone app? Apps test well with the 26–35 demographic. And the dog, well... we never kill dogs. *Ever*."

Ultimately, I chose to novelize this story because I grew tired of the hurry-up-and-wait nature of filmmaking (though I'm not opposed to the proper film treatment, emphasis on *proper*) but mostly because it was the kind of story I liked to read growing up. *Pet Semetary, The Damnation Game, Ghost Story*, and others calibrated my childhood definition of horror; I don't believe a good story needs to hit a scare quota by page fifty. The best stories, the ones that resonated the longest with my own taste, were the ones that slowly built to a climax of both spiritual and psychological conflict. Just like the past caught up with Professor Rineheart, much of my own childhood haunts came out through this project. I'm certainly a little more weary around paintings. And I *finally* quit smoking after finishing this novel.

Art can be devouring. I hope *Forsaken* provided you with a fraction of the fear and enjoyment that consumed me in its creation. If so, then like our protagonist, I shall make my peace and find balance.

Thanks for reading!

—Andrew Van Wey

Started in Chuncheon, South Korea
August 2010

Finished in Breckenridge, Colorado
August 2011

ONE MORE THING...

If you enjoyed this story, please consider joining my reader group at **andrewvanwey.com.** There, you'll find exclusive behind-the-scenes offers, reader recommendations, and a **FREE** copy of my novel *Grim Horizons: Tales of Dark Fiction.*

See you there!

ALSO BY ANDREW VAN WEY

Novels

Forsaken: A Novel of Art, Evil, and Insanity

Head Like a Hole: A Novel of Horror

By the Light of Dead Stars

Tides of Darkness

Blind Site: The Clearwater Conspiracies (Book One)

Refraction: The Clearwater Conspiracies (Book Two)

Collections

Grim Horizons: Tales of Dark Fiction

ABOUT THE AUTHOR

A child of the eighties, Andrew Van Wey was born in Palo Alto, California, came of age in New England, and lived as an expatriate abroad for nearly a decade. He currently resides in Northern California with his wife and their Old English Sheepdog.

When he's not writing Andrew can probably be found mountain biking, hunting for rare fountain pens, or geeking out about D&D and new technology.

For special offers, new releases, and a free starter book, please visit andrewvanwey.com

facebook.com/andrewvanwey
amazon.com/author/andrewvanwey
instagram.com/heydrew
goodreads.com/andrewvanwey

www.ingramcontent.com/pod-product-compliance
Lightning Source LLC
Chambersburg PA
CBHW020306030826
48979CB00029B/2260/J